BOOKS BY RODERICK MACLEISH

Fiction

A Time of Fear
The Man Who Wasn't There
The First Book of Eppe

Nonfiction

The Sun Stood Still
The Guilty Bystander
A City on the River

The First Book of Eppe

The
FIRST
BOOK
of
EPPE

An American Romance

RODERICK MacLEISH

Random House New York

Published in the United States by Random House, Inc., New York, and
simultaneously in Canada by Random House of Canada Limited, Toronto.

Library of Congress Cataloging in Publication Data
MacLeish, Roderick, 1926–
The first book of Eppe.
I. Title.
PZ4.M164Fi   [PS3563.A3183]   813'.5'4   79-26560
ISBN 0-394-50424-0

Manufactured in the United States of America
24689753

For Beverley
sempre

"America, you have it better . . ."
                    —Johann Wolfgang von Goethe

"America is a mistake."
                    —Sigmund Freud

The First Book of Eppe

One

SET FREE

THE FIRST THING YOU NEED when they let you out of the insane asylum after seven years and four months is a car. Nobody can get far in America without one.

This country, as a matter of fact, has a very ambivalent attitude toward feet. People used to walk everywhere and not think anything about it. Then we discarded the habit. Most suburbs built after the Second World War have no sidewalks. The foot had become the most despised part of the American anatomy. Now, all of a sudden, using your feet to jog or walk to work has become a cult thing. Like water wheels, feet have undergone several metamorphoses—from useful to disdained to quaint. Still, nobody can live without a car.

Nobody, that is, except the paralyzed, the ancient or the incarcerated. Since all of my limbs were in working order, I was twenty-four years old and had just been released from Craigie Glen (don't let the name fool you; it's a flowery Scottish label on an expensive private mental institution full of droopers, mumblers, people with habits repulsive to convention and some screaming loonies), I fitted none of those catagories. Therefore, I needed a car.

I reached that conclusion in the worst possible circumstances —at four forty-five on a miserable February afternoon. I was standing at the corner of a boulevard and a side street in Cleveland, Ohio, where I didn't know anybody. Night was coming on, it was pissing rain, I was four hours out of the nut house, had two hundred and sixty-seven dollars in my pocket, and a burning desire to find success and perfect love and I had hit upon my first American truth—I had to have a car.

The great thing about truth is that you can always act on it some other time. I picked up my suitcase and duffel bag and started to think about a direction. If you don't keep moving in this life you'll turn into a benumbed thing that hangs from trees.

The boulevard looked like the entrails of a radioactive snake. It was lit up with neon signs advertising dirty books and movies and places where they sold foot-long hot dogs or hero sandwiches. There was a huge purple cross proclaiming that Jesus not only saved but cured acne or something. The last few letters had gone all weak and flickery.

The side street was more promising. It was lined on both sides with old brownstones. Some were boarded up but others were obviously occupied. One of the things I remembered from the last time I was free was that where there are old brownstones in run-down parts of cities, there are rooms for rent.

My memory was sound. I saw a sign in the window of the fourth house on the right. I went up the steps and rang the bell. Somebody had taken a lot of trouble with that front door. The paint had been scraped off to show the carved, paneled wood underneath. There was an arched-glass transom over the door with the number 117 on it and a Boston fern hanging in the hallway inside.

The lock rattled. The door opened and a round-faced guy in a white shirt looked out at me. He had gray thinning hair. "Hi," he said in a kind of welcoming chirp.

"I saw the sign about the room," I said.

"Sure," he answered. "Come in out of the rain." I knew that accent. He was from Boston.

The hallway inside was painted white. A big bare room off to the right was painted white too. When I first saw that house, as a matter of fact, every room was painted white.

The round-faced guy held out his hand. "Hebba's the name," he said.

I shook hands. "Bill," I answered, which was a lie.

He looked me up and down, an easy smile on his face, taking in my soaking clothes and duffel bag. Then he looked back at my face. "Leave your stuff," he said. "Come on back." He led me down a narrow hallway to the kitchen, where a girl was sitting at a table scraping parsnips into a bowl.

She was big, bigger than the guy, well over six feet with the breadth to match, and, I thought for a moment, one of the plainest young women I'd ever seen. Her face was sloped, her hair was the color of wet sand and she had hardly any chin at all. All the material intended for a chin had gone into her teeth, which were like a gopher's.

She looked up as we came in and my first impression went blooey. She smiled. She was beautiful.

"Bill," Hebba said, "say hello to Lulu. He's come about the room."

She wiped her hands on a dishtowel and shook mine. "Cool," she said, still smiling. "Look at you! You're a drowned rat. How about some coffee?"

"Yes, ma'am," I answered. I'll say one thing for me—I have good manners. I'll probably say a good deal more about myself in the course of recounting my adventures. But my good manners are the main point at this stage.

Lulu got some cups off a shelf and poured out three coffees. I took off my wet coat and we all sat down at the table.

"Are you at school around here?" Lulu asked me.

"No, ma'am," I said.

She made herself all beautiful and huggable by smiling again. "Now, you have to stop calling me ma'am."

She was about my age. Hebba was a lot older. I wanted to explain to her that *everybody* my own age was older than me because I'd been locked up since I was seventeen. But that would have been admitting where I'd just come from and I wasn't ready to do that yet.

"If it's okay, then," I said, "I'll call you Lulu."

"And him Hebba," she said. "His real name is Herbert."

Hebba smirked at me. "That's Yiddish for Herbie."

"Really?" I asked. Languages interest me.

He laughed. "Not really. Only in the North Bronx."

"How much is the room?"

"How much can you afford?" Hebba asked.

"I've got two hundred and sixty-seven dollars," I said, "and no job. But I'm going to start looking as soon as I get settled."

"What line of work are you in?" Hebba asked.

I had a little fit of abash. "I don't know how to do anything," I said.

"There are two other people in the house besides us," Lulu said. "There's a welder named George on the second floor, where we live, and a girl named Amelia on the third, where you'll be. You share the bathroom with her." She was talking as if the business of my living there was all settled.

"How much rent do you want?" I asked again.

"Don't worry about it," Hebba said. "Listen, we can work that out after you get a job."

"But that's illogical," I said. "You don't even know me."

He turned to Lulu, indicating me with his head. "What we got here is a guy who thinks it's logical to stay out in the rain because he doesn't know us."

"How do you know I can pay?" I asked.

"So what do we lose if you can't?" Hebba answered. "Go on. Schlepp your stuff up to the third floor."

"And if you only have two hundred and sixty-seven dollars,

you'd better eat with us until you find something to do," Lulu said. "Dinner's at seven."

As I went upstairs my bewilderment explained why goodness has such a hard time in this world. It's simple and the human race can't cope with the simple any more than it can accept the obvious. Since Ur of the Chaldeans, at least, everybody's been looking for the catch. Good people screw everything up. There isn't any catch to them.

The room they'd given me was small and neat. There was a poster on the wall illustrating various species of grasshopper, a little dresser, a table, a bed and one chair.

When I got up there the bathroom door at the end of the hall was closed and I could hear splashing and other sounds associated with the cleaning of the body.

I didn't have much to unpack. I'd left Craigie Glen with two suits, five shirts, two pairs of shoes, socks, underwear, three ties, nineteen books and assurances that I not only was sane now but always had been. My possessions all fit in the little room. I put my books in a line across the dresser and stacked the rest on the table.

I listened. The splashing had stopped. I went out into the hall. The bathroom door was open and a stark naked girl was standing in front of the mirror brushing her hair.

"Excuse me," I said, turning back to my room.

She looked at me. "For what?"

"Because," I said, feeling a conflict between horniness and good manners well up inside of me, "people of the opposite sex who meet for the first time usually have clothes on."

"That's symptomatic of the whole trouble," she said, starting to brush her hair again.

It was long brown hair. She had shoulders round as billiard balls, good-looking breasts and those square hips you sometimes see on tall, slender women. In fact she had a pelvis on her like the front end of a 1922 Rolls-Royce.

"My name's Bill," I said, lying again. "They told me downstairs you're called Amelia."

_{⊰ 7 ⊱}

She nodded and went on brushing her hair. "If you want a pee, come on in."

"It can wait," I said. "I'm going to live here."

She turned and looked at me again. It was a long, deciphering gaze.

I went back to my room and lay down on the bed. Since this is a true and candid account of the experiences I had in my twenty-fourth year, there isn't any point in denying that the sight of Amelia naked had filled me with instant, boiling lava. If you got caught doing anything sexual at Craigie Glen, it was considered a sign of retrogression and they threw you in Carpenter I, the section where they keep the real howlers. Aside from a little pawing and snorting with several girls, I had been a functioning celibate for seven of the ruttiest years of a young man's life. It wasn't natural.

But there had been nothing I could do about it at the institution and there was nothing I could do about it now. I switched on my guerrilla-leader fantasy. In this one the Russians have captured America and I am a lean, nature-wise strategic genius living in the hills somewhere. My men and I have discovered that a whole Soviet division is going to come through a valley. We've buried tons of dynamite along their path, brushing dust over the tracks and replanting the bushes. At the climax of the fantasy I am standing high among the rocks watching through binoculars as the Russians approach. The dynamite goes off. There is a terrific battle full of smoke and yelling. But there's no blood, no human wreckage of any kind. We win.

I must have drifted off to sleep for a few minutes. When I woke up, Amelia was sitting beside my bed looking at me. She had put on a bathrobe and had her chin propped in her fist.

"You want to lay me," she said. It was an accusation.

For a moment I was too sleep-fogged and astonished to answer.

"Just because you saw my tits and ass," she said.

I considered her statement for a moment. It was true.

"That's true," I said.

"See?"

I used up a few more seconds by having a good look at her face. It was narrow. She had brown eyes and a straight, delicate nose. It wasn't the face of someone who goes around laughing a lot.

"See what?" I said.

"You regard me as an object."

"You are an object," I answered. "So am I. So is everybody, along with all the other things they are."

"You don't want to know what else I am. You just want to use my body to make yourself feel good."

"What the hell brought this on?" I asked.

"Pathetic," she said.

I sat up. "You left the bathroom door open. I'm a male, and naked females arouse sexual urges in me."

"Go get a job in a sperm bank," she said, rising. "You're the kind of man who refuses to recognize his true feelings about women."

"I've been out of touch lately. Tell me about it."

"It wouldn't do any good. I threaten you. Go take a leak. I'll be late for my meeting." She went back to her room and slammed the door.

It was a jargon new to me. I understood her basic point perfectly well. But I was baffled about why she was trying to make it with me, a man she didn't know. That conversation concerned something more than its words.

I have discovered that people will go to amazing lengths not to say what's really on their minds. They will invent whole new vocabularies and systems of logic. They will join movements, go crazy or even jump off bridges before they'll say they hurt when they hurt, want when they want, declare love or admit they're scared out of their skulls. Decoding your fellow human beings can be a wearisome pain in the ass but it has to be done with those you care about because we talk to each other in signs and signals seventy percent of the time. I decided that Amelia was worth decoding. I was curious about what all that jibbertyjabber really meant. Besides, I liked her. I had a pee and went downstairs.

The kitchen was full of the aromas of fresh bread, a stew with herbs in it and the leftover cinnamon-and-apple smells of pie. While Lulu set the table Hebba showed me the downstairs of the house.

They didn't have much furniture. The walls were stark and pure. Hebba said he was doing the woodwork. The parts he had stripped had that glow of antiquity brought back to life. The plants hanging in the windows and clustered on old planks set across cinder blocks were so lavish and green that you knew they were in a place that was right for them.

A big blond guy with a beard came in from the wet. That was George, the welder. It was of considerable comfort to me that none of them used last names. I wondered if that was for my benefit. Hebba and Lulu seemed to have picked up on the fact that I didn't want to discuss myself in much detail.

So, instead, they talked about themselves while George, the welder, ate his dinner and never said a word. It turned out that Hebba did come from Boston. He said something in passing about having had a business. Lulu didn't tell me where she was from, they didn't say whether they were married nor make any embarrassing effort to explain the difference in their ages. That first evening I understood that Hebba and Lulu were very relaxed about their lives. They knew it was okay, so I knew it too.

What they actually *did* was buy abandoned houses from the city and fix them up. This was their third.

"Is that *all* you do?" I asked as we started in on the pie.

"That's it," Hebba said. "I'm the electrician, plumber and carpenter. Lulu's the designer and stonemason."

"*Stonemason?*" I said, astonished.

She laughed. "Sure. It's cool. Symmetric."

"Where did you learn to be a stonemason?" I asked.

"From a book," she said. "You can buy books on how to do anything." It's a fact. In my subsequent travels I took to buying books on an astonishing variety of crafts, subjects and ways of living life. I found one in Pennsylvania on how to cure stomach trouble with birch-bark brew. I bought books on greenhouse building, abolishing anxiety, creative anxiety, raising exotic birds for fun and profit, the subversive uses of Roberts' Rules of Order, canoe construction, love-making, chain-saw sculpture and meditation. Some guy in New York who must have been very scared wrote a best seller on how to develop a hideous personality so that you could push everybody else around. Judging by what they'll pay good money to read, the Americans have some very weird aspirations.

"What do you do with the money you get from selling your houses?" I asked.

"We finance the next house," Lulu said.

"But what are you eventually going to do?" It was a question that interested me keenly.

Hebba was sitting with his arms on the table. He was a man of subtle mannerisms—pursing his lips in a half smile, then opening his face up in a full one. "Listen," he said, "this *is* eventually. We're having fun, that's what it's all about."

"Don't you ever worry about the future?" I asked.

He laughed. "That's all I ever used to worry about—house, mortgage, station wagon, tuitions, all those future payments. You know, hero, you can spend all your time thinking ahead and never notice the present."

The kitchen was silent. I couldn't think of what to say. He had stopped me dead as we were approaching the subject most on my mind by assuming an attitude that had never occurred to me.

"I suppose that makes sense," I said. I felt inexplicably anxious.

"Hebba doesn't mean it's wrong to plan your future," Lulu said. "It's just that he's had more time than you to find out what he really wanted to do."

"Sure," Hebba said. "You have to go through the old process of elimination. I found out I was happiest working with my hands. Believe me, I tried a lot of things before I understood that." He put one of his hands on Lulu's arm and laughed. "A few other people too."

"He's worried about his future," Lulu said to Hebba.

"I'm not exactly *worried*," I said.

"Don't talk about it if you aren't comfortable," Hebba said. They were all looking at me, even George, the welder, who hadn't said a word all evening.

Rain was splattering and streaming on the windows. I wanted to be a success but I've never thought out what that precisely meant. From what I had gathered before they locked me up in Craigie Glen, successful men led lives of regularity and invisibilities. A successful man went to his office every day. He had invisible parts of his life—bank accounts, stocks, bonds and arrangements—which gave him an air of comfort that you don't detect in your average cabdriver or gravedigger.

"I don't know how to do anything," I said. "I'm almost a quarter of a century old and I've never succeeded at anything in my life or even tried to. I'd like to know what it feels like."

"There's success and success," Lulu said, standing up and stacking some dishes in the sink.

"I guess I'll have to be like you," I said to Hebba. "I'll have to try a few things before I find out what I'm good at."

"Well," he answered, hesitating a moment before he continued. "Listen, what you're good at may not be what you enjoy most. Just because a guy goes to law school, it doesn't mean he's got to spend the rest of his life as a lawyer—unless he feels obliged."

I knew all about *that*. I come from Obligationville.

Lulu put her arms around my neck and kissed me on the top of my head. "Just don't break your heart chasing after somebody else's definition of success, honey. You be your own man. Make up your own definition."

"Wander a little," Hebba said. "Fall on your face a few times." He grinned suddenly. "Most guys are happier if they've broken their nose once or twice."

They just let it go at that. They hadn't made me feel foolish or new at life. I could have hugged them all. But, as I have remarked before, people will go to amazing lengths not to express what they're really feeling, including me.

There was an evening paper on the kitchen counter. They said I could have it.

I went upstairs, got into bed and started reading the jobs column in the Want Ad section. There were openings for unskilled people at car washes, as waiters, baby-sitters, domestics and laborers. Somebody wanted somebody to look after an elderly invalid.

None of that sounded promising. I wanted a job where further things might happen, a real starting place on my search for success. One experience leads on to another in this life, but not usually at car washes.

At last I saw something interesting. "Sell discount auto parts by telephone," the ad read. "Commission. No experience necessary. Great Lakes Discount Auto Parts Company." I decided I'd try for that.

I switched off the light and lay there thinking that things hadn't started off badly. I knew some people, I had a roof over my head and a job possibility. I heard Amelia come in. I wondered what she'd been trying to say to me.

Just before I fell asleep I wondered where my father was. I wondered if I'd ever see him again.

Two

SOME EXPLANATIONS

I SUPPOSE IT ISN'T FAIR to go on with the story of my adventures without telling you who I am and why I was put away in Craigie Glen for more than seven years, and clearing up a few other matters.

To begin with, my name isn't Bill. It's Sherborne Eppe. When I was a kid my natural nickname was "Bornie," which embarrassed me no end because it was unique. Small boys are great conformists. My mother should have considered what people would call me before she gave me her maiden name as my first name.

My mother, however, never devotes much thought to the ramifications of things she wants to do. She is a singularly strong-minded lady while, at the same time, being quite weak-minded. What I mean is this: not many ideas find their way into my mother's head, but if one ever *does* get in there, you can't blast it out with nitroglycerine.

Her redeeming feature is that she is a very handsome woman. She has what they used to call good carriage. She is dark-haired with limpid hazel eyes that disguise her real disposition, which is that of a constipated rhinoceros. My mother has spent her entire life in pursuit of what she wants. When she finds something she wants, anybody who happens to be standing in the way had better have his New England Life policy paid up.

After she and my father separated she decided that she wanted Raoul. She'd just had our house in Cambridge, Massachusetts, done over and needed to have someone to put in it besides me. She was a woman hungering for something. Whatever it was, Raoul contained it.

I could understand at least a part of his appeal for her. He was a very undemanding and unannoying man compared to my father. He came from Guatemala and was handsome in a bloated sort of way. He looked like a retired sport. Raoul spoke eleven languages but I never heard him say anything challenging, provocative or even interesting in the ones I can understand—and I have been multilingual since childhood thanks to long, tense vacations in Europe with my parents. Raoul had no profession that I know of. He did nothing. As an art form.

It may seem that I maligned my father in comparing him to Raoul. I was speaking, however, of the comparison that existed in my mother's mind. To her, my father was demanding because he is intelligent. He annoyed her because he spent most of his time thinking about matters that had nothing to do with her. He is what you might call a dreamer, a visionary. A rare bird.

My mother could not penetrate him. Nor could she move him with her limited but noisy emotional artillery. This included shrieking, throwing furniture and announcing her impending suicide. My father is impervious to loud sounds made by women and children. He had enough money to buy a warehouse full of furniture. And, I think, he came eventually to believe that the absence of my mother from this world would improve it.

He left her in my fifteenth year. We talked about it out in the garage. "What are you going to do?" I asked.

"First," he said, "I'm taking you and Clarissa with me when I go."

I was astonished. Clarissa was our English maid. I was astonished because *I* had developed a horny interest in her. When you discover that your father has scored with the woman who gets star billing in your own raunchy fantasies, you feel a certain awe. It is as if an adolescent baseball fan found out that his father had been a heavy hitter with the Boston Red Sox.

"Then what are you going to do?" I asked.

"Then," he answered, "I'm going to try to find the meaning of life."

"But great men have been trying to do that for centuries," I said.

He nodded. "I know. But nobody's tried lately. Big questions embarrass people nowadays."

He had something there. We've settled for microbiology instead of God.

My father, I ought to tell you, is the son of the retired Episcopal bishop of Massachusetts, a decrepit old divine of unshakable faith in the New Testament and the Social Register (not, necessarily, in that order) who is still alive to this very day. The Eppe family hadn't much inherited wealth but it *does* have social position won in the typical American fashion; the Eppes assume they're genteel and so, therefore, does everybody else. My father, Roger Crucial Eppe, went to Harvard College and did investment counseling until he was forty-five. Then, out of his dreams and visions, he pulled off a huge commodity coup in hog bellies or codfish cheeks or something that made him the first genteel *and* rich Eppe. Shortly thereafter he quit his job and decided to go off and find the meaning of life.

His plan to take me with him, however, hit a snag, the megasnag of the twentieth century—my mother. She wasn't having it. There was this huge legal battle over me with enough Sherborne and Eppe family lawyers involved to stage a successful invasion of Corsica. During it, the judge called me into his chambers and asked whom I'd like to live with. "My father," I said. The judge had had this discussion with me in the presence of my mother and father, which was black-belt stupidity because it improved neither their relations with each other nor hers with me. In the end my mother got custody of me.

My father was angry and upset. I was his only child and he was genuinely fond of me and I of him.

"I don't know how your mother won," he said to me. "If I thought I could get away with it, I'd kidnap you. I'm sorry, sport. You can at least spend the summers and Christmas with me. If things get too bad, let me know."

Things were already pretty bad. I was making a career of being thrown out of New England prep schools. I was more interested in dreaming about perfect love and becoming a great man than I was in studying. My fantasy life obliterated the learning that the masters were trying to shove into me. We were beginning to run out of schools that would accept me. I drove my mother crazy, and now my father, who was my friend and ally, was leaving. I don't know why my mother wanted to keep me. I guess I was one of her possessions. My mother is very big on possessions.

That autumn I went to St. Stephen's. They accepted me because my mother's cousin was headmaster. This man, Lowell Sherborne, was a triumph of packaging over content. He was the most distinguished-looking person I have ever met—a square face, glittering blue eyes, crisp, steel-gray hair and a brisk, purposeful stride. Inside, he was oatmeal. He found life and boys impossible to cope with. Periodically, he would call me into his office to discuss my dismal academic performance. He could never think of anything to say except that maybe I'd be happier at another school. I'd answer that there *weren't* any other schools. Then we'd stare at each other. St. Stephen's was a High Church academy in cold country where hockey was the favorite winter sport. I have weak ankles, I can't skate very well and am not, by nature, given to violence.

I came home for Christmas and found that Raoul had moved in. From the beginning I was out of sync with him and he regarded me as a surtax that went with my mother.

My father wrote to me all the time, wonderful letters, addressed to an equal and full of speculation on the nature of things. Those letters helped because I was feeling marooned. My mother and cousins had long since written me off as a fifteen-fingered dingbat, and even my closest friends were considering the possibility that I might walk off a cliff before attaining my majority.

My one, unwavering ally was my mother's mother. The relationship between them was a genetic mystery. It was as if Florence Nightingale had given birth to Typhoid Mary.

My grandmother's name is Anne Lowell Sherborne. She was seventy-eight when my father left my mother. "That wasn't a separation," she told me, "that was a man running from an avalanche."

She is a tall, vivid old lady who was, at one time, the scandal of *her* family. The best years of her life were spent in Paris in the twenties, and she thought the world had been going to pot since Isadora Duncan died. My grandmother has a house on Beacon Hill, another one in Pride's Crossing, twenty-four million dollars and the unflinching opinions of someone who combines those kinds of assets with an unchallengeable position among the Brahmin families of Boston. She has more practical views and fewer complexes than anybody I've ever met. "Your mother," she told me on another occasion, "is God's fault, not mine." My grandmother was always threatening to sell her property and move back to Paris.

She liked my father and me. We were unusual. When I was doing my revolving-door number among the Ivy League schools of New England, my grandmother was unfazed. "Groton," she told me after I'd been expelled from it, "turns out men with dead-fish handshakes who talk as if they had two throats. That isn't what you want to be, is it?"

"I don't think so," I said.

"Let's play backgammon," she said. "Five hundred dollars a game."

"I can't afford it," I said.

"I'll put it on your bill," my grandmother answered.

I had been playing backgammon with her since I was eleven, always for astronomical sums which I never paid. She recorded my debts with a gold pencil in a leather notebook. A few days before the events which propelled me out of Boston and into Craigie Glen she told me I owed her nine million four hundred and forty-four thousand dollars.

After my first year at St. Stephen's I went to India, where my father and Clarissa were living in a village. It was the dirtiest place I've ever seen. The air was full of smoke; hump-backed cows wandered around crapping in the street. There were swarms of scowling little kids who were obviously going to be the thugees of the future.

A low brushy hill with caves in it was outside the village. A sect of holy men lived there. They were aiding and abetting the general atmosphere by smearing their bodies with mud and cow poop. They spent their time sitting in the caves, rolling their eyes, sticking splinters into themselves and chanting *oom oom*. "They're trying to attain higher consciousness," my father told me. I asked what that was. "Obliviousness to existence," he said, "oneness with the cosmos." I asked if he thought there was much of life's meaning to be discovered in such goings on. "I doubt it," he said. He had run his Indian inquiries into the ground and, besides, Clarissa had come down with a virus and was off her head half the time. They left that place shortly after I did.

I got through another year at St. Stephen's and went off to England to see my father in the summer. He and Clarissa were living in a cottage in Wiltshire. He was reading German philosophy, Eskimo anthropology and early English history at the time. He took me for walks across the wide rolling countryside that was spiked with strange hills, some of which had been built by men in ancient times. My father told me about the tribes of wild Celts that had retreated across those sweeping vales when the Romans came, about the forts the Romans had built and then about the armies of raggedy Saxons marching west after *their* invasion of the British Isles.

I would stand in tree-lined lanes just before dark, looking out over the vast emptiness of it all. In my mind I could conjure up the mobs and legions of various civilizations that had crossed that place—some hairy, some in armor. They are all dead. The generations that came after them for centuries are dead. My father and I standing in the soft gloom of evening were on our way to being dead. The country will remain until the end of the world. Nobody owns it because it outlives everybody in profound, immobile silence.

When I returned to Cambridge on the first of September my mother told me that St. Stephen's didn't want me back. They'd had it with me. "Raoul," she said, "thinks that you belong in a military school. I agree with him. I don't know why I never thought of it myself."

We were having that conversation by the swimming pool. Raoul was spread out all over a deck chair working on his tan. He was wearing sunglasses and had a beer belly. It was covered with curly, coarse hair that was mostly gray.

To this very day I don't understand what triggered off the events that followed, me being a nonviolent person and all. Perhaps it was my indignation at the thought of being sent to a military school at the age of seventeen. But, as honestly as I can recollect, what suddenly activated me was the sight of those gray hairs on Raoul's big brown stomach. I don't know why they should have offended me. But they did. Suddenly and mightily.

I have told you that my ankles are weak. But the rest of me is terribly strong. Among other things that I should mention is the fact that I am six feet tall and can lift the front end of a Volkswagen when I want to show off.

As nearly as I can remember it, I threw *both* Raoul and the deck chair into the deep end of the swimming pool. Then I jumped in after him. My mother started screeching loud enough to wake James Russell Lowell from the dead. She ran for the telephone. Some boys from the neighborhood got there first. Then the Cambridge police. By the time I was pried loose from Raoul he was a very soggy Guatemalan.

That did it as far as my mother was concerned. I had already sullied her social position by being thrown out of some of the best schools that money can buy. In my character I incorporated most of the qualities that made her loathe my father. And now I had damaged one of her possessions. Raoul and I ended up in the hospital—me in the psycho ward.

There was an uproar that lasted for about a week. The police were all for booking me on attempted homicide. A platoon of Sherborne and Eppe lawyers fixed that. When the doctors finished draining Raoul they got around to me. They looked at me and then had whispered consultations.

My Sherborne grandmother came to see me too. They tried to keep her out of the hospital but couldn't because she had donated the wing I was in; she threatened to take it back and give it to the Animal Rescue League.

They let her into my locked room and she sat down on the edge of the bed. She was wearing a tweed suit, her soft gray hair was combed back in sweeps from her face and tied with a black ribbon. "The law," she announced, "is what Dickens said it was. A ass. Too bad you *didn't* drown that man. He's a greaseball."

"He can't help coming from Guatemala," I said.

"Coming from Guatemala hasn't anything to do with it," my grandmother answered. "He can be an Eskimo for all I care. A greaseball is a man who lives off women—that's what we called them in my day. 'Gigolo' was a word the French stole from the Italians. I've talked to my lawyers and your cousin Percy. He's expiated the sin of being born one of us by becoming Suffolk County District Attorney, in case you didn't know. They've checked into this man Raoul. He's made a career of women with more money than brains. That's the best description of your mother I've heard in ages."

"That all may be true, Gran," I said. "But I think I'm still in a lot of trouble."

"I think you are too," she said. "But you're young. Just tough it out."

I was startled. "Where did you learn that expression?"

"From that chauffeur I hired last month," she said. "He's very verbal. I'm updating my language. When I told him on the way over here that they were thinking of indicting you for attempted murder, he said 'Bullshit.' "

"Gran," I said, "do you know what that means?"

"It's a form of disdain, I believe."

"Don't use it at the Myopia Hunt Club," I said.

She stood up. "If you say so." She studied me for a moment with her bright, deep eyes. "I can't help you, Bornie."

"I know, Gran."

"But I love you."

I'd never heard her say it flatly before. "The feeling's mutual," I answered.

"Tough it out," she repeated. She gave me as much of a hug as was in her Brahmin nature. "Someday we'll look back on all of this and throw up," she said.

An eminent professor of the mental sciences was called in from the Harvard Medical School who happened to be another of my mother's cousins. He asked me a lot of questions about dreams, fantasies, masturbation and mother fixation and then announced that I had a nervous disorder. And that was how I came to be sent to Craigie Glen in central Ohio.

As I look back on it now, years later, I can see that the decision to lock me up in an institution solved a lot of problems. The first one was continued coexistence with Raoul. When you've tried to drown a man it tends to spoil your relationship with him.

Then, too, my departure for Craigie Glen ended several conflicts in my mother's life. I was one of her possessions but not one she wanted in her general vicinity. My incarceration was a simple explanation for all the embarrassments I had caused her —I had been perverse and a general screw-up, I was never going to make it to Harvard, I preferred my father's company to her's. It was all explicable now. I had fallen out of my tree. My mother became instantly endowed with universal sympathy because she'd had to put up with a deranged son. I don't think she'd tried martyrdom up to then. She got addicted to it after they put me away.

I don't know how familiar you are with expensive private mental institutions. Actually, I'm an authority on only one. Craigie Glen was another planet. It was a society with its own system of values. The outside world, for instance, puts a high premium on normalcy. At Craigie Glen they prize abnormality because that's the business they're in. If they could find in you some aberration of the mind they hadn't seen before, you became a member of their aristocracy. A guy I knew who liked it there and wanted to stay pretended to go blind on Tuesdays. The authorities and the psychiatrists just loved that.

But most people didn't like it there and wanted to get out. So everybody who wasn't totally off his head spent most of his time straining to act normal. The Craigie Glen definition of normalcy could be pretty bizarre. When a friend of mine named Steve Clipper was told that he would be considered restored to sanity if he could go for two weeks without wetting his bed, several of us formed a conspiracy, staying up all night in shifts to get Steve to the bathroom every hour on the hour. In that way he managed to get through two weeks with dry sheets. He was pronounced cured.

Physically it was a very beautiful place, set among the hills of the upper Ohio Valley with rolling lawns, big trees, old Victorian buildings, tennis courts, a swimming pool and shaded walks.

Where you lived at Craigie Glen depended on what they could find wrong with you and how bad they decided it was. If you were *really* crazy they put you in Carpenter I for men or Carpenter II, the ladies' equivalent. I never made it to Carpenter I—although they threatened to put me there once as a punishment—but I understand it was God-awful. The sick wards were full of people exploding or getting ready to.

The cottages were at the opposite end of the residence scale. They were attractive little buildings scattered around the campus where eight or ten people lived together with only one attendant on duty. You had to put in a lot of time acting ferociously normal before you got to live in a cottage.

I ended up somewhere in between—a hall in the main building called Fitzpatrick I. It was for men only and they kept the doors locked. I had some interesting and unusual dormitory mates. The one who became my best friend was a gaunt old dope fiend from New Jersey named Mr. Fletcher. When the craving was on him he'd lurch along the halls groaning and holding up his trousers with both hands. At other times he was a very funny and erudite man. He'd tell me stories about all the institutions he'd been in—and there were a lot of them—and he would recite poetry to me and tell me what to read.

There was a tense, writhing stockbroker who sat at the end of the main hall playing dominoes all day with anyone who could stand him, and a Chinese who spent most of *his* time in the common room doing crossword puzzles and periodically shouting, "I'M NOT THAT KIND OF PERSON!" There were alcoholics drying out; a Jesuit priest of sweet melancholy; a distinguished-looking television executive from New York whom I would sometimes hear sobbing in his room. There was a stocky, silent guy about my age who was too sick to be in Fitzpatrick. One day he attacked me with a squash racket, and if I weren't as strong as I am, I'd be dead.

The attendants had an office on the hall—they were called "aides" at Craigie Glen. Some were men, some women, most of them were young. I half fell for one of the girls who worked nights. Her name was Dusty and she used to bring me candy bars.

After I arrived they put me through all sorts of tests and assigned me to a psychiatrist named Dr. Primrose. He was to be the master of my destiny for the next seven years and a few months, and that was a decidedly bad situation. Dr. Primrose was crazier than almost everybody in the place. He was even tenser than Fitzpatrick's resident twitcheroo, the stockbroker. Primrose would roll pencils up and down his desk, bug his eyes out, sweat, clear his throat, fling himself out of his chair, ricochet off the walls and sit down again. He was always at himself—scratching, clutching, picking at his orifices and yanking his ears.

In our first interview I asked Dr. Primrose what the matter was with me. He said I had too powerful a fantasy life. I said I'd spent my whole life dreaming about love and becoming a great man. Precisely, Dr. Primrose answered. I needed to get in touch with reality. They were going to give me a course in accounting.

I don't know which of the great psychiatric philosophers discovered that accounting and reality were synonymous or, for that matter, what was so hot about reality. But I was in their power and wanted to get out of there. So I took the accounting course. I also attended classes in woodworking, pottery, leather tooling and picture painting. They tried to keep you busy at Craigie Glen. We had sports, escorted walks around the grounds, safe, dull movies on Saturday nights and dances with women from Fitzpatrick II. Those were the most decorous parties I've ever been to because we were all trying to act so damn normal. A bunch of unbalanced Trappists is what we were.

During the first year I worked so hard at behaving myself in order to get out that it never occurred to me that maybe I wouldn't. I devoted my brain to making contact with reality. That was almost my undoing. The more I contemplated reality, the more I realized that I was in Craigie Glen mostly as a solution to my mother's problems with me.

I spent the better part of the second year trying to accept that reality. Once I *had* accepted it, I didn't like it one bit. All that was needed for me to become a permanent resident was my mother willing it and the institution's ability to go on defining me as a psychotic. Since my mother and Craigie Glen were organisms that lived by their own rules, I was trapped. One winter afternoon I made a break for the main gate during an escorted walk. It took four aides to catch me and get me back. They threatened to throw me into Carpenter I as punishment. After that I gave up reality and went back to my comfortable old way of mental life.

My mother wrote to me once a month. But I never heard from my father at all. I wondered where he was and how he was coming along in his search for the meaning of existence. I had no doubt my mother had worked out a way of keeping him from communicating with me. I had letters from my grandmother for a month. Then they stopped too.

My fourth year was a bummer. Craigie Glen was getting embarrassed, I think. While I was a profitable enterprise for them, it must have been obvious to *somebody* in the place that I wasn't crazy enough to merit so long an incarceration. So they had another crack at me—more tests, prodding, poking and questioning. One autumn afternoon Dr. Primrose called me in and told me I was a schizophrenic. As he announced this he was all knotted up in his chair, kneading his crotch and grinning in triumph as if he'd just informed me I'd won the Nobel Prize for Distraught.

The rest of that winter is a blur. They pumped me full of chemicals that were supposed to unlock the secrets of my past. Then they zapped me with electric-shock treatments that made me forget the past and everything else, including how to tie my shoes. Winter fixed itself on the Ohio Valley. I remember in fragments only: bare trees swaying and creaking, small dim rooms filled with machinery that intended me no good, ice like teeth around the edges of the windowpanes. I recall somebody yelling, but I don't know if it was me or not. Two faces stay with me—Mr. Fletcher, the cadaverous old junkie, sitting by my bed reading Wordsworth's poetry aloud, and Dusty, the aide who used to bring me candy bars, holding me and crying.

When the inside of my head began to unscramble, it was spring. I didn't feel very changed after all that drugging and blasting. All they'd done was wreck that part of my brain which is in charge of remembering numbers. To this day I can't remember numbers.

Dr. Primrose came to see me. He wriggled around my room and said I wasn't cured yet. It would take time. It took the better part of three more years, but not to be cured.

Everything was pretty much the same as it had been when I left the realms of the reasonable the previous November. The Chinaman, the stockbroker and the crying TV producer were carrying on in their usual fashion. Dusty, however, was gone. She'd left a note with Mr. Fletcher. She said she quit because she couldn't stand what they were doing to me. She told me to be brave and go on believing. Mr. Fletcher thought she was in love with me.

I never saw or heard from her again.

Mr. Fletcher was not only my best friend, he was one of the main reasons why I didn't really go bananas during my seven years and four months at Craigie Glen. As I've told you, he was a drug addict. He'd spent most of his life in mental hospitals or practicing habits that get you put in mental hospitals. He was very tall, with reddish hair, and he had a reddish mustache which disguised the fact that he hadn't many teeth left. His face was pockmarked and he was too skinny for his clothes.

When he wasn't going through his terrible fits of craving, he read books. That's what he made me do. "They attack your mind in these places," he said. "Well, you beat the sons of bitches by improving yours."

So I read. That was considered a good thing to do in the Craigie Glen ethos and they gave you all the books you wanted. That explains my splattered education. I read novels during my years at Craigie Glen. I read American, British and Christian history. I read a book on theoretical mathematics, even though I can't do long division. I read theology and reams of mythology, no science except a bug book by a Frenchman named Fabre. I already knew how to speak French and German. I taught myself Spanish, classical Greek and some Russian.

My curriculum was odd and incoherent. That's because I read what Mr. Fletcher told me to read most of the time. The books I got were a reflection of what *he* was—a bagful of contradictions, a Catholic, a mystic, a political radical and an Irishman of great taste and violent prejudices.

I drenched my mind with books and that, along with my

reversion to fantasy, kept me sane. Mr. Fletcher and I sat up late arguing about literature. Dr. Primrose jittered in and out of my existence, the upper Ohio Valley turned bare, cold and dead, exploded into three more springs, three more summers and autumns. Then, suddenly, something happened that gave me back my life.

It was on the second Friday of my eighth December in Craigie Glen. An aide came to take me over to the building where the psychiatrists had their offices. Like a pigeon homing for a coop he hates, I walked down the hall to Dr. Primrose's room. The aide stopped me. "You're seeing Dr. Feldman today."

"Who's Dr. Feldman?" I asked.

He opened a door. "In here."

I found myself in an office I'd never seen before. There was a desk covered with papers, a bookcase along one wall, modern paintings illuminated by track lights, a sofa, a chair with a smoked-glass table between them. There was a box of Kleenex on the table. It stood there as a hint that the man who occupied this office believed it natural for people to cry and blow their noses.

Dr. Feldman was sitting at the desk when I came in. When he stood up—he was a tall, trim man—and held out his hand I was almost tempted to like him. He had one of those faces whose awkward parts come together in a harmonious whole. He wore thick glasses.

He waved me toward the sofa and sat down in the chair opposite, crooking one elbow on the back and folding his hands.

"What's going on?" I asked. "Why aren't I seeing Dr. Primrose?" I thought this might be the prelude to some new chapter in my life at Craigie Glen. The only certain thing about new chapters in that place was that they were bound to be worse than the previous ones. The very fact that I instinctively liked the man sitting across that low table from me made me wary. I had become a professional inmate.

"My name is William Feldman," he began. "Two weeks ago I came here as the new chief psychiatrist. I've been reading your file, Mr. Eppe. Tell me about yourself."

"If you've read my file, you know everything," I said, getting my guard up higher, as it were.

"No," he said, breaking into a warm, homely, squinty smile, "I've read what *other* people think about your case. I want to know why *you* think you're here."

"Look," I answered, "I'm an accused man without a lawyer. If this is leading up to more treatment for schizophrenia—"

"You're not a schizophrenic," Dr. Feldman said. "There isn't a scrap"—he held his thumb and forefinger slightly apart to show how big a scrap is—"of evidence to indicate schizophrenia. None of the classic symptoms." He turned his near-sighted eyes onto my face. "Not even any of the obscure ones we sometimes run into. Now, tell me why you're here."

There aren't any personal truths in mental hospitals. You are whatever they say you are. You give up trying to think honestly about yourself and spend all your time trying to work your way out of their diagnosis of you. It had been a long time since I could remember the real reason why I was in Craigie Glen. Now, all of a sudden, here was the head diagnostician himself telling me I didn't have the disease they'd treated me for, damn near killing me in the process.

I didn't know what to make of it. I stared at him, torn between suspicion and a big effort to get back thoughts I hadn't had for years. He stared back at me, but not like an inquisitor. More like somebody who regards you as an equal but knows it's hard for you to speak because you aren't sure of him yet.

Then I began. And once I began, it was as if the river of what I *had* been broke its sluices, and the current swept away the denizen of the grotesque world I had become. Never before or since have I talked for so long at one stretch. It got easier as I went on because of a confidence which grew in me that I *was* telling the truth, that my truth was real and not an accommodation of somebody else's definition of me.

I gave him all the facts—what it was like in our house when I was a kid, about my parents' separation, my daydreams and my failures at school. I told about my father and how much I missed him. I was even fair when I described my mother, including all the good points I could think of. I told about throwing Raoul into the swimming pool, about my coming to Craigie Glen and learning how to fit in because I thought I'd never get out.

Dusk fell outside the office windows. The sun turned into a rose-and-orange smear in the western sky. The lights went on across the grounds, earthbound stars in the frosty Ohio night. Dr. Feldman gave no sign that he wanted me to stop or that he had any other business in this world. Sometimes he sat with his hands folded and his thoughtful gaze on me, sometimes he would tilt his head back and laugh when I said something wry (I had thought up to then that psychiatrists got drummed out of their regiment if they laughed) and sometimes he made notes on a yellow pad. But through all of it, total absorption beamed out of his brain through those thick glasses.

It was a little before eight by the time I was finished. "Christ," I said, "it's been four hours."

"How do you feel?"

I'd told so much truth by then that I decided they couldn't hang me for telling one more. "I feel like I used to feel, which was pretty good most of the time," I said. "I'd feel great if somebody believed me."

He put his pad on the smoked-glass table. "I believe you," he said. "As I told you, I've read your record at Craigie Glen and I've done some other checking on you." He leaned back in his chair, laced his fingers together again and looked at the ceiling. "I kept asking myself . . ." He paused and shook his head. "Damn. Words. I can't find the right ones to say this as I'd like to. I'm not as verbal as you are. I kept asking myself why a young man who'd had perfectly normal reactions to his kind of life should be kept in an institution all this time." He swiveled half-way around in his chair and looked back at me. "I wanted to check, to see if *you* thought you should be here."

"Not me," I said.

"You do know there's nothing wrong—abnormal—about you, don't you?"

"They almost had me convinced," I said. "It's been seven years and four months."

He picked up a bound folder on top of a stack of them. I assumed that the stack was me. He opened the folder. "Dr. Primrose discussed your fantasy life with you," he said.

"That was their first diagnosis," I said. "Before they sent me up to the majors with schizophrenia."

Feldman suppressed a chortle. "It really isn't funny." He closed the folder and shook his head again, compressing his slightly off-center mouth into a grimace of disapproval and amazement combined. "God, the knee-jerk analyses that go on in this profession. Look, Mr. Eppe, these fantasies of yours . . . Now, I'm not trying to suggest anything to you, ways you should think about yourself, but—" He spread his arms and shrugged. "Fantasy of the kind you were engaging in seems quite logical to me."

"I'm glad to hear it," I said.

"You come from two families that many people would consider great. Let's call them families that are, at the very least, success-oriented, conscious of their position in the community, that kind of thing."

"They are."

"In many such families there's a need for failures, people they can measure themselves against," Feldman said. "Maybe you were their chosen failure. I expect that from early childhood you were subtly *ordered* to fail—not by words, but by signals, attitudes toward you." He spread his arms wide again. "Now, if that *was* the case, your daydreams were arguments against such a demand. Look at what you fantasize about: being a great man . . . successful. I'd say that's a very healthy fantasy to have."

"First you tell me I'm not a schizophrenic," I said, "now you tell me my fantasies are healthy. Next you'll be saying I don't belong here at all."

He stabbed a finger at me. His voice became quiet. "That's exactly what I'm saying." He dropped his hand back into his lap.

"As for Craigie Glen's part in the fraud that you are a mentally ill person, that's not for you and me to discuss."

"Fraud or no fraud," I answered, "my mother won't let me out of here."

"Your mother," said Dr. Feldman, "hasn't anything to do with it. Do you remember signing some papers about the time of your twenty-first birthday?"

"No," I said, "I'm afraid I don't. I was pretty screwed up with shock treatments and drugs that year."

"You were committing yourself," Dr. Feldman said. "You can leave this place any time you like."

"You mean I can just walk out?" I cried.

He nodded slowly, still gazing at me. "On ten days' notice." He raised his hands. "You're a free man. What I'd *like* you to do is stay a few more weeks. I want to spend some time with you, just to make sure you're all right. If you're willing to do that, I'll see you every day. Meanwhile, I'll take you out of Fitzpatrick and have you put in a cottage."

I was too stunned and happy to think straight, but I did know the last thing I wanted out of Craigie Glen. "I'll stay," I said. "But in Fitzpatrick. I've been there a long time. I have friends there. That's where I'd like to end. It just seems right."

"Seems," he said, grinning his squinty, affectionate grin. "That's why I want you to stay a bit longer. I want to see how things seem to you, how you seem to me." The grin faded. "We can create problems in hospitals like this as well as solve them."

"You're telling me?"

"All right," he said. "Come in tomorrow morning at ten o'clock."

"I'm glad I don't have to see Primrose anymore," I said.

"Dr. Primrose," he answered, "is no longer with us. As of this afternoon."

I took Mr. Fletcher into my room after supper and told him what had happened. He sat on my bed, legs crossed, gaunt old arms resting in his lap, one wrist lying on the other. For the first time I noticed an ageless glitter in his eyes that neither life nor drugs could have put there. "Seven years," he said. "Seven. Hmpf."

"And four months," I added.

He nodded. "And four. Seven and four. I knew the day I met you that this is when it would end."

I didn't ask him how he knew, nor doubted that he did.

I saw Dr. Feldman every day for six weeks. What he did was reel me backwards to the boy I had been when I entered that place so that I could understand the man I was now. Then, one day, we decided that both our curiosities were satisfied. "What are your plans?" he asked.

"Stay away from my mother," I said, "and find my father."

"If I were you, I'd try to make some of those daydreams of yours come true," he said. "There are worse fantasies than love and success, Bornie."

"That's my main plan," I said. I had a sudden thought. "Since I'm starting all over again," I said, "could I borrow your name for a while?"

He held out his hand for the last time, smiling that wise, near-sighted smile for the last time. "Good luck, Bill."

And that was how I happened to find myself standing at the intersection of a boulevard and a side street in Cleveland, Ohio, on a rainy February afternoon, realizing that the first thing you need when they let you out of the insane asylum is a car.

Three

MY BEGINNING

THE GREAT LAKES DISCOUNT AUTO PARTS COMPANY was a warty little figment of the American dream. In the reveries of success-seekers like me there is the Ultimate Suite—a huge office equipped with all the gadgetry of command from multiconsole telephones to electronic charts which will, at the push of a button, tell you how the Shreveport division is doing. The person sitting in command, pushing the buttons, issuing the orders and feeling invulnerable to life's doubts and humiliations, is the dreamer of the dream, *self* as the Augustus Caesar of the U.S. free enterprise system.

Great Lakes was obviously supposed to be just a way station on Mr. Rafe Haddon's progress toward the Ultimate Suite. But somewhere along the line Mr. Haddon's destiny got screwed up, he lost his capacity for fantasy, his hair grew thin and his middle part fat, and he never learned that you don't wear white socks with black shoes. He made the fatal mistake of settling for what was.

What was turned out to be a big warehouse in a dismal part of town. The top floor was a large dirty space presided over by

Mr. Haddon and his bony, disappointed secretary, Miss Esmee Dupont. Actually, she liked to be called Mademoiselle Dupont. "I am of French ancestry," she said to me one day, gumming her upper plate. "Not your common Wilmington DuPonts. *The* DuPonts." Trying to be polite, I said something in French. She looked at me as if I were talking Navajo.

Mademoiselle Dupont sat outside the half-glass office where Mr. Haddon spent his days swinging around in his chair, a telephone stuck to his ear, wheedling with people, screaming at people and asking people if they *really* thought he'd do that to them.

He was a lump. I'd like to give a more precise description of Mr. Haddon, but that's what he was—a lump of overstuffed, underexercised, pale, anxious, furious American flesh. Most people pass through periods of beauty in their physical development. But Mr. Haddon must have gotten through his very, very quickly. When I knew him he was about forty-five and given to flatulence.

The warehouse beneath the office was filled with tons and tons of carburetors, mufflers, radiators, hub caps, exhaust pipes, windshield wipers, fans, tubes, bolts, nuts and everything else required for the functioning of cars.

When I first went to work for Great Lakes, the warehouse was the domain of a kid with long greasy hair who went into convulsions one morning from whiffing antifreeze. His place was taken a few days later by a black man named Hannibal. On initial acquaintance I thought that Hannibal was the meanest spade I'd ever met in a life that, admittedly, hadn't intimately encountered many people of Negroid ancestry, mean or otherwise. He was six feet four, with a huge Afro hairdo and muscles like auto springs. The first time I went down to the warehouse to get an order from him he scowled as if he'd have liked to kick me through a brick wall and devour my remains for lunch.

Those sections of the top floor that weren't filled with Mr. Haddon, Mademoiselle Dupont, cardboard boxes, dusty files, leaning stacks of catalogues, insects, crud and order pads were divided up into little plywood booths for the salesmen. They were either young guys like me on the way up or older men on the way down. The place was a patch of allegorical turf in front of Dante's entrance to hell. The three younger salesmen weren't ready to abandon all hope. The two older ones already had.

We each had a territory. I got New England, probably because I put down my true home as Cambridge, Massachusetts, along with my false name, which belonged to Dr. Feldman. Every morning they gave you lists of telephone numbers which had to be handed back when you went out for lunch or quit at the end of the day. It was forbidden to copy down any of the numbers on the lists. Mademoiselle Dupont watched us like a beady-eyed old eagle.

You would call a garage or auto-parts dealer on your list, find out what they needed, try to get them to buy the Great Lakes special of the week and then fill out an order form. When you had enough order forms you took them down to Hannibal.

I got paid eighteen percent commission on everything I sold. It wasn't hard work. The customers seemed eager to buy. My first week I made two hundred and thirty-one dollars. Mademoiselle Dupont made me sign a tax form saying I'd been paid a lot more.

The discipline got to you. Working for the Great Lakes Discount Auto Parts Company was like being a member of the palace guard in the Principality of Paranoia. You had to do everything by Mr. Haddon's dippy book: orders in handwriting, not printed; sit sideways in your booth, never with your back to Mademoiselle Dupont; keep the phone calls brief.

One day a guy in Ellsworth, Maine, was telling me about a time he saw a pair of moose making little meece in a blizzard. I started to laugh. Mr. Haddon came flying out of his office, demanding to know whom I was talking to. I told him it was a dealer. He grabbed the phone and shouted, "Who's this?" He listened, grunted and handed the phone back to me with a foul-mouthed warning. For several days thereafter Mademoiselle Dupont glared at me as if *I* had been the one caught doing it to a lady moose.

It was, I decided after a while, a very strange setup. I checked around and discovered that we were selling at about forty percent discount. In my mind I assembled all the oddities about Great Lakes and had a big think about them. The truth dawned on me: I was selling stolen auto parts to people who knew they were stolen, and my signature on a doctored tax form was Mr. Haddon's way of getting something on me in case I ever got something on him. I thanked whatever gods were in charge of me that winter that I wasn't using my true name. But neither my gods nor I were operating on a full quota of brains. Had we been, I would have gotten out of there fast.

Meanwhile, I was starting to live a real life for the first time in more than seven years. That took some getting used to. It wasn't easy switching from the contrived, tight ways of Craigie Glen to being with people who started from the assumption that you were normal until proven otherwise. Being free to come and go and do whatever I pleased was a strain at first. The rhetoric of the times is filled with talk about freedom. Actually, I have concluded, freedom makes people feel unanchored and nervous. There is, in most of us, a secret and voluptuous yearning to obey rules.

I took my first week's pay home to Hebba and Lulu, feeling all proud and contributory. I tried to give them a hundred dollars and we had a skirmish. They said it was too much. They had the damnedest lack of avarice I've ever seen. We finally settled that I'd pay them fifty dollars a week for rent, breakfast and dinner whenever I wanted it. I kept fifty dollars for spending money and banked the rest as savings toward a car.

During the time I lived there the Cleveland house underwent a beautiful, almost mystic metamorphosis. The original woodwork began to appear from under coats of paint and decades of indifference. Hebba went off and found an old hotel that was being demolished. He bought a whole bathroom—marble washstand, claw-and-ball bathtub, john and floor tiles—which he installed on the second floor after tearing down a few walls. I came in one cold evening and found the living room repainted in a soft, mustardy color of the kind you never know exists until you see it. There was real genius behind what happened to that house.

It was also a bend in the river of American life where all sorts of people were caught and held for brief periods. Somebody was always coming through on the way to Schenectady or Palo Alto or coming *from* some other point on the map. Sometimes there were only four of us at dinner—Hebba, Lulu, George and me—and sometimes Amelia joined us. At other times we'd be feeding twelve or fifteen.

Furniture and pictures assume a harmony with the personality that collects them. So do the friends of those people who have the mysterious capacity for attracting others to them in large numbers.

Hebba and Lulu's friends were a very mixed bag. There was a Boston banker; a Jesuit priest from Washington who cracked jokes about the Pope; a Chilean who'd been to Harvard; a gentle, funny kid studying the trumpet at the New England Conservatory of Music; a middle-aged English journalist with a raspy voice and an infinite capacity for gin who was brought around by a reporter from Indiana who seemed to be famous for a series he'd done on a flasher from Kokomo. There was another Englishman—he wrote thrillers and naval histories; a loud-mouthed Irish-American from New York who never quite knew when the party was over; the unoccupied, the preoccupied; people who never talked about what they did, and people who didn't talk about anything else; an ex-spy with a severe case of mental health and a rumbling laugh; a bald former diplomat; and a guy from Maine who discussed poetry with me for a whole evening and who, I discovered later, was a United States senator.

At Craigie Glen they thought the news—which was about the real world—was bad for you. We had no TV or radio news programs, no papers or magazines. But word filtered through about big, flagrant events like Vietnam and Watergate, riots, sex and the theory that God had gone off and died because the Methodists had discovered He was a Zen Buddhist, or vice versa. I had, in other words, a general idea of what had gone on. What I'd missed was how the texture of the country had changed, how it danced now, the canticles of a whole new time.

The first thing I picked up from listening to Hebba and Lulu's friends was the subject of the current conflict. At the time I was put away, the Americans were fighting about wrongs—the war, Richard Nixon and other such interruptions of reason.

Now *right*s were crashing together like a bagful of bottles falling downstairs. Everybody and everything had rights. There was the public's right to know and individual people's rights not to be known about. Oil companies were promoting their right to punch holes in the world while environmentalists whooped it up for the rights of the world not to have holes drilled in it. I heard a lot of talk about sexual rights (the country now had three official sexes), property rights, squatter's rights, racial rights, the right to live, the right to die, the right to be born, the right not to be born, the right to smoke, the right not to have smoke blown at you, the right to say anything you please, the right not to have to listen to displeasing sentiments, Polish rights, atheist's rights and, for all I knew at the time, the rights of five-year-old children to piss in each other's ears.

I also found out that problems were the fashion and pleasure of America. Food additives were a problem, so were violence on television, schools, potholes in the streets, Jesus freaks, books that people didn't read, books they did read, trains, dope fiends, parents, Indians, breeder reactors, children, cities, suburbs, beer cans and elm blight.

I came to understand that nobody gave a damn about solutions. Americans got their satisfaction out of their problems. Millions of them were anxious by nature, and discussing national problems made them feel anxious and together.

While I was absorbing these and other instructive facts

about how my country had changed I was trying to grapple with a problem of my own—Amelia.

We were living together on the top floor of Hebba and Lulu's house but not acknowledging each other. Amelia had retreated after her accusative self-presentation on the night I arrived. She still brushed her hair naked with the bathroom door open. She'd say "Hi" when I came home and I'd say "Hi" back and come over all horny. At dinner she talked around me. She wasn't aggressive but didn't make contact, either. The situation bugged me because it was so incomplete.

So I tried to do some deducing. On that first night we met, Amelia had been asking questions: how limited was my attitude toward women, could I see them as people? She'd been waiting for my answer but she didn't want it in words.

Having decided that that was the problem, I realized I'd been stupid. I'd been playing courtship games with her, which, when I stopped to think about it, was just what she suspected in me.

On the way home one Friday night I steeled myself not to look at her as a naked woman, when I saw her as a naked woman. My lust was a fence I had to look over in order to see her as a person.

When I got to the top floor she was brushing her hair as usual. She looked down the hall and said "Hi."

"Hi," I answered. "How did it go today?"

"All right," she said, turning back to the mirror.

"I'm crummy," I said. "Mind if I take a bath?"

The rhythm of her brushing slowed but she didn't look at me again. "Go ahead," she said. "Want me to run it for you?"

"Please," I answered. I went into my room. I heard the gushing of bath water. I undressed slowly, trying not to think of all the ways that physiology and I could wreck everything in the next ten minutes.

Stark naked, I threw the towel over my shoulder and walked down the hall to the bathroom. Amelia was still brushing. I sidled past her, touching her bare hip and reminding myself with every muscle in my brain that I was there to talk to somebody, not to perform a lot of subtle maneuvers on a woman.

I turned off the water and stretched out in the tub, trying to be calm. One of the annoying things about me is that I tend to jabber a lot when I'm tense.

"Tough day?" she asked, still looking at herself in the mirror.

"Sort of. I've never had a job like this before. I'm still trying to figure it out."

She put her brush on the washbasin and looked down at me. "Mind if I ask you a question?"

"Go ahead," I said.

"Have you ever had *any* job in your life?"

I stared at the bathtub faucets for a few moments. When all else fails, tell the truth. "No," I said. "This is the first job I've ever had."

"How old are you, Bill?"

"Twenty-four," I said.

"You mean you're twenty-four years old and you've *never* had a job?"

I nodded.

"Have you been in school?"

I looked up at her. "No, I haven't been doing that, either."

She picked up her hairbrush. "You must have a very rich and indulgent family." She left the bathroom and went into her own room, closing the door.

So much for trying to act out your premises, I told myself. I was still cussing out the inappropriateness of my approach to her when she came back in her dressing gown and sat down on the john seat. "What kind of food do you like best?"

"French, I guess. My father used to take me to some pretty good French restaurants."

"What about Greek?"

"I've never been to a Greek restaurant."

She sighed, but it wasn't an irritated sigh; it was supposed to ·

be a funny imitation of one. "You're twenty-four years old, you've never had a job before and you've never been to a Greek restaurant. What've you been doing, living in a cave?"

I laughed. "You'd be surprised at how close you are. Let's go have a Greek dinner."

"Okay," Amelia said, "but we go Dutch. I imagine you're as broke as I am." That was her way of saying she was sorry she'd accused me of coming from a rich and indulgent family. Things were improving. For the moment, anyway.

It was raining, with expectorations of snow coming in on the wind from Lake Erie. Amelia drove us to the other end of town, to another parish of dismal in the gray diocese of Cleveland. The sign of a restaurant called Athena was a warm beckon in the middle of a block of houses fit only for the dead.

It was a noisy, low-ceilinged place full of smoke and garlic. We had to sit at the bar for a while. I was feeling more relaxed but cautious. I didn't want to do anything false or let off great vapors of sudden intimacy. Amelia and I were still only ankle-deep in the possibilities of friendship.

We talked about some of the people who had been staying at the house lately. She told me that she worked as a computer programmer and was divorced. As we both dismantled our outer defenses, I told her stories about the Great Lakes Discount Auto Parts Company. She laughed at some of them and slapped me down hard when I referred to Hannibal as a spade. She was very principled about racism and sexism and such. I was about to answer that I meant nothing derogatory when I used such a term, but after a quick check of myself, I wasn't so sure I didn't.

Questions hovered in the smoky air like the low front in the February night outside as we moved to a table and ordered dinner. Over the first course she told me more about herself—she came from Oregon and was thirty-one. Her former husband was a professor of mathematics.

"Bill," she finally said, "you haven't spoken a word about your past. Is there something you're ashamed of?"

"I'm not ashamed. I don't know how to be the next thing after what I've just been."

"I don't believe in intruding on people's secrets, but all of us have been wondering something about you."

"All of who?"

"Hebba, Lulu, George and me."

"What have you been wondering?" I felt uneasy.

"Everybody likes you. You mustn't think they don't."

"I won't," I replied. "What have you been wondering?"

"Whether you've been in prison."

I didn't answer for a moment. I could see instantly how such speculation would start about me. It fit.

"No," I said, "I haven't been in prison." I shut up again, struggling with several impulses that were suddenly charging around in my brain. "Have you ever heard of a place called Craigie Glen?"

"The mental hospital," she said.

I nodded. "That's where I've been."

I was hanging by my fingernails in the effort not to say any more, not to explain it all and prove that I wasn't crazy, when Amelia said, "Somebody made a dreadful mistake about you. What an awful thing to do to a perfectly normal man."

I fell in and out of love with her all within ten seconds. "You said that you were *all* wondering about me. How do you know George is wondering? I've never heard him say anything."

Amelia laughed. "You can tell by the expression on his face when we were talking about it," she said. "I actually heard George say something once."

"What was it?"

"He was helping Hebba move that big dining-room table down to the basement. He slipped and dropped it on his foot and said 'Shit.' "

They were playing one of those pulsating Greek dances on plucked instruments in the smoke around us. The remnants of dinner were on the table between us as reminders of the evening's various satisfactions.

We drove home, talked to Lulu in the kitchen for a while and then I went upstairs. I got into bed and tried to read. I was full of a gratification that I didn't want to define, so I slipped into my king fantasy.

In that one I've been made king of a small arid country in some one-eyed corner of the world. The people have had a terrible time with their previous rulers, who were corrupt, cruel and self-indulgent. In the king fantasy I'm trying to make their lives better with all my knowledge of how the developed part of the world operates. I move out of the palace and turn it into an orphanage, dress simply and get technical advisers from Israel and foreign aid from the United States.

Realistically, I know that partisans of the old order are still around, and so are revolutionaries who will try to overthrow me before I can carry out my plans to get the country cleaned up and the people educated and aware enough to hold free elections (in which I will be elected president by a love-charged landslide, of course). I really ought to have spies out listening, but that's the kind of thing my terrible predecessors did. I leave that problem to one side and proceed on with imagining myself talking to the peasants, installing a medical-care system and marrying a girl from one of the hill tribes (she's very beautiful in an Egyptian sort of way) as proof of my benevolent intentions.

Amelia came upstairs and went into the bathroom. I lay with my book on my chest, half floating in pleasurable memories of the evening, half thinking about getting somebody from the British Treasury to come and design a modern economic system for my kingdom.

I heard Amelia leave the bathroom. A few minutes later she came in and sat down on the side of my bed. "I'm not going to tell the others what you told me tonight," she said.

"Okay," I said.

She pondered me for a moment with her dark eyes, in which I could watch her mind working out how to say something.

"It must be awful in one of those places," she said. "Is it?"

"It's more unreal than awful," I answered. "You live a life full of things they won't let you do."

"Have you ever made love?"

"No," I said. "And it worries me."

"Why does it worry you?" Her question was solicitous, not accusative.

"Because someday I'll fall in love with somebody. I'll know how to get pleasure in bed but I won't know how to give it."

Amelia looked at me in the soft light of the bedside lamp. Then she took my face in both hands and kissed me. I hadn't known until that moment how much she wanted that unspoken question answered. It never occurred to me. She stood up and took off her dressing gown. It was as if I were seeing her body for the first time.

She got into bed with me and turned off the light. She taught me how to give—and receive—pleasure.

I never made love to Amelia again for the rest of the time I lived at Hebba and Lulu's. But the first time, being *my* first time ever, was one of the most fortunate events of my life. And she became my friend.

Four

LOVE AND PERIL

PONCE DE LEÓN was looking for the fountain of youth when he discovered Florida, the world's most celebrated peninsula for the elderly. Some guck in Sir Alexander Fleming's test tube came up penicillin. You never know when one of life's directions is going to take you someplace else.

The various components of my life on March 18, 1980, weren't pointing in any particular direction, but I wasn't looking for one, either. I was living in a comfortable and interesting environment, and I'd just lost my virginity. I was getting enough sleep, had all my original teeth, and like most of the rest of the populace, I sat more than I stood, went to the dry cleaner's once a week and was forming the usual number of opinions, reasonable and otherwise.

Then, on March 18 several events, connected to one another by that symmetry which the ignorant call coincidence, changed everything.

It was a Tuesday. The air was sharp and the sky so blue that you couldn't believe that storms had ever been invented. I got out of the house early and decided to walk to work. I took a new street east—a way I'd never been before—and passed a used-car lot where there was a blue Volkswagen with "Priced For Quick Sale" written in soap on the windshield.

You will recall that buying a car was the first thing I decided to do when I got out of Craigie Glen. I went to the little shack that was the office of the used-car establishment. A guy gave me the keys. Inside, the Beetle was clean but smelled musty. The engine seemed to start and run properly. I went back to the shack and asked how much. They wanted five hundred.

I had four hundred and ten dollars in my bank account and a devout if untested belief that anything not for sale in a chain store can be haggled over. I am a mechanical ignoramus and knew I needed a second opinion before I started bargaining. I put fifty dollars down to hold the car and said I'd be back.

The weather was cold and bright outdoors that morning, but the barometer was falling in the offices of the Great Lakes Discount Auto Parts Company. Mr. Haddon was whirling around in his chair like a hyperactive dervish, screaming into the telephone. Mademoiselle Dupont's knotty fingers flew across her desk, nervously rearranging the arranged. The salesmen were cussing and getting wrong numbers. I don't know if they all arrived infected with individual pestilences of their own or whether they had cross-pollinated each other with fury and misery. Anyway, it was going to be a bad day. As Mademoiselle unlocked her desk drawer to give me my lists Mr. Haddon hollered through the glass that if I got in late again, I'd be out on my ass. I said "Yessir" and went to work.

That week's special was fan belts. We were loaded with them. Our suppliers must have knocked off the biggest fan-belt works in the country. I started calling dealers in northern Maine, and by midmorning I'd sold sixty dozen fan belts and a grand heap of other purloined goods.

I took my orders downstairs to Hannibal. I couldn't tell if he had caught the virus of foul dispositions that prevailed upstairs or whether he was just being his old sweet self. "Don't screw around, man," he said as he took the papers from me.

"Who's screwing around?" I answered. "I'm just standing here living and breathing."

He started shuffling through my orders. "You're screwin' around with Haddon," he said. "He don't like you one damn bit."

"What'd I do to him?"

"Listen, smart-ass," he said, "it ain't what you *do*, it's the way you act." He turned around and looked down on me. That's right, looked *down*. Big as I am, I'm an undernourished midget compared to that huge hunk of aboriginal malevolence. "What's a cat like you doin' in a place like this, anyway?"

"Making a living like everybody else," I said. "Listen, Hannibal—"

"You don't need to make no livin'," he said. "You talk rich. Like you don't belong here. Haddon don't know what you is except you think you're better than him and got some goddamn funny reason for being here. Now, you watch out and stop screwin' round, you hear me?"

"I can't help the way I talk," I answered. "And I've got just as much right to earn a living as anybody else. Besides, Haddon's crazy. You'd see that yourself if you weren't so damn dumb."

"Don't tell me what I see and don't see, smart-ass. You just watch out or maybe *I* give you something to watch out for."

"Cut the crap," I said. "How'd you like to make twenty bucks?"

He glared at me with his discolored eyes from beneath the edge of a woolly hat he'd pulled down over his ears. "Doin' what?"

"I found a car I think I'd like to buy," I said. "It's in a lot near here. If you'll come up and check it out, I'll give you twenty bucks."

"Whether you buy it or not?"

"Whether I buy it or not."

"Come down at twelve-thirty," he said.

I went back to the office feeling irked. I looked across the room at Mr. Haddon. He was holding the telephone to one side of his head and pounding his desk. It was probably true that he didn't like me, but it was irrelevant. He poured all of his emotional energy into scheming, being paranoid and staying one jump ahead of the failure beast that stalks this world's marginal operators.

I flipped over to my Rhode Island list and dialed a garage in Warwick. It was run by a Portuguese guy I liked, and I thought that talking to him would lift me out of all the poisonous vapors that were floating around that morning.

A female voice answered on the other end. I asked for Serge.

"Who?" she asked.

"Serge Texiera."

"Not *again*," she said in tones of exasperated resignation.

Wrong number, I thought. I was about to hang up when I imagined I detected something. "Have you been crying?" I asked.

"Oh, Edward," she said, "stop kidding around. I really don't want to talk about it anymore."

"This isn't—"

"Facts can be discussed into mush," said the girl's voice. "What's happened has happened. We can't make it rehappen or take back anything."

I tried again. "I think—"

"We agreed on silence, a clean break," she said. "Suture it off. Go get drunk. Sail your boat. Be irrational for a while."

"Miss—"

"Please," she said. "It's been a bad enough day already. Purvis just got killed."

I had blundered into a terminating love affair which included a murder. That's a situation nobody could abandon. I glanced at Mr. Haddon and Mademoiselle Dupont. They were wrestling with their furies and anxieties and not paying any attention to me. "This isn't Edward," I said to the girl on the telephone.

There was a pause, denoting surprise, at the other end of the line. "Oh?"

"I dialed your number by mistake," I said. "I was trying to call Texiera's garage."

"Extraordinary," the girl answered, her voice de-escalating from its tone of plea and anxiety. "You sounded like—well, somebody I know. Now you don't. Say something more."

"Murder will out," I answered, not being able to think of anything else.

"You have a nice voice," she said. "It's mellifluous. You aren't five feet three, are you?"

"No," I answered. "And I haven't got any dueling scars, either."

She laughed softly and suddenly as if mirth had escaped from her by accident.

"And I'm not Edward," I said.

"That's in your favor too," she answered.

"Which brings me back to my original question," I said. "Have you been crying?"

"Why do you want to know?"

"Well, I stumbled on you, I thought you had been."

"If I *had* been crying—"

"Were you?"

"—what would you do about it?"

"Cheer you up."

"That's nice," she said. "But—well, asking somebody if they've been crying is a sign of intimacy. I haven't the wildest idea who or where you—"

"You haven't read Oliver Catchpole," I said.

"Oliver who?"

"Catchpole. He wrote *Instant Intimacy*."

There was a minute pause at the Rhode Island end of the line. "Tell me what he said."

"Chapter Six," I answered. "If you misdial the telephone and get a crying girl on the line, tell her you put on torn underwear that morning. That establishes instant intimacy."

I heard a sound that could have been a blip of Ma Bell's static or a half-stifled giggle. "Tell me, Childe Harold, did you put on torn underwear this morning?"

"Clean but definitely torn."

She laughed again, laughter that sounded as if it were wrapped up in velvet. "Okay, we're intimate. What happens now?"

"Well," I said, "it's a safe intimacy. I'm almost six hundred miles away from you, so I'm not going to drive my Cadillac convertible up onto your front porch or anything."

"Six hundred miles?"

"Something like that."

"Just my luck," the girl said. "I get a nice new intimacy and it's six hundred miles away."

There was an implication of flirt creeping into the conversation that attracted me—along with my burning curiosity about the death of Purvis.

"Stop being arch," she said, "and tell me where you're calling from."

"Cleveland," I said. "Why were you crying?"

"It's pretty hard to describe—ah—*factually*," she answered. "The facts wouldn't make any sense without the context."

"Then tell me the context," I said. "Look, people say things to total strangers on airplanes that they wouldn't say to their best friends or their psychiatrist."

"Are you a psychiatrist?"

"No," I answered. "You're avoiding the question."

"Have you ever been treated by one?"

"Once," I said.

"What did he say was wrong with you?"

"My mother."

Her laughter came forth again, low and full of pleasure. Anxiety had vanished totally from her voice. "I'm sorry. Maybe you didn't mean that as a joke."

"I did," I said, "even though it's true."

"Hm. Do you laugh at all your problems?"

"Not all," I said, "some—especially large, loud and unsolvable ones like my mother."

"That's novel," the girl answered. "Not pitying yourself. I like it."

"Tell me why you were crying."

"Well—" She took a long breath. "I'd been feeling palsied in the spirit this morning, anyway—"

Edward, I told myself. I liked her original phraseology, I liked her alto voice and the way she spoke, as if she cared about the shape and sound of each word.

"—and then my cat, who was born the same year I was, got run over about an hour ago by this great, oily, gritty truck."

"*That's* who Purvis is," I said.

"Of course. Who did you think he was?"

"When you mentioned at the beginning of this conversation that Purvis had been killed I thought somebody had been murdered."

"Oh." Her voice turned consoling. "I'm sorry to deprive you of drama—"

"I'm fine."

"—but Purvis was definitely a cat. A twenty-three-year-old cat." For the briefest instant I thought she might start crying again.

"From which I deduce," I said, "that you're twenty-three."

"Very shrewd," she answered.

"I'm twenty-four," I said.

"Our lives almost match."

I had an odd feeling I knew her from somewhere. I decided to try a show-off. In Craigie Glen, Mr. Fletcher had made me read a lot of poetry, and catchy phrases from it had stuck to my memory. "Maybe our eternities match," I said. " 'When this grave's dug up again, some second guest to entertain—' "

"When *my* grave's dug up again," she corrected me. "Are you a John Donne man?"

I was having a good time. I was enjoying her distinct, beckoning personality. "I guess you could call me that," I said.

"What's your name?"

"Bill Feldman."

"Mine's Elizabeth Watts." She switched to a droll, imitation Georgia accent. "Folks round the plantation call me Beth."

I was liking her more and more, the realization of how I knew her was coming closer and closer. "You did that pretty well," I said.

"I stole it from somewhere. *Light in August*, maybe?"

"I don't think so," I said.

"Oh, well. Anyway, I don't want to leave you with the impression that I'm a lady who has hysterics over dead cats. What happened this morning just gave me a chance to have a good, self-indulgent wallow. Life, the last twist of the knife and all that. What do you do in Cleveland, Mr. Feldman?"

"Bill," I said.

"Bill it is," she said.

"I sell discount auto parts," I said. "Temporarily."

Her low laughter came flooding through the telephone, giving my plywood salesman's booth and the gritty environs of the Great Lakes Discount Auto Parts Company a burnish of enchantment. "I'm glad it's only temporary. You've saved this day for me and I'm having a reverie about you. I couldn't construct imaginary pleasures about a man who had given over his soul to discount auto parts."

Whammo! When she said the words "reverie" and "imaginary pleasures" I suddenly knew who she was: in voice, manner and approach to me she was the very embodiment of a girl I'd invented in one of *my* fantasies! It was uncanny and thrilling. I glanced at Mademoiselle Dupont just as she was glancing at me. But I didn't care. "Tell me about it," I said to Beth.

"It's bright and clear here this morning," she said, "and the air is stiff. I was imagining you were quite tall—"

A fellow fantasist to boot! She was an *embellishment* on my invented girl!

"—and we were walking around a place called Beavertail—"

"On Jamestown."

"God Al—mighty!" she murmured. "I don't believe it. You mean you *know* Beavertail?"

My Eppe grandfather, the bishop, has had a summer house on Jamestown since the Last Supper—which is how I knew. "It's an island at the end of Narragansett Bay," I said.

"Now, this is almost . . ." She hesitated. "A twenty-four-year-old John Donne man who knows Beavertail . . ."

"Coincidence," I said. "More of a coincidence than you'll ever realize."

She didn't answer.

"Are you still there?" I asked.

"Yes, sorry. Still here."

"My name isn't Edward," I said.

"I know," she said softly. "Forgive me."

I had a quick look at Mademoiselle Dupont. Both she and Mr. Haddon were having hard looks at me. "Beth," I said, "I've got to hang up pretty soon . . ."

"I've disappointed you," she said.

"No, you haven't. I have to hang up because of the circumstances I'm in. They're pretty goofy and when I tell you about them, you'll laugh. But I can't now."

"Then when will you tell me?"

"I'll call you tonight from home," I said.

I had become so absorbed in her that my real surroundings had completely evaporated like a bad odor in a sweet wind. Mademoiselle Dupont was glaring at me with ferocious curiosity.

"Do you really think you'll call me again?"

"Tonight," I repeated. "I promise."

"I'm scared of promises," she said. "They're like storm warnings. Just tell me quickly—"

"I'm tall."

"I teach school and write poems."

"Do you like chocolate ice cream?"

"Peppermint," she answered. "We'll work something out. Oh, *please* call me tonight . . ."

Mademoiselle Dupont was rising to her feet like a killer bird gaining altitude for the final pounce. Mr. Haddon had ceased howling down the telephone and was eyeballing me as if I'd kneed him. I turned my back on them—a violation of their nutty rules—and hunched over my desk. "Give me your number," I whispered.

Beth gave it to me. I scribbled it on my list.

A stumpy paw with an American flag tattooed on it grabbed the list off my desk. I looked up. Mr. Haddon was standing over me, his potbelly smothering his belt buckle and his piggy face full of gnash and fury. Mademoiselle Dupont was jittering and accusing behind him. "He wasn't selling!" she cawed in a voice that sounded like a band saw going through a railroad tie.

"Who're y'talking to, Feldman?" Mr. Haddon barked.

I hung up the phone so excited that it took me a full ten seconds to become properly alarmed. "I was calling a customer in Rhode Island," I said. "I dialed the wrong number."

"He talked for ten minutes!" Mademoiselle Dupont screeched.

Mr. Haddon started to grab at me, considered my size and muscle for a second and made the sensible, cowardly decision to stop short of physical violence. He handed the list to Mademoiselle Dupont. "I wanna know who you were talking to!"

The other salesmen had stopped work and were looking out of their booths at me.

"I was calling a garage in Warwick, Rhode Island," I said. "Look, Mr. Haddon, I'm doing very well today. I've sold sixty dozen orders of the special. Now, if I can just—"

He glared at me, his speech centers paralyzed by that anger which, my experiences among the mad had taught me, is accumulated over a whole lifetime and is invested in moments that frighten you. "You can go to lunch," he finally said. He marched back to his office and slammed the door. Mademoiselle Dupont put my list in her drawer and locked it with the smug expression of a grade school teacher confiscating smut. They were members of some subspecies, those two.

I didn't give a damn. I was full of blooming rapture.

I haven't told you yet about my love fantasies. There were two kinds. The first involved fleshy, tousled-haired women with whom I had an amazing variety of sexual adventures on sofas, beds, porches, desert islands at high noon and in cars. The women I made up for those kinds of fantasy didn't have well-worked-out characters. They didn't need them.

Then there was an imaginary girl about whom I began to daydream when I was nineteen and incarcerated in Craigie Glen. She was my ultimate fantasy.

She was a mixture of that poise and mystery you see in faded photographs of beautiful women from the last century—a mixture of that and the cheerful confidence of girls I had known or glimpsed in my own life. I saw her in everything from faded muslin dresses to blue jeans. I imagined her in a gazebo with the music of Aaron Copland filling the summer air around her. She kept dead flowers pressed between the pages of books and she was well-read. She also had a sense of humor.

Her character entranced me even more than her beauty—which was of some unusual, out-of-the-mold type. In my imaginings of her—which often came after I had exhausted my inventive powers with scenes of lurid debauchery—the girl in the gazebo had a clear-edged, witty exterior. Underneath, a brilliant but receptive mind was at work on some great talent she possessed. She thought original thoughts and expressed them in well-tempered, almost *carved* language. I understood her at every layer.

We loved each other, a wise love moderated by the previous tempests of our individual lives. Though she was an individualist, she was dependent on me—we never discussed it. I was the protector of her great, unspecified talent. On her side, her love for me was sensible and perceptive and helped to keep my screw-up–prone life on a straight course. She was proud of my accomplishments, I was proud of hers.

Now, amid the inconclusive reality of my days, I had heard the girl in the gazebo on the telephone—trying to free herself from the tempestuous ardors of Edward (whoever he was), mourning her dead cat, speaking her clear, precise language, a poet. I'd heard her laughing because I'd made her happy.

I put on my coat, went down to the warehouse and gave Hannibal instructions on how to get to the used-car lot. At the bank I withdrew all my money. I really needed that car. As soon as I could afford to leave Ohio I was going to go to Rhode Island and find Beth.

Hannibal walked around the Volkswagen, kicked its tires, bumped his huge body up and down on the front seat, looked at the engine and turned it on.

We drove around the block. "Transmission's half gone," he said. "Sumbitch probably stuffed her with sawdust. How much he want?"

"Five hundred dollars," I said.

We drove back to the car lot. "This man," said Hannibal to the owner, "is gone give you three hundred and fifty dollars for it."

"I'm losing money," the owner said. He was gray, freezing and wore rimless glasses.

"No, you ain't," Hannibal answered. "You paid seventy-five for that pile of crap and got some asshole to fix her up so she'd get out of the lot."

The owner looked at him in misery. "Four hundred."

"Three-fifty," Hannibal said. "You screw around an' the price goes down to three hundred."

"Three-fifty," the owner said in a voice like Cornwallis surrendering.

Hannibal turned to me. "Gimme my money."

I gave him twenty dollars and thanked him for saving me a lot of cash.

"That's because you're a smart-ass who don't know what he's doin'," he said. He turned his head covered by that God-awful hat and glared at me. "Or *do* you know what you're doin'?"

"Goddamn it," I said, parking the car in front of the warehouse, "what's this all about?"

"Haddon thinks *he* knows," Hannibal said. "Man, you better watch your ass."

Well, he was right. But it was too late. When I got back upstairs to the office I was ordered into Mr. Haddon's office. "Close the door," he said.

I closed the door and stood before his desk. He was about two degrees paler than his usual dead-flounder hue and had himself under some kind of eerie control for the moment. "There are two ways we can do this thing," he said.

"What thing?"

"Ah, *c'mon*, Feldman . . . if that's your real name. *You* know what I'm talking about. If you want to forget what you saw here and make yourself a few bucks, we can arrange that." He grabbed a wad of his right side and scratched himself. "Personally," he said, "I don't think you can prove a damn thing."

"Mr. Haddon," I said, "I don't have the wildest idea what you're talking about." I had more than a wild idea, but I didn't want him scared of me. I wanted to go on working until I had enough money to drive east and find Beth.

"We traced that call you made this morning."

"Look," I said, "I'll tell you exactly what happened. I was calling Texiera's garage and I misdialed. I got a girl on the line and talked to her for about ten minutes. You can take the cost of the call out of my pay."

Suddenly he couldn't hold it in any longer—all that the daddies, mummies and deceptions of his life had done to him. "I'll take more than that out of you!" he yelled. "I can get people who know how to fix spies! Bottom of the river! Goddamn FBI! I'll sue the balls off you *and* J. Edgar Hoover!"

I could understand the terrible apprehension he lived with, being a criminal and all. But what I had done to trigger off his terror was beyond me. "J. Edgar Hoover's dead," I said.

"You're gonna be, too!" he hollered. "The lime pit, Feldman!"

"I'm not from the FBI," I said. "I just want to get back to work. Can I have my list, please?"

"You can have your legs and arms chopped off!" Haddon shouted. He had a nice color in his face now. Purple. His neck was so swollen that I thought his collar was going to behead him. "The government's fulla Commie spies!" he yelled. "You get your Commie ass out of here! You're fired!"

I went to my booth, got a couple of books and picked up my coat. The other salesmen were watching me in meek, I'm-a-good-boy silence. Mademoiselle Dupont's fists were clenched in some inexpressible fury. I looked quickly around the room for the last time, noticing things for a plan I was already formulating.

"Bottom of the river!" Haddon shouted as I walked toward the door. "Both legs broken, Feldman! The lime pit!"

I had several feelings to untangle as I drove home. On the one hand I was a veritable symphony of enthrallments over Beth. On the other hand, I had two problems: I was jobless again and the list with Beth's telephone number scribbled on it was locked up in Mademoiselle Dupont's desk. I had to have that telephone number. Without it, I'd never find Beth.

When I got home Hebba was stripping down an old oak chest in the basement. I sat on a crate and told him everything that had happened. In the weeks I had known him I had come to regard Hebba as a very wise man.

After I'd finished he folded his arms and thought for a moment. "Listen, hero," he said, "are you sure they're fencing stolen auto parts?"

"That's what it's got to be. Haddon's scared to death that I know *something*."

"But you haven't any proof?"

I shook my head.

"Then you can't go to the police."

"I don't especially want to," I said. "They're all in hell already. What I want is that New England list. Hebba, I'm going to break into that place tonight. I won't even steal the list. I'll just copy down Beth's telephone number."

"You're a real original, Bill," he said. "What makes you so sure this girl is what you think she is?"

"It's hard to put into words," I said. "I think there are people we've always known in our imaginations."

"There are dumber ways of falling in love," he said. "How are you going to get in?"

"The fire-escape door's bent," I said. "I could pry it open with a crowbar."

"Want me to come with you?" Hebba asked. "Me and George?"

"I appreciate the offer," I said, "but I'd better go alone. I could use a crowbar."

He handed me one from his workbench. "Take care of yourself, hero. We'd hate to lose you."

The sun set into a streak of clouds like a frozen lake that evening. The wind came up after dark and whooped around in the eaves just above the windows of the third floor. I wanted to tell Amelia about how I'd fallen in love, but she had to go to a meeting.

The shutters were rattling and the power cables were swaying above the street as I left the house a little after ten. The Volkswagen gagged and shuddered a few times before it started. As I drove east, bits of snow blew through the headlight beams like the ghosts of last summer's insects. All around me the city was empty. The avenues were abandoned to the wind.

I parked near the alleyway that ran behind the Great Lakes Discount Auto Parts Company. The building was blacked out and loomed in dirty misery against the sky.

It took me only two sprints across the width of the alley to run far enough up the side of the building to get my hands on the bottom rung of the fire escape. It swung down. I climbed up to the third-floor door and took Hebba's crowbar from inside my jacket. I stuck it between the fire door and the jamb. After two hard jerks on the crowbar the bent door swung open. I was in.

I don't mind telling you that I was as tense as a shock absorber as I pushed the door closed behind me. My heart was pounding in the middle of my chest, and my hands were both sweaty and cold.

There was a dim reflection of light from the alley on the glass of Mr. Haddon's office. I stood still until I could make out the familiar shapes of that cruddy office. My solar plexus was tying itself in granny knots as I went over to Mademoiselle Dupont's desk. Her sour, untouchable odor still hovered where she sat. I inserted the crowbar into the slit at the top of her drawer, wrenched it open, shuffled through the file, and—with a mental cry of triumph—pulled out the list.

At which point the lights went on.

I looked up in panic—which is to say that I looked up into the working end of a revolver held by Mr. Rafe Haddon, who was standing ten feet away holding the gun with both hands, Kojak-style. Hannibal was only five feet away. Mademoiselle was behind them wearing a fur coat that must have been made from a diseased kangaroo.

"Stick 'em up!" Mr. Haddon shrieked.

I was paralyzed. I looked at Hannibal. He looked back at me.

"Upupup!" Mr. Haddon screamed.

"Shoot him in the foot!" Mademoiselle howled. "Shoot him in the leg!"

"Don't do anything you'll regret," I said, flinging up my hands which flung the list across the room. It landed at Hannibal's feet. Mr. Haddon was jerking the gun around in spasms of mixed exultation and worst fears realized. "If you don't calm down," I said, "that thing's likely to go off."

It went off. The glass wall behind me exploded and a file cabinet in Mr. Haddon's office gave a grinding death rattle as the bullet ripped through its sides and partitions.

Hannibal was nearest, toughest and didn't have a gun. At the same instant as the glass came down all over my head and shoulders I dove for him. It was like hitting the side of a Franklin stove, but to my surprise Hannibal reeled across the room, smashed into Mr. Haddon and they both went down in a heap. I made for the fire door as Mademoiselle Dupont hopped up and down screaming "Rape!" "Murder!" and "Shoot him in the leg!"

I yanked open the door, lunged through it, shoved it shut, jammed the crowbar into the place where the lock should have been, and went down that fire escape with an agility that would have made a baboon proud. As I dropped to the ground I could hear Hannibal pounding on the fire door and roaring, "Sumbitch jammed it!" Crazy. With his strength he could have ripped that door off its hinges.

I didn't have time, however, to speculate on the nature of such things. As I rounded the corner out of the alley I could see Hannibal coming down the fire escape. To me, he looked like King Kong.

My gods hadn't totally abandoned me. The Volkswagen started with the first twist of the key. I slammed it into gear and roared away from the curb, nearly hitting a car that was coming out of the alley at the same speed. For an instant I saw Hannibal behind the wheel. He was all teeth and eyes as I hurtled past and hung a sharp right, burning half the rubber off my tires.

The headlights of Hannibal's car lit up my rear-view mirror. I pushed the accelerator to the floor. Stop signs and red lights flew past. Behind me, the headlights were holding steady, neither gaining nor falling away.

I was in one of the keenest panics I've ever experienced in my whole life. I was either going to be killed in a car crash, mangled by that black monster pursuing me or arrested by the police—with my luck perhaps all three. What was worse, I hadn't gotten Beth's telephone number. I had truly screwed up again.

I had the Volkswagen up to seventy as I entered the tree-lined streets of a suburb. I was driving like a demented stock-car jockey. Twice I had to perform automotive miracles to avoid hitting cars whose drivers assumed I was going to observe stop signs. And always those headlights were shining in my rear-view mirror. Hannibal wasn't trying to catch me, not yet. He was stalking me.

I roared into an area of dark streets. In my desperation I turned off the headlights and took a sharp left, hitting the curb so fast and so hard that my car flew five feet and landed in a skid that turned it completely around. I was facing a driveway. I gunned the engine, shot between two houses and stopped.

Out on the street I heard a horrid, screamy sound as Hannibal took the corner on two wheels. His car rocketed past the head of the driveway. In the distance I heard the same screeching as he went around another corner looking for me.

He wasn't stupid, though I'd called him that. He'd figure out what I'd done and he'd be back. I reversed the car out of the driveway, set off down the street he'd taken and turned right, praying that Hannibal had turned left.

I drove for ten blocks before I dared turn the headlights on again. By that time I was entering open country. I turned left and drove for miles and miles, away from Cleveland. I finally saw a big green sign with luminous letters which said I was approaching Route 80, the Ohio Turnpike, heading east.

That was the direction I'd planned to take eventually, but not now. I thought about Hebba, Lulu, Amelia and George, the silent welder, and wondered if I'd ever see them again. I wondered what they'd think had happened to me.

I got onto the turnpike going east. I hunched down in the cold. However badly I'd messed things up, I had made an important discovery—the business life was not for me.

Love was ahead of me and peril behind me as I was swallowed up in the dark night of Ohio.

Five

DASHFORD'S TRUTH

MISERY IS A WHOLE COUNTRY. Once it gets you, everything else visible, audible and olfactory takes on a general wretchedness.

I had driven all night. I was rusty and huge-eyed with fatigue. There was less than a gallon of gas left in the Volkswagen. I had twenty-seven dollars in my pocket, and all my worldly goods were back on the shores of Lake Erie where the general management of the Great Lakes Discount Auto Parts Company was possessed of a baleful lust to see me dead and buried.

I was sitting in a diner across a potholed road from an industrial mess called the Farnham Brothers Pottery, Inc., which was snorting smoke and steam into the cold air. The rising sun was doing its best to blind me. I was trying to eat some eggs that tasted as if they'd been scrambled in the lard from a buffalo's hump and drink a cup of tepid battery acid that the menu claimed was coffee.

Those were my practical circumstances that freezing winter dawn. The misery they were aiding and abetting was my realization that I was a born loser. I had lost Beth's telephone number. I had lost my job. I had lost Hebba's crowbar, and as if to confirm my hopeless proclivity for misplacement, I had lost my way the previous night. I had somehow gotten off onto a highway that eventually ended up running parallel to the Ohio River. I didn't want to be there, especially not on the outskirts of a dismal factory town named East Heidelberg.

As I said, misery is a whole country; everything around you contributes to its landscape. Across the road at the Farnham brothers' factory gates a guy in a raincoat, wool scarf, earmuffs and mittens was trying to pass out leaflets to men arriving for the morning shift. They were all numb with sleep and cold, and not one of them took a leaflet. It was a spectacle of such utter rejection that it seemed designed especially for my state of mind. God hated East Heidelberg and everybody in it that morning.

After the last worker had passed through the gates, the leaflet man stood looking at the factory as if he were trying to figure out why it didn't love him anymore.

After a few minutes he crossed the road to the diner, sat down on a counter stool and ordered a cup of coffee. He must have been about forty, but he still looked boyish. Several strands of brown hair flopped over one side of his forehead. He had a sixteen-year-old's goofy grin as he turned around to me. "Hi," he said.

"Hi," I answered despite my desire to be left alone to concentrate on my gloom.

He tasted his coffee. "Christ," he murmured so that the tired, breastless girl behind the counter couldn't hear him, "that's pretty bad, isn't it?"

"It's terrible," I answered. "So are the eggs."

He slid into the booth opposite me. "Want to read something?" He sounded as if he were offering me dirty literature or state secrets.

"Sure," I said.

He handed me a leaflet. It had his picture at the top and his name, Ben Dashford, printed in large, exciting letters underneath. It said that he was a candidate for mayor and that if people voted for him, all sorts of virtuous things would happen to East Heidelberg. The streets would improve along with the air quality, there would be a new wing on the high school, a medical center, community college, minority rights and no more sexism in the city government. In addition, an unnamed but obviously insidious and familiar force would be vanquished.

Ben Dashford was leaning forward with his arms on the table and that expectant kid grin on his face. "What do you think?" he asked.

I was completely ignorant about politics. It had played the same role in our house as my father's character, my deportment, the inadequacy of servants and the general unspeakableness of those members of the species who didn't have Anglo-Saxon names or subscribe to the Boston Symphony Orchestra. Politics, in other words, was a weapon in my mother's war against my father. I knew who was President, and I gathered from my mother's periodic whoopings that Irish Catholic Democrats were blighting the history of the world. Aside from those facts, I was a political imbecile.

"It sounds pretty good to me," I said.

"How about voting for me?"

"I'd like to, but I can't. I don't live here."

"Too bad," Ben Dashford said. "What's your name?"

In the bloat and mist of my fatigue, I realized that I couldn't be Bill Feldman any longer. Mr. Haddon had a contract out on that name. I was too tired to be anything but myself—and risk all the consequences thereof. "Sherborne Eppe," I said. "My nickname's Bornie."

He held out his hand and I shook it. "Call me Ben," he answered; "everybody does. Say, are you all right?"

"I'm pretty tired. I've been driving all night and I have to find a place to sleep before I move on."

"Where are you going?"

"Rhode Island," I said.

"There's an apartment over my garage. You can sleep there."

He was one of those people who can't resist being generous to everybody they meet.

Having had a good deal of experience of human nature with its varnish off in the madhouse, I knew that instant nicers like him can sometimes be difficult in other ways. But the vision of a bed was as alluring to me as a Bedouin's vision of a water hole. "I'm very grateful," I told him.

Ben Dashford beamed. "You can drive me home. They slashed the tires on my car while I was at a meeting last night."

I got the impression that East Heidelberg wasn't just indifferent to him, it was downright hostile. Maybe it was because he was trying to change the place.

Doing that made sense to me as we drove through town. I'd never experienced anything with a worse case of the uglies than East Heidelberg, Ohio. Main Street was made up of squat brick and stone buildings with cheap glass façades and Rexall drugstore signs stuck on them. There were gas stations and a MacDonald hamburger stand interspersed in between. Dogs had done their leg-lifting on the frozen piles of snow, and grit had been scattered over everything. I saw a few signs of human life—fat ladies carrying shopping bags, murderous-looking teen-aged boys, and cops sitting in their cruisers drinking coffee out of Styrofoam containers. It was a perfect setting for my mood of self-disgust that morning. East Heidelberg was the very personification of American Drab.

The only things I saw which were not old and dirty were election posters. Some extolled a man named Kronenberger, others a black candidate named Mitchell Parrish. There were a few Dashford stickers, which were mostly defaced with mustaches or dirty words. I asked about Kronenberger.

"Oh, he's a dip stick," Ben Dashford said. "He belongs to a man named Copernicus Thall. So did our late mayor. So does everything else that makes money out of the government of East Heidelberg."

"I guess Thall is who you're out to defeat," I said.

Dashford nodded. He looked out the car window at the frozen corpse of a cat draped over a fire hydrant. "He's run this place for thirty years. He's a lawyer, he's on the town council and he owns real-estate and construction companies." Dashford looked back at me. "Thall's a genius. Do you know, fourteen grand juries have tried to get something on that bastard and they've all failed. He controls the Germans. They're the biggest bloc in the population. They founded the place."

"What about Parrish?" I asked.

"Mitch is a good man. He's got the black vote, which is getting so big it scares Thall. Mitch's trouble is that the whites are afraid that he doesn't give a damn about East Heidelberg. They think he just wants the blacks to get what the Germans have." He grinned again, as if it were all a big funny game. "That's why Thall's yahoos are slashing my tires and hassling my campaign people." His grin broadened into something like delight. "They're trying to make a martyr out of me so that all the anti-Thall whites won't vote for Parrish."

"Ben," I said, using his first name with some difficulty because I wasn't raised to instant familiarity, "why are you running?"

He shrugged. "I came here nineteen years ago to be an English teacher. I married a local girl. Now I'm the assistant principal of the high school. I guess I'm a true believer. I have concern for my fellow-man."

I felt an inexplicable little shudder of anxiety.

His house was on a high ridge above town in a section, I learned later, called Society Hill. Below us East Heidelberg's urban smear, warehouses and factories were black against the icy glare of the Ohio River in the morning sun. "They make bathroom fixtures in the potteries here," Ben said as we walked up the drive. "East Heidelberg is the Urinal Capital of the World."

There were cars parked all over the place. A couple of large dogs came woofing and wagging down to greet us. An army of cats ate from dishes set out on a plank in the snow.

We went into the kitchen. The back of the house seemed to

be filled with people, most of them women and high school kids. Through a door I could see them sitting at a large table, talking on the telephone, waving large pieces of paper and yelling. A lady in a green sweater and blue jeans came into the kitchen followed by a wailing little girl I took to be a couple of years old. This lady was all bone structure. She had a large nose, good jaw and long ash-colored hair. She was in a state. "Ben, for Christ's sake, what happened to that check you got from the East Ward's committee? Shut up, Victoria."

Ben's grin became slightly embarrassed. "I gave it to Miriam," he said. "She's the treasurer."

"Miriam has neuralgia," the lady said. Behind her, telephones were ringing and somebody was loudly explaining Ben Dashford's position on sewers.

"That's not my fault," Ben said. "This is Bornie Eppe. My wife, Lydia."

"Hi," said Mrs. Dashford. "Shut up, Victoria. And we can't find the goddamn check, and the radio station wants its money before they'll run any more spots."

The little kid started banging her head against the oven door of an old-fashioned gas range stove. In the back room someone was hollering over the telephone at a printer.

"I'm just the candidate," Ben said, "what do I know about anything? Bornie here's driven all night. He's going to bed down over the garage."

Lydia Dashford looked at me as if I were the last thing she needed. "If there are any cats up there, throw them out," she said. "Victoria, quit that—you'll get all bloody. Ben, they've announced the memorial service for Arnie Schwab. It's at two this afternoon. Kronenberger and Mitch are going to be there."

"I'm not," Ben said.

"Oh, shit," Lydia said, rolling her eyes to the ceiling. "I knew you'd say that. Why not?"

"Because they'll try to keep me out. I don't feel like getting beaten up."

Victoria started to crawl under the stove. In order to do

something, anything, to avoid conceding that I was listening to the argument brewing between the Dashfords, I bent down, grabbed Victoria by the ankles, hauled her out, swooped her up and tucked her under my arm. That used to amuse me when I was a little kid. It amused her. She stopped crying and began to laugh and wheeze. Lydia Dashford missed a beat, gave me a quick glance and then started in on Ben again. "The Pittsburgh TV station's going to be there. It'll be worth *thousands* in publicity if they filmed you being kept out."

Ben tried changing the subject. "Nobody took any pamphlets at Farnham's," he said.

"You should have made a speech. When are you going to learn to yell? Honest to Christ, I don't think you *want* to be mayor."

Ben couldn't think of anything to say to that. He looked hot, meek and angry, all at the same time.

Victoria had wet her pants down one side of me, which reminded me of how much I needed to do the same thing. I was so tired that my brain was going on and off like a lamp with a faulty switch. The back room full of quarreling, explaining people was beginning to sound like a demented football stadium.

"Ben," I said in desperation, "I think you ought to go to the memorial service if the other candidates are going to be there."

They both looked at me, surprised.

"If you'll let me stay here overnight," I said, "I'll go with you. I'm pretty big."

Ben looked me up and down, then east to west. His dopey grin spread across his face. "You've got a deal," he said.

"Well, thank Christ *somebody* can talk some sense into you," Lydia said. "Bornie . . . Is that your name—Bornie?"

"Yes, ma'am," I said.

"Go to bed. I can't stand people with unfulfilled imperatives. I'll wake you up at one-thirty."

"Make it one," Ben said, trying to hold on to a little piece of authority.

I put Victoria down and heard her start to bellow as I let

myself out of the back door. I walked across a space between the house and the garage and went up a flight of wooden stairs. The apartment was ice-cold and a little cobwebby. But it did have a living room, a bedroom and bath. I used the latter, took off my boots and trousers and got into bed. I lay there tight with fatigue. I tried to turn on my fantasy of the girl in the gazebo, but it only reminded me of how miserable and stupid I felt about losing Beth's telephone number and my conviction that I'd never talk to her again.

When fantasy fails you, all that's left is sleep.

It was summer and the grass was green. I was walking toward a bluff with music all around me and a salt marsh ending at the edge of the sea far below. I knew the gazebo behind me was empty.

Suddenly a door marked "Private" flew open and Hannibal jumped out, all teeth, eyes and death. He grew eleven feet tall and grabbed at me with hands as big as waffles. I was running down the fire escape with my father calling me. I landed in the alley and he grabbed me by the shoulder. I tried to explain that we had to run because Hannibal was coming on like the Wabash Cannonball, but it didn't seem to get through to him. I struggled to break away, but not really wanting to go away because I'd been looking for my father a long time and was anxious to discover if he'd found the meaning of life. He was shaking me.

I woke up. Dr. Primrose really could have had a field day with that dream if he'd known about it.

I opened my eyes and looked up into Lydia Dashford's face. "It's ten past one," she said.

I sat up. "I'm sorry."

"Don't be sorry. I'm sick of men being sorry. Here." She put a tray on the bed. Victoria was standing looking at me as if I were her long-lost teddy bear.

Someone had turned on a kerosene heater. The apartment was warm. Afternoon sun was streaming in through the dusty windows. I drank from a hot cup of tea on the tray and ate a piece of cinnamon toast. Lydia sat down on the edge of the bed. "Are you awake?"

I took another gulp of tea. "I think so."

"Then listen carefully," she said. "There are some things I have to tell you and there isn't much time. Do you smoke?"

"No, ma'am," I said.

She took a pack of cigarettes from the pocket of her jeans and lit one. She exhaled a blue-gray freshet of smoke into the sunlight. "Arnie Schwab—the man they're having the memorial service for—was mayor of this city."

"Ben told me he'd died," I said. I was still a little disoriented and trying to make up my mind whether I liked Lydia Dashford or felt sorry for Ben.

"Arnie left us two and a half weeks ago, supposedly in a Turkish bath in Pittsburgh. Actually it was in a massage parlor, a whorehouse." Her urgent demeanor collapsed for a moment. She put her long slender hand over her face and started to laugh. She looked at me. "Christ, it's like a bad novel, isn't it?" That resolved my problem. She was strong, witty and grown-up. I liked her.

I laughed back. "It's great so far."

"All right," she said. "Now listen, Bornie. Arnie belonged to Copernicus Thall. So does Billy Kronenberger, who's winning this election so far. Thall has his people run this garbage scow of a town so that he gets advance notice on what property the city, the state or the federal government is going to buy around here, then *he* buys it through his real estate company. He buys low and sells high on inside information. He's made millions on city construction through Kronenberger's building company—Thall's people see to it that Kronenberger's bid is always the lowest, then Thall gets a split. Can you remember all that?"

I finished my tea, ate another piece of cinnamon toast and nodded. "I think so. But why are you telling me?"

"You seem to have some kind of influence with Ben," she said. "If you can get him into that memorial service, he'll have to make a speech. He has to say what I've just told you."

"At a *memorial* service?" I asked in astonishment.

Lydia nodded. "The damn election's only nine days away and Ben hasn't made a ripple yet. He's got to pull off a shocker. That's the place to do it."

"But he must know all of this himself."

She nodded. "I've told him. I don't think he wants to know." She crushed out her cigarette on the instep of her right sneaker. "Will you try to make him say those things—for me?"

"But if *you* can't—"

"Resisting me is his only way of fighting me," she said. It was a blunt revelation made in Lydia's version of a loving tone. "Look, if you do this, you can stay here for a week. And I won't tell anybody you're on the lam."

I felt apprehension and thought about Mr. Haddon's possible connections.

"A man on his way to Rhode Island with no baggage in his car," she said. "That's—"

"I'll do it in return for room and board," I said, possessed suddenly of a hunch that it was time to breach gentlemanly conduct, "but not because you've threatened me. In fact, I react pretty badly to threats, Mrs. Dashford."

She stood up. "I brought you a razor, toothbrush and some soap while you were asleep. They're in the bathroom." She looked down at me with a summer light flickering in her eyes.

She took Victoria by the hand and paused a moment before going downstairs. "Call me Lydia," she said. Then the summer light came on full and she smiled again. "Move your ass, Bornie Eppe. There isn't much time." She wasn't such a tough lady, after all.

In fact, I was beginning to have a fantasy about her before she had closed the door. In it I was her husband, I was older, I was settled down and the object of her profane, accusing, loving attentions. That wasn't my first spirited-lady fantasy, but it was the first I'd had about an older woman. I liked it.

As I drove Ben Dashford down to the center of East Heidelberg, he talked about how much it meant to him to be mayor if he could. He was a nice man despite his instant niceness. It was just that he occupied three different chambers of his life and was trying to handle them all at once. The first was his past, which held some fiend of self-doubt in it. The second was the present, in which Lydia personified the fiend without wanting to. Ben Dashford's third chamber was the future, a glowing and serene state in which he imagined himself as mayor doing good things. I didn't doubt that he really *wanted* to do good; he was just having trouble getting from here to there.

The cold air had brought me fully awake and I had a moment of resolve. "Ben," I said, "you've just hired me to be your bodyguard for this afternoon, but I'd like to give you some advice if you wouldn't be offended."

"Hell, no," he said, giving me his kid grin. "I can use all the advice I can get. I'm losing."

"Well," I went on, "I don't know anything about politics but I'll bet it's like the rest of life. People who are difficult aren't necessarily nice, but they are interesting and other people tend to pay attention to them."

He didn't answer for a moment. He sat staring through the windshield. "Lydia's been talking to you," he finally replied.

I told him yes.

"It goes against my grain," he said. "Running a man down when he's dead . . ."

"Being dead doesn't mean he was good when he was alive," I answered.

He was still thinking about that as we pulled up in front of a large ungainly church. It was named for St. Dismus, which seemed appropriate to the occasion. In a book Mr. Fletcher, the dope addict, made me read at Craigie Glen, I'd learned that St. Dismus was a thief who repented. I could imagine Arnie Schwab engulfed in repentance—if he'd had time—as his life left him in a whorehouse.

The broad steps of the church were crowded with people. The Schwab family—widow and nine kids ranging from a small fat one to a sullen girl with acne about my age—were in the middle, all wearing black. Almost everybody else was dressed up and feeling awkward. The only mourners in work clothes were three mean-looking guys on the sidewalk. One was young and lean. The other two had potbellies, and one of *them* wore a hard hat. They were our reception committee.

We got out of the car. Hard Hat held up his hand. "You ain't invited, Dashford," he said. "This here's just for Arnie's friends."

I'll give Ben credit. He didn't try his goofy grin. "It's a public memorial service," he answered. "My friend Mr. Eppe and I are going in."

The young guy was looking me over, trying to figure if he could take me. I was scared but I knew he was, too.

"You could get hurt trying," Hard Hat said to Ben.

People began to move down from the steps and gather around us. Potential bloodshed is an irresistible attraction. There was a churning to our right. I saw a portable TV camera hoisted onto a bearded fellow's shoulder. A blond girl with a notebook in her hand was watching us.

"If I'm kept out by force, it'll be on TV," Ben said.

It took a couple of seconds for that to sink through the layers of Crisco surrounding Hard Hat's brain. "I don't give a shit about no TV," he said. "You ain't comin' in here. Neither one of you."

I decided it was time to do my dangerous, silent-stranger act. I walked back to my Volkswagen, grabbed it by the bumper and offered a gallopy little prayer that I was still as strong as I'd been at seventeen. When I lifted the front end of the car off the ground, I thought my reproductive organs were going to end up somewhere around my knees, but I held it off the pavement for longer than I ever had in my life. The TV camera was on me. Slowly I lowered the Volkswagen to the ground and then went back and stood beside Ben.

"Now, ain't that cute," Hard Hat said to me. "Whaddya want to bet that the three of *us* could throw that fuckin' car over onto Ontario Street?"

Suddenly the young lean one made his move. Before I knew what was happening he was right up against me and a switch-blade was pricking my Adam's apple. "We don't need to throw no car," he said in a voice that sounded like slag tumbling down a heap. "This cocksucker's gonna get himself turned into hamburger if he don't clear out of here."

I was just trying to see how far apart his legs were so that I could give him a knee in the groin—I've seen that done in the movies—when a quiet voice said, "That will do."

To my immense relief the young guy stepped back and re-clasped his knife.

A short, slender man in a tweed suit was standing on the sidewalk to our left. He must have been about sixty, but he had dark hair parted in the middle like an old-fashioned druggist's. "Well, Ben," he said, "I didn't think you'd turn up this afternoon. Mitch Parrish is here, but he never had a bone to pick with Arnie. Of course Billy Kronenberger is inside, too. But you—you surprise me." He spoke in a low, cultivated voice.

"But you made sure there'd be trouble if I *did* come," Ben said. He slapped on his grin. "I'm grateful, Thall. People will think you're scared of me."

Copernicus Thall turned to the three hoods. "You can go home now," he said. To the young guy he added, "Don't you know that switchblades are illegal in Ohio?"

"No, sir," said the knifer, suddenly humble.

"I'd get rid of it if I were you," Thall said. "It would be a pity if the police found you with it." He took out a handkerchief and coughed heavily into it. His face became red but not disorderly. He put the handkerchief back in his pocket and turned to me. "I don't believe I've seen you before, young man."

"This is Sherborne Eppe," Ben said. "He's just come to town."

Thall gave one of those wintery smiles that you hope is amiable but suspect is disdainful. "I'm glad to meet you, Mr. Eppe. Welcome to East Heidelberg. If you're an associate of my friend Ben Dashford, you must be a great idealist. I hope we'll visit together one day."

The insidious people of this world come in unexpected forms. When I first heard about Copernicus Thall I imagined him as Rod Steiger playing Al Capone. Now I had to admit that I was impressed.

As we mounted the steps the girl TV reporter squirmed up beside me. "What's your name?" she asked.

"Eppe," I said.

"Eppe birthday," she said.

"Epicenter," I quipped. "What's yours?"

"Barbara Defere."

"Only de brave deserve Defere."

"Haw, haw," she said. Then she grinned. "Look, Eppe—"

"Bornie Eppe," I answered. "I've already made up all the ones about Bornie."

"Oh, well," she said. "Look, Bornie, if you're with Dashford, I want to talk to you. I cover this part of Ohio for Pittsburgh television."

"I'm not important. Ben's the one you ought to talk to."

"I talk to Ben all the time. What was all that about on the sidewalk?"

"I think Thall's guys were trying to keep us out," I said.

She took a card from her notebook and handed it to me. "Anybody who stands up to Copernicus Thall is important in his own right. Call me."

I took the card and said I would.

That afternoon was the first time I ever saw the inside of a Catholic church. As I've told you, my grandfather used to be the Episcopal bishop of Massachusetts, so I'd done time in *our* churches. It was not that my immediate family was religious. My father, as a matter of fact, told me that in his opinion the Christian religion went out to lunch sometime in the fourth century and hadn't gotten back yet. We went to church because of my mother, who, if not devout, was very big on connections. She had married a powerful connection with the Episcopal church and she wasn't about to give it up any more than she'd surrender her membership in the Junior League.

Episcopal churches try to make you feel proper and comfortable; Catholic churches go in for drama. There were statues of Mary and Jesus showing off His bleeding heart. I immediately noticed one stained-glass window that portrayed a martyr being roasted alive with a pious expression on his face. The organ was making tuneless groans that were supposed to represent lament. There was a skinny, scowling priest up front, and every pew was packed. Ben and I found seats on the aisle; Barbara Defere and her cameraman stayed in the back.

I don't know if Arnie Schwab was a crowd pleaser in life, but in death he could really pack a church. I'd only been in East Heidelberg a few hours and all I'd heard about Arnie and the Thall machine was from the Dashfords. I believed Lydia when she said that the mayor had died in a massage parlor. Also I'd had confirmation that there was something fishy about the late lamented's political connections because one of Copernicus Thall's hoodlums had tried to knife me.

I was, therefore, keenly interested in the first speeches. The priest got things going by saying that we had all come there to celebrate the life of Arnie Schwab, whom everybody loved. After that, one of the older Schwab kids got up and said that Arnie had been the best dad in this whole world and that his mother, who was too overcome, wanted everybody to know that Arnie had been the best husband in this whole world. Everybody murmured about how sweet and touching the Schwab kid was.

Then came Billy Kronenberger, a tall square guy with a very small head who was Thall's candidate to succeed Schwab. Kronenberger was no Cicero when it came to making speeches. But he gave ten minutes to ascribing the standard American virtues to Arnie Schwab—he had been a veteran, a good citizen, a member of four fraternal organizations, a free-enterprise businessman who had devoted himself to the civic affairs of East Heidelberg.

Following all of that, the priest delivered a homily on the Christian family in general and the Schwab family in particular, most of which I missed because I was having this fierce, hissing conversation with Ben.

"See how it is?" he said. "What would I look like if I got up there and told what I know?"

"At least you wouldn't look like everybody else," I hissed back urgently. I had to make him speak. I'd promised Lydia. "Besides, everybody knows this is all hooey."

"But his *family's* here!" Ben roared in a whisper. "I can't get up there and say he died in a—"

"They were here when he was alive. They aren't stupid!"

"You don't know the Schwabs," Ben murmured. "That son who spoke is almost old enough to vote and he can't spell horse. I tried to teach him in sophomore English—three years running."

Maybe it was the incongruity of the proceedings, but suddenly I was feeling all involved and indignant. "I thought you had concern for your fellow-man."

"Well," Ben muttered, looking down at his hands as if he were defying them, "I do."

"Then tell them the truth that's supposed to set them free," I whispered.

By this time Mitchell Parrish, the black candidate, was up front having *his* innings. He was a handsome man with a handlebar mustache. Aside from Copernicus Thall, Mitchell Parrish was the only male resident of East Heidelberg who wore a three-piece suit as far as I knew. He was soft-spoken and had piercing eyes.

He was also very subtle. He said he had known Arnie Schwab for twelve years—and then never mentioned him again. Instead, Parrish gave a political speech whose main point was that people have more in common than their external appearances might suggest. He mentioned brotherhood.

There was a good deal of coughing and squirming when Parrish had finished. In all that mass of white countenances there were only four or five black faces down close to the pulpit. Parrish had suggested that people overlook the difference. It was time to get back to platitudes.

Ben had been sitting in a sulk while Parrish spoke. Suddenly I felt desperate. There was one of those throat-clearing, uncertain pauses that rustle across public occasions when nobody's quite sure what's supposed to happen next. In his chair near the altar the priest was glaring out over the audience, expecting somebody to do something.

I did something. I got up and said, "Ladies and gentlemen, Ben Dashford is now going to pay his—" I stopped. "Ben Dashford is going to speak now," I said.

I felt mean, but I knew I had to blast Ben into action and I couldn't think of any other way of doing it.

I suppose at that moment he wanted to murder me. It would have been illogical if he hadn't, because he knew that Lydia had put me up to it. He muttered, "Aw, Bornie," and the next thing I knew he was on his feet walking slowly toward the front of the church. I can tell you, I felt like a lizard because I'd never done anything like that to anybody in my life.

"Ladies and gentlemen," he said in a steady voice, "I suppose you know who I am. I'm the assistant principal of the Von Steuben High School, and like Billy Kronenberger and Mitch Parrish, I'm a candidate for mayor. I wish I could tell you that I've come here to say a few respectful words about Mayor Schwab. But I can't, because I don't know anything respectable about him."

The audience came awake like a catfish in a pond that's been charged with electricity.

Ben took a deep breath. "Arnie Schwab was a crook who was put in office by Councilman Thall over there, and Arnie made—wait a minute, I've got the exact figure—over thirty-eight thousand dollars selling trucks to the city while he was running it."

Somebody shouted. The priest was out of his chair, hurrying toward Ben. Ben didn't even look at him, he just stiff-armed him away.

"Arnie Schwab's life was a lie," Ben went on, raising his voice over a sudden tumult of mutters, grunts and exclamations, "and his death was, too. Arnie didn't die in the Turkish bath where he went once a week for his health. He died in a massage parlor—a brothel!! *Where three naked women were doing unspeakable things to him!!*"

Mrs. Schwab screamed. Her children were flopping all over themselves trying to get to her. Four men were running down the aisle toward the front of the church. Three black guys from Mitch Parrish's contingent just below the pulpit jumped out in front of them. A fistfight started.

"Copernicus Thall has made millions selling real estate to this city under illegal bids!" Ben shouted, trying to talk and watch the fight at the same time. "He's the real owner of Kronenberger Construction, fronted by Billy Kronenberger, *the next man Thall wants to install as your mayor!*"

By that time there was pandemonium. Women were screaming and trying to drag out their children, and men who seemed to be supporters of Ben were clawing their way up the aisle, past the fighters. A lady climbed up on a pew and screamed, "Tell 'em, Ben!," at which point a bluish-white light went on and Barbara's cameraman started filming the festivities. The priest was jumping up and down and shouting something about it being sacrilege to take pictures in church. At the risk of life and limb I got to my feet and looked over at Copernicus Thall. He was a filament of enigmatic calm in the middle of the chaos, sitting beneath the barbecued saint with that late-December smile on his face. Then somebody fetched me a rounder on the side of the head and my own lights went out.

By the time I was sensible again we were out on the sidewalk. The street was filled with police cruisers with their red and white flashers revolving. Several bloodied-up, handcuffed men with their finery all torn and their shirttails hanging out were being hustled into a paddy wagon. Two of them were black and laughing fit to kill. Blacks don't seem to take getting arrested very seriously. I guess they've been picked on so much they're used to it.

The cops were herding people away from the steps. I was propped up against the church wall with a circle of men around me, the cameraman taking pictures of me and Ben wiping blood off my right temple with his handkerchief. "How do you feel?" he asked.

"Like Mount Everest fell on me," I said. "How about you?"

He grinned. "I didn't get hit at all. Everybody did except me, and I started it. How about that?" He was filled with the exultation of a man who has survived a dreaded experience.

He was also one of those people who enjoy the highs of their life so much that they forget how they got there. On the way back to Society Hill he was exuberant. "Do you think they got the idea?" he asked me.

"What idea?"

"Well—that I'm a reformer! That I want to be mayor for their sakes!"

That wasn't an easy question to answer for several obvious reasons having to do with the difference between Ben Dashford's character and the electorate of East Heidelberg. But he didn't even notice my noncommittal mumble. He was still chattering about how he'd been the only speaker at St. Dismus' who really laid it on the line. He never once referred to how I had kicked him into laying it on the line, which was fine by me.

When we got home Ben was filled with secretive glee. He refused to tell Lydia what had happened at the memorial service, just saying it would be on the news at six. Lydia washed my head cut and bandaged it. Along with not being as tough as she pretended to be, she was also a very wise lady. She only tried to pry details out of me once. When she had finished bandaging my wound she said, "Well, are you going to be staying here for a week or not?"

"I don't want to spoil Ben's fun," I said. "You decide after you've seen the news."

She gave me a quick kiss on the cheek and said, "You're a son of a bitch, Bornie Eppe," without meaning it at all.

I played with little Victoria, the demon pants-wetter, until it got dark. About a dozen people gathered in the living room and we all hushed up as the news came on. First there was a spinning globe, and then a rather used-up man said, "Violence in the East Heidelberg election tonight. We'll have that—with pictures—after this message." The message was about dog food and foot-odor pads. The dilapidated announcer came back on and said, "The special election in East Heidelberg, Ohio, to fill the seat left vacant by the death of Mayor Arnold Schwab erupted into violence and serious charges of political corruption today. Barbara Defere was there."

Suddenly the screen was full of the uproar in St. Dismus'. People were screaming and cursing, the camera was swaying and jolting; you could see the fistfight in the aisle and several other brawls besides. The sound faded and Barbara's voice said, "The riot in St. Dismus' Church started when one of the candidates—teacher Ben Dashford—told those attending a memorial service for the late Mayor Schwab that Schwab had died in a Pittsburgh massage parlor, not a Turkish bath, as had previously been reported, and that another candidate, William Kronenberger, had paid kickbacks on city construction contracts to Councilman Copernicus Thall, who was also accused of illegal real estate transactions."

The riot on the TV screen switched to a picture of Barbara. "It was obvious from the beginning of the memorial service that some faction in East Heidelberg city politics didn't want Mr. Dashford to attend the service at all."

The next thing was pictures of Ben, me, the three hoods and Mr. Thall on the sidewalk with people crowding around us. "When Dashford and his campaign aide, Sherborne Eppe, arrived at the church there was an attempt to stop them from entering," Barbara's voice said. She let the pictures tell the story —with the cusswords by Hard Hat and the knifer blipped out. I watched myself cross the sidewalk, lift my Volkswagen and then come back to stand beside Ben. You could just barely hear Mr. Thall's voice as he broke up the confrontation. Barbara came back on the screen. "After the police had cleared the church, I asked Councilman Thall about Dashford's charges."

There was Copernicus Thall standing on the steps as calm as ever. "Ben Dashford," he said into Barbara's microphone, "is a very idealistic and somewhat excitable man. Now, we all know that irresponsible charges are made in the heat of campaigns, we all regret them, and when it's all over, we just forget them."

"But are Mr. Dashford's accusations true?" asked Barbara's voice.

"All I know about Arnie Schwab's death is what I saw and heard on your television program, Miss Defere."

"What about the charges that you accepted kickbacks from Kronenberger and that you're the real power in East Heidelberg politics?"

Thall laughed. "I wish I were a real power in something," he said. He patted Barbara's arm. "Sounds like a conspiracy theory to me, doesn't it to you?" He tipped his hat and walked off down the pavement.

There was a quick shot of me with Ben hovering over me, and then Mitch Parrish was in the middle of the screen. Underneath him was his name printed in white followed by "Candidate for Mayor."

"I don't know if the charges are true or not," Parrish said into the microphone. "I'm an attorney and I'm certainly going to demand an investigation of the matters raised by Ben Dashford in there."

"Does Copernicus Thall really run East Heidelberg?" Barbara's voice asked.

Parrish hesitated for a moment. "I'd say Mr. Thall is a power to be reckoned with in this city," he answered quietly.

Finally Barbara appeared on the screen again. "Sixteen people were arrested in East Heidelberg this afternoon, seven injured including Dashford's campaign worker Eppe—none of them seriously. Until today Ben Dashford has been a poor third in a field of three in the East Heidelberg election. Now he is the *focus* of that election because of the serious charges he has made. As one observer remarked after the riot at St. Dismus' Church, 'Ben Dashford has blown the manhole cover off this town. Whether it'll get him elected or not is anybody's guess.' This is Barbara Defere, News At Six."

There was loud applause in the Dashford living room. Somebody turned off the TV set and somebody else turned on the lights. People were hugging Ben and smacking him on the back and shaking hands with each other and saying "How terrific!" and "Let's have a drink." Lydia was still sitting on the floor, hands clasped around her knees, and looking at the dead TV screen with a smile on her face. I had seen that expression on somebody before but I couldn't remember who it was.

The telephone kept ringing for the next few hours. People were calling up Ben and congratulating him for being the last honest man in this world. Maybe a lot of East Heidelberg was indifferent or hostile to him, but that dirty sock in the laundry of American life had its quota of idealists and Concerned Citizens, too. Still, one of the campaign ladies in the back room told me, the Dashford faction was pretty small potatoes compared to the vote controlled by Thall and its main rival, the black population.

My head had stopped feeling as if there were a drop forge inside it, but I still ached when Ben, Lydia and I sat down to dinner at nine o'clock. I was back to gloom again, wondering if we'd *really* accomplished anything by offending man and maybe upsetting God at St. Dismus' Church that afternoon.

Ben was full of triumph and a rare dose of self-esteem, and Lydia was getting tired of telling him he'd been wonderful. He couldn't get enough of congratulation.

"It's going to take more than one riot to get you elected," Lydia said, "and you only have eight days left. Now look, Ben, this goddamn campaign is a mess—"

"Aw, c'mon, honey," Ben said. "We've got a *whole new lease on life!*"

"No, we haven't," she said. "You've had *one good moment.*"

He didn't answer. He was trying to hold on to feeling splendid about himself.

Lydia reached over and put her hand on his. "Ben. Darling. I'm not trying to detract from what you did this afternoon. It was wonderful. *You* were wonderful."

Ben looked across the table at me. "Here comes the 'but,'" he said.

"Oh, for Christ's sake," Lydia sighed. "Ben, is there *any way at all—*" She stopped. She knew there wasn't any way. "Look, I have an idea. A hunch."

Ben sighed. He looked at his watch. "All right, let's hear the hunch. That League of Women Voters meeting starts in fifteen minutes. It'll take Bornie and me ten to get there."

"Bornie's not going with you," Lydia said. "A couple of the kids had new tires put on the car. You can drive yourself, Ben; Bornie and I are going to plan what you do tomorrow."

"Bornie?" he asked, looking back at me.

I was as astonished as Ben was. "Look, Lydia—"

"We need an activist," she said. "We need a fresh perspective. You like Ben, Ben likes you. Stay here until the election and work for us."

I felt panicky, as if I'd misrepresented myself by my deeds at St. Dismus'. "Lydia, your hunch about me is all wrong. I don't know the first thing about political campaigns . . ."

"Welcome to the club," Ben said. He was grinning again.

"I've never been in East Heidelberg until today . . ."

"That's your biggest asset," Lydia said.

"I need to find a regular job so that I can make some money to get to Rhode Island."

"We'll pay you two hundred dollars," Lydia said.

"Three hundred," Ben put in, "and your keep."

Lydia saw her opening. "Ben's absolutely right," she said, "three hundred."

I couldn't think of any more arguments. It was the stupidest idea I'd heard since being subjected to some of Mademoiselle Dupont's social theories, but it had three hundred dollars riding on it, a place to sleep and only nine days for me to screw things up with my political ineptitude.

Ben was beaming because Lydia had said he was right about something. That was the final argument. I couldn't reject him.

"All right," I said, "I'll try. But—"

"Great," Ben said. He got up. "I have to go. What's on the schedule for tomorrow?"

"Bornie and I will work it out," Lydia assured him.

Ben kissed her. "Don't wait up late," he said.

After he had left I told Lydia, "I think you've just made the biggest mistake of your life." My relationship with her was different from the one I was developing with Ben. Blunter.

Lydia lit a cigarette. "As if you knew all the mistakes I've made in my life."

"Look, Lydia," I said. "I really have to know what's going on."

She shook out her match, exhaled, pulled back the sleeves of her green sweater and put her arms on the table. "I don't know who you are," she said, suddenly gentle, "or where you came from, and I don't want to know. But you're sensitive. You must see how things are between Ben and me."

"I can see it," I said. You'd have had to be a toad not to. "But where do I come in?"

"Ben and I are caricatures. All the bad books, jokes and theories made up about strong women and weak men leave out one thing—that a woman like me could love a man like Ben. I do, even if he drives me up the goddamn wall and it isn't much of a marriage at the moment. Ben decided he should run for mayor, not me. It was the first initiative he's taken in years and I want it to work. But he's such an idiot that he doesn't know *how* to make it work. You can get him to do things."

"Things you want him to do."

She nodded. "I know about politics. That's why I want you

with us. You can organize protest demonstrations against the Thall machine."

"I don't know how to organize a demonstration. I've never even seen one."

"Don't give me that crap, Bornie. How old are you?"

"Twenty-four."

"You mean to sit there and tell me that you went through the Vietnam years and never demonstrated?"

"Yes, ma'am."

She looked at me through the serpents of smoke curling up from her cigarette. "You're weird," she said.

There are worse things.

The back room was empty, Victoria was asleep upstairs. Lydia got some towels and light bulbs and went across with me to the garage. The sky was so black that it had a purplish hue. Stars were scattered across it to the rim of the world.

Lydia put a bulb in the lamp beside my bed and hung the towels in the bathroom. She came back to the bedroom. "Do you understand everything I've said to you, Bornie?"

"I understand."

"All the nuances?"

"Sure," I said. Something was happening. I didn't add any more words.

"I want to get into your goddamn bed!" she cried suddenly, "but I don't want you thinking that's why I—"

"I guess I'd better turn out the light," I said.

In bed she threw herself against me with muscle power that was almost equivalent to mine. I had to use all my strength to force her back so that I could caress her. She writhed and wept, and then her angular body wrapped itself around me. Her legs tightened onto my leg and her hands clutched the back of my neck as she shuddered and had the first convulsion.

Before I could press my mouth onto her body, she gasped, "Don't fall in love with me, please, for God's sake!"

"It's okay," I said. "I'm already in love with somebody."

"Oh Christ! I'm glad! Yes! That!"

I was inside of her with her arms and legs riveting me to her as we arrived together at a summer city filled with summer light.

She gently pushed me off and leaned over me. She kissed me a dozen times and said "Thank you, thank you."

Afterward she lay beside me in the dark with her head on my arm and a cigarette in her fingers. "It means a lot to you to have Ben win, doesn't it?" I asked. "For his sake."

She turned her head and kissed my shoulder. "That's one reason," she said peacefully. "The main one."

"What's the other?"

Lydia looked at the ceiling. The last light that the stars could manage came through the windows, making her face rounder, softer and younger.

Her hand came down and she drew on the cigarette. Its dying ash was hot and vivid for a moment and then subsided in the dark.

"Copernicus Thall is my father," she said.

Six

MY POLITICAL EDUCATION

ON MY SECOND DAY THERE, East Heidelberg didn't look as fearful as it had on my first. The place hadn't changed; I had. I still considered myself a contender for the Inept Championship of Ohio because I hadn't gotten my hands on Beth's telephone number. But I was free of that desolation which comes with wandering this world despising yourself, not knowing anybody, knowing of no way *to* know anybody and having no place or purpose to which you can attach your life.

East Heidelberg was the beneficiary of my improved state of mind. It was still a dump—an infinity of altered moods couldn't change that fact. But it was now an interesting dump.

That second morning began with a rackety whoop. It seemed as if every newspaper, wire service and broadcasting company this side of Zanzibar had heard about the riot at St. Dismus' Church. They all wanted interviews with Ben. By nine o'clock the driveway was full of vans with call letters on them; television crews were standing around in the snow while reporters added to the general disorder of the back room by trying to find somebody to plead with or persuade. There was even a stringer from the New York *Times*. That was when I came to understand that the news business likes scurrility almost as much as it is attracted to lust, gore and politicians who can't live up to their promises. The Dashford campaign was in the scurrility business that day.

When I walked into the kitchen, Lydia wasn't speaking to me. She put some bacon and eggs on the table and went to the back room. I could hear her pithy contributions to the noise and bewilderment for a few minutes. She let rip with an epithet and said she'd try to fix something. Then she came back into the kitchen. "Look," she said, "I'm sorry I was a shit to you last night. You couldn't understand without my explaining it to you, but I want you to—"

"Then why not explain it to me?"

"Because I want you to get my goddamn husband down here and talk to these reporters!" she retorted. *"I've* tried three times."

"You're making me his press secretary?"

"You've got to do something to justify your existence," Lydia answered, "besides being Ben's persuader. We need a structure around here."

I hadn't the wildest idea what the job entailed, but she was right about the state of the Dashford campaign. It had about as much structure as a nervous breakdown. So I cleared all the reporters out of the back room, put them in the front of the house and got one of the ladies to serve them coffee. Then I went upstairs to deal with Ben.

He was sitting on the edge of his bed in his shirt, underwear and socks looking at a picture of himself on the front page of the East Heidelberg *Echo.* He gave me his kid grin, a strand of brown hair was falling over his forehead. "Pretty good, huh?" he said, showing me the newspaper.

"It's great," I said. "And there's more of the same waiting for you downstairs. About twenty reporters. You'd better talk to them before you make your Rotary Club lunch speech."

He started to put on his trousers, had one leg in and then

stopped. "What am I going to say to them?" he asked the room as much as me. "I said it all yesterday."

I'd had a picky nag working at me since I'd goaded him into making that speech at St. Dismus'. "Ben," I said, "can you prove all those things?"

He put his other leg in his trousers, pulled them up and buckled his belt. "Yeah. Sure. It's all in a folder in Lydia's dressing table."

The dressing table was a symbol of Ben and Lydia's intimacy, which I'd intruded on. I had a spasm of guilty squeam as I took out the folder. In it was a mass of photocopied checks, bank statements, scribbled notes and pages of real estate contracts; I also found a witnessed and notarized statement attesting to the true circumstances under which Arnie Schwab took leave of this life. I read everything carefully while Ben finished dressing, trying to get it all straight in my mind. I guessed Lydia had compiled the folder.

"Okay," Ben said, putting on his jacket, "I'm ready. What do we tell them?"

I hadn't known Ben Dashford long, but I had a sense that he was a big-picture man, a visionary of what ought to be. He wasn't very interested in the precise details and squiggles of the present condition.

"I imagine those reporters want proof of the accusations you've made," I said. "I think you ought to go down there and tell them how you're going to clean up East Heidelberg, and then turn over the details to your press secretary."

"I haven't got a press secretary."

"Lydia just appointed me."

"Well," he said, smiling. Delight was spreading through him. It makes a man feel important to have people who are extensions of himself, picker-uppers of his minutiae. "Good idea," he said. "Do you understand all that stuff?"

I made a little prayer to my gods to see that I did and we went downstairs.

The press conference was held out in the snow. Ben wore a

lumberjack shirt over his suit which gave him that man-against-the-elements look that Americans like in their political candidates and beer-commercial actors. The shirt was my idea.

By his own voluble standards, he was brief. He told the reporters that Copernicus Thall was the real issue in the campaign. He rattled on a bit about good and evil—meaning himself and Thall—and then turned the press conference over to me.

I was scared as I went to the microphones. I had the folder in my hand and the hand was shaking, but I had gotten myself into this and there was no way out.

The first question *was* about proof of the charges that Ben had made the previous day.

I held up the folder. "It's all in here," I said as cameras whirred and people wrote things in their notebooks. My gods swooped down and gave me the right words at the right moment. "Mr. Dashford doesn't want to give you *his* version of the situation in East Heidelberg," I said. "He wants to hand over everything he's got and let you draw your own conclusions." I added a little commercial. "Mr. Dashford believes in a free press and thinks we've got an intelligent one." I said I'd have the contents of the folder Xeroxed and distributed.

There was a clamor about deadlines and urgency, and we finally agreed that copies of what was in the folder could be picked up at two o'clock.

Just before the press conference began, Barbara had arrived in her TV station's van. She had jollied up the atmosphere by cracking jokes. Afterward, as Ben chatted with the reporters and posed for pictures throwing snowballs at his dogs, Barbara came over to me. "I've been at Copernicus Thall's office this morning," she said.

I couldn't resist trying to make her laugh. She was, in fact, a vault full of giggles waiting to be opened. "Thall right with me," I said.

"Bornie gain as a great wit," she answered, "ha diddy ha. Listen, honeypot, Thall wants to see you."

I sobered right down. *"Me?"*

"Little you," she said. "Today. Dashy quick."

Being summoned had, in my life, usually meant that someone with authority has discovered one of my screw-ups. I hadn't done anything to Copernicus Thall but he was connected to Lydia, and making love to her had left me with an uncomfortable feeling I'd been trying to suppress all morning.

Having just begun to learn about real sex, I was also beginning to learn about its complications. When I went to bed with Amelia neither of us was committed to anybody. But Lydia was in love with Ben in her own exasperated way, and I had this vision of Beth shimmering ahead of me. Sex is part of your intention toward somebody you love and there's no getting around it, no matter what stories you tell yourself to justify your behavior. So here I was feeling guilty because Lydia's father had summoned me.

I drove to Copernicus Thall's office in the middle of East Heidelberg. Since I had begun to slip back into gloom about myself, the city had retrogressed too. It looked squat, filthy and barren of human possibility in the raw midday light.

Barbara had given me Thall's office address and said she'd meet me in a coffee shop across the street after I'd talked to him. Driving through the dismal streets, I thought back to what had happened the night before. I had been surprised, to say the least, to hear that Lydia Dashford was Copernicus Thall's daughter. "Do you see him much?" I asked her.

Lydia went right on looking at the ceiling. "We haven't spoken for eleven years," she said. There was no change of tone in her voice to indicate whether that suited her or not.

"You must really hate him," I ventured.

Her face in the remnants of starlight got angry and tight. "*Hate* him?" she said, turning to look at me.

"Look, it doesn't take much sense to figure out that you're the real brains and force behind Ben's campaign. If Ben can't win, he can at least do a lot of damage to your father. He did this afternoon. You were the one who made me make him do it."

"*Hate my father?*" she repeated, furious and incredulous.

She threw her cigarette across the room, jumped out of bed and yanked on her jeans, sweater and sneakers. "You dumb bastard!" she cried before she slammed the door. I put out her cigarette so that the garage wouldn't burn down, and returned to bed to consider two mysteries: the mental processes of those people who expect you to know what they're thinking without being told and the strange power that Copernicus Thall seemed to cast over his surroundings.

I parked my car across the street from a big lump of a building made out of square blocks of gray granite with ornate Victorian trim around the windows and a legend, "Arnheim Brothers," in concrete letters over the front entrance.

Inside, the tiled front hall was smudged with guck brought in from the sidewalks on many galoshes. There was wood paneling that hadn't been polished for a long time, a rickety elevator and a dim building register. The law firm of Thall, Stern and Arnheim was on the fourth floor.

A corpse in a frayed uniform took me up to that floor and pointed me in the right direction. The waiting room of Copernicus Thall's law office was crowded with people—old women in shawls with envelopes in their hands, fat men of various ages, young guys in work clothes twisting their caps in their hands and looking at the floor. They all had the expectant patience of supplicants.

I gave a lady my name, she repeated it into the telephone and then told me to go right in. I was embarrassed as she said it in front of those other people; they all wanted something and had been waiting a long time; I didn't and hadn't.

Mr. Thall had a big office—huge, in fact—on the corner of the building. It was furnished in a style to show off the occupant's self-confidence and comfort with a little erudition thrown in to keep the unerudite off guard. There was a large marble fireplace with busts of men who looked ancient and brainy on each end of the mantel, a Persian carpet on the floor, an oil portrait of some Supreme Court Justice or other by one of the Peales over the fireplace, heavy drapes, red leather chairs and two desks—one roll-top and closed, the other vast, lit by a long green-shaded light and fitted out with brass pen holders and letter slots. On the wall facing the desk there was an Edwardian-era portrait of a lady in a black hat, coat and muff. She was so beautiful and mysterious that I used up an extra couple of seconds looking.

"Striking woman," Copernicus Thall said, getting up from behind his desk.

"Yes, sir."

"My mother." Thall put his hands in his pockets and looked across the room with proprietary pleasure at the picture. "That was painted in 1914 by Robert Suzanne, Mr. Eppe. He was a very fashionable and expensive artist. In 1912 my mother was a housemaid."

There wasn't any reply to that. There never is when someone you don't know suddenly tells you an intimate truth about himself.

Thall gave me his thirty-below smile and held out his hand. "It was very courteous of you to come so quickly. I admire courtesy. Please, sit down."

I understood part of his power already because it had made me feel easier. Copernicus Thall had the gift of projecting himself as a superior member of the species and giving you the impression you were his equal. He was also unhurried in his ways. He returned to his chair behind the desk, tilted back, took the Phi Beta Kappa key that hung from a gold chain across his vest and studied it for a long moment of hush. Then he looked at me. "Well, Mr. Eppe."

I waited, suppressing my tendency to babble.

"Tell me about yourself," he said.

"I'm just an ordinary man," I answered.

"No," Copernicus Thall said, "the one thing you aren't is ordinary, Mr. Eppe. You came to East Heidelberg yesterday and suddenly this city is in an uproar." He swung around and looked out the windows. "All the components for uproar have always existed here, of course. But they were ignited when you arrived." He swung back and looked at me again.

"Mr. Thall, that's just coincidence."

He dropped his Phi Beta Kappa key. "Let us tell each other the truth," he said. "I think we will understand each other better if we do."

Copernicus Thall was sitting behind his big desk looking all orderly and dignified and shellacked eight times over with his courtly manners. But something from his subsurface was leaking through to me. This man hired knifers to scare people, or worse, and I concluded that he was now making threats. Veiled, as they used to say. I began to get mad.

"I'll start," he said. He swung himself around again so that he could look out the window at the glories of East Heidelberg. "What Ben Dashford said yesterday was essentially true."

"Including the part about you really running this city?"

Still looking out the window, he nodded, a very small, distracted nod. "Yes, I do. Somebody has to. Furthermore, since we're telling each other the truth, I'll add that I know where Ben got his information. From his wife, Lydia, who happens to be my daughter.'" He half looked at me. "Did you know that?"

"Yes, sir," I said. "Where did Lydia find out all of those things?"

"From her mother, I expect," he answered, as if he were saying something of no consequence.

His detachment was really getting to me. It was the same inexplicable sort of anger that the hairs on Raoul's stomach had aroused in me. "So you're telling me that you're a crook and that your wife and daughter are out to get you," I said. I was glad there wasn't a swimming pool in the vicinity. I might have thrown him in it, he was that pompous, dainty and aloof from all the vile things he did or caused to be done.

Thall swung his chair around slowly so that he faced me. He began that subzero smile, but his frail, elegant body was overtaken by a spasm of coughing. He got out a handkerchief and busied himself with his miseries while I looked at the portrait of his mother and wondered why he had summoned me, a total stranger.

He folded his handkerchief and put it back in his pocket. "Excuse me," he said. "No, that is *not* what I'm telling you, Mr. Eppe, although I admire your spunk and candor for expressing yourself so bluntly."

I didn't say anything. I was enjoying my spunk and candor too.

"I'm explaining the facts of life as they prevail in this city," he went on. "When you have been in East Heidelberg for a little while, you will notice things. For instance, there is racial tension here, but there has never been a race riot. That's because I've told the police, the leaders of the German community and the church that I won't tolerate violence. I am able to do that because I own the police, the leaders of the German community and the church in this city. How do you suppose I came to own them?"

It was a rhetorical question. It was supposed to prove that Copernicus Thall's thievery was really Robin Hoodery because he used the money to keep East Heidelberg racially calm.

"Go up and down the Ohio River," he said. "Everywhere you will see potteries closing, but there are three of them open and operating here. That's because arrangements have been made concerning their property taxes, labor contracts and electricity bills. There isn't much unemployment in East Heidelberg, Mr. Eppe. For black or white."

"Mr. Thall," I said, "I was raised to be polite and I don't enjoy saying rude things to people. But if you're trying to tell me you haven't gotten rich off all the corruption I've heard about in this city, I just plain don't believe you."

He dropped the temperature a few degrees with his smile. "Of course I've gotten rich. If you wish to use the word 'corruption,' that's your business. To me, my share of East Heidelberg's political profits is a management fee, a surtax these people pay for government that works."

"You're just a councilman. Nobody elected you to impose surtaxes. Or don't most people know you run this place?"

"People know what it suits them to know," Thall answered quietly. "Your average man, Mr. Eppe, doesn't worry about how the system works as long as it works for him. Oh, he'll throw up his hands in horror when reformers like Ben Dashford or the newspapers make a fuss about corruption in city hall. But people really aren't bothered by such things. They don't feel victimized. It's the *public* that's being cheated. Most people don't think of themselves as members of the public. That's somebody else. An abstraction."

I couldn't make up my mind whether he was a complete realist or the most cynical man I'd encountered since the proprietors of Craigie Glen, who would certify a telephone pole as paranoid if you paid them enough to do it. Realists and cynics aren't the same thing, despite what cynics tell you. I didn't want to believe what Copernicus Thall was saying, but there was a wrinkled texture of truth to it.

He wasn't telling me all this to keep his jaw limber on a winter afternoon. He had something in mind for me, I suddenly realized, and I was so busy waiting for him to spring it that I forgot all about being mad. But he wasn't going to be rushed.

"You can't buy every German in East Heidelberg," I said. "How do you get *them* to do what you say?"

"Ethnicity." The word seemed to amuse him. "I understand that people write doctoral theses nowadays about the ethnic question. It doesn't require a thesis to be understood. Ethnicity is a form of collective conceit, Mr. Eppe. If a man doesn't think much of himself—and in secret most men don't—he takes his pride in his tribe. If you're an Irishman, you'll vote for another Irishman. It's a way of voting for yourself. You think the Irish leader owes you something because you're Irish too. The Germans here think I'm a German."

By now he was really amused. He was taking me into his confidence and he wanted me to share the joke. He wasn't threatening anymore. "Aren't you?" I asked.

He smiled. It wasn't his freezing smile. "Do you know who Copernicus was, Mr. Eppe?"

"Sure. He was a Polish astronomer."

"You and I may be the only two people in East Heidelberg who know that." He hooked his thumbs into the pockets of his vest and looked at the ceiling. "I was born Copernicus Thalewski. In Philadelphia. After I graduated from law school and began looking for a place to settle I came here and found the city populated mostly by Germans—as it was in those days. So I changed my name to Thall. It has a nice Germanic ring to it."

"Mr. Thall, as long as we're telling the truth—"

"You haven't told me yours yet," he said, still contemplating the ceiling.

"I will. I promise. Who do you think is going to win the election?"

He lowered his tired, thin face and looked across the desk at me. I noticed once again that his dark hair was parted in the middle. "If the issue was competence instead of ethnicity," he said, "Mitchell Parrish would win easily. He's the one man running who is equipped to be mayor of East Heidelberg. Billy Kronenberger belongs to me, which is *his* only qualification. Ben Dashford is a fool. Not all idealists are fools, but he is." He stopped as if he were saying it all over again to himself. "I will not permit a fool to get control of this city."

That fetched me up sharp. Copernicus Thall had just conceded that he might let somebody else take over. He was sidling up to the reason why he'd summoned me. But my sense of him was to let him take his own time about it. "What would happen if the blacks won?" I asked.

Thall swung his chair slowly around so that he could look out at the city which was his grubby treasure. "Oh," he said in that distracted way of his, "I suppose they'd be virtuous at first. Parrish would keep them under control and run things decently enough. They'd become vengeful after a while." He looked at the sooty façade of the hotel across the street. "They have a lot to take vengeance for. Within six months there wouldn't be a German bureaucrat or city contractor in East Heidelberg. They'd all be black. You'd be amazed, Mr. Eppe, at how quickly the redressed grievance of former vassals becomes the *droit du seigneur* of the new establishment." He glanced at me. "I presume you know the meaning of the phrase."

The big office had become enveloped in a kind of suspension of time and sound. Copernicus Thall had slipped into a disguised sadness. I was infected by the depth, stillness and mystery of it. "Yes, sir," I said. "And if the blacks won, you'd be out."

He nodded. "I'd be out. East Heidelberg wouldn't be my responsibility anymore."

The silence held us dangling together for a few moments. "Mr. Thall," I said, "do you believe in anything?"

He contemplated the dirty city. Finally he said, "I believe in our Lord Jesus Christ, in the miraculous character of His holy mother, Mary, and I think I believe in the infallibility of the Pope on matters of faith and morals." He thought about that for a moment. "Most Popes. I also believe in my own immortal soul." He stopped again. "I believe in repentance and salvation." He turned away from the window. "And now, Mr. Eppe, your truths."

As quickly and briefly as I could I told him about how I'd arrived in East Heidelberg by accident, how I met Ben and got caught up in the Dashford campaign. I told him that I'd embarrassed Ben into making the speech at St. Dismus' because I had promised Lydia I'd try. I didn't say anything about going to bed with Lydia.

"I don't suppose you'd care to tell me what you were doing before you came here."

"No, sir. I'd rather not."

"It doesn't matter." He tapped the leather surface of his desk with a sharp pencil. "I expect, Mr. Eppe, that you'd do rather well in politics if you chose it as a trade. You have good instincts."

I wasn't sure whether to take that as a compliment, considering the source. "Mr. Thall, why did you ask me to come see you?"

He looked up at me. "I was wondering if my son-in-law would make a deal before election day."

"With you? No, sir."

"I didn't mean with me," Thall answered. "Another reason for asking you to come here today was that I wanted to converse with you. I envy you, Mr. Eppe. You're a true innocent. I saw it in you yesterday. You thought that lifting your automobile would impress those men threatening you and Ben. You thought that Ben's speech would make a great difference, that it would change East Heidelberg." He smiled again. "Innocents have several advantages in life. They see things directly and clearly. No one hates them, so they can talk to anyone." He leaned forward almost like a conspirator. "You have great power, young man. Use it wisely."

"But for what?"

"I have confided in you, Mr. Eppe. I have been candid with you about the true political situation here." He looked at me in silence. "It is my belief that you now know who should be mayor of this city. I believe further that only an outsider can go back and forth between the various parties and make suitable arrangements."

He was like a fourteenth-century cardinal. He'd been devious for so long that he'd gotten out of the habit of saying things directly. But I got his drift. It scared me and bewildered me as to his motives.

I stood up. "I'd like to know one more thing."

"You may ask it."

"Why haven't you spoken to your daughter for all these years? That seems pretty stupid to me."

The old cold smile came back to his face. "You still wonder if I believe in anything," he said. "Lydia married outside the Church, Mr. Eppe. Ben Dashford is an atheist. I could not accept her marriage to such a man."

Well, he did believe—and powerfully, too. He believed in God but not in man. He believed I was innocent and he had spent the last forty-five minutes trying to corrupt me with his view of politics. And he hoped he'd failed.

"You've got a nice granddaughter," I said.

His smile held. "I'm told she favors me."

"She's determined," I said. "You ought to get to know her, Mr. Thall."

The distraction came over him again. He nodded. "Pride and desire," he said. "The proud deny what they desire, Mr. Eppe, for fear they will be repulsed."

I wondered if, in all his complicated life, he had ever come so close to true confession. I went to the door and just before I opened it, I turned back to him. He looked small behind the huge desk and all alone in his vast office. "Mr. Thall," I said, "last night I asked Lydia if she hated you and she called me a dumb bastard."

"Thank you, Mr. Eppe," he said. "I'm happy to hear that."

I went across the street and found Barbara in the hotel coffee shop.

"What did he want with you?" she asked after I'd ordered some tea.

"I can't tell you," I said. "It was a confidence."

"Copernicus Thall gave a confidence to you?" she asked in astonishment. "Don't get all rashy mad, honeypot, but you're a new boy in town—and come down heavy on the *boy*."

"Maybe that's why he chose me," I said. "It's like pouring out your heart to a stranger."

She made a smirk. "There's a theory that old Thall has a pocket calculator where his heart's supposed to be. And if he *has* got one, he doesn't pour it out. I'll bet he even lies in the confessional."

"He has his own devious way of confessing," I said.

"And you won't tell Barbie-doodle what he said?"

I shook my head. "I can't."

"Some pal you turned out to be," she said.

"Look, I have to do something. How would you like to be in on the result? Somebody's got to report it right."

"Peachy," she said. "You're my pal again."

"Okay," I said. "Tell me where to find Mitchell Parrish."

Her eyes widened a little. "He's always at Packard's pool hall on Ohio Street after eight. Say, what're you up to?"

"Meet me at Ben's around ten," I answered. "Then you'll see."

I raised my head. The afternoon sun was trying to get through the layers of dust and grease on the windows of the coffee shop. It was all a smeary glare, real East Heidelberg light.

"I was surprised that Thall confessed to me," I said. "Why do you think he did it?"

"You can never tell what the dying will do."

"Dying?" I asked in astonishment.

"Yeah," she said, suddenly empty of impending giggles. "Copernicus Thall won't make it to Christmas."

Seven

VICTORY

THE NEWS THAT Copernicus Thall was dying hit me like a train. It confirmed my impression that—in ways as devious as an Armenian can opener—he was using me to achieve a purpose. And it left me perched on the train's cowcatcher hurtling at one hundred miles an hour right back into that whole country which is misery.

There's only one thing to do when you arrive at that kind of territory—start moving again. Eventually you'll get to the border and end up somewhere else. Chronically unhappy people have settled for the stationary condition. They either can't or won't put up with the struggles and perils of getting to the border.

I drove back to the Dashfords' in the cold light of late afternoon growing more miserable by the minute. If I accomplished the purpose Mr. Thall had in mind for me I was going to cause a lot of shrieking and garment-rending. Yet I had to do it. My motives were partly moral. Morality is a system of logic that goes against all the available evidence. It can get you burned at the stake—and if I *didn't* do what Copernicus Thall wanted, he'd probably have me rubbed out.

I had to get out of East Heidelberg fast. The way out was going to be unpleasant.

The unpleasantness began the moment I walked into the Dashfords' kitchen. The back room was full of its usual ravings and disorder. Lydia was at the stove stirring a potful of something with one hand, holding a telephone in the other and trying to shake her kid off her leg. Victoria was clutching with both arms, alternately howling and biting her mother's knee.

"Rover boy is back," Lydia said. "Not you," she told the telephone, "somebody else. Victoria, *lay off!!* Goddamn it, Bornie, you're supposed to be the press secretary around here. I'm sorry," she said into the telephone. "Look, I'll call you back." She hung up while I unwrapped Victoria and held her upside down, which made her squeal and wet her pants.

"I *am* the press secretary," I said.

"Every effing reporter in Ohio and Pennsylvania's been calling about that stuff you handed out today," Lydia said, her voice rising. "*I* can't deal with them all and Ben's out canvassing and the back room's filled with idiots." Her angular face was flushed with fury and cookery, and a strand of hair flayed the air around her forehead.

"I've been seeing your father," I said.

Lydia's anger was choked off in mid-yell. It plunged into some cold well deep inside her. She glared at me for a full thirty seconds, her face going pale and her eyes turning into agates. It was pretty scary.

"Put that child down," she said.

"She'll start screeching again, Lydia."

"Let her screech. You have some explaining to do."

I followed her into the living room. She slammed the door. "All right. Start talking."

There was so *much* to explain that I had a hard time deciding whether to say it all or settle for the minimum and let subsequent events be the explanation. I was also having problems swallowing. "I talked to him," I said. "I think I understand what you do about him."

"I don't want to hear a lot of shit about understanding," Lydia retorted. "When I told you that Copernicus Thall was my father I wasn't appointing you our emissary to him. *He's the enemy*, you treacherous bastard! You're supposed to be on our side!"

"I'm not on anybody's side. I didn't ask to get involved in Ben's campaign. You asked me. You offered me three hundred dollars if I'd stay."

"It's a free country," she shot back. "You could have refused. But once you accepted, you accepted what Ben and I are trying to do. You signed on to help beat my father, not become his buddy!"

"He can be beaten. But not by Ben. You know that yourself."

Her answer was more furious glaring at me. There's a huge and special reproach in the anger of a woman you've made love to.

I cranked up my courage. I didn't have much to lose, anyway. I took one of those deep breaths which are prefaces to statements you know are going to be unpopular. "Lydia," I said, "I think you're trying to do two things. First, you're trying to make Ben into a man so that he'll love himself and be easier for you to love. Second, I think you love your father too and know him pretty well, even though you haven't spoken in all these years. You know he's dying and worried about his soul, even though you probably don't believe in souls yourself."

"Bullshit," she snapped. "I *demand* to know what you—"

"I think you want your father out of power because you know he needs clean time to repent and die contented."

"Oh, balls," she said. But she didn't add anything.

"I think you got trapped," I went on. "You encouraged Ben when he decided to run. Then Mitch Parrish got in and that threatened Ben because the anti-Thall vote would be split. After that you didn't know what to do until I came along. You hoped I could do something. I think I can."

"What?" she asked.

"Make some of Ben's visions come true."

"Visions, my ass!" she said. "Ben wants to be mayor. This campaign's the biggest thing that ever happened to him!"

"And losing would be the worst thing that ever happened to him. But if what he wants can happen to East Heidelberg—"

"Don't tell me what he wants," she snapped. "I *know* him. I live with him!"

"But you don't listen to him."

"What the hell do you know about it? I *demand* to be told what you and my father have cooked up."

"I've got to talk to Mitch Parrish tonight. I'll be back here about ten. Everybody thinks I can make Ben do things." I was edging out toward the end of a limb that could snap at any moment. "I'll try."

Lydia's flush was back. Her fury was out of its well and hot on her surface. "You double-crossing son of a bitch!" she shouted. "You and my father and Parrish! You've got it all doped out between you, how to sell Ben Dashford down the river! If you think we're going to pay you three hundred dollars for—"

"Goddamn it, Lydia, I'm trying to give you people what you really want. I wish you'd all stop being so stubborn!"

She walked out, slamming the living-room door again. The worst affront to pride is discovering the desire that lies behind it.

I stood there amazed at my audacity in talking back to Lydia. As you may have gathered, I'm not one of those powerful personalities who can force their point of view on everyone around them. I knew that most of my own understanding of conditions tended to be impractical. But this time I was sure I was on to the right one because it came from Copernicus Thall. Whatever else he was, that man knew how to size up situations.

I heard a small scratching on the door. I opened it. Victoria was standing there with the expression of a pygmy adoring a totem pole on her round dirty face.

"I don't feel like playing right now," I said. The fact that I had correctly predicted that my mission would cause a lot of shrieking made me even more miserable. And the garment-rending was still to come.

Victoria staggered into the living room and grasped me around one leg.

"I'm not going to pick you up and let you pee on me," I said, trying to be stern. "Your whole family's crazy. They all love each other and spend their time feuding with each other." I walked across the room, wearing Victoria like a shin guard, and sat down in an easy chair. She put her chin on my knee and looked up into my face. That kid really adored me. If she grew up to be anything like her mother or grandfather she'd prove it by shooting me.

I looked down at her. "I don't suppose *you* can tell me which is more important to your father—getting to be mayor or having East Heidelberg reformed?"

Victoria gnawed on my knee. Then she wiped her nose on it. She recommenced staring at me with her arms still clutched around my leg.

"Everybody wants your grandfather out." I went on just because I needed somebody to talk to, even a little kid who could neither understand nor talk back. "Your grandfather wants out himself. But his pride and face won't let him just quit. He won't even *say* he wants to quit. He connived his way into power and now he has to connive his way out in accordance with his religious principles and he's using me to do it because he thinks I'm the lamb of God or something."

Victoria had let go of my leg. She'd climbed up onto the chair and was trying to poke her finger in my eye.

"Your father likes and trusts me," I said, "and now I'm supposed to go see Mitchell Parrish and arrange to have *him* win the election. If I don't, your grandfather will murder me, and if I do, your mother will never speak to me again." I looked at the kid. She'd stopped trying to put out my eye and was staring at me again with her face about two inches away from mine. She was rapt.

"Why me?" I asked her. "It isn't fair."

Victoria made a loving gurgle. "Pow," she said.

I drove downtown and parked on Ohio Street. The ghetto was almost deserted, its life going on out of public sight.

Packard's pool hall was one of the out-of-sight places. It was full of smoke, men, the talk and jokes of another language. A big fat guy with a cue in his hand came over to me in a slow lumber and asked what I wanted in that tone of voice which tells you you don't belong. I said I'd come to see Mitchell Parrish.

" 'Bout what?"

"It's personal," I said. "Well, political."

"He don't just see anybody," the fat guy said. Somebody was black. Anybody was white.

"I work for Ben Dashford," I said.

"Gimme your name."

"Sherborne Eppe."

"Wait here."

He walked away, rolling as if his feet hurt and his beef was too much to bear. Down the length of the pool hall the games began again. Laughter floated through the smoke and the low hot lights over the tables.

Suddenly I didn't know where to look or what to do with my hands. I was even uncertain about the propriety of leaning on a glass counter. They knew I was there but they had decided not to know it. I was standing at the back door of *their* house now.

Fatty came back, taking his own good sweet Christian time about it. He pointed to a door at the rear of the pool hall. "In there," he said.

I walked the length of the place feeling invisible. I thought of Hannibal, who was out there in the winter night somewhere tearing down mountains and tipping over buildings looking for me. As a general principle black *is* beautiful. But not universally.

I opened the office door at the back of the hall. Two of the guys I'd seen being arrested at St. Dismus' were sitting in low chairs with papers in their laps. One of them had a large bandage on his head. Mitchell Parrish sat behind a desk, tilted back, reading something.

I've already told you that he was handsome, with a handlebar mustache, and that he wore three-piece suits. When you got into his immediate presence you recognized his solidity. Some people telegraph that sort of character—no self-doubt, but no arrogance either, a man loaded with knowledge that was always ready for use.

He looked up. "Sherborne Eppe?"

"Yes, sir," I said.

Parrish rose from his chair and held out his hand. "How's your head?"

"It's okay," I answered. I looked at the guy with the bandage. "How's yours?"

He laughed. "Those krauts pack some kind of wallop. You and I know."

Parrish introduced me to both of them, but their names slipped by me because I was focusing on the man I'd come to see. We all sat down. Parrish tilted back in his chair again and looked across the desk at me. "How's Ben?" he asked.

"All right for a man who's losing."

Parrish nodded. "There can only be one winner."

"Do you think you can win?"

"It's possible. Why do you ask me that?"

Now it was my turn to think before answering—or try to think. My mind was full of the political education that Copernicus Thall had tried to give me. I'd had a few hours to consider what he'd said and there were parts of it I didn't want to be true.

"Mr. Parrish," I said, "I'm a go-between. I hope you'll excuse me from telling you how I came to be here . . ."

"Don't say anything you don't want to," he answered. "And speak for yourself as well as for whoever sent you."

That's what I wanted to hear. "I haven't really been sent by anybody," I said. "I just got caught in the middle of a situation. I can understand all the parts of it because I'm not involved in any of them."

"Fair enough."

"I think I can make something happen."

"But before you do that," he answered, smiling a little, "you have a question."

I nodded.

"Shoot."

I took another of those deep prefatory breaths that come before a statement you'd just as soon not make. "Mr. Parrish, somebody told me today that if you win, the blacks will become what the Germans have always been in this place."

He raised his right hand, crooked a finger and placed it on his mouth. He looked at me, being very thoughtful. So did the two other guys. I couldn't tell if I'd made them angry or not.

"That's not one question," Mitchell Parrish finally said. "It's about twenty or thirty."

"Yes, sir."

"I wonder about several things," he said. "How I can persuade you that I'll act on the answer I give you now—whether you'll think I'm giving you the answer you want to hear because you've obviously come here with a proposition." He tilted forward, put his arms on the desk and clasped his hands. "I'll begin by asking *you* a question. Is there someone or something in your past that you resent?"

There wasn't any point in denying it. "Yes, sir. I think I resent my mother. I try to pretend I don't and I kid a lot about her." They were all looking intently at me. "But I have resented her."

"Do you spend a lot of time on it?"

I thought a moment. "I guess I used to." Dr. Feldman had made me see that I was unconsciously resenting. It was a waste of energy.

"Has it screwed up your life?" Mitchell Parrish asked.

"It did for seven years."

He nodded. "It's almost impossible to be born black in this country and not grow up with profound resentments. The system gets us both ways. It creates barriers against us because of our skin color and then lets us suppress ourselves in our own rage."

"Yes, sir."

"Stop calling me sir," Parrish said quietly. "It sounds patronizing. That's a resentment."

"Okay, Mitch."

He gave me a sudden, brief smile with his eyes and that part of his mouth visible under the handlebars. "Revenge, as the saying goes, is a dish best eaten cold," he went on. "We blacks have to beat the resentment rap and get into the system self-controlled and with clear heads. That's why I'm running for mayor of East Heidelberg. Would you want to be mayor of this dump, Bornie?"

"Not me," I said.

"I don't either. But if I *do* become mayor it'll be to show the Germans that the blacks aren't as corrupt and racist as they are. We'll be as fair as we can. Stanley and Bud here have drawn up lists of which city employees will stay and which will go. A lot of whites will stay on, including the police chief if he can make his men stop hassling our people."

"*Are* blacks less corrupt than Germans?"

"You're asking the wrong question," Parrish answered softly. "You're asking if blacks are human beings. It isn't a matter of racial virtues and vices. *The* question is—can I run this place better than Copernicus Thall?"

"Can you?"

"I hope so. I also know what the road to hell is paved with."

We all sat in silence for a while. I used the time trying not to be disappointed. I'd come hoping that Mitchell Parrish was going to be Sir Galahad. He turned out to be a realist who promised to do the best he could. Still, he was the only game in that miserable town. My depression was thicker inside of me. "Okay," I said at last, "here's what I think can happen."

We talked and bargained for almost an hour. When I left,

the guy with the bandaged head—I think he was Stanley—
walked me to my car. We shook hands. "You staying around
here?" he asked.

"No," I said. "Whatever happens, I'm leaving tonight."

"Too bad," he said. "Mitch needs a press secretary. Look
pretty good if he was a honky."

We both laughed, but I don't think either of us really
thought it was funny. "Take care of yourself, man. Hear?" he
said.

I promised I would.

I drove back to Society Hill, and as I reached the curved road
that led to the Dashfords' I suddenly understood what had been
picking at me all day.

I'd seen a lot of ignominious things done to and by the
human character, but I'd always had this belief—unspelled-out,
yet lurking in me—that there is a basement of nobility under
most people's visible structures. Maybe I just *wanted* to believe
that. Still, wanting to believe and believing are almost the same
thing. Now I wasn't so sure about the nobility.

In East Heidelberg I'd gotten to know a cynic who claimed
that all men are vile, and a promiser who admitted that he
wasn't sure he could carry out his promises. There had been
doomed love and angry love—all of it was churning around a
fool who, maybe, was taking a big ego trip on his virtuous desires
and proclamations. Nobody had displayed any nobility.

I parked in the Dashfords' driveway and thought about it
for a couple of minutes. I was pissed-off because abandoning my
belief made me feel like an exile from my whole life up to then.
My gods had really deserted me on the road to East Heidelberg.

I pulled myself together, told myself to be a man and do the
last thing—go inside and disabuse the nice fool of his illusions.
Then I could leave that place forever.

Lydia was sitting alone at the kitchen table, smoking and
thinking in the sudden silence of the house. She looked at me
with about the same expression she'd use if she found a dead rat
in her apple pie.

"I have to talk to Ben," I said.

"Got your stiletto with you?" she asked.

There wasn't any answer to that. I just left the previous statement lying on the table. After a weighty, hate-filled pause, Lydia went into the hall. "*Ben!*" she yelled up the stairs.

There was a muffled answer from the second floor.

"Get your ass down here!" Lydia shouted. "Your best friend wants to see you!"

Ben came into the kitchen followed by Lydia. He had on pajamas with pale-green stripes and he was grinning his kid grin as usual. More than the usual amount of hair was falling over his forehead. "Hi, Bornie," he said in the conciliatory tone of a man who knows everything and who, out of compulsive niceness, wants to be agreeable about it.

"Hello," I answered.

"What we need is a cup of coffee," Ben said. He looked at Lydia. "How about it, honey?"

"Make it yourself," she said. She was leaning against the side of the kitchen doorway, sleeves pulled up on her sweater, arms folded.

Ben sat down at the kitchen table, still grinning at me. "Well. What've you been up to, Bornie?"

I took my third deep breath of the day. "I guess I'd better give it to you all at once," I said. There wasn't any point in trying to persuade him I hadn't instigated anything, that I was really just the messenger. "I saw your father-in-law today," I said. "In his own way he wants to let go of East Heidelberg. But he won't dump Billy Kronenberger to let you become mayor." I took my fourth deep breath. "There are three reasons, Ben. Mr. Thall doesn't approve of you. He doesn't believe you can win. And if you *did* win, he thinks you'd be a lousy mayor." I'd said it. Half the bad news was delivered.

Ben was sitting with his arms on the table, head cocked a little to one side. He nodded, still grinning. He was like a village idiot who's about to be lynched and doesn't quite grasp the fact.

"Tonight," I said, "I had a talk with Mitch Parrish. He's agreeable to adopting most of your platform if you'll pull out and get your people and your campaign organization behind him."

Ben didn't bat an eye. "What parts won't he adopt?"

"The community college and the medical center. He says East Heidelberg can't afford them."

"We could get federal loans . . ."

"I don't think Mitch has thought of that," I answered. "Maybe you could talk to him about it."

"Or you," Ben said. "You've gotten a good grasp on the situation here, Bornie. Everybody likes you."

I shook my head. "I'm leaving East Heidelberg tonight."

"You're *what?*" Lydia asked from the doorway.

"Leaving," I said.

"You mean you *aren't* going to work for Mitch?"

"Of course he isn't," Ben said. "Don't be a damn fool, Lydia." He looked back at me. "What about the streets, sewers and clean-air ordinances?"

"Parrish will go for all that," I told him. "It depends, of course, on who gets a majority on the city council. But he thinks the money saved by wiping out corruption will pay for those parts of your platform—and maybe a new wing on the high school, too. He'll still run on black rights."

"Well, I'm for black rights," Ben said.

Suddenly he seemed to be a man waking up from a long sleep. The grin on his face—which was just a nervous and niceness habit—spread out into a real smile of delight. "You know," he said, "I think we've got something here! I have the best campaign organization outside of Thall's. Mitch has the numbers. If we add our people—" He turned to Lydia. "What was our last registration count?"

The cold rage had left her eyes. Her arms were still folded, but not as an expression. "Wait a minute," she said. "About seven thousand—"

"Mitch has fifteen, maybe eighteen thousand blacks," Ben

said, all charged up with the injection of new possibilities, "and we can use our people to get them to the polls! Hey, Bornie, what would you think if we challenged Kronenberger to a debate over the radio? Mitch would wipe the street with him. Then we can keep hammering away with all the stuff we've got on the Thall machine . . . we could pick up another twenty-five hundred . . ."

Lydia left the door, crossed the kitchen and knelt down beside him. She put her hands on his shoulders. "Ben," she said, shaking him a little, "Bornie's telling you you're out! *Finished!*"

"Finished, hell . . . Almost everything we've worked for is really going to happen!" He looked up at me. "Mitch is an honest man. He'll do what he says." His mind was totally enraptured by the vision of his reforms and improvements. He was asking me for affirmation that it was really possible.

"I think he means what he says," I answered, hedging my bets, as it were. I didn't want to get into a discussion about what paves the road to hell.

"Good," Ben said. "Bornie, where's Mitch right now?"

"In Packard's pool hall on Ohio Street."

"Get the number," Ben said to Lydia. "I'm going to call him."

"Yes, Ben." She stood up. She was bewildered, and Lydia Dashford wasn't a lady who bewildered easily.

Nobody said anything until she came back with the telephone number. Then Ben stood up and shook hands with me. "I wish you were staying, Bornie."

"You're going to be fine," I told him.

"Yeah," he answered. He was being pulled back to excitement again.

There was a knock on the back door. Before any of us could answer, the door opened and Barbara's head appeared. "Finished talking dirty?" she said. "Can the kids come in now?"

"Hey, Barbara." Ben grinned.

She stepped into the kitchen, closed the door, pulled off her mittens and hat. "What's going on?"

"Ben's out of the election," I said. "He's putting his organization behind Mitch Parrish."

Barbara stared at me. "The hell he is."

"The hell he isn't," I answered. "I'm still his press secretary —for a few more minutes, anyway."

"God's best damn," Barbara murmured.

"It's true," Ben said, still grinning at her. "This time we're *really* going to get rid of Thall."

"Can I use the phone?" Barbara asked. "Gotta get this on the eleven o'clock news."

"Go ahead," Ben said. "Then I'll call Mitch. Damn! It's wonderful!" It was just like the hours following the riot at St. Dismus'. Ben Dashford was a percolator of enthusiasm and not giving a thought to how his pleasurable circumstances came about. "Make sure we hear from you," he said.

"I will," I answered. "You're a great man, Ben."

The kid grin reappeared for a moment. "Do you really think so?"

"I really do," I said. I really did.

After he'd left the kitchen Lydia just stood contemplating me. What was happening inside her was unreadable.

"I've got to go," I said. "I'll turn out the lights in the apartment. What about the heater?"

"I don't care," she said. "Look, do you mind telling me about yourself or do you want to go on being an enigmatic stranger who appears and changes the whole goddamn world?"

"I kind of like being an enigmatic stranger," I said. It was one of my favorite fantasies, as a matter of fact. Mystery man.

Lydia took a roll of bills from her jeans pocket. She held it out to me. "You've earned this."

After all I'd been through, putting up with East Heidelberg and nearly losing my faith in human nature, I thought I *had* earned it. "Thank you," I said, taking the money.

She crossed the kitchen and gave me a hard kiss. "You're a son of a bitch, Bornie Eppe," she said without meaning it.

I went outside feeling released. I was my old self for the first time since I'd gotten caught in East Heidelberg's plumbing. Whatever else had happened, I had discovered that politics was not for me. Too many people invest their souls in it, and as Mitch Parrish said, there can only be one winner. There aren't enough Ben Dashfords in politics to make it comfortable.

Barbara was standing in the drive looking off east at the stars on the curve of the world. "Now where are you going?" she asked.

I told her I didn't know.

"Then you'd better come home to Pittsburgh with me until we figure out what to do with you," she said.

My gods were back. "Okay," I said.

We crossed to the garage and walked up the dark stairway to the little apartment. I could hear cats scuttering around in the beams and blacked-out corners.

I switched on the living-room light. "I haven't got much," I said. "Most of it's in the bathroom."

Barbara turned on the bedroom light. She screamed.

I bolted out of the john. When *I* saw what was in the bedroom I went into shock.

Hannibal was sprawled out with his hands clasped behind his bull neck. That terrible woolly hat was half covering his eyes, and his big filthy boots were smearing the bedclothes.

"Hello, smart-ass," he said.

Eight

THE OLD, OLD MAN

FOR A MOMENT that was several eternities I couldn't move. Nor could I say anything. My mind and bowels froze as I stood in the apartment over the Dashfords' garage staring at what I was sure was the first harbinger of Kingdom Come.

"Who in the name of sweet Jesus is *that*?" Barbara asked. Her eyes, too, were riveted on Hannibal. Encountering him un-expectedly was like finding a McCormick reaper in your bath-room.

"He's come here to kill me," I finally managed to say to her. "You'd better get out of the way. He isn't very accurate."

Hannibal's red-shot eyes glared at me from under the rim of his woolen hat. He looked at Barbara, then back at me. He unclasped his hands from behind his head and made a noise that expressed loathing, contempt, blood lust and several of his other natural sentiments. He swung his legs off the bed and stood up, rearing before us like one of those radioactive creatures in a Japanese horror movie that grow to monstrous size. He took off the hat.

"Good evenin'," he said to Barbara with a sort of brutish

courtesy. "There's something you better know right off. This man here tell so many lies he wouldn't know the truth if it tore his own leg off."

My fear became voltages of instant anger—they're more or less the same thing, anyway. "You're the liar!" I blurted, my voice coming out both gulpy and shrill.

"You shut your mouth," Hannibal said.

"He's been following me ever since I left Cleveland!" I yelled, even though Barbara was right beside me.

Hannibal made his noise again, a rumbling snort like a volcano that's about to blow. "He such a smart-ass that if *somebody* don't follow him around, he gone get his pecker caught in the wringer," he said to Barbara. He made a little bow. "And I do beg your pardon."

"You got it, honey," she answered, still giving him her undivided attention.

I had a fleeting glimpse of myself in one of my fantasies—frightened but ballsy in the face of deadly peril. I forced my voice down a few octaves. "He's a gangster," I said, making myself look at Hannibal. "A guy named Haddon sent him after me. They're both gangsters."

Hannibal began to make that wheezing sound in his vocabulary of horrible noises that was supposed to represent laughter. "That Feldman," he said to Barbara, "he's so goddamn stupid that he don't know if I *was* gone kill him he'da been dead the first night. Dumb sumbitch thought he could outrun a Pontiac in a little old piss-ass Volkswagen. Then when he goes to hide out he gets his picture on the teevee so the whole fuckin' world can see him. Man, he's some FBI!"

I was so tight I was shaking. "That's crap," I said.

"Even gave the peckerhead time to get out of the building," Hannibal went on. "Made like I couldn't open the fire door." He shook his head. "That Feldman," he repeated. "You better watch out, lady. He liable to lean against the house and knock it down."

Standing in the door between Hannibal and me, Barbara was looking bewildered. "Who's Feldman?" she asked.

"That's what this cannibal thinks my name is," I said. "It's too complicated to go into right now."

My spurious courage was calming me. It was true that Hannibal could have killed me on the way out of Cleveland and he'd obviously had plenty of chances since he'd seen me on television. He could have been stuffing me through the floorboards of the Dashfords' apartment right then and there instead of running off at his big fat mouth.

"Sumbitch lies so much he don't know his own name," Hannibal said to Barbara.

"Look," she told us both, "if you two clowns want to have a discourse, I wish you'd talk to each other instead of me. I just do the laundry and feed the gerbils around here."

I took a deep breath. "Okay," I said to Hannibal, "now that you've found me you can go back to Cleveland and play with your parts."

"Say," Barbara murmured, "what've you kids been up to?"

"I mean auto parts," I said. "He steals them and sells them."

"You tell any more lies," Hannibal said, "I'm gone fix your mouth so you can't chew your soup with it. I ain't never stole no auto parts and you know it because you're a FBI."

"Are you really an FBI agent, honeypot?" Barbara asked me.

"Of course not. This idiot thinks I am because Haddon told him so. Haddon's paranoid."

Hannibal put his woolly hat back on his head. "I ain't goin' back to no Cleveland nohow," he said.

"That's why he's chasing me," I explained to Barbara. "Haddon thought I was going to blow the whistle on him."

Barbara studied Hannibal for a moment as if she couldn't believe that what was huge, ugly and evident about him was the total truth. "I don't think he *is* chasing you," she said.

"You listen to that lady," Hannibal said to me. "She's got sense, which you ain't. Dumb sumbitch never would listen."

Well, I've already conceded that not listening when I should is one of my faults. I get a particular perspective on a situation so fixed in my mind that I don't hear the alternatives. My perspective on Hannibal had been sheer terror. The alternative—that he meant me no physical harm—couldn't find a comfortable place in my brain.

"I think he likes you," Barbara said.

"You don't know him," I told her. "He's never liked anybody or anything in his whole life."

"Lies," Hannibal said. "Godamighty, listen to him lie. Where we goin'?"

"*I'm* going to Pittsburgh," I said. "I don't know about—"

"Then let's shake ass," Hannibal said. He peered around the low-ceilinged bedroom. "This place fulla spiders."

Even monsters are capable of pathos. They may not feel pathetic but they can assume the posture. Here was big horrrible Hannibal with his hat slipped down over one eye and an expression like World War Three on his face admitting that he was scared of spiders and wanted to go to Pittsburgh with us. I didn't find him all that touching, but Barbara seemed to. "You can come, too," she said. "But you'll have to share the bedroom with Bornie."

"Who's Bornie?" he demanded in a belligerent grunt.

"Him," Barbara said, jerking her head at me. "Feldman, the FBI agent."

"*Thass* his name?"

"That's what he's calling himself this week," Barbara said. "Sherborne Eppe."

Hannibal got all convulsed with wheezing and bumped his head on the sloping rafters. "Shee-*yit!*" he hollered when he had himself under control. "Sherbert Eppe! They named the sumbitch after a ice cream parlor!"

It was on that note of hope and dignity that I left East Heidelberg, Ohio, forever. As Hannibal and I followed Barbara's van along the highway to Pittsburgh, the Urinal Capital of the World didn't seem so bad in retrospect. At least when I was there I didn't have Hannibal attached to me like some large volatile leech of unknown intention.

The glow of the dashboard lights on his face made him look like a Nigerian Beelzebub. I was having a hard time getting rid of my fear and truculence. I considered the possibility that he hadn't murdered me in the apartment because Barbara would have been a witness. We drove in silence. Beyond the spread of the Volkswagen's headlights the night was metallic and cold with tree branches like mantis legs black against the starry sky.

Hannibal shifted in his seat. "Man can't fight something he can't see," he said.

I should have kept quiet, but I was tense and therefore chattery. "Like a ghost," I said just to say something.

"Shee-yit," he grunted. "Like a *FBI!*" He gave me a filthy look. "A po-lice come after you, you can hit him with a brick because you can *see* him. You can't *see* no FBI." He unzipped his jacket and slid his hand inside.

Oh, Jesus, I thought, a knife. It had never occurred to me that he'd assault me with anything other than his fury and muscle.

He pulled out something flat wrapped loosely in an old brown piece of paper. "Can't fight 'em, join 'em," Hannibal said. "Now, you remember it was me give it to you, smart-ass."

"I don't know what you're talking about!" I said loudly between dry swallows.

"You *remember* that, hear?" he rasped. "I'm puttin' it on the back seat and you *take it!*"

"I don't want it! What is it?"

"*Watch your drivin'!*" he roared.

I wrenched the wheel just in time to keep the Volkswagen from smashing head-on into a roadside wall of rock covered with ice. We bounced back onto the concrete at sixty miles an hour.

"You're giving me that because you think I'm an FBI agent!" I screamed. "*I am not from the FBI!*"

Hannibal shoved his hands into his jacket pockets, scrunched down in his seat and snorted. "You just keep your eyes on the road," he said. "Stop screwin' around, you hear me?"

My metabolism was back to normal after we'd gotten about

five miles closer to Pittsburgh in the freezing gloom. That is, I was normally terrified, tense and enraged. "You're always calling me dumb and a smart-ass," I said. "How can I be an FBI agent if I'm dumb and smart-ass?"

"Ain't no FBI gone *show* he's smart," Hannibal grunted.

He thought my personality was a disguise. I gave up.

When I woke up in Barbara's guest room the next morning, the world was a gray blank. Mist had slithered around the house and oozed over the side of a ridge, spreading across the river valley and wiping out the sight of the city. I could hear Pittsburgh faintly, the humming rivulets of traffic, an occasional beep and toot, but those were just sounds that framed the silence of a foggy winter day.

Hannibal's bed was empty. I got up and was about to go into the bathroom when I noticed his package on the table. I twitched. It brought back the terrors of finding him in the Dashfords' apartment. But I was still alive and curious, so I sat down on my bed and unwrapped the crinkled brown paper.

When I saw what was inside I came vividly awake as if my mother, Dr. Primrose, Rafe Haddon and the combined choruses of Harvard and hell had jumped out of the closet yelling at me in unison.

All the salesmen's lists from Mademoiselle Dupont's locked drawer lay in my lap! I flipped through them, my heart pounding until I found the New England list. Beth's number was still there—right opposite Texiera's garage in Warwick, Rhode Island.

I cut myself shaving and nearly slipped twice in the shower. Scenes from my gazebo-girl fantasy were tumbling through my mind.

She looked up from her writing desk in the library, smiling and deeply happy that I was back. I had been away for a long time. As we lay between Irish linen sheets in our vast bedroom after making love she described how much she'd missed me and needed me. Later, sitting in the gazebo in our dressing gowns, having a drink and holding hands, I modestly told her about some epic accomplishment I'd just pulled off. She didn't comment, but her eyes looking into mine were filled with pride. That evening we went off to have dinner with the President of the United States.

Downstairs in the kitchen Barbara was cooking breakfast and Hannibal was sitting at a table glaring at the day as if he were trying to figure out a way of killing it. "I've got to make a long-distance call," I said. "I can pay for it."

"Breakfast's almost ready," Barbara said, flipping a curly piece of bacon onto a paper towel.

"It can't wait," I said.

"Okay, sugarplum," Barbara said. "If it's private, go up to my bedroom."

"You keep this lady waitin'," Hannibal said, "and there ain't gone be no breakfast to wait for."

Barbara handed me a cup of coffee and I went upstairs. Her bedroom was a pretty, disorderly place. Long window drapes had been opened to let in the dim light. The bedcovers were half pulled back, and the aroma of old perfume, dry and sweet, hovered in the air. I imagined myself coming awake in that bed beside Beth after a long sleep. The gazebo girl stretched her arms, yawned in luxuriant pleasure and ran her hand over my face . . .

"Nobody's waitin' on you!" Hannibal bellowed from downstairs. "Shake ass!"

I slammed the door, sat down on the bed and dialed Beth's number.

Electronic circuits and junction boxes muttered across the eastern fifth of the United States; my own circuitry jangled in anticipation and my heartbeats accelerated as a telephone buzzed twice in Rhode Island.

A man's voice answered. "Harold Watts."

"Is Beth there?"

"Just a minute."

I waited. The Copland music swelled and late afternoon sun lay in long, golden shafts across the lawn, nearly reaching the gazebo. "Oh, Bornie," the girl was saying to me, "that's *brilliant*, absolutely—"

"Hello?"

"Beth?"

"This is Elizabeth Watts." Her voice was muffled.

"It's Bornie."

I heard a faint clink like a fork against a plate. "*Who?*" Her voice was even thicker.

"Are you eating?" I asked.

"Mm," she mumbled. "Waffles." She swallowed. "Sorry. I got up late. I've *got* to have breakfast. Don't care about lunch or dinner, but I *have* to have breakfast. Who did you say you were?"

"Bornie."

There was a moment's pause. "I don't know anybody named Bornie."

Then I remembered my first call to her. "Beth, this is Bill. I got you on the phone from Cleveland by mistake."

Another pause.

"It was the day your cat died," I said.

"Oh, sure," she said. She was working on the waffles again. "I remember you."

"I said I'd call back."

"And you didn't," she answered, swallowing. "Oh damn!"

"I can explain," I said, my visions evaporating.

"I spilled on my skirt," she said. "Wait a minute. I can't handle this plate and the telephone—hold it." She put down the phone. My heart was beating faster—but with anxiety. "Okay," she said.

"I said I can explain why I didn't call you back that night even though I promised I would."

"You don't know of a quick way of getting maple syrup out of tweed, do you?"

"No," I said. "Listen, Beth—"

"You promised me you'd call me back and you didn't," she

said. "So you broke a promise. I told you I didn't like promises. You offered something I didn't want, then you took it back. Now you want to explain and I'm in a hurry. It's a fugue that ends in nothing." She said all of that in brisk, almost cheerful tones.

I was wrenched up with awkwardness. "At least let me tell you the circumstances."

"That's the second time you've alluded to a circumstance," she said. "Cleveland must be a very dramatic place."

"I'm not in Cleveland anymore," I said. "I'm in Pittsburgh staying with this friend of mine named Barbara—"

"Who?"

"Barbara Defere."

"Ahah!" Beth cried. "*She's* your circumstance." She switched on a British accent. "*Teddibly* decent of you to clear up the the misunderstanding and we—will—watch—your—future—progress—with—"

"Goddamn it, Beth!" I shouted. "*Listen* to me!"

"*No!*" she snapped back. "I really don't want to. Go manipulate somebody else. I've been that route, Bill—"

"Bornie," I said.

Silence for a moment, cold, foreboding silence. "First you're a man in Cleveland who calls himself Bill, now you're in Pittsburgh with a new name . . ."

"It's my real name," I said, trying to think fast of a way of making myself plausible without telling the whole story of the last ten years of my life, which she obviously wasn't in any mood to listen to. "My name is Sherborne Eppe," I said. "My mother is Mrs. Roger Crucial Eppe, who lives on Brattle Street in Cambridge, Massachusetts. That's the truth."

" 'Truth, like a bastard, comes into the world never without ill-fame to him who gives her birth,' " she answered. "What number on Brattle Street?"

"I didn't get the first part."

"Me quoting Hardy quoting Milton," she answered. "Poetry. What number on Brattle Street?"

I damned Craigie Glen for destroying my capacity to remember numbers. "I forget," I said, "but you could check—"

"Check, prove, verify," she said, "figures don't lie but liars figure. *I don't want to check up on you!* I don't give a hoot if you're Sherborne Eppe or Genghis Khan!"

"Mrs. Roger Crucial Eppe—" I said again.

"—who lives at some number on Brattle Street you can't remember, your own mother." Her voice was scaling down to the honeyed alto register which had originally attracted me. "The first time you called you were trying to get ahold of Serge Texiera's garage. I didn't know it then, but I know it now—Serge Texiera's supposed to be mixed up in a stolen-auto-parts racket operating out of Cleveland. You were selling auto parts. Do you work for the Great Lakes Discount Auto Parts Company?"

By that time I needed antifreeze in my bloodstream. She wasn't the girl in the gazebo. She was Sherlock Holmes.

"I used to," I said.

"I thought you were fate," she said, "a lovely, benevolent accident. You called me on a miserable day, you made me laugh, you quoted John Donne, you knew about Beavertail, you were my age, you said you were tall, though that's probably a lie—"

"I *am* tall," I said. In my mind's eye I was a short, awkward seven-year-old who broke vases.

"You made me feel like an ass because I *did* believe in fate," she went on. "I was vulnerable, damn it, I needed something to look forward to, I was wretched when you didn't call back that night—"

"Look, if you'd—"

"—and then when you *do* call back, you've run away from Cleveland, you've changed your name, you can hardly wait to tell me you're with this girl named Barbara Defere—"

"*I'm trying to explain!*" I shouted.

"Explain, explain, explain. I've been burned in the fires of a thousand explanations that don't change anything, and never again, Bill, Bornie or whatever your name is."

"Bornie," I said helplessly.

"Besides, you're a crook and the police are probably going to catch you and beat your brains out and I'd remember how lovely I thought you were the first time—"

"Beth!"

"—and it would make me cry and I've got maple syrup on my skirt and I'm late and I can't afford you and I wish you'd never called back at all."

The telephone made a funny sound as she hung up, a chirp of abruptness and finality.

I felt humiliated, stupid and grotesque. Even if she hadn't hung up on me, I wouldn't have been able to think of anything to say. Her admission that she'd thought I was enchanting when we first talked just made everything worse.

So I began to get mad, which is what you do when you're humiliated. First I was mad at myself for thinking that a girl I'd talked to on the telephone just once was the embodiment of my ultimate fantasy. Then I came over all chagrined for even having fantasy girls.

Being angry with myself didn't help much. So, I switched focus and got mad at Beth. I concocted an instant counter-fantasy of her: she became a neurotic, near-sighted girl with thick, blistered lips and legs made sinewy from jogging. I was lucky to be rid of her. I went downstairs.

Barbara and Hannibal were finishing breakfast in the kitchen. There wasn't much left for me. "Thanks a bunch," I said to Hannibal, taking the last piece of toast and pouring myself another cup of coffee.

"Trouble with you," he said, "you can't decide what to do with your mouth. If you sit up there talkin', you can't be down here eatin'."

"That's known as folk wisdom," I said to Barbara. "He's the Socrates of Cleveland."

"C'mon," she said, "cut it out, both of you. We were just talking about how cute you are."

"If *he* thinks I'm cute, I'm moving to Canada," I said, spreading jam on the toast.

It wasn't lost on me that *she* thought I was cute. She was wearing a thin silk dressing gown; she was sitting hunched forward with her arms on the table and her breasts spilling over them. I could see her cleavage. Her hair was uncombed—she had that just-out-of-bed look that makes you think powerfully about being *in* bed—and her round, grinning face without make-up seemed voluptuous and inviting.

The sudden loss of one fantasy means you have to substitute another one fast. I had an instant picture of Barbara and me rolling around on the sun-baked beach of a desert island making wild and noisy love.

"Don't be a sorehead," she said. "You're a nice-looking boy. I was telling Hannibal that I'm going to speak to my program manager about you unless you've got other plans."

"Man's gotta know how to do something before he has plans," Hannibal said with a mouthful of breakfast.

I ignored him. I was trying to go on being angry, but a feeling of loss, of having nothing to look forward to, was spreading through me. "I don't care what I do," I said, "but I don't know anything about television."

"They've got a problem at the station," she said, "or they're about to. Maybe you'd be the answer. I won't tell you any more until I talk to them. But if they like you they'll train you."

Hannibal slurped down the last of his coffee. "If they're gone put him on the teevee, it'd better be a program where nobody says nothin'," he mumbled. "You let him start talkin' and they gone call it the smart-ass hour with ole Sherbert in person."

I was considering busting him over his big Afro-ed head with a kitchen stool when there were two sharp shrills on Barbara's doorbell.

She pulled her dressing gown together and went out into the front hall. I heard a female voice jabbering in calamity. "Hannibal!" Barbara called. "Bornie! Quick!"

Hannibal flung down his napkin and lumbered out into the hall with me behind him. A small middle-aged woman with a turned-up nose was standing on the front steps clutching her hands in anguish. She was dressed in a tweed suit. She looked at Hannibal imploringly.

"It's her grandfather," Barbara said. "He's fallen out of bed again."

I wondered how a woman her age could have a grandfather. She must have been close to fifty.

"And his nurse quit," she said. "I've just *got* to be at the university by ten for my course."

"Where you live?" Hannibal asked.

She pointed across the street at a little one-story house, dingy-white, with about as much character as a pine coffin. "He's on the back porch," she said.

"Too cold for a old man to be on the porch," Hannibal grunted, crossing the street.

"I've had storm windows put on," the little woman said as she trotted after him. "It's really quite comfortable, I assure you." Barbara and I were following them. Barbara was holding together the front of her dressing gown, which squeezed her cleavage higher and tighter.

We went through a living room whose furniture and pictures were meant for a larger space, and a kitchen with old-fashioned appliances and a green-and-white linoleum floor.

The back porch was, as the lady said, really a room. It looked like a mixture of junk shop and infirmary. There was a ratty old sofa piled with dusty-looking books, a shoe box full of postcards, a Gladstone bag also coated with dust, a set of andirons and a cage made out of rusted chicken wire. A few ancient pictures propped against the wall and an armchair piled with worn underwear and shirts stood among oxygen tanks, bedpans, tables covered with medicine bottles, hypodermic needles, vaporizers and other trappings associated with invalids. A hospital bed had been shoved up against some windows that gave a view of a bare and dismal backyard. The covers were half off the bed, and the oldest human being I have ever seen in my life was lying on the floor in his bathrobe and pajamas.

He was huge. That is, he was the remnant of a very big man, swollen in the middle and bulky-boned at his extremities. His head was completely bald. The years and years of his life had drained him; shadow lay where tissue, muscle and flesh had been. His eyes were wet sparkles in two dark craters, and he had a hooked nose.

Hannibal squatted down beside him. "What you doin' on the floor, old man?"

The embedded eyes rolled to look at him and the gummy old mouth grinned. "Waiting for the A train, Johnny," he said in a voice like a wood rasp scraping the top of tin cans.

"You hurt yourself fallin' down?"

"Hell, no," the old man said. "I've had practice. Done it lots of times."

"Oh, Grandpa," the little woman said.

The old man shifted his eyes toward her. "Shut up, Harriet. I like this fella."

"Then we better get you back on the bed so you can like me some more," Hannibal said.

"Good idea," the old man answered. "You ever know Charlie Pankstaff?"

"That's one man I never did know," Hannibal said. I, the Volkswagen lifter, started forward to help him, but Hannibal had already slid his arms under the old man's shoulders and knees. He stood up as easily as if he'd been holding a pillow instead of a human carcass that must have weighed two hundred and twenty pounds.

"Charlie was totally crazy," the old man said as Hannibal set him on the bed. "Anybody who'd burn down his own house because he had a fight with his brother about the dog crapping on the sofa is a plain and simple lunatic. Hee! Hee! Hee!"

The little woman called Harriet busied herself rearranging the covers, tucking them in and getting the pillows fixed under the old man's head. "Please try to behave, Grandpa," she said.

"Behave like what?"

"Oh, Grandpa," she said again.

"Oh, Grandpa," he mimicked her. He looked up at Hannibal. "She's got bad nerves. I don't know where it comes from. Daisy had nerves like a plow horse."

"You act nice, old man," Hannibal rumbled.

"What'll you do if I don't?"

"Whop you."

"I'm too old to whop."

"No, you ain't," Hannibal said.

The old man cackled *hee hee hee* some more. He looked over at his granddaughter standing beside the bed clasping and unclasping her hands. "Where'd you get your bad nerves, Harriet?"

"He plagues me," Harriet said to Barbara.

The old man reached out and took her by the sleeve with three fingers as knobby as tree roots. "You're a good girl, Harriet. Don't carry on. Did these fellas know Daisy?"

"No," Harriet said. "I'm sure they didn't know Mother. Now you try to take a nap while I make arrangements for you. The nurse has quit."

"Good," the old man answered. "Dried-up old bagful of farts." He fell asleep as abruptly as a puppy.

We all went back to the living room. "This is Harriet Luddington," Barbara said. "Bornie and Hannibal."

Mrs. Luddington shook hands with us, lingering at Hannibal for a moment. You could see that she had been small, cute and precocious at one time. She'd never quite graduated from her girlhood character. The earnestness was still in her manner and her accent was a mixture of New York and Ivy League. "He seems to really *like* you," she said to Hannibal. "He hardly likes *anybody*. I just don't know what I would have done without you. I mean, he's unmanageable without help. And now that we don't have a nurse again—"

"How old is that man?" Hannibal asked.

"Ninety-seven." Mrs. Luddington sighed and clasped her

hands again. "I've *got* to be at the university by ten for my course," she said, "and I promised two little black—two little underprivileged boys that I'd take them to the library. I won't be able to start calling around to get another nurse until at least this evening . . ."

Meeting the old cadaver on the back porch had diverted me from my temper and moroseness, but I wasn't ready to abandon them altogether. I was feeling even more empty and trapped in the unpromising present. "I'll sit with him," I said.

"You better tell us what to do," Hannibal said to Mrs. Luddington.

"Nobody needs you," I said. "*I* can handle it."

"You stop screwin' around," Hannibal said. "What we got to do for that old man, lady?"

Mrs. Luddington sighed again and looked at us anxiously. "I'm afraid he talks a lot."

"That's all right," I said. If the old man talked, I wouldn't have to say anything to either him or Hannibal. I could be alone with my mood.

"I mean a *lot*," Mrs. Luddington said.

"Don't matter," Hannibal said. "Now, what we got to do?"

Mrs. Luddington gave us a short course on the care, feeding and emptying of a ninety-seven-year-old man. The way she talked was weirdly impersonal. If you can take a real sorrow of this world, like dying people, the sane locked up in insane asylums or the prevalence of clap among Eskimos, and reduce it to a social problem, then you don't have to feel anything personal about it. I wondered if Mrs. Luddington thought of the old man on the back porch as a specimen or her grandfather.

When she had finished describing our duties I asked her what course she was taking at the university.

"The Sociology of Death," she told me. "It's *really inter-esting*. It *really* is."

Specimen, I told myself.

Mrs. Luddington filled us in on a few other details. Her grandfather's name was John S. Pennydine and he had been a bank president. She shook hands with me, giving me her college-sophomore-twinkle smile. "I'm *really* grateful to you," she said. "I just don't know *what*—well . . ." After a few moments of knotting and unknotting herself with the inadequacy of her expressed gratitude, she left.

"Good luck, guys," Barbara said. "Old man Pennydine's kind of fun. Ask him about how he won the bank in a crap game. Gotta get dressed and go to work. Supper'll be about eight."

I stood in the front door watching her trot back to her own house. Beneath the silk dressing gown she had one of those wide, symmetric women's bottoms that you just want to run your hands over, and I felt a little bit better—a *little* bit.

Mr. Pennydine was lying on his back with his gnarled old hands twisted together where the covers crossed his chest. He was awake, looking at the ceiling with an impatient expression on his face. The light from the oily sky outside glowed on his skull, nose and jaw. "I suppose Harriet's gone off," he said without looking at us. His voice sounded as if it were coming out of a dusty tunnel.

"Yes, sir," I said.

"She's always taking those goddamn courses," he said at the ceiling. "Art history, social science—whatever the hell *that* is—appreciation of this, appreciation of that, pottery. Lobotomy." He stopped his recitation and chortled. "They should have given Charlie Pankstaff a lobotomy. Earl could have used one, too." He turned his head to look at us standing in the middle of his possessions and medications. "You fellas know Earl?"

"No, sir," I said.

"He's divorcing Harriet, she's divorcing him, maybe they're divorced—I don't remember. Earl's a grouchy son of a bitch. He comes from Montana. He thinks the niggers and the Jews and the Communists are taking over. Taking over *what?* I asked him one time. 'Everything,' he said. We were having lunch. I said I didn't see any Communists under the table or in the parlor. That was the day Earl called me senile and I called him a horse's ass and Harriet ran upstairs crying." He paused again, worked his gums and thought about it. "That Harriet. She's spent her whole life preparing for a future that went by last Tuesday. I don't know where she gets it. Must be her Muller blood. The Pennydines have more sense. I wonder where they put that silver cigarette lighter of mine, the one the Major gave me. The nurse quit, didn't she?"

It was the first thing he'd said in a few minutes that I could respond to. But Hannibal beat me to it. "She quit," he said.

"And Harriet's hired you to stay with me until she can find another one." He said it like an accusation.

"I'm afraid so," I said.

"Don't be afraid, Johnny," Mr. Pennydine said, turning his head to look back at the ceiling. "I'd rather spend my time with a couple of fellas than one of those creaky old nurses. You don't get the young ones on a job like this. We've had four nurses since Christmas." Pause. "Mary Jane got a dollhouse for Christmas one time. That Swede girl broke it sitting on it. I wouldn't mind if they had a Swede girl looking after me, they're horny and young. The nurses can't stand me because I talk so much and I can't stand them because none of them has any more juice than a pipe wrench. When I get so that I hate one of them I fall out of bed. They can't lift me back—I've still got my weight, you know—and it gives them an excuse to quit." He said *hee hee hee* a couple of times.

It appeared that he had accepted the idea of Hannibal and me. Hannibal made himself comfortable on the wicker chair near the bed and I pushed some things aside on the sofa, sat down and prepared to let my mind drift. I noticed a faded, brown-hued photograph of a girl on Mr. Pennydine's bedside table. She had frizzy blond hair and an impish smile. Not my type. Too scrawny.

"Did they tell you I owned the bank?" the old man asked as if he were trying to locate us in his recollections.

"Unh," Hannibal answered. Christ knows what *that* meant.

"And I suppose they told you I won it in a card game, me and a Chinese fella."

"Lady said it was a crap game," Hannibal grunted.

"Card game," Mr. Pennydine said, looking down at his twisted, lumpy left hand. "Anyway, it's a lie."

"Which part?" Hannibal said. "You didn't own no bank?"

"Oh, I owned the bank, all right," he answered. "But I didn't win it in any card game. I talk a lot. I'm damn sure they told you that."

"Lady mentioned it," Hannibal said.

"People like me talk a lot because their brain only works out loud," Mr. Pennydine went on. "If you talk a lot, sometimes you run out of real facts, even if you've lived as long as I have, so you throw in a couple of lies to liven things up. Only they aren't *really* lies, Johnny, because they give the *idea* of what it was like and what you were like at a particular time." He stopped talking and shifted himself. His insides gave out a fearful gurgling sound and Mr. Pennydine clutched his stomach. I was snapped into alarm, but Hannibal flapped his hand to shush me.

The spasm passed. Mr. Pennydine lay breathing for a minute or so. Then he worked his mouth around a little. "Now, the facts about how I got the bank—it was, Jesus, let's see, nineteen and twenty-nine. No, that was the year the stock market went to hell and A. D. Hardeville blew his brains out in my garage right in front of my Pierce-Arrow. It was a white Pierce-Arrow and you can imagine the mess. It's still out in the garage at the place in Sewickley, all cleaned up, of course. I never sold a car I got after nineteen and thirty-four. I got the Pierce-Arrow before that, but I kept it. I got a Buick touring car, two Cadillacs, one of those Lincoln Continentals and a Rolls-Royce I bought off a fella when Lucretia and I were in Liverpool, England, in '54. Lucretia thought I was perverse. 'Your daughter gets killed in a crash,' " he said, suddenly pitching up his voice until it became uncanny, a scolding woman, " 'and you start collecting cars! You've lost your mind, John S. Pennydine!' "

He stared up at the ceiling for a moment. "No, I haven't," he answered in his own voice. "Daisy's death and my cars haven't got anything to do with each other. *'You've got five automobiles already!' "* he screamed so piercingly in the woman's voice that it made me jump. "'You're trying to break my heart!'" The accusation was flat and categorical. It made Mr. Pennydine seethe in inarticulate fury for a while. I knew how he felt. Then he resumed his own voice. "*You* were the one who wanted her to marry that son of a bitch, not me! Just because you thought his father could get me into the Duquesne Club! *That* was the reason, Lucretia! I never did like Eddie Muller *or* his father!" Mr. Pennydine grunted at his own riposte. "I'm glad Eddie's dead, too, I don't care who knows it."

He lay in the gloom reliving an episode that had been long in its grave. "Shit," he said softly. "Still, I knew how Lucretia felt because *I* felt the same way, even though she never believed I did. Never cared about anything or anybody again after that car rolled over on Daisy and Eddie. I don't give a good goddamn when I die. Sooner the better." A tear rolled out of one of the dark caverns on his face. It became a slender, gleaming rivulet over his cheekbone. "Makes me mad when I think how Lucretia wouldn't understand I felt it just as deep as she did. She wouldn't *say* I did. Never would." He turned his head and looked out at Mrs. Luddington's backyard. "I suppose she was a good woman. Aunt Dexter would have called Lucretia Pennydine a good woman. Lucretia was Major Clarence's niece. Aunt Dexter would have told me that I married good sense, good blood and a good connection. I suppose that's *why* I married Lucretia." He turned his head and looked at Hannibal. "Do you suppose that was it, Johnny?"

Hannibal nodded. "That was the reason," he said, "and my name ain't Johnny, it's Hannibal."

He seemed to have a perfect understanding of that decayed old man's mind. Up to that day I never thought Hannibal could understand anything subtler than a camshaft or a fistfight.

I squirmed around on the broken sofa, trying to get comfortable, trying to switch off Mr. Pennydine's talk and get back to my broodings, but what he was saying was too intriguing.

"'Marry up,' that's what Aunt Dexter used to tell the girls. 'Marry up. Don't ever marry a traveling man or a railroad man.'

Buck Ransom's uncle got killed by a Swede who worked fireman on the Rock Island line. Just picked up a barrel on the depot platform and hit Buck's uncle with it. Squashed him flat. I didn't see it but I heard about it. I never saw a dead person until I was seventeen and that was Harry Pitt. He was deader than a old mackerel. Just lying right there where we found him." Mr. Pennydine reclasped his hands on the coverlet and turned back to look at the ceiling. He thought about Harry Pitt for a little while.

" 'Marry up.' Aunt Dexter always said that drummers, traveling men, were the worst. They all stayed at the Great Northern Hotel and Aunt Dexter thought it was hell reincarnated. She was always going on about how the Great Northern was full of profane, fornicating men who'd be the ruin of the girls if they got the chance. She thought that was the worst place in town but it wasn't. There were eight bars on Main Street—Jo Daviess County, Illinois, was wet in those days, you know—and a shed behind Manson's livery stable. *That* was the worst place in town if you believe that fucking out of wedlock is the road to hell or grows hair on the soles of your feet. The Swede servant girls would meet young fellas in the shed behind Manson's. It was a regular diddling emporium except in the wintertime. I never knew where the screwing went on in the winter and I never knew another boy who found out, either. Boys can sniff out screwing, you know. They're burning up to do it themselves but they don't have the chance or they don't dare, so they go around thinking about it, imagining it, talking about it, making up lies about it and watching if they can. Hee! Hee! Hee!" His laughing turned to gasping which turned to choking. Hannibal handed him a vaporizer and Mr. Pennydine heaved on it for a few minutes.

"Sometimes me and Buck Ransom would get ourselves up on the rafters of that shed and spend the whole evening watching. It nearly drove us crazy. There was this one girl, Nanny Borogrove, she wasn't Swede and she wasn't a servant. Me and Buck were kind of in awe of her the way boys are over an older girl who's wicked. Somewhere along the line Nanny decided it

didn't matter. I think she learned it from their hired girl, Ilse."
He considered for a moment, holding the vaporizer in his right
hand. His huge chest moved up and down, his eyes alive in the
shriveled wreckage of his face. "I *know* that's where Nanny got it.
I just remembered. One night me and Buck were up in the
rafters trying not to laugh at each others' hard-ons, and Nanny
and Ilse were down in the hay doing it with Harry Clarence's five
boys. All five of them. They took turns. That was the longest
screwing bout I ever saw. My God, how those girls carried on."

I began to picture what he was describing—the two girls
spread out in the hay, long old-fashioned skirts crushed around
their waists, exposing their white flesh, their legs wrapped
around the bare buttocks of a Clarence boy. I imagined the
groans and screechings of lust, all seen and heard from the cobwebby rafters far above. I got horny as I listened.

". . . *way* past midnight when we got out of there," Mr.
Pennydine was saying. "I didn't dare tell Aunt Dexter where I'd
been, so I made up a story. I lied, she knew it and she gave me a
licking and I wondered if I was going to go to the bad place. I
believed in eternal consequences in those days. Punishment.
I was a literal, confessing Christian when I was eleven years old. I
remember watching Nanny and her family in the Elder River
Baptist Church. She'd be singing hymns and kneeling down to
pray with the rest of them and I wondered how she could do it.
Only me, Buck, Ilse, the five Clarence boys and God knew that
Nanny Borogrove had broken the commandments, and it was a
miracle to me that the floor didn't open up and swallow her right
then and there. I knew *Nanny* was going to the bad place for
sure. I forgot about such speculations when I grew up—most of
the time, anyway—but I was certain back then." He began to
cough again, out of control, and his face turned purple. He
sprayed himself with the vaporizer, trying to blast open his old
lungs and tubes.

"You need to go to the bathroom?" Hannibal asked the old
man.

Mr. Pennydine shook his head. He couldn't answer for a time. He just lay there, huge and helpless, fighting for air.

"Not yet, Hannibal," he gasped after a while. He began to get his regular breathing back. "I'm working on strangling myself just now. *Later* I'll go to the bathroom and turn my insides out." He cackled in a combination of laughter and respiration. "Don't worry about getting old, boys. You can spend your time guessing which part of you is going to finish you off first."

"You go on with the story," Hannibal told him.

Mr. Pennydine turned to look at him. "You mean you *like* hearing it?"

Hannibal nodded.

"I'll be a son of a bitch," Mr. Pennydine said. "What was I talking about?"

"That girl," I said.

"Thanks, Johnny."

"*My* name isn't Johnny either," I said. "It's Bornie."

"Don't worry about it, Johnny," he said. He lay still for almost a full minute, his hands working at each other on the coverlet and his eyes seeing something far beyond the ceiling. "Florida Watson," he said finally. "I've never gotten her out of my head and that's funny because I'm a man who's spent a good part of his life thinking about women—"

You and me both, I said to myself.

"—and forgetting about most of them: ones I knew, ones I made up in my own brain, this girl and that, wife and daughter. I never put Daisy or Florida out of my mind, but most of the others I did. I was even acquainted with a one-legged woman one time. I remember *that* year and no mistake. It was nineteen and three and the newspapers were full of those Wright boys from Ohio and their flying machine and that picture show, the first long one, *The Great Train Robbery*. That one-legged woman ran the laundry and she was ugly as the south end of a mule going north, but smart. She knew about life, Hannibal, even parts of it she hadn't lived. I talked it over with her when I realized I was crazy about Florida Watson. I'd just moved to

Pittsburgh and didn't have anybody else to go to for serious advice. And she told me that if I wanted to be a banker, which I did, it was more than going to the bank every day, it was a whole way of living, and a girl in Florida's line of work just wouldn't fit in, so I'd better choose. Well, I thought in those days I could always find somebody else to love, so I chose. Yes, sir—I got the truth from the woman in the laundry." For a few moments he contemplated the cracks in the ceiling. "I *guess* it was the truth. I guess it was best the way things worked out between Florida and me, best if you believe you have to get ahead in the world. I'm lying here more dead than alive and I'll be goddamned if I know why you have to get ahead in the world. You're going to end up in the boneyard whether you've done well or badly. But everybody says it, so it must be so. Get me some orange juice, will you, Johnny?"

I went out into the kitchen, out of hearing range of Mr. Pennydine's droning, dry old voice. The door of Mrs. Luddington's refrigerator had pieces of paper stuck to it with magnets shaped like garden beetles—schedules of Public Television broadcasts and chamber music concerts, snipped-out quotes from Sigmund Freud, Loren Eiseley, and a recipe for coq au vin. I poured a glass of orange juice and went back to the porch.

"He was a reasonable man," Mr. Pennydine was saying. He took the glass from me and sipped from it and then clutched it to his chest with both hands. "Thanks, Johnny. Major Clarence was a reasonable man. He knew us young fellas were itching to get away on Saturday afternoon and have some fun. The bank closed at one, but he'd pay us off at twelve and tell us to scoot along, that is, those who weren't needed. I was just a messenger in those days or maybe I'd had my promotion to assistant teller, I forget. An assistant teller stood behind a cage and ran errands for a teller or checked balances or accounts, that kind of thing. Mine was a man named Reuben Jackson. He was bald and he'd been a teller at the bank for nineteen years before he quit to take a job with the carnival as bookkeeper. He married the tattooed lady." Mr. Pennydine thought about Reuben Jackson for a few minutes.

Then he chortled. "No, he didn't. That's a lie, the part about his marrying the tattooed lady. But he *did* go off and work for the carnival. He was fifty-one and I think he was lonely. He'd been living in the same rented room for eleven years. I heard later he died in a drugstore fire in Bardstown, Kentucky, but I don't know if it's true. I don't know what Reuben Jackson would be doing working in a drugstore. Maybe he just dropped in. Reuben was older than me—what was I talking about, Hannibal?"

" 'Bout havin' fun on Saturday afternoon," Hannibal said.

"Oh, we had fun on Saturday afternoons, all right," Mr. Pennydine said. "At least when I was a young fella. I was working in the bank, and me and Charlie Ream would go over to Bingham's saloon. I don't suppose you boys know that place. Bingham's."

"No, sir," I said.

"Well, maybe it burned down. Anyway, that was where all the young bucks went on Saturday afternoon. There was Dick Stannard, who worked in that big dry-goods store, he was going up fast, and Ed Weaver, who was a clerk at the coal company, and Billy Mason. Bingham's was the place where the fight started between Julie Stein and the Polack. They had a free lunch, ham, cheese, beef, *all* kinds of cheese, sausage and pickles and fresh bread. Billy Mason was the one who won the bet he could run out of the saloon and jump on the trolley car balancing a mug of beer on his head, and he did it, too. You could get a glass of beer for a nickle and a shot of whiskey for fifteen cents. Fred Nasby got so drunk one time that he ate some sawdust off the floor, and there was a photograph of John L. Sullivan, personally autographed. They had a picture of Corbett, too, but it wasn't personally autographed. Me, Dick, Charlie and Ed spent most of Saturday afternoon in Bingham's listening to the gossip—a lot of the sporting crowd drank in there—and watching Billy get up to his pranks. I saw them throw old Teddy Sewell out of Bingham's one time because he didn't have enough money to buy a drink. I don't think he even wanted one. He just wanted to hang around with his friends. He'd been a famous jockey in his day, but by then he was old and in ragged clothes and they threw him out. He wasn't bothering anybody. It's a terrible thing to expel a man from the comfort of his friends and his familiar surroundings. Teddy never came back. He was shamed, I think. Maybe he took to drink. Now, our crowd never got as drunk as Fred Nasby did the time he ate the sawdust, because around five o'clock we'd go over to Mrs. Downey's. That was a parlor house. It was a big old board house but I don't recall what street it was on. I don't remember street names anymore, don't have to, I'm not ever going anyplace again. You had to ride the trolley about ten blocks and then walk two more blocks west to get to Mrs. Downey's. We'd all go. A girl cost two dollars in those days. It wasn't like you read about in books. There wasn't any piano player, no gambling of any kind. Just whores. It was a clean, sanitary establishment. *I* never caught anything there. But then, after the first few times, I didn't go with any girl except Florida Watson. Have I told you boys about Florida Watson?"

"You mentioned her," I said.

The overcast was turning blacker. Raindrops were splashing here and there on the glass, and a wind had come up. It rattled the storm windows, attracting Mr. Pennydine's attention. He took another sip of orange juice and turned his sapped, ruined face to look out. "It was a wet day," he said, "and only the second time I ever saw her cry. Even then I didn't see her cry much. She did the goddamnedest thing. She *shook hands* with me and then walked away with her back to me. Never said a word, just went up the avenue. It was a wet day and her buttoned-up boots had dead leaves stuck to them. A beer wagon was coming down the avenue pulled by four horses. One of them was white. I felt like killing myself." He gave a grunt and put the orange-juice glass on the bedside table beside the photograph of his daughter—at least I assumed the girl in the picture was Daisy. "Maybe I should have," Mr. Pennydine said. His stomach was making those alarming, gurgling noises again and his feet were beginning to twitch under the covers. "I never got over it—*goddamn!*" He clutched his middle and began to groan seriously.

Hannibal got up and went over to the bed. "Time for you to go to the bathroom," he said.

"Can't," Mr. Pennydine gasped, holding his stomach and beginning to shake. He rolled on his side. "Can't get up . . . don't want to shit the bed like a goddamn baby. Oh Jesus . . ." He closed his eyes and screwed his face into a horrible grimace. "Don't ever be an old man . . . don't ever be old . . . can't be a man . . ."

Hannibal got his hands under Mr. Pennydine's armpits and drew him off the bed. "You hold on 'til we get to the bathroom," he said.

"Can't," Mr. Pennydine groaned. But he was on his feet, bent over, clutching his middle, with Hannibal holding him up and making him shuffle and stumble through the clutter toward the kitchen.

"You can hold on," Hannibal said, "you jes hold on and be proud of yourself."

"I'm holding on," Mr. Pennydine grunted as they heaved up the steps into the kitchen. "That was the last time I ever saw Florida Watson . . . should have killed myself . . ."

It was horrible, seeing all that pain and memory mixed up together. I sat on the sofa watching the rain on the windows. I didn't even have any thoughts, just pieces of Mr. Pennydine's recollections whirling around in my brain. I felt as I did that evening long ago standing in an English lane listening to my father describe all the civilizations that had come and gone across Wiltshire. The people Mr. Pennydine was talking about were probably all gone. He never did finish what he started out to tell us—how he got control of the bank.

He was shuffling, straightened up, when Hannibal brought him back from the bathroom. His face wasn't contorted any longer. He got slowly into bed with Hannibal helping him and pulling the covers over him. "The human body's a nonsensical thing," Mr. Pennydine said. "It rots. You put stuff in one end, it just comes back out the other end. Maybe I'll starve myself to death. Be more comfortable." He looked up at Hannibal standing over him. "Say, you're a nigger, aren't you?"

I tensed, but it was all right.

"That's what they tell me," Hannibal said.

Mr. Pennydine nodded. "I thought so. When you get to be my age you sometimes forget to notice things. I've always said the niggers were just like everybody else and I'm not saying it now because you're standing there, Hannibal. I'm so goddamn old I don't have to be nice to anybody. No future in it. I saw a colored fellow named Jack Johnson beat Jim Jeffries for the heavyweight championship in Reno, Nevada. It was in nineteen and ten, maybe eleven, and Dick Stannard, a friend of mine who worked in a dry-goods store and ended up getting control of it, Dick and me and this fellow named Billy Mason, we went all the way out on the train to see the fight. I ate some fish at a Fred Harvey's and damn near died of the ptomaine. But we saw the big fight, we saw Jack Johnson beat Jeffries. Hot—you wouldn't believe the heat out there. I think about the heat sometimes, I have days when I can't get warm at all. Then, when they made me president of some association of bank presidents or other, I heard a colored professor give a lecture on monetary policy in Cambridge, Massachusetts. It was in nineteen and fifty-six, he had ideas that *I'd* never heard of ever. Goddamn it, I wish I knew where they put that silver cigarette lighter of mine. The Major gave it to me. You don't see a silver cigarette lighter over there, do you, Johnny?"

I poked among the things heaped on the sofa. "No, sir," I said.

"Son of a bitch put it *somewhere*. What was I talking about?"

"Black fella giving a lecture," Hannibal said.

Mr. Pennydine looked puzzled. "A lecture on what?"

"Monetary policy," I said. "In Cambridge, Massachusetts."

"I remember," the old man said. "I was there. I thought of something. I heard that colored professor give that lecture, and sometime around nineteen and ten, maybe it was eleven, I saw a colored man named Jack Johnson beat Jim Jeffries for the heavyweight championship. Now, what I thought of is this: if a member of a species is the strongest man in the world and another member of the same species is smarter than most other men, why isn't that species just the same mixture of humanity as the white one? Look here, Hannibal, Warren G. Harding wasn't a nigger, was he?"

"Not that I heard of," Hannibal said.

"Well, he was a pompous damn fool," Mr. Pennydine answered. "I used to call Harding a horse's ass, but bad language upset Lucretia and made her carry on at me and I got enough of that as it was. Anyway, Harding was a white damn fool. You know any colored damn fools, Hannibal?"

"You bet your ass I do."

Mr. Pennydine's toothless mouth spread into a grin like an old baby's. "Well, there you are. White champions, colored champions, white idiots, colored idiots. *I* don't know what all the fuss is about." He looked across the porch at Hannibal slouched in the wicker chair. "You're pretty big, big as me. You ever fight?"

Hannibal shook his head. "Not for money."

The old man worked his gums for a moment. "How do you make your money, then?"

"Cars," Hannibal said.

"Fixing 'em?"

"Any car you can name," Hannibal said.

Mr. Pennydine thought about it. "I got a white Pierce-Arrow in my garage out in Sewickley. Nobody's driven it for years. If you can fix it up, you can have it. You're a good boy, Hannibal."

"I ain't no boy, old man."

"Every fella under sixty is a boy to a ninety-seven-year-old man," Mr. Pennydine said. "I'm trying to tell you you're a good fella. You're good to me. Now, do you want that car or don't you?"

"Wouldn't mind," Hannibal said.

"That's settled, then," Mr. Pennydine said. "I don't want you misunderstanding when I say you're a good boy. Sick of being misunderstood, had thirty-seven years of it from Lucretia. She even picked on me when I changed things in the bank after I got control of it. She said I was dragging her uncle's memory in the mud. Lucretia was Major Clarence's niece, you see, and he was dead by then. Blood clot. But he'd been going soft in the head for years. I knew banking, I knew everything there was to know about it because I'd done everything *in* the bank. I started as a messenger. Trouble is, I didn't *act* like a bank president and that's what got under Lucretia's skin. She said I was a hick, even though she knew I did better than the Major himself." He considered Lucretia for a while, getting madder by the minute. "I doubled the assets of that bank, more than doubled them before I got through. But Lucretia would never credit me with it. She was always getting at me about my personality. I usually just took it."

The rain was making a steady roar on the windows now. Mr. Pennydine's lungs and digestive tract were easier. He stared at the ceiling saying nothing for a long, long time.

"I was never comfortable with Lucretia, it was never natural," he said. "You can live with a woman for thirty-seven years without it ever getting natural."

This time he was silent for so long I thought he'd died. Then he took a deep breath. "The last time I saw that silver cigarette lighter was the day of Daisy's funeral. The Mullers wanted her and Eddie to be buried side by side. I wasn't having any of it. There was a fight about it and they didn't speak to us at the funeral and we didn't speak to them."

Another long patch of silence. He was looking at the ceiling, the gray light touching the ridges of his face and the rain's shadow streaks reflected on his shining head. "Dick Stannard was the one who got me to buy the estate in Sewickley. Never liked it, but Lucretia did. 'You can afford it,' Dick said to me. He was right about that. I was practically running the bank by then and getting well paid for it. I was smart, knew the business and the Major had always taken an interest in me. He had only one child, Harry, named for the Major's twin brother out in Illinois who was father of five boys I knew. *This* Harry Clarence, the Major's kid, was a disappointment, went to prison, as a matter of fact, you boys probably heard about it. 'You're just like my own son,' the Major would say. He knew I didn't have any people of my own anymore, not after what happened to Aunt Dexter and Mary Jane, she was the youngest, the last of the girls left at home when it happened. So the Major took an interest in me right from the beginning, maybe because his brother sent me to him. It was a help and a hindrance when I was a young fella. The Major was a Methodist. He didn't hold with carrying on in any form. I've never been interested in sport except for prize fighting, but I took to reading the sports pages on Sunday so I'd be ready on Monday morning when the Major asked me what I'd done on Saturday. I'd tell him I'd gone to the ball game." He stretched his head around to look at me. "I wasn't going to tell him I'd been drinking with a rowdy crowd at Bingham's saloon and then going to the whorehouse, was I?"

"No, sir," I said.

Mr. Pennydine turned his face back to the windows and looked at the rain. "I don't regret it," he said. "I don't care if it was a pack of lies. When I was a boy I thought that lying got you sent to the bad place. Then I forgot all about it. I don't think anybody this side of the undertaker's knows. Even if my lies to Major Clarence *did* matter, they were worth it. I was crazy about Florida Watson and she was crazy about me. On Sunday afternoon she used to come around to old Mrs. Cawley's where I was boarding. She'd sneak into my room by climbing up over the shed and we'd spend four or five hours doing it for free. First woman who ever put her tongue in my ear. She was a little slip of a thing with red hair and hardly any tits at all. First woman I ever did it with stark naked."

For a while he lay considering what he had said.

"Autumn," he muttered. "They used to burn the leaves in

the street. *I* don't know why they stopped doing that. Florida liked walking through the smoke. I don't suppose she ever forgave me in her own mind. Maybe she did. I sometimes daydream that she did."

Slowly he turned his head on its side and looked at Hannibal. "It wasn't just screwing, her and me," he said. "I took Florida on the all-day trolley excursion. I took her to the ball game and the picture show, that first long one, *The Great Train Robbery*. I saved up and we went to Klein's for oysters. I took Florida to a dance one time. It was put on by the Epworth League, some man recognized her and we were asked to leave. Now, your average girl would have cried over that, Hannibal, but not Florida. Walking home, I remember she had her hands held behind her back and she was taking long, slow steps as we talked about it." Mr. Pennydine's voice became soft, almost like a girl's. " 'You have to understand, John. Some people get nervous seeing a whore in proper places. It's all right for a girl to be in a parlor house, out of common sight.' She stopped right in the middle of the pavement and laughed. 'That man who recognized me comes regular to Mrs. Downey's. He likes Maybelle Chew and she's *fat!*' I said the man was a hypocrite and Florida said he wasn't. 'It's just that when a whore gets into a respectable place it makes him feel ashamed and unnatural, don't you understand?' I understood but I didn't want to. That winter I got the flu bad. Florida went to Mrs. Cawley and said that she was my sister come from Illinois to take care of me. Mrs. Cawley was a good old soul who believed everything you told her. Florida stayed with me for eleven days. When I got the chills she'd crawl into bed with me and hold me, calling me honey dear and warming me with herself. When I got the sweats she hung a wet towel over the headboard of the bed and slept on the floor with two quilts and a bolster that Mrs. Cawley had fixed up for her. She made my meals down in the kitchen, chattering away to Mrs. Cawley about Aunt Dexter and Jo Daviess County, Illinois. She knew what to say because I'd told her all about myself. Those eleven days were like her and me were married. She never did talk much about herself except that she came from Ashtabula, Ohio, and her mother was in the county home. She was nineteen years old and hadn't hardened to the life she was leading. It was just like her and me were married. She'd sit by the bed reading to me. She couldn't read very well, she had to take the words slow, bending over with one finger on the page, tracing the sentences."

He stopped again, turned his head back so that he could look at the ceiling. He was running down. His voice was disintegrating into a gravelly whisper broken by moments when he spoke but no sound came from him.

"I don't remember much of what she read to me except that it was mush, love stories and the like. Sometimes she'd cry over the people in the stories. That was the only other time I ever saw Florida Watson cry."

The power of the rainstorm had slackened. It broke the wet sheen on the windows with minuscule splatters, and I could hear it hissing on the roof of the back porch. Mr. Pennydine was almost asleep, worn out from his hours of talking. He had taken me completely out of my own life and put me right in the middle of the lusts and regrets of his. I leaned forward. "How did you get control of the bank?" I asked.

"Hush up, smart-ass," Hannibal said softly. "Let the man sleep."

Mr. Pennydine was breathing deeply. His eyes at the bottom of their shadowy craters were closed. I thought he *was* asleep.

"Won it in a card game," he muttered, "me and a Chinese fella."

Nine

THE RETURN OF FLORIDA WATSON

IN HIS OWN DECREPIT AND GARRULOUS WAY, Mr. Penny-
dine was a work of art. His life, as he told it, became a panorama
of American textures and sentiments. He had the power to evoke
an Illinois prairie town ninety years before, Pittsburgh from the
perspective of a twenty-year-old man in 1903. He could inject you
with a sense of his own life's conditions—what it was like to be
on the way up, and also on the way out, in a cage of drying bones
and rotting flesh.

After our first day with Mr. Pennydine a new nurse was
hired, but the old man wouldn't have anything to do with her.
He flung himself out of bed and stayed on the floor until Hannibal and I arrived.

Then, a few days after *that*, he began to turn against me.
He'd cut his flow of gab and spend whole minutes glaring at me.
One evening I asked Hannibal what I had done wrong.

"It ain't what you done," he said, "it's what you is. You
remind him of him."

"When he was young?"

"And havin' fun," Hannibal said. "Ain't his fault. Be better if you go 'bout your business, if you can get off your ass and find some."

So I stopped spending my days with Mr. Pennydine and began to think about the various chapters and departments of my own life. My unfinished business from the past was finding my father. I would have sold you most of my adolescence and its artifacts and occupants for a dollar ninety-eight, but not my father and grandmother. It had taken strong character and a clear mind to have faith in me when I was a kid—but both of them had, and I loved them.

I decided that since I had no idea where my father might be pursuing his inquiries—he could be anywhere from Alice Springs, Australia, to Arkansas because life's meaning might be in either of them—the best thing was to try to contact my grandmother.

I couldn't, of course, remember her telephone numbers in either Boston or Pride's Crossing. I dialed information for both places, but they had no listing for an Anne Lowell Sherborne.

I put down the phone in Barbara's kitchen and looked out at the sunny, cold day. I'm one of those people who don't easily consider worst implications. I hadn't seen or heard from my grandmother for over seven years. She would be eighty-five now but, I told myself, a lot of ladies live to be eighty-five, especially old Boston ladies with strong opinions. I preferred to reflect on the possibility that my grandmother had become a glamorous old recluse with an unlisted phone or had carried out her threat to teach Boston a lesson by moving back to Paris.

The only other solution was to call my mother and ask about my father and my grandmother. I would have preferred to call Scotland Yard, tell them I was Jack the Ripper and ask if they wanted to see me. I temporarily abandoned the unfinished business of my past until I could think of a better way of handling it.

Hannibal became Mr. Pennydine's nurse, for nurse's pay which seemed to suit him very well. He spent his days listening to and tending the old man while Harriet Luddington tore around Pittsburgh in the anxious pursuit of self-improvement. She didn't have time to take care of her dying grandfather. She was too busy studying death. Death was very big that year.

So, as far as I was concerned, was the resumption of life. I had been foolish to try to cram Elizabeth Watts into my gazebo-girl daydream. I'd never even seen her, I'd only talked to her twice on the telephone. I had to deprogram myself before I could start on another fantasy. I worked hard on my new imagining of Beth as a near-sighted Rhode Island schoolteacher hunched over her kitchen table scribbling mawkish poetry to compensate for the self-imposed frustrations of her life. I didn't forget those sinewy jogger's legs, either.

I was abandoning spiritual love in my dream world and taking up rack-and-pinion sex. Barbara was somebody I *did* know, she was physically and aromatically real. I made her the leading lady of my lurid imaginings, whose settings proliferated in my mind to include staircases, apartments on Memorial Drive in Cambridge, and an Armenian rug dealer's showroom after business hours. In all those places, in scenes that would have gotten my brain banned in Boston, I had fantasies of Barbara and me making it.

She was older than I, around thirty, and a pleasant, funny lady—both of which fit my lascivious imaginings. The trouble was, in real life she acted motherly toward me. Considering my actual experience of maternal attention and my pulsating, glandular reaction to her at the breakfast table every morning, being Barbara Defere's surrogate kid was the last thing I had in mind.

After Hannibal and I had been at her house for a while she came home one evening all bright-eyed and excited. "Buy yourself a suit, honeypot," she said. "Big Ned wants to see you."

"Who's Big Ned?"

"My program manager," she said, tossing her hat on the sofa and pulling off her coat. "I told him you were smart and crushy-cute."

From the kitchen Hannibal let out a derisory belch that sounded like a baseball hitting an empty oil drum.

"We'll talk about it when Godzilla's gone," I said.

After dinner Hannibal, as usual, went out to Sewickley to work on Mr. Pennydine's Pierce-Arrow. As Barbara and I washed the dishes and I mentally ran my soapy hands over her curves and embankments, I asked her what sort of job she thought I could get in television.

"I can't talk about what they have in mind," she said, "but if they think you're what they want, it'll go in stages. First they'll teach you rewrite, then you'll put in some time as an investigative reporter."

"I thought all reporters investigated," I said.

"Haw haw. Get yourself some stripey ties. Big Ned'll think you're a Yalie."

The next day I drove around Pittsburgh looking for discount clothing stores. After going through three of them I found a suit which, by accident, hadn't been made for a pool shark or Rafe Haddon. I bought some imitation Brooks Brothers shirts, two ties and some new shoes.

The day after that I arrived at Gateway Center at noon. It was a glade of aluminum skyscrapers near the point where the rivers met. I found the television station on the fourth floor of one of them. Barbara came out to the waiting room, said I looked yummy enough to pour chocolate over, and led me down a corridor. We passed control rooms full of permanent dusk where red lights glowed and men sat at consoles watching banks of television sets. Dante, who was a student of fates worse than death, would have been very interested in those men.

Big Ned turned out to be a guy named Ned Plotkin who was about five feet three inches tall. He had large blue eyes, sandy hair that was getting thin and a permanently bemused expression on his face. He got up from behind a desk in his office, whose pale-green walls were covered with plaques and testimonials. "Hello there, Sherborne Eppe," he said in a deep, melodic voice that was way too big for him.

We shook hands.

Ned beamed at Barbara. "Well," he said. "So this is him."

"It ain't Geronimo," she said. "Treat him nice, Neddy, he's my pal."

"Oh, I'll treat him nice," Big Ned answered, looking up at me as if I had just been delivered from the Boston Museum of Fine Arts. "You're a good-looking boy, Sherborne Eppe."

"I'm not exactly a boy."

"Ha ha," Big Ned said, grinning. "I love it."

He picked up the telephone and asked somebody named Art Olsen to come in.

We sat down. Big Ned smiled at me. He folded his hands together on his desk and smiled some more.

I was getting nervous. I smiled back.

"Gooood," he said as if to encourage me. I felt like a chimpanzee that had suddenly recited the multiplication table.

"Barbara tells me that you were Ben Dashford's press secretary," Big Ned said.

"Yes, but—"

"Say. Is he a homo?"

"I don't think so," I said. "He's got a wife and daughter."

"Ah well," Big Ned said. He took out a cigarette and shoved it into a long black holder. He smiled at me as he did it. Throughout the rest of our conversation he clinked the holder against an ashtray. "Ever been on television?" he asked.

"No," I said. "And I haven't any experience in journalism despite the fact that I was Ben's press secretary. That was an accident."

"The right man doesn't need any experience."

"For what?"

"We're going to give you a screen test," Big Ned said.

"But I thought Barbara said there might be a *news* job—"

Big Ned smiled some more. "Yes," he said, "this is the news business."

I was still trying to figure out what screen tests had to do with the news business when an earnest man came in. He was short, muscular and had the last crew cut I ever saw on an indoor American north of the Mason-Dixon line.

"Art Olsen," Big Ned said, "this is my new pal, Sherborne Eppe."

Olsen peered at me with a mixture of solemnity and anxiety. "Glad to meet you, Sherborne," he said. He secmed to be scrutinizing me for symptoms.

"Well?" Big Ned said.

"Mpf," Olsen answered. "Let's look at him on camera."

"Art's our news director," Big Ned told me. He smiled proudly as if I were a mineral deposit and Olsen a mining engineer.

They took me past the chamber where the doomed men watched television forever, and into a smaller control room. It, too, was in twilight.

I was introduced to Peterson, a tall, amiable man in an anorak. "Ever done this before?" he asked.

"No."

"Well," he said, "there isn't a hell of a lot to it. C'mon."

He took me into a studio filled with cameras, lights hanging from the ceiling, and men standing or sitting around waiting for something to happen. There was a dais with a desk and chair on it facing the cameras. Peterson showed me how to sit, hold a dummy script and read off a Teleprompter which rolled down words in front of the camera lens.

"That's one of Bronson's scripts from last month," Peterson said as I sat down at the desk. "Pretend you're *telling* the words on the Teleprompter to me or somebody you know. Have a glance at the written script once in a while. The camera lens is behind the prompter. Look into it as if you were looking into the eyes of the person you're talking to. Now try it."

The words began to roll down the Teleprompter. I sat up straight. "The mayor of Pittsburgh declared a snow emergency today," I said, "after seven inches fell on the city. The declaration from City Hall means—"

"Good," Peterson said. "Nice and natural."

"Some of the phrasing doesn't *read* conversationally," I told him.

"Try ad-libbing around it," Peterson said, "but keep the meaning. You can run through the copy a few times. Don't be nervous."

"There's nothing to be nervous about," I said.

He grinned at me. "You've got it. The guy over there's the floor manager. When he points you toward the second camera, turn to it. The camera with the red light showing is the one taking your picture. Good luck."

He went back to the control room. The prompter man ran through the script with me twice. I got the sense of what the words were about.

"Stand by," the floor manager said.

I told myself to pretend I was a television newscaster. I was trying to decide whether to be John Chancellor or Walter Cronkite when the floor manager pointed at a camera and a red light went on. I made a split-second decision to be me. "Good evening," I said, even though it wasn't in the script, "you obviously know we had snow today. Seven inches in Pittsburgh. The mayor has ordered a snow emergency, and here's what it means." I looked down at the dummy script in my hand and back at the camera. "All parking on snow-emergency–posted streets is banned, cars parked on those streets after eight this evening will be towed . . ."

A few minutes later as I was reading the fourth item in the news, Peterson's voice broke in through the intercom. "That's it. That's a buy."

I went into the little control room. Big Ned, Art Olsen and Peterson were looking at a replay of my performance on a couple of television screens. I was in full color. I got absorbed in the taped replay because I'd never seen myself as other people saw me. On the television screen I looked and sounded as if I knew what I was talking about.

Olsen walked me back to the newsroom. He was noncommittal about my performance. Big Ned hadn't reacted either. He had just squeezed my arm and chortled, "Don't call us, we'll call you. Like it? Ha ha." I decided I hadn't impressed them as much as I had impressed myself, and I began to think about where I could find a job so that I could stay in Pittsburgh and have unseemly adventures with Barbara.

While I waited to take her out to lunch Art Olsen introduced me to Bronson Hake, the station's star anchorman. In person he looked even more used up than he did on the six and eleven o'clock news. He was a triumph of expensive tailoring which could hold in everything except his face. It was evolving from Errol Flynn good looks into a wrinkled paunch on the front of his head. He had a deep, whiskey-mellowed voice to which elocution came as naturally as snoring did to Hannibal.

I told Hake I had used one of his scripts to take a screen test. "I changed some of the words around," I added. "I hope that was all right."

"Okay with me," Hake said. "It isn't my prose. I don't write."

"I guess that's because you're so busy out covering stories."

"Reporters and camera crews cover stories," he mumbled.

Later, at lunch, I asked Barbara exactly what Bronson Hake *did*.

"He reads the news, sugar," she said, "and that's it. That and trying to stay off the sauce."

"But millions of people think he's an authority on everything!"

She nodded.

"It's a funny business," I said.

"Like getting measles is funny," she said. "You'll see."

"I don't think I will. They didn't seem very impressed with my screen test."

"That's a good sign," she said. "If they thought you were a dummy, they'd take you out to lunch. If they liked you, they'd throw you down the stairs so you wouldn't ask for a big salary. Joe Peterson's sane. He thought you were a natural. Mind doing the grocery shopping for me?"

"I haven't anything else to do," I said.

It was a sunny, windy afternoon with spring trying to get started. You could almost smell the impending balminess in the air. After I put the groceries in the car I wandered around the ratty streets behind the façade of the Gateway Center looking for a bookstore.

I found one among the pawnbrokers and Army surplus stores and went inside. The place was nearly empty. A young man with a beard was reading behind the cash register. There was a woman thumbing through an atlas and sniffing. It was very quiet. Except for the sniffs. I went to the paperback section and found Prescott's *Conquest of Mexico* and four novels. I was on my way to pay for them when something caught my eye. Then it hit me like a roundhouse right.

I backtracked to the poetry section. There, on a shelf just below eye level, was a book turned front-cover-outward for display. The title was printed in dark-green letters on a glossy white background:

MANFRED—AND AFTERWARD

Beneath that there was a little sprig with leaves on it and then:

POEMS 1977–1980

The bottom line was the one that shattered my equanimity like an anvil falling through a greenhouse roof:

By Elizabeth Watts

At epic moments my mind runs to irrelevancies—such as throwing Raoul in the swimming pool because the hairs on his stomach were ugly. Looking at Beth's book, I wondered if my new shoes weren't half a size too narrow.

I turned away, picked up a volume on do-it-yourself swimming pools, set it down and turned back to the poetry. I looked at

Manfred—And Afterward for a whole minute while the woman with the atlas made an especially voluble sniff—it was really a snort—and blew her nose.

I took Beth's book off the shelf and turned it over. The back cover was a black-and-white photograph of Elizabeth Watts. I immediately recognized that she was a being of beauty beyond anything I had ever conjured in my simplistic fantasies. Her hair appeared to be ash-blond; it was curved over the right side of her forehead in a graceful wave. Her nose was narrow. She was smiling slightly. Her eyes were large and, to me, they reflected her soul's profound sentiments.

She was wearing a light-toned turtleneck sweater and was leaning on her forearms. Her hands at the bottom of the photograph were long and graceful. One wrist was encircled by a plain silver bracelet.

Those eyes of Elizabeth Watts stared into mine. She *was* the gazebo girl—but of a beauty magnified ten times that of my imaginary one. She was polished and glowing with life—perhaps fate's abrasions and her own deep feelings had done it. The sound of her alto voice swept across my memory; I recalled how cocky I'd been in my first conversation with her, how paralyzed, fumbling and angry in the second. I couldn't stop staring at the photograph, which incarnated the happiest daydream of my life. I couldn't stop the bitter, surging realization of how I had blown my chance to make the daydream come true.

The name EDWARD KARNOW was printed at the bottom right-hand corner of the picture in tiny type. I felt a small adder-sting of jealousy. I opened the book and read the blurb about her on the inside jacket flap:

Elizabeth Watts was born in 1957 and attended Princeton University. She won the U.S. Poet's Circle Award when she was eighteen years old. *Manfred—And Afterward* is her third collection of verse. Her first, *Firebrake*, was nominated for a National Book Award. Her poetry has appeared in *The New Yorker*, the *Atlantic Monthly*, *Harper's* and a number of smaller magazines.

Miss (she insists on the title) Watts is an Associate Professor of Modern Literature at Brown University. Her father is the United States Attorney for Rhode Island.

I closed the book and put it back on the shelf. I needed protection from it. That book was a thundering denunciation of me for screwing up my chance to capture the affections of a stunning and accomplished girl. There was no escape. She was a shimmering mirage turned real, and I was lower than a worm. A worm's assistant.

I walked around the bookstore, came back to the poetry section, opened *Manfred* in the middle and read:

> Once stolen, there is nothing left to steal;
> Once informed, all my wondering ceases.
> I come, by you, of age,
> Absolved of speculation's rage,
> Blessed, cursed by a new genius to feel.
> Fantasy lives as my desire increases . . .

I couldn't stand it. My mind was white with jealousy, self-loathing and a whole lot of other emotions that had been mashed up in my psychic blender and tasted horrid. I took the copy of *Manfred—And Afterward,* paid for it along with my other books and left.

Driving home, I couldn't abolish from my mind the clean, pensive beauty of Beth's face, the awesome listing of her accomplishments, the rapture over Manfred in her poem. I haven't hated many people in my life, but that afternoon I conceived a hatred for Manfred because he, clearly, was everything manly I was not.

I had also discovered the answer to several minor mysteries of my own inconsequential life: Beth's father was the U.S. Attorney for Rhode Island. After Mr. Rafe Haddon traced my call to her, he must have found out what Mr. Watts did and that was why Haddon thought I was from the FBI. It also accounted for how Beth knew about the Great Lakes Discount Auto Parts Company and Haddon's racket. Her father told her.

As I turned into the short unpaved strip of driveway beside Barbara's house, my Volkswagen gave a sudden lurch, made a ghastly grinding sound and nosed forward, smashing my chest into the steering wheel.

I sat for a moment until Mercury, Venus and a few of the other bright objects of the universe stopped whipping around in front of my eyes, and then I got out. Both front wheels were folded inward, there was a mess of oily parts scattered around under the car. I kicked the front door so hard that I dented it. The end of a perfect afternoon.

My solar plexus felt as if it had been punched; so did my self-esteem. I put away the groceries and went upstairs. I stretched out on my bed and tried to lose myself in Prescott's *Conquest of Mexico* but it didn't work. I read the first page eight times.

Jealousy hurts; it is the father of all miseries. Jealous people have a compulsion to poke around trying to find more to be jealous about so they can feel even worse. We are a strange species.

I closed Prescott, took Beth's book from the bedside table and opened it to the first poem. The title was "Railroad Platform."

> Magritte men with apples for faces
> Read the news, expecting no news
> On that dateless day.
> The stiff, zinc-flavored air implied
> Early snow. An explosion of train
> Going the wrong way
> Shook down grit instead. Time, according
> To a brick tower's clock, had stopped.
> In Westchester county
> There was arctic silence that morning,
> Silence doing body counts and claiming
> Despair as its bounty.
> The dead waited for the eighteen fifteen

Or smoked in yellow-walled kitchens
Trying to contrive
Strategy for the coming evening's siege.
Amid and of that carnage I looked up
And there you were—alive.

It was unbearable. With the self-pitying truculence of a
climber that knows the mountain he's dreamed of is too much for
him, I threw Beth's book in a bureau drawer and turned my
mind full blast to a fantasy of Barbara and me in a half-filled
bathtub.

When she came home around seven I was still upstairs.
"Borniekins!" she called. "I got news!"

I went down to greet the object of my unfettered, substitute
desires.

"You're in!" she said, throwing her arms around me. "You
did beautifully, baby!"

I participated in the hug and did a little pelvic grinding,
which she didn't seem to notice at all.

"You're what they're looking for," she said. "Big Ned wants
to take you to lunch tomorrow."

For a moment I couldn't quite grasp what she was saying. I
had put the screen test completely out of my mind. If the television station wanted me, the day wasn't a total wipeout, after all.
"Jesus," I said, "that's amazing. Let me buy you dinner."

"Can't," she said. "Got a date. Be at the station at noon and
wear a different tie."

When Hannibal came home he inspected my Volkswagen
and pronounced it a total wreck. When the front end collapsed, it
had wrenched the transmission loose. "I got ripped off," I said.

"No, you ain't. Sumbitch fetched you from Cleveland to
here."

"It would have been cheaper to ride the bus," I said.

He called me an asshole and said he'd sell my car to a junk
dealer in the morning. When I told him I was going to be on
television he said that television didn't have any more sense than

an alligator and went off to Sewickley. Barbara left for her date. I spent the rest of the evening being jealous of whoever *she* was seeing and imagining myself as a famous network newscaster. I would be rich and respected, my mother would be driven nuts with shame, I'd find my father, my grandmother would know she'd been right about me all along, Beth would see me and wonder—I chopped off speculation about Beth. There was no future in it.

The next day Big Ned Plotkin took me out to lunch in a restaurant filled with Muzak and men in appropriate suits. "Like trains?" he asked me after we'd ordered.

"I don't have any special feelings one way or another."

"I have a train set," he said. He smiled.

I felt befuddled. I smiled back.

"I like your head-on shot," he said, clinking his cigarette holder against an ashtray. "We had a meeting yesterday afternoon. We reviewed all the video tapes."

I waited.

His eyes opened a little wider so that he was looking at me with the moist gaze of a cocker spaniel. "Say, you didn't get hurt in that riot at the East Heidelberg church, did you?"

"Not badly. Mr. Plotkin—"

"Ned," he said. "If we're going to work together, we can't mister each other. Bad for morale, hm?"

I felt even more befuddled. "You mentioned something about reviewing videotapes," I said.

He nodded. "You've met Bronson."

"I had a talk with him yesterday."

"Bronson's getting old," Big Ned said.

The waitress brought our drinks—a ginger ale for me, a double martini for Big Ned. He took a large sip from it and lit another cigarette. "Say, if you're free for dinner tonight you could come around to my place and we could have something to eat and have a look at the trains."

"I'm really sorry but I'm busy tonight," I lied. "You were saying something about Mr. Hake."

"Bronson's getting old," Big Ned said again as if Hake were doing it on purpose. "He has about a year and a half left. We've been looking for a replacement. Somebody young, somebody who has—*appeal*. You do nice eye contact."

"Thank you," I said, wondering what the hell he was talking about.

"Love your body language," he said, sipping at his martini. He set down his glass and smiled at me. "*Nice* body language. Art Olsen wants a man who writes his own stuff, does interviews. Sales thought you were marketable."

"Ned," I said, "I don't want to give you any false impressions. I don't have any experience in television or journalism—I don't know if I can write and do interviews."

"That's why we want you now," he said. "We're going to train you. Trains. Remember the trains, hm?"

I didn't want to remember the trains. I didn't want to smile in case it made him think I was interested in his trains. I had run out of physical and verbal vocabulary.

"We'll start you on dayside rewrite," he said.

"I don't know what dayside rewrite is."

He pretended to convulse with laughter. "I like it." He clinked a couple of more times against the ashtray. "Then we'll move you on to investigative reporting. Put you on the air." Big Ned Plotkin smiled his mysterious, molasses smile. "We can't promise anything, Bornie. There are imponderables. Bronson doesn't know we're thinking of retiring him. The station doesn't know how audiences will react to you. A lot of your future is up to you." He clinked and sipped. "*Love* your body language," he said.

And that's how I got into television. Queasily.

There isn't much to writing news prose for TV. For one thing, it has practically no adverbs or adjectives. Its content is nothing but facts which don't tell you much about the real world. Still, they were paying me three hundred dollars a week, which was a lot more money than I had ever earned before.

My immediate boss was Art Olsen, the news director. I have

already told you that he was a very earnest man. He was deeply concerned about the staff's happiness. Art loved it when somebody got sick; that gave him a chance to telephone and send flowers.

The sales manager had a smile like lockjaw. It never left his face. He was overweight, with slicked-back hair, a man who looked like a Kewpie doll smeared with Vaseline. He'd come grinning into the newsroom and yell at Art Olsen, "You guys had a tenement fire, two county indictments and all that shit from Iran on last night. Isn't there any *good* news, for Christ's sake?" His smile was as meaningless as a baby's gas-pain grimaces.

And then there was Big Ned. He became a slightly supernatural being to me—always materializing out of nowhere, driven by unutterable desires. One day I got that feeling you read about in ghost stories—that eyes were upon me. I looked up. Big Ned was standing beside my chair looking down at my typewriter. "Mmmm," he murmured, *"good!"* He waved his hand around indecisively for a moment and then gripped my shoulder. "Getting the old hang of it, eh?"

"I guess so," I said, wishing he'd let go of me.

He gave my shoulder a squeeze. "Smart boy," he said. "Smart." He started, as if an idea had just occurred to him. "Say! How about coming over to my place for dinner tonight? I could show you my trains. Remember the trains?"

I felt as if someone had poured transmission fluid in my bathing suit. "That'd be nice, Ned," I said, "but I can't tonight."

"Too bad," he answered. His face assumed the indecisive expression of the repulsed.

That evening I asked Barbara about the top executives. "How do those guys manage to run a multimillion-dollar television station?" I asked.

"Like Noah ran the ark," she said. "God helps a lot."

In the next few weeks I began to make Big Ned Plotkin tense. He had taken to ignoring me as we passed each other in the hall. That tactic started after my rejection of his third dinner invitation. Charlie Harris, the senior rewrite man who was teaching me, told me that Big Ned had asked him if I was a homo. I began to worry about my career at the television station.

It didn't take long before I got so that I could write television prose with its grabby leads and short sentences. One day when Charlie Harris was out having some root-canal work done (Art Olsen sent him a dozen roses) I did Bronson's personal commentary. I was of the opinion that the beginning of Mitchell Parrish's administration in East Heidelberg was promising. That was Hake's opinion that night. It was all goofy, but it kept me employed and anxious about whether I'd make it to the next stage—being an investigative reporter.

Along with learning the TV news business, I stepped up my campaign to conquer Barbara. I figured that since my body had attracted Amelia and Lydia Dashford, maybe it would have the same effect on Barbara. I reflected upon my limited experience at seduction and decided on a plan.

One Friday evening I got home around seven-thirty. It was cold and raining and I wanted a hot bath, anyway. Barbara was in her bedroom. Hannibal was out at Sewickley. So I went upstairs, started water gushing into the tub and undressed in my room. I threw a towel over my shoulder and stepped into the hall stark naked.

The barometrics of sensuality hung in the air. There was the rush of hot water—an intimate sound implying steam, perfumes and languid relaxations; the rain was beating on the windows making indoors desirable because outdoors was so wet, chilled and gloomy. In the kitchen I had seen a half-empty ice tray and a bottle of bourbon. Barbara was having a drink, which suited my purposes perfectly.

I started down the hall toward the bathroom, trying to make a noise in my bare feet so that she would know I was there. As if fate were the Cecil B. DeMille of my scenario, Barbara suddenly opened her bedroom door as I passed it. Warm light spilled from a lamp over the length and breadth of desirable me. I stopped.

She was wearing her silk dressing gown and had a drink in her hand. "Well," she said kind of softly, "will you look at that?"

The ON THE AIR sign of my brain started to flash. I tried to think of a suave, tasteful reply. "I forgot to buy a bathrobe," I said.

Her eyes lowered slowly and stopped in a gaze at my anatomy south of my navel. I tensed. This was the ultimate moment.

"That," Barbara said after a few seconds, "is the messiest appendix scar I've ever seen. They must have done a real rush job on you, honeypot."

I couldn't help it. I started to laugh. My fiendish plot of seduction dissolved into the relief of mirth. I leaned against the wall and guffawed. Barbara Defere was a lady who appreciated her own sense of humor. She began to laugh too. Finally she shoved her drink into my hand. "Go take your bath and have that, stud-baby," she said. "Then you can take me out to dinner."

We went to a French restaurant a few blocks away and it was old times again. I told Barbara about my emergency appendectomy at St. Stephen's, she told me about being in love with Bronson Hake and how she had settled for that, even though Bronson was a drunk and a man fading from life's possibilities. She hoped I would replace him at the TV station because when he was off the air he didn't booze it up so much.

Hannibal was working late. I went to bed, turned off the light and lay listening to the traffic in the city below. I thought about Beth and decided that I would be what Mr. Pennydine was—a man who had loved one woman for his whole life. Like him, I had lost the woman I loved forever. Since I no longer needed to bother myself with the complexities of love, I could make other fantasies come true. I decided I would become a great man. I would be admirable and carry with me an aura of mystery and tragedy which I would never discuss.

Somebody gripped my shoulder. In my sleep my brain whisked Big Ned Plotkin into the dream I was having. The grip tightened and I was shaken so hard that my teeth felt as if they were back where my ears should have been.

I looked up into Hannibal's face. He was already dressed

and the bedroom light was on. "Get your ass up," he said. He wasn't wearing his usual scowl, the one that expressed his loathing of man, God and the universe. He looked as if he was upset at something specific.

"What's going on?" I asked, trying to come fully awake.

"That lady's downstairs."

"Which lady?"

"One that lives 'cross the street. You get your pants on, hear me?"

I dressed and we went downstairs. Harriet Luddington was sitting in Barbara's living room in a quilted bathrobe wringing her hands.

Barbara looked up at me. "She thinks her grandfather's dying."

"I gave him his medicine at ten," Mrs. Luddington said as if I had accused her of something. "He seemed all right . . ."

"Have you called the doctor?" I asked.

She nodded. "He said he'd come. They usually don't make house calls. But this one's *really* nice. I mean, *really*."

We went across the street. The rain had stopped. The sky was full of stars and there was no longer a bite in the winter air. As we passed through Mrs. Luddington's kitchen the clock told me it was after four.

Mr. Pennydine was lying flat and still on his hospital bed. For a moment I didn't want to look because I thought he was dead and I'd never seen a dead person before. Hannibal went over, bent down and put his great big head sideways on the old man's chest. He listened. "Still alive," he said.

"I took his pulse when I came down to check on him," Mrs. Luddington said. "It was irregular." She looked at her grandfather—pale, immobile, eyes closed in their pools of shadow. "I must have done something wrong."

She was making coffee in the kitchen when the doctor came. Only Hannibal was out on the porch with Mr. Pennydine. He had plunked himself down in the wicker chair and was sitting with his hands folded, looking at the old man.

The doctor, who was Chinese, took out his stethoscope and did a lot of listening. He got Hannibal to roll Mr. Pennydine over and listened to his back. Then he took out a kit, filled a hypodermic needle with something and stuck it in the old man's arm. Mr. Pennydine opened his eyes after a while. "I never stole a thing in my life," he said.

"You hush up, old man," Hannibal told him.

Mr. Pennydine looked up at him. "I know you," he said. "Buck?"

"Hannibal," Hannibal said.

"Oh hell, yes," Mr. Pennydine mumbled. "I'm getting so old I'm going soft in the head. I thought you were Buck Ransom for a minute. You ever know Buck Ransom?"

"Never did," Hannibal said.

"You would have liked him. Buck and me used to get into all kinds of scrapes. I heard he died in a drugstore fire in Bardstown, Kentucky."

"That was the bank teller," Hannibal said.

"You're right," the old man answered after a moment. "I get mixed up. I don't know what happened to Buck. At least I don't think I do, but I'll tell you a story about him and me—"

"Try to rest, Grandpa," Harriet said.

"For what?" Mr. Pennydine answered. "Rest up for what? I'm not going anywhere and you know it, Daisy."

"I'm Harriet," Mrs. Luddington said.

"Of course you are," Mr. Pennydine said peevishly. "Nobody ever said you weren't. Where's Hannibal?"

"Right here," Hannibal said. "Now, you be quiet."

"What'll you do if I don't?" Mr. Pennydine said, grinning like a child starting to play a familiar game.

"Shake you out and hang you up to dry," Hannibal answered.

"I'm too old to shake out and hang up."

"No, you ain't," Hannibal said.

Mr. Pennydine cackled *hee hee hee* and then closed his eyes and fell asleep.

In the kitchen the doctor had a cup of coffee. We were all sitting at the table waiting for his verdict. "What made you think something was wrong?" he asked Mrs. Luddington.

"He always wakes up between three and three-thirty," she said. "He has to—" She shrugged and smiled her middle-aged cute-girl smile.

The doctor nodded.

"Then he usually wants to talk for a while," Mrs. Luddington said. "But when I came down this morning he didn't move and I thought he was *dead*."

The doctor set down his coffee cup. "He probably did wake up and then fainted."

"Fainted?"

"He's got what we call aortic stenosis," the doctor said. "You can hear it in his heartbeat."

"What does that mean?" Barbara asked.

"That he's going to die very soon."

"How soon?" Hannibal asked.

The doctor closed his bag. "Considering his age and everything else that's wrong with him, it could be a matter of days, perhaps a few weeks at most."

Mrs. Luddington looked a little blank. "Death should be a meaningful life experience," she said to nobody in particular.

"We can move him to a hospital if you want," the doctor said, rising, "but that might upset him and kill him."

"No," Mrs. Luddington answered. "I want him here. I want his death to be meaningful."

The doctor stood up. "Just avoid anything that would cause emotional disturbance—and no alcohol."

Hannibal looked at the doctor. For once his face had a thoughtful expression on it instead of ferocity. "You mean he— can't have no booze?"

"That's right," the doctor said.

Hannibal went out to the porch to check on Mr. Pennydine and then crossed the street to join Barbara and me. We were all sobered.

Hannibal sat down in Barbara's living room. "I'm sorry," I said to him. "I know he's your friend."

"Hush up," he said. "Let a man think."

I figured that was equivalent to letting a mole dig the Panama Canal, so I didn't wait around for him to finish. I went back to bed.

When I woke up, the room was filled with morning light. Clouds were scudding across the sky, driven by one of those melting March winds. I got dressed and went downstairs. Barbara was in the kitchen. "I was just coming to get you, Borniekins," she said. "Hannibal's off somewhere and he wants you to sit with old man Pennydine."

"Where's he gone?"

"Beats me," she said. "He isn't exactly the gabby type." She looked out at the clouds rushing east across Pittsburgh. "I know that anybody who's ninety-seven is living off his interest," she said. "But it's still sad."

I put on my jacket and went across the street. Mrs. Luddington was agitated. "I have my encounter group at eleven. And there's a seminar at Carnegie this afternoon that I said I'd—"

"We'll look after your grandfather," I assured her. "It's Saturday and I have the day off. Hannibal will be back soon."

"I hope so," Mrs. Luddington said. "Grandpa is upset already because he isn't here."

"It'll be all right."

"The doctor said he wasn't *supposed* to get upset."

"I'll calm him down."

"I should be back by six at the latest," she said, clenching and unclenching her hands. She was one of the guiltiest people I've ever met and one of the slowest departers.

After she'd gone I went out on the porch. Mr. Pennydine was lying on his back staring at the ceiling. He rolled his huge hairless head on the pillow and looked at me. Since his face was so caved in by time, it was hard at first to see what expression was on it. "Who're you?" he demanded.

"Bornie," I said.

"Never heard of you. I suppose Harriet's gone off."

"Yes, sir."

"Where's Hannibal?"

"He had to go do something. He asked me to come over and keep you company until he gets back. I'm his friend, the guy who came with him the first day. Johnny."

Mr. Pennydine looked back at the ceiling. He gripped his old hands together on his chest. "I remember. Sam Delancey's cousin."

There wasn't much point in arguing with him. If he wanted me to be Sam Delancey's cousin, that's who I'd be. I sat down in the wicker chair. "Yes, sir," I said.

"Or his brother. Which one are you?"

"His cousin," I said.

He thought about that for a while. "You couldn't be. Sam Delancey's cousin got killed by a Swede who worked fireman on the Rock Island line. Hit him with a barrel."

"That was Buck Ransom's uncle."

"Don't tell me about Buck Ransom," the old man said. "He was *my* friend." He turned his head to look at me again. He was irritated. I worried that he'd become so upset that he'd die before Hannibal could get there. "I never met a Delancey who wasn't a liar," he said. "Sam Delancey was the worst of them, your brother. I remember one time, it was New Year's, nineteen-hundred, no it wasn't, that was the night the Algonquin Theater burned down in Chicago and Aunt Dexter read us all about it in the *Inter-Ocean*. There was a boy named White Fox got killed in that fire. I never knew him, but Aunt Dexter knew his people and she told the girls . . ."

He was off. He forgot all about me—that is, the me who was Sam Delancey's cousin or brother. I was just someone to listen, a part of his furnishings. It was a wonder to me that he needed anybody there at all in order to talk. From the Algonquin Theater fire he wandered into his trip to England in the nineteen-fifties, he retold the story about buying a Rolls-Royce, had the fight with Lucretia about cars again. That got him around to his

most durable theme, Florida Watson and their happy time together, especially the eleven days when he had the flu and she
took care of him in Mrs. Cawley's boarding house. His agitation
subsided and his voice became soft.

As I said, Mr. Pennydine was a work of art. He could make
his fantasy of Florida Watson breathe, speak and occupy turn-of-
the-century settings. He could put me on a city street with her,
holding her hand and walking with her through the pungent
smoke of burning leaves; I was *on* the trolley with her, pressing
against her hard thin body. Most of all, the old man infused me
with the terrible suffocation of his regret as Florida Watson, her
tears contradicting the brave expression on her face, shook hands
and walked up the avenue on that last wet day.

I was sitting immersed with him in his mixture of happiness
made perfect by constant retelling and his desperate desire to do
it all over again, when Hannibal walked in.

Mr. Pennydine stopped recollecting. "It's about time you got
here," he said. "Who's this fella?"

"Friend of mine," Hannibal said. "How come you still lyin'
in that bed, old man?"

"Because I got to," Mr. Pennydine said.

"What you got to lie there for?"

I wondered if Hannibal had gone crazy.

"I got to lie here because I'm so goddamn old I can't do
anything else," Mr. Pennydine said. "You know that, Hannibal."

"You just *think* you can't do anything else because they
told you so," Hannibal said. "You know what day it is?"

"I haven't known what day it is since I don't know when.
Don't ask me a lot of damn fool questions. Tuesday, Sunday, it
doesn't make any difference to me."

"It's Saturday," Hannibal said.

Mr. Pennydine stopped talking again. He stared at Hannibal.

"You know what we do on Saturday."

The old man looked confused. Saturday was one of his principal memories and I could *see* the uncertainty in his eyes.

"You better go to the bathroom before we get you dressed," Hannibal said. He moved to the side of the hospital bed, got his arms under Mr. Pennydine's shoulders and helped him to an upright position on the floor.

"Have you lost your mind?" I demanded.

"Shut up," Hannibal said, steering Mr. Pennydine toward the steps leading up into the kitchen.

"Yeah, shut up, Johnny," Mr. Pennydine said, bent-over and shuffling with Hannibal's arm around him. "We know what we're doing." He began to cackle.

Once the old man was in the toilet Hannibal came back to the porch and started taking clothes out of the closet.

"What the hell are you up to?" I asked him.

He didn't answer. He laid out the clothes on the wicker chair—underwear, trousers, socks, a pair of boots, shirt, sweater and a suede shooting jacket.

I grabbed his arm. "The doctor said he was supposed to stay calm!" I shouted.

"Then you calm yourself," Hannibal said.

"What are you going to do with him?"

Hannibal turned on me with a terrible expression on his face. He pointed through the kitchen door to the bathroom. "That there's a dyin' man, smart-ass," he said in a sotto-voce roar. "Nothin' gone save him, so he's gone die happy."

"And *you're* going to make him die happy?"

He glared down at me. "Whether I got to bust your head open first or not," he said. "Now you take your hand off me and either come along or leave us be. But if you come along, *Mistah* Sherbert, you keep your big mouth shut and just listen and don't screw around, you hear me?"

There was a grimness in him, an urgency that I knew I couldn't oppose. So I let go of his arm and sat down on the sofa. Hannibal brought Mr. Pennydine back and dressed him. The old man seemed full of anticipation, even though I was sure he didn't know any more about what Hannibal was doing than I did. As we headed for the front door he shuffled along, clinging to Hannibal's arm and grinning in toothless pleasure at the prospect of going somewhere.

The most beautiful automobile I had ever seen in my life was parked in front of the house. It was a convertible touring car, tall and squared off. The wire wheel spokes and all the other chrome parts glittered in high polish; the body was snow-white and the seats inside were made of red leather.

"Son of a bitch," Mr. Pennydine said as Hannibal helped him down the front steps. "It's my Pierce-Arrow . . . and that's funny. I had the idea the other day that I gave that car away to somebody."

"A colored fella," Hannibal said.

"That's right!"

"Well, you didn't. It's still yours, old man."

"Son of a bitch," Mr. Pennydine repeated.

With some difficulty we heaved him into the back seat and made him comfortable. Hannibal and I got in up front. The engine started as if Mount Vesuvius were under the long hood. It roared and then settled down to a menacing purr.

"Did I ever tell you boys about the time A. D. Hardeville shot himself in my garage?" Mr. Pennydine asked loudly from the back seat.

I was about to say he had, but I remembered Hannibal's threat. I decided to keep my mouth shut. I didn't know the rules of the game.

"Put a pistol to his ear and blasted himself all over this very car," Mr. Pennydine informed us as we moved away from the curb. "Right by that front fender there. He did it to get back at me. The dumb bastard had been buying on margin, even though I'd told him not to. When the stock market went to hell in nineteen and twenty-nine, Hardeville tried to borrow a hundred and fifty thousand from the bank to cover himself. Well, we couldn't loan him that kind of money. He didn't have any collateral. So he killed himself in my garage. Dick Stannard said it was vengeance and I believed him."

We drove down a hill and turned into a main street. People

were stopping to gawk at the Pierce-Arrow, even two cops in a cruiser.

"She runs good," Mr. Pennydine said.

"She runs real good, old man," Hannibal answered. He was driving as if the car were made out of spider webs and cut glass.

"Major Clarence gave me this car," Mr. Pennydine said. "It was just before he died of a clot. I think he knew that Lucretia and me weren't a perfect match and he wanted to give me something for pleasure."

He jabbered on about Major Clarence as Hannibal drove deep into a crowded neighborhood of old stores, stark wooden houses, wires crisscrossing overhead and vacant lots littered with trash around the legs of billboard stands.

Hannibal parked in front of a saloon called McCarry's Bit of Ireland. We opened the back door and got Mr. Pennydine out with considerable difficulty. His legs didn't bend very far and he gripped the back door with his gnarled hand, grunting and gasping a little until he was on the pavement holding on to both of us. A few people had gathered around to look at the car. Hannibal scowled and they stepped back to give us passage.

McCarry's was dim and smelled of beer. There were two or three round tables with wooden chairs standing in the middle of the tiled floor. The place was almost empty, but even with my limited knowledge of booze joints I could see that it was a genuine saloon, not a cocktail lounge.

A heavy man with red hair came out from behind the bar as we lowered the old man into a chair. "Well, if it isn't Johnny Pennydine!" he said. He winked at Hannibal.

Mr. Pennydine looked up at him. "I don't recall you," he said. "What's your name, Johnny?"

The fat man guffawed. "Why, *Johnny*'s my name! How've you been?"

"I'm fine," Mr. Pennydine said. "This is Hannibal. I forget who the other one is."

The bartender shook hands with us. "Pleased to meet you, gents. What's it going to be, Johnny?"

Mr. Pennydine looked at the bar. "Where's the free lunch?"

"Ah now, you came too late," the bartender said. "It's all gone." He winked at Hannibal again.

"I wouldn't mind a boilermaker," Mr. Pennydine said.

Jesus, I told myself, he's as good as dead already.

"And what about you, gents?" the bartender asked.

"Same," Hannibal said, sitting down.

I sat too. "I'll just have a beer."

"Two boilermakers and a beer," the bartender said.

We sat like figures in an old-fashioned American barroom joke: Did you ever hear the one about the black guy, the white guy and the ninety-seven-year-old man who'd blow out his last gasket if he so much as touched a drop of whiskey?

Our drinks came. Mr. Pennydine lifted his shot of bourbon. His hand shook, but he got the glass to his lips and threw down the whiskey with one gulp. He picked up his beer and grinned. "Goddamn," he said softly, "that feels *good*." A little spasm hit him as the bourbon reached his brain. Hannibal put his hand on the old man's wrist so that the beer wouldn't spill.

Somebody put some money in the juke box. A slow Irish jig filled the dim bar. Mr. Pennydine sipped at his beer, grinned again and looked down at the table. "I remember one time Billy Mason and Fred Nasby made a bet to see which one of them could dance longest on one leg. Billy won. There used to be a piano player in here then. I don't know where he's gone. Maybe he died in a fire. I knew a man who died when a drugstore in Bardstown, Kentucky, burned down."

"You recollect the time Billy Mason bet he could run out and jump on the street car balancin' a beer on his head?" Hannibal asked.

Mr. Pennydine burst out laughing. "And he did it, too!"

"He sure did," Hannibal said.

The old man sipped some beer again and wiped his mouth with the back of his hand. "Yessir," he said, "Billy did it." The whiskey was getting to him. His voice, never exactly a model of clarity in my experience, was thickening. "I wonder where Billy and Dick are now?"

"They went to the prize fight," Hannibal said. He slid his glass of bourbon in front of Mr. Pennydine.

The old man crooked his fingers around it. "That's what we should have done, Hannibal. But it's a long way to Reno, Nevada, and hot when you got there."

"And you got to sit up on the train," Hannibal said.

Mr. Pennydine nodded. I watched him as you'd watch a drunken tightrope walker, knowing he was going to fall. "And like as not get the ptomaine," Mr. Pennydine said.

"There's that," Hannibal acknowledged. He was watching too, but for something else. He was waiting, I sensed, for a particular moment to come.

The record of the Irish jig ended. There was almost silence. Two men were talking in a booth at the back. Mr. Pennydine picked up the shot glass and carried it in his trembling hand to his mouth. "Goddamn," he muttered. Again, the little spasm hit him. Hannibal pushed his beer glass across the table. Mr. Pennydine's hand took it. "Yessir," he said slowly, heavily, "it's a long way to Reno, Nevada. It's a long way to Bardstown, Kentucky. It's a long way back to Jo Daviess County."

"You remember Manson's livery stable?" Hannibal said. "You remember sittin' up in them rafters watchin'?"

The reminder of Nanny Borogrove, Ilse and the five Clarence boys yanked Mr. Pennydine from his torpor. He grinned at Hannibal. "*Remember?*" he said. "Why, you bet I remember. I never saw two girls carry on like that in my life. They just couldn't get enough of it."

"Time we went along," Hannibal said.

"Went along?" Mr. Pennydine asked. "Where are we going?"

"You know, old man," Hannibal said.

Mr. Pennydine thought for a moment. Then he grinned. "I'll be a son of a bitch," he said. "I completely forgot. Is it time?"

"It's time," Hannibal said. "Let's go."

"And we don't even have to ride the trolley," Mr. Penny-dine said. "We're in the Pierce-Arrow."

We got him to his feet. The bartender came out again. "Don't stay away so long, Johnny," he said.

"I won't," Mr. Pennydine answered. "We've got to go now. You know, Florida's never seen my Pierce-Arrow."

"Is that a fact?"

"That's a fact," Mr. Pennydine said. "She always thought I'd amount to something."

It was a little more difficult getting him into the car this time because he was drunk. It was darkening toward late afternoon. The warm wind had blown itself out to the east and the sky was overcast.

"Roll down the windows so we can feel the breeze," Mr. Pennydine said as Hannibal started the engine with a roar. "Roll down the windows, boys."

Store lights and window lights in dingy apartments above the street were gleaming in the dusk. Hannibal guided the big car carefully into the traffic.

"You know the way, Hannibal?" Mr. Pennydine asked. "It's about ten blocks and then you go two blocks to the west. It's a plain wooden house."

"I'll find it," Hannibal said.

I glanced in the rear-view mirror. Mr. Pennydine was smiling and running his hand over the red leather seat. "I'll tell her why Major Clarence gave me this car," he said. "I'll tell her it was because the Major knew that Lucretia and I weren't right for each other. It's a grand car. It's grand."

Those were the last words he ever spoke in this world. When we stopped at the next light I looked around at the back seat. Mr. Pennydine was sitting with his hand on the red leather and the smile still on his face. He had died anticipating Florida Watson's pride in his car.

We took him home, carried him inside, put on his bathrobe

and pajamas and got him onto his bed. I didn't feel as if I was helping with a dead man. It was just Mr. Pennydine, not talking for once.

That evening Mrs. Luddington did some dutiful crying and called the undertaker. Hannibal waited at her house until a black hearse had taken away the mortal remains of John S. Pennydine. Then he came across the street to Barbara's. "You ever tell," he said to me, "and I'm gone break you in so many pieces you can't wiggle your feet."

"I won't tell," I said, "but you'd better worry about that bartender."

"I ain't worried about no bartender," Hannibal said. "That man got paid a lot of money."

"What'd you do," I asked, "rob a bank?"

"Smart-ass," he said.

Later he drove off in the Pierce-Arrow, and Barbara went out to have dinner with Bronson Hake. I was left alone. I decided to watch television, but it was boring.

I went upstairs, got Beth's book and read through to the last poem, which was about her waking up one morning on Martha's Vineyard all alone. It was raining and Manfred had apparently left her for good after he got all wrathful, neurotic and unmanageable. The last poem ended:

> But now you are just pain
> And God decreed this rain.
> It has nothing to do with me.

The poem was poignant and it moved me. I put down the book so I couldn't see her face on the back cover, and turned on a fantasy about my own future as a famous and successful man living in an elegant house, a gracious host, popular and respected, but cloaked in the mystery of bachelorhood. I would, of course, be seen with fashionable women but never form a permanent attachment. I was working up a scene in my drawing room late one night after all my guests had gone except for a beautiful, intelligent lady in a black evening dress. She had just told me that she was in love with me and asked why I couldn't love her. I was touched and broke my vow of silence. "Once, when I was a young man," I was saying, "I fell very deeply in love—"

The telephone rang.

I got up from the living-room sofa and went out into the kitchen. "Barbara Defere's residence," I said into the phone.

"Well, thank God," Beth's low, clear voice answered. "Do you know how many ways there are to spell Defere?"

I was in an instant state of stupefaction and delight.

"Little *d*, big *F*," she said, "big *D*, little *f* . . . Bornie, it's Beth. Remember me? I was supposed to be Serge Texiera's garage."

"Of course I remember," I said, beginning to emerge from shock. "The last time we talked you said you couldn't afford me."

"Is that a payback?"

"A what?"

"Are you reminding me of what a rat I was to you to get back at me for being a rat to you?"

"No," I said, "I promise I'm not. It's just that I'm so surprised that you phoned . . ."

"Are you pleased?"

"Well, *naturally* I'm pleased."

"So am I," she said. Her voice softened. "You see, I *was* terribly disappointed when you didn't call me back the first night—"

"There was a reason. A lot of them."

"I know," she answered. "I'm sure there was—were. But this is now, that was then, a time will be when we talk it all into order. The main point is that I was making you into somebody else and that's not fair."

"Were you making me into Manfred?" I asked.

"What do you know about Manfred?"

"I've been reading your book," I said.

There followed a moment of silence. I looked through the kitchen windows at Pittsburgh glittering and winking far below.

"I don't quite know what to say," Beth answered.

"Those poems got to me. I can understand why you were suspicious of me. Manfred really gave you a bad time."

"Pain, pain, pain," she said, almost with indifference. "Everybody suffers from something. It mustn't become a habit."

"Is Manfred gone?"

"Gone?"

"Out of your life?"

"Manfred's a book of poems," she said enigmatically. "Bornie, one of the reasons I called—"

"You're very beautiful," I said, anxious not to break the spell of subtle intimacy that was reconnecting Beth and me.

"I saw a picture of you, too," she said. "You really *are* tall."

I felt a small pang of anxiety bump against the familiar rapture her voice aroused in me. "Where did you see my picture?"

"Do you remember something else?" she asked. "You gave me your mother's name and part of her address?"

"Yes," I said. The mere mention of my mother made my stomach knot and my scalp tingle—conditions not conducive to the perpetuation of rapture.

"I called her—you see, I didn't *really* mean I couldn't afford you—I called her and said I was a friend of yours and she insisted that I come and see her. I drove up to Cambridge today. She wants to know where you are."

Old alarm bells were going off inside me. "You didn't tell her, did you?"

"No, silly, I didn't tell her. Do you know something?"

"Tell me," I said.

"Your mother's crazy," Beth said. *"Miss Watts!"* she bellowed suddenly in an uncanny and spine-tinglingly accurate imitation of my mother's supersonic intimidation screech, "I *demand* to know where Bornie—"

"She calls me 'Sherborne.'"

"Oh, right, sorry—I *deee-MAND* to know where Sherborne is THIS INSTANT! Blah, blah, blah. She's really awful—but she's beautiful, too."

"Yes," I said, "she is. What else?"

"Bornie, you must have had a really horrid childhood."

"It wasn't that bad. Besides, all childhoods should be abolished. You just have to live them down."

"Do you *really* mean that?"

"There goes my big chance to be a psychological hero," I said. "No, I haven't lived down my childhood completely. I've got all kinds of faults, flaws and bad thoughts."

"I like the way you tell the truth," Beth said.

My unease evaporated before the aural stroking of her alto voice. I was getting excited over the way the conversation was going. "Listen, Beth," I said, "I'm not doing anything important. I could quit my job here and leave for Rhode Island—"

"No," she said, "not yet. Bornie, your mother's obsessed with putting you back in a mental hospital. She was raving around about lawyers and protecting income."

"I don't get it."

"I didn't either. She talks in wallops and blabs. She threw me out when she realized I wasn't going to tell her where you are."

"Jesus, I'm sorry," I said. "You shouldn't have to put up with that."

"I don't understand what it's all about, but she's absolutely determined to commit you. She told me you are unbalanced and dangerous. She even said you tried to kill a man."

"I threw him in the swimming pool," I said.

Beth giggled. "Did you really?"

"I really did."

"That's funny, but your mother isn't. She's going to have you locked up."

"She can't," I said. "I'm over twenty-one and they let me out of the last place she sent me because the new chief psychiatrist discovered I'd been sane all along."

"They're building a case against you," Beth said in tones of warning and alarm. "In all that mishmash of talk I found out that she knows you were mixed up in that Cleveland auto-parts racket—I don't know whether to be thrilled or dismayed that you tried being a gangster . . ."

"I can explain—"

"Some other time," Beth said. "Listen to me. Your mother claims you signed some federal tax forms with that other name you were using and that you started a riot in a place called East Heidelberg."

My pleasure went blooey, my mind's springs began to jangle in alarm again.

"She's got somebody following you, Bornie. Somebody's watching you. It's probably a private detective."

"Jesus wept," I said.

"They're waiting for you to build a record of unbalanced behavior. Your mother as good as told me that. You've got to be careful. Oh, Bornie, it's revolting! That poor, weak, angry woman . . ."

"Listen, Beth," I said, "we'd better stop calling each other. I don't know exactly what could happen to you if we go on like this, but my mother's unpredictable. She's got more lawyers than the Chrysler Corporation. She's feeling threatened by something and you've got this great career going and your father's a U.S. Attorney. You just don't need the kind of trouble that comes with me."

There was a protracted silence at her end of the line.

"Are you still there?" I asked.

"I'm still here," she said.

"What are you doing?"

"Trying to make Manfred shut up so that I can listen to my instincts about you."

"What do your instincts tell you?"

"That you really mean what you just told me."

"Beth," I said. "I'm pretty immature in some ways. When

we first met by accident on the telephone, I conjured up this great fantasy about you. I fell in love with your voice."

"Interesting . . ."

"Why?"

"I—" She paused. "Well, I can understand how that could happen."

"Then when I saw your photograph on the back cover of *Manfred—And Afterward* and read some of your poems, I decided that you were unattainable. That's a form of fantasy, too."

"We must have read the same novels when we were children."

"But everything you've just told me is real life," I went on. I tried to nail down the rest of my thought in succinct language, but I couldn't. "I think it would be better if you went on being my fantasy of the unattainable woman and stayed clear of my trouble."

There was another long silence in Rhode Island.

Finally she asked, "Do you know what the writing of poetry is about?"

"No," I said.

"It's seeing a shape in the half light and trying to make it come clear," she said.

I couldn't think of any response to that because I didn't know if the message I was receiving was what she meant.

"That's why I don't want you to come to Rhode Island yet," Beth said. "I want you to stay in the half light and keep on telephoning me until I can make you come clear."

"I guess that's the way you have to court a poet," I said.

She laughed softly. "That's the way you have to court a poet. Don't give me up, Bornie."

"I won't," I said. I was calm again and profoundly happy.

"Good night, dear friend. Please be careful."

"I will," I said and carefully hung up the telephone.

I sat becalmed in the kitchen for a long time trying to get a grip on the realization that a girl of a beauty and nature beyond my greatest fantasies had loving feelings about me—the same me my mother, for reasons past all knowing, was trying to put back in an insane asylum. Thoughts of my mother led to wondering about my father. Somewhere out there, on Mr. Pennydine's first night in the kingdom of the dead, my father was trying to discover the meaning of life.

It was all too much to think about.

Ten

GOD'S CASHIER AND A FAINTING HORSE

ON MONDAY, Carlos Morales came to work at the television station, on Tuesday we buried Mr. Pennydine and on Wednesday they promoted me to investigative reporter. Considering what I subsequently investigated, I'm not sure the promotion was worth it. More on that after these messages.

I can't tell you much about Carlos except that he came from Panama, he was blond, wore a flowered shirt, a huge brass belt buckle and had amazingly long eyelashes. He was, in fact, beautiful. Big Ned smirked as he brought Carlos into the newsroom after lunch on Monday. "This is Eppe," he said to Carlos, "the one I was telling you about."

Carlos held out his hand and said, "Ease great pleasure to meeting you."

I shook hands with him. Carlos' smile was like pale light. "I hope you'll enjoy it here," I said. "If there's anything I can do to help . . ."

Big Ned's gloating expression broadened into the grin of a

man who's about to burst into the last laugh, which, as everybody knows, is the best. "He's going to replace you on dayside rewrite," he said.

Carlos had a beatific look on his face as if he were thinking of cozy dinners and model trains. He wandered over to an AP machine. "Does he know English well enough to be on rewrite?" I asked.

Big Ned did his pretend convulsion into laughter. "We're an equal-opportunity employer," he said. "I love it."

The burial of John S. Pennydine was in a funeral parlor at ten o'clock the next morning. I made Hannibal buy a suit for the occasion—it was the only thing I was ever able to make him do. He, Mrs. Luddington and I were the entire congregation of mourners. Mr. Pennydine had outlived everyone he knew. He had even outlived Pittsburgh's memory of him. Barbara couldn't come to the funeral because she was on assignment.

So the three of us sat in the front pew of an empty chapel while fake sunlight streamed in through fake stained-glass windows and recorded organ music wafted on air which had been sprayed with a piney-woods scent. It was an inappropriate setting if you believe that life and death are epic matters. It was like going to a great king's coronation in a Sears, Roebuck store.

On the way home in the Pierce-Arrow, Mrs. Luddington was full of guilty anxiety as usual. "I hope I bought the right coffin," she said. "Do you think he'll be comfortable?"

"Lot more'n he was a week ago," Hannibal said, driving with great care and precision.

"You've done a beautiful job on this car," Mrs. Luddington told him. "I mean, *really—beautiful!* My grandfather said he gave it to you."

"He was a old man," Hannibal said. "Didn't know what he was talkin' 'bout half the time."

"But he must have *wanted* you to have it," she said, "I mean, even if it was just at the moment he said it. I'd feel *terrible* if I went against any of his wishes." She looked pleadingly at Hannibal.

"Don't want you feelin' terrible," he said. And that's how we got the 1926 Pierce-Arrow for keeps.

The next morning Art Olsen asked me if I had ever heard of the Jesus Christ Church of Holier Than Thou. We were sitting in his cluttered little office. Out in the newsroom Bronson Hake was bellowing at Charlie Harris, the head rewrite man, and Charlie was trying to teach Carlos Morales how to conjugate the verb "to be." From what I could hear through the closed door, Bronson was roaring that in parts of the previous evening's broadcast he had been made to sound like Pancho Villa.

"The Jesus Christ Church of Holier Than Thou is in Andrewstown, Pennsylvania," Art said. He squinched his pugdog face into a solemn expression and ran his hand over his crew cut. "It's one of those evangelical outfits."

"What do you want me to find out?" I asked.

Art looked even more serious. "Holier Than Thou is run by a man named Rhett Hinkley. Now, I don't want to prejudice you from the start, Sherborne, but a lot of people think Holier Than Thou is a racket. Hinkley's a showman, a charismatic, and his business has been booming since the epidemic hit."

My brain connected. I knew I'd heard of Andrewstown. It was southeast of Johnstown, the center of an area in which a mysterious disease had appeared. I'd written stories about that for the evening news. The disease, as yet undiagnosed and of unknown source, had afflicted a large number of people with splitting headaches, muscle weakness, respiratory problems, disorientation and other symptoms including something called "formication"—that's with an *m*, not an *n*—which creates the sensation that bugs are crawling on your skin. In fact, the epidemic—which was spreading—was popularly known as the Bug Plague. "What's the disease got to do with the Jesus Christ Church of Holier Than Thou?" I asked.

"None of Hinkley's followers have caught it," Art said.

I looked closely at him. He was as solemn as ever. "You aren't joking?"

He shook his head and picked up a document. "This just

came in from the Public Health Service. They're doing all sorts of studies around Andrewstown by various population categories." He tossed the document across the desk. "Read page seventy-four, Sherborne. Nobody who belongs to the Jesus Christ Church of Holier Than Thou has gotten that disease."

I turned to page 74. Art was right. I felt a prickly sensation at the roots of my hair as if some holy bug were trying to burrow into my brain with a message. "Maybe Hinkley's discovered a preventive version of faith healing," I said.

"That's what he's selling," Art answered. "He's running services every night and on Sundays. He's packing people in because they're frightened and they think he offers some sort of spiritual immunity. And Hinkley's making more money than ever before."

"Weird," I said.

"Well, not really. The Public Health people think there's a behavioral pattern connected with the disease and that when they discover the source they'll find out why the Holier Than Thou congregation has been immune. What we want *you* to find out about—if you can—is the money."

"What about it?"

"There's an awful lot of it, and nobody knows what happens to it. Most wealthy evangelical sects use their money to set up universities, buy television time. Some of them establish missions in ghettos or in underdeveloped countries." Art looked solemnly at me. "Rhett Hinkley doesn't do any of that. He doesn't even spend money on running Holier Than Thou. All the work is done by volunteers—from the bookkeeping to the janitors." He crinkled up his face into his earnest frown again. "We've been interested in Holier Than Thou for some time now. We even sent a reporter out to Andrewstown for a couple of days last year but he didn't come up with anything. Now the stakes are higher because of all the money Hinkley's making—and we've had a call from a local clergyman who thinks Hinkley's up to something, that something's going to happen."

"Like what?"

Art shook his head. "I don't know. The clergyman—his

name is Tom Dawson—said he had inside information about Holier Than Thou but he wouldn't discuss it on the phone. I want you to go out there, talk to Dawson and dig up everything you can about Hinkley's finances."

"I'll give it my best shot," I said.

"An investigative reporter has to be tough and hard-nosed. I want you to keep that in mind."

"I will."

"There's something else," Art said, lowering his voice as if the walls had ears. After all the bizarre things I'd seen at that television station, ears growing out of the pale-green walls wouldn't have surprised me a bit. "Ned Plotkin's out to get you, Sherborne."

"I know," I whispered back.

"The rest of the management thinks you have promise."

"I'm grateful."

"Do your best in Andrewstown. Your job depends on it."

I murmured that I would and went out into the newsroom. Charlie Harris was trying to show Carlos how to spell Pittsburgh. I told Barbara I was going off to investigate the Jesus Christ Church of Holier Than Thou. She gave me a big hug and said, "Knock 'em dead, sugarplum."

The day I sold my Volkswagen I had resigned myself to the probability that Hannibal would come with me when I left Pittsburgh. He hadn't had anything to do since Mr. Pennydine died and he showed no inclination to go out looking for gainful employment.

When I got home and told Hannibal I'd been assigned to go to Andrewstown for the TV station he made his usual eloquent declaration about shaking ass and went upstairs to pack. I followed him to our room and told him we were going into an epidemic area. "You gone be glad I'm along when you get sick," he said. He operated on the theory that I couldn't cross a street without falling into a manhole unless he was with me.

We were clear of Pittsburgh's eastern rubble by noon and

out on the open highway. It was a sunny day of benevolent temperatures. We had rolled down the side windows, and the zephyrs of spring rushed over me as I sat in the front seat beside Hannibal. The stark branches of trees were blurred in a haze of green as new leaves returned to try life for another year.

We had a sandwich in Johnstown and drove southeast. Hannibal turned off the highway at a sign that said "Andrews-town—2 miles." We were in farm country and the road was dirt.

"There's got to be a more direct route into the town than this," I said. "Look at those ruts and potholes. You'll wreck the car."

"This car," Hannibal said, "gone last to the end of the world unless some asshole like you drives her."

"Well, *I* wouldn't be idiot enough to risk it on a crappy road."

"What *you* don't know, smart-ass, is that when this car was built, 'most *all* roads in the country was like this one."

We were having that argument going around a bend. Suddenly Hannibal jammed on the brakes and we came to an abrupt, mud-sprayed stop. A horse was lying across the road in front of us. It was a very large horse, reddish brown, and it looked dead. There were ditches on both sides and no way around. "And all the roads were blocked by dead horses in 1926," I said.

Hannibal told me to shut up and we got out. He walked over and squatted beside the horse's head while I surveyed the countryside.

A farm was spread out on either side of the road. There was a two-story house, a barn, some outbuildings with two rusted cars and a partially dismembered tractor adding to the charm of the setting. Some of the fields were plowed, but the one to my left was pasture. A portion of the barbed-wire fence was pushed over into the ditch. "That's how the horse got out," I said to Hannibal.

"He ain't dead."

I went back to where Hannibal was crouching. The horse's eyes were closed but he was breathing, the huge rib cage rising and collapsing like an engine in neutral gear. "Do you suppose he got hit by a car?" I asked.

A door slammed up at the farmhouse.

Hannibal looked at me. "Now, how you think I'm gone know if he got hit by a car? If he did, he's lyin' on the side that got hit."

A man in a khaki shirt and heavy work shoes came striding up the road with a bucket of water. "Afternoon, gents," he said. "Sorry about this."

He was tall—not as tall as Hannibal and me, but of a rugged build—and, I guessed, in his mid-thirties. The work of his life had stained him here and there—embedded etchings of grime on his hands, a hot, leathery burn on his face and networks of muscle and large veins on his arms. He had the aromatic aura of perspiration and barnyard about him.

Hannibal stood up. "What's the matter with that horse?"

"He faints," the man said.

"He *what*?"

"Faints," the man said again. "Mostly from excitement." Holding his bucket of water, he looked down at the horse. "Dumb son of a bitch. A dog can make him faint too, so can firecrackers. He spends every Fourth of July flat out." Suddenly he grasped the bottom of the bucket and flung the water over the horse's head with a violent splash. "C'mon, Charlie, get up off that road!"

The horse opened his eyes with a snort, flailed his legs around and then heaved himself up on all fours. He shook like a dog and made a loud, blubbery equine noise.

"He's been working on that barbed-wire fence all morning," the man said. "He wanted to come over to the house where *I've* been working on the goddamn tractor. That horse there loves me and hates me at the same time. When he finally got the fence knocked down he probably passed out from excitement. Stupid bastard." He kicked him in the rear. The horse lashed out with both hind legs, jumped over the ditch and trotted back into the field with a loose, arrogant gait.

The young farmer looked disgusted. "I should have been harrowing with that horse, but he's slow. If I could have fixed the tractor, I'd have done twice as much as me and Charlie could do. But I didn't fix the tractor and the day's half shot and that, gents, is the story of my life." He looked at the Pierce-Arrow— tall and gleaming white with mud splotches on its chrome wheels. "That's some kind of car you got there."

"It was built in 1926," I said. "My friend restored it."

The man looked at Hannibal. "Know anything about tractors?"

"Got four wheels and a engine?"

"Yep. And it's busted."

"Lemme have a look at her."

"Listen," I protested, "I've got to get to Andrews—"

"I'll take you in my pickup," the man said. He held out his hand. "Will Timberlake's my name."

We shook hands with him, introduced ourselves and drove him back to the farmhouse in the Pierce-Arrow. "I've got to fix the fence or that damn fool horse'll be on the road again," Timberlake said. "Come inside and meet my mother."

The Timberlake farm was poor, but not a rural slum like a lot of small farms you see. I could hear the distant *umpf* sound of a rooting pig, and the lazy caws and croons of chickens in the spring sunlight. Several large black-and-white cows were mooning around on a bushy slope behind the barn.

The buildings were solid and the house had been painted recently. Two aluminum-and-plastic chairs were on the front porch; someone had filled a large wooden tub with earth for flowers.

There were *plastic* flowers on the inside hall table and an imitation hooked rug on the floor. We went into a sunlit living room filled with little china figurines on the mantel, in a curved niche, on tables and shelves. The place was furnished with a matching set of chairs and sofa covered in a purple-and-brown fabric. A gray-haired woman sat at a large table putting slips of paper in envelopes. After she licked each flap and pressed it down she said, "Thank you, Jesus."

"Ma," Will Timberlake said, "this here's Sherborne Eppe and Hannibal."

The woman, who must have been in her early sixties, looked up and smiled a slightly off-center smile. She had on rimless glasses and wore a flowered dress. She stood up. "It's a pleasure to welcome you to our home," she said.

"Charlie fainted on the road, which is how I met these guys," Timberlake said. "Hannibal's going to see if he can do something about the tractor."

"Thank you, Jesus," Mrs. Timberlake answered.

"Hannibal's the name," Hannibal said.

Mrs. Timberlake smiled her bent smile again. "Thank you, Jesus."

"For Christ's sake, Ma," Will said with exasperation, "will you cut it out?"

Mrs. Timberlake turned to me. "Will's going to burn in eternal perdition," she said with no more reproach or passion than if she'd been giving me the weather report.

Suddenly Will smashed his clenched fist against the pine-paneled wall with such a reverberating thud that china figurines jumped all over the living room. One—a frilly shepherdess—fell to the floor with a crash. "She drives me nuts!" Will yelled, his face suddenly furnace-bright. "She's had Jesus like the hiccups ever since Hinkley got ahold of her!"

Mrs. Timberlake stood with her hands folded against the front of her flowered dress as if nothing—neither fire, water, death, pestilence nor her son's furies—could perturb her. "I am holier than thou," she said to Will. "Would you gentlemen like a piece of coffee cake?"

Will raised his fist again, then dropped his hand to his side, open and loose. "They don't need any coffee cake!" he told his mother. "*I* need to get that tractor fixed, prop up the goddamn fence and go meet Grace."

"If you go into that house, you're not to upset the Reverend Hinkley," Mrs. Timberlake answered. "You do as Grace says."

"One of these days I'll do more than upset the bastard," Will said. "C'mon, Hannibal."

After Will and Hannibal had gone outside, I followed Mrs. Timberlake into the kitchen. She interested me because she was so serene and because she was the first human example of the Reverend Rhett Hinkley's handiwork I'd encountered. While she was putting a percolator on the stove I asked her why Will might upset the Reverend Hinkley.

"There's a great struggle going on over Will," Mrs. Timberlake answered. "He's a battleground with Jesus and the Reverend Hinkley on one side and Satan on the other."

At that point I was unfamiliar with the Holier Than Thou jargon. "I don't think I understand what you mean," I said.

"Satan hates the holy people," she answered, "so he's made Will sick with lust for Grace Hinkley, our Reverend's daughter. Now, under ordinary circumstances Grace would make a fine Christian wife for Will. But she's got God's work to do. Jesus needs her to help her father save people from the plague."

"The Reverend Hinkley must be a powerful converter," I said.

"*Powerful?*" Mrs. Timberlake echoed, taking a platter of coffee cake from the refrigerator. "Why, you ought to hear him, Mr. Eppe. That dear man can preach like the prophets of old. If Grace married Will, the Reverend Hinkley says, he'd take her mind off God's work. The Lord Himself is opposed to that marriage. How do you take your coffee, Mr. Eppe?"

"Black," I said. "Mrs. Timberlake, I've always been under the impression that God's ways were unknowable."

She cut a slice of crumbly coffee cake and put it on a plate. "The Reverend Hinkley knows. He discussed it with Jesus and explained it to me after."

"The Reverend Hinkley has *discussions* with Jesus?" I asked.

"In person," she said. She didn't bat an eye, metaphorically or otherwise. She really believed what she was saying, and that gave me my first whiff of Rhett Hinkley's power.

Back in the living room Mrs. Timberlake resumed stuffing envelopes while I drank my coffee and tried the cake. I asked her how long she had belonged to the Jesus Christ Church of Holier Than Thou.

"Three years, four months and nine days," she answered in the happy tones of a girl recounting the time she has been in love. Mrs. Timberlake pressed down with her arthritic fingers to seal an envelope. "Thank you, Jesus," she said. She looked through the picture window at the sunny afternoon and the cows on the slope. "Mr. Timberlake passed on in 1976," she said, talking more to herself or God than me, "the last year Will was in the penitentiary . . ."

"What did he do?" I asked.

Mrs. Timberlake looked back at me and smiled. "Will? He got into a fight with a state trooper and hit him over the head with a cuspidor. He didn't mean any harm. Will's just got a temper." She started stuffing envelopes again. "But, you know, Mr. Eppe, at the time it seemed like more than mortal flesh could bear. I tried to keep up the gas station in Charleston—that's Charleston, West Virginia—but without Will and his father I just couldn't manage. So I sold out and moved here. This was my brother's place. He passed the same year."

A clock ticked in the hall, filling up the pause while she stuffed another envelope. "Thank you, Jesus. I said to myself, 'Helen Timberlake, you're going to be a lonely old woman before you can say Jack Robinson.' Then one morning I turned on the radio and heard the Reverend Hinkley—he has a weekly program, you know." She smiled at me again. Her weathered and reduced face was beautiful. "That very night I went to my first meeting in Andrewstown. I made my witness eight days later and I became a member of a blessed family."

She laughed as she picked up another envelope. "Sometimes there aren't enough hours in the day to keep up with all the doings of my family. There are the prayer meetings—every night now since God sent the plague—the regular meetings, the ladies' circle, the Sunday School, the love-donation hours at the center . . ." She looked at the envelopes on the table. "Thank you, Jesus. I've sealed two hundred and three of these since breakfast and there are one hundred and ninety-seven to go."

I put down my coffee cup. "What are they?"

"Letters of witness and salvation," she said. "Do you know, Mr. Eppe, the ladies' circle is sending one to every single solitary household in two counties?" She touched a pad of papers. "These are the witness forms. Anyone who can't come to the tabernacle and make his witness personal can fill out one of these and send fifteen dollars and they'll have *made* their witness. Isn't that wonderful? They'll be included in the endless chain of prayer—"

"And they won't get sick," I said.

"That's right. And everyone who sends in his witness form and the fifteen dollars will get a personal, inspirational message from the Reverend Hinkley."

I remembered the news reports on the mysterious Andrewstown epidemic I'd done for Bronson Hake. It had started about five weeks before. They'd closed the schools in Andrewstown for a week until it was discovered that most of the victims were adults. By the time I started writing about the epidemic, the news was full of briefings about air- and water-borne bacteria, descriptions of the symptoms—some of which were pretty awful —and all the labyrinthian clinical guesswork of science that's hard to reduce to television prose. More than a hundred people were down with the enigmatic illness, nobody died and it didn't spread much beyond a thirty-mile radius around Andrewstown. Gradually the epidemic slipped down in the hierarchy of horrors, political errors, cute features and graphically visual automobile accidents that was the stuff of our nightly television news. It became just another typical American disaster—full of complicated technology, shrieks of blame, officialdom stumbling around looking for answers, and public anxieties over an invisible threat. The anxiety was still big around Andrewstown, judging from the way the Reverend Hinkley was packing in the populace. "Why do you think the epidemic started?" I asked Mrs. Timberlake.

She sealed another envelope, thanked Jesus and answered, "Why, I *know*, Mr. Eppe. God sent the plague as a sign."

"Of what?"

The clock was ticking in the hallway. Mrs. Timberlake's amiability dissolved into a sort of quiet firmness. "The world is full of sin, Mr. Eppe. You know that, and that's what God's trying to warn us about. Why, look at Mary De Mola right here in Andrewstown. Mary's had a good upbringing, even if her family *is* Catholic. She's got a fine husband and two nice children. I'm not a gossip, Mr. Eppe, it's unforgiving and un-Christian to gossip, but *everybody* knows that Mary runs around. Now she's sick and so's her eight-year-old, little Paul. And Bill O'Brien —well, don't talk to *me* about that man's carryings-on. His poor wife, Ethel. Bill's one of the sickest. They thought he was going to die two, three weeks ago."

"I'm a television reporter," I said. "We're thinking of doing a series on the Reverend Hinkley."

Mrs. Timberlake brightened up immediately. "Why, that's wonderful!" Next, she looked at me skeptically. "You will tell the truth, won't you?"

"I usually try to."

"I mean, about Mr. Hinkley being the *way*," she said. "The sickness can't touch the holy people. Have you made your witness yet, Mr. Eppe?"

"I don't think so," I said, feeling a psychosomatic spasm of recollected sin and wondering if baptism and confirmation by my grandfather, the bishop, counted.

"Then I am holier than thou," she said without the slightest trace of arrogance or superiority. "You ought to go to the meeting tonight."

"I plan to," I assured her.

I had gotten two impressions from Mrs. Timberlake. She was obviously full of peace and happiness because of the Reverend Rhett Hinkley, while he—seen *through* her—was an outrageous bunkum artist. Yet his congregation wasn't getting sick, while people like Mary De Mola and Bill O'Brien were paying for their sins with splitting headaches, weak joints, respiratory failure, nausea, hair falling out and the squeamy feeling of bugs crawling all over them. Maybe, I thought, God has a grisly sense of humor.

Out in the barnyard I found Hannibal lying under the tractor, tugging with a wrench, sweating and grunting "Sumbitch" at some inanimate object, which meant that he had found the ideal mixture of machinery and an outlet for his primordial truculence.

Will took a shotgun from the cab of his truck and put it in the barn. "Wouldn't do me a hell of a lot of good if they found me with a weapon," he said as we both got into the truck. "I've done time. I guess Ma told you that."

"She mentioned it," I said.

Before he started the truck, Will ran his hand over the panel of hair lying like a cleaver blade on the side of his head. "Ma doesn't approve of me," he said. "Never has." He spat out the window, which was meant to demonstrate defiance but which actually displayed his chagrin. "Ma's all right," he said. "She's just got an overdose of Jesus and she talks too much."

"I was locked up for seven years," I said.

Will turned and looked at me with his pale-blue eyes for a moment. He began to grin as he turned back to steering the truck. "No kidding," he said. "What'd you do?"

"I assaulted a Guatemalan," I said.

His grin turned into a light smile of recognition. "What do they call you?"

"Bornie."

"Okay, Bornie," he said.

His farm was in hilly country and the midafternoon sun was drying the winter wet from the fields and wooded slopes. A flight of small birds burst from a row of bushes and scattered over a stubby pasture as the pickup truck swayed and splashed through puddles on the dirt road.

It was beautiful country, fresh with early spring, yet the

appearance deceived. Pestilence hovered in the air that looked so clear; it was a gaseous, invisible presence.

Will braked the pickup to a stop at the junction of the dirt road and a six-lane highway. I saw two billboards—one faded, one blaring new in the bright sunlight. The first one read:

ANDREWSTOWN—HOME OF THE JESUS CHRIST CHURCH
OF HOLIER THAN THOU!

Rev. Rhett Hinkley, Evangelist and
Pastor
Services Thursday Evenings at 8 P.M.
and Sundays at 10 A.M. Every Week of
the Year

THE MESSENGERS!
THE RESURRECTION SINGERS!

The second, newer and whoopier sign read:

*I will send the pestilence among you; and
ye shall be delivered into the hand of the
enemy.*—Leviticus 26:25

HEAR THE PROPHECIES AND SALVATION MESSAGE OF:
THE REVEREND RHETT HINKLEY
WORLD FAMOUS EVANGELIST AND PREACHER!

BE SAVED FROM SICKNESS AND SIN! WITNESS
CHRIST FOR SPIRITUAL AND PHYSICAL HEALTH
AT:

THE JESUS CHRIST CHURCH OF
HOLIER THAN THOU!

Services Every Night at Eight!

THE REVEREND RHETT HINKLEY!

Put on the whole armour of God . . .
—Ephesians, 6:11

That second billboard was twice the size of the first one. It was painted in luminous colors so that automobile headlights could pick it up at night.

"Hinkley's been happier than a pig in shit since the plague started," Will said as he turned the pickup truck onto the highway.

"Is it really true that nobody from Holier Than Thou has gotten sick?" I asked.

"That's what they tell me," Will said.

"Do you have any theories about why?"

Will chortled. His knotty Adam's apple twitched in his throat. "It sure as hell isn't because Rhett Hinkley and Jesus have beaten the microbes."

"You don't seem to like Hinkley much."

"Can't stand him. He can't stand me, either. He ran off Grace's first husband, but he can't run me off and it drives him nuts. I suppose Ma told you about me and Grace."

"Yes."

"He doesn't want me taking her away," Will said. "Old Hinkley can't get along without her. She thinks he's Jesus Christ."

"He must be an extraordinary man," I said.

"Beats the shit out of me how he does it," Will said. He drove in silence for a few moments more. The highway in front of us was white and dry in the afternoon sun. "It isn't that Grace is *scared* of her old man, it's—hell, I don't know. Six, seven months ago I was over there and Hinkley said something mean to her—he's one mean son of a bitch—and Grace started to cry. I got so mad I rammed his Lincoln Continental with the pickup. Hinkley was in it. I haven't seen him since. Grace makes me stay away from him."

Andrewstown was a pretty place with old houses sitting on side streets that were lined with tall trees. Dead leaves lay matted on the lawns.

"There's something you ought to know," I said to Will. "I'm a television reporter. I was sent here from Pittsburgh to find out what I could about the Reverend Hinkley."

Will glanced at me, his ruddy face and blue eyes glowing with sudden pleasure. "You're *investigating* him? No kidding?"

"No kidding."

"You may save his life," Will said. "If you find out enough to run that bastard out of the county, I won't have to blast his ass off with my shotgun."

I didn't know if he was speaking in the rural jargon's natural euphemisms of violence or whether he really meant it. I'm not very fluent in rural.

"I'd appreciate your help," I said.

"You got it," he answered. "I don't know much about Hinkley except that I hate his guts, but I might dig up a couple of people who do. Who're you going to talk to first?"

"The only name I've got is the Reverend Tom Dawson."

Will nodded. "I know Tom—he's a nice guy but kind of goofy, and he isn't much of a preacher. If he gets twenty people in that church of his on a Sunday, he's doing real good. He can't even make a living at it. Tom drives a morning delivery route for the milk company over in Johnstown. What kinds of things do you want to investigate?"

"I'm told that Holier Than Thou takes in a lot of money."

"Like a dung heap draws flies." Will slowed down as we got to Main Street—which ended at a river. "I don't know if I ought to tell you this—" He paused. "What the hell. There's this lady named Betty Darius at the bank. I used to bang her when I came up here summers to visit my uncle. We were just kids. Me and Betty are buddies now. She sure as hell knows about Hinkley's money. She's assistant cashier. 'Course it wouldn't be legal for her to talk about bank business, but maybe if I told her you and me were friends . . ."

"I'd appreciate an introduction to her."

"You got it. Like I say, I'm not sure she'll talk." Will turned into a side street, drove three blocks and swung the pickup onto a gravel driveway curving around before a sprawling Victorian house made of dark, gloomy stone. There was a wide lawn.

Through a row of trees and bushes I could see, in the rear, the top of an ugly concrete building with air-conditioning vents on the roof. "What's that?" I asked.

"That," said Will, wheeling the pickup around to the rear of the house, "is the Jesus Christ Church of Holier Than Thou, where the folks come to fork out their money to the Reverend Rhett Hinkley, world's champion savior from the Bug Plague and personal buddy of Jesus H. Christ." He braked the truck in front of the back porch. "The part you see there is the auditorium. The offices are on the other side."

We got out, mounted some steps, crossed the porch and opened the back door into a high-ceilinged, old-fashioned kitchen.

A young woman turned around by the stove. She was pretty in an unadorned, tired way. Her hair was dark-blond and pulled back in a bun. I noticed her shoes. Shoes are a great index to a person's view of themselves. This lady's shoes were brown, plain and dull. "There you are," she said, putting down a wooden spoon and wiping her hands on a towel. She came over to us and gave Will a kiss on the cheek.

Will kissed her back and said, "Grace, honey, this is Bornie Eppe from the Pittsburgh television station."

Grace Hinkley shook hands with me. She smiled—one of those wan smiles your heart goes out to—and turned back to Will. "Daddy's home," she said. "I think you'd better leave."

"Screw Daddy," Will said. His face was getting florid. I'd only known him for a few hours but I'd already learned to read his complexion like a barometer of his approaching moods. He pinked up if he was pleased or preparing to lose his temper.

Grace Hinkley put her hand on his arm. "Will, we've been very lucky, we've had every evening together because Daddy's holding meetings every night. Now—"

She was interrupted by the sound of footsteps. They were coming from a dark passage that led into the front of the house.

"*Please*, Will," Grace said with plaintive urgency.

Will was about to make one of his defiant declarations when the Reverend Rhett Hinkley stepped from the shadows of the passage into the sight of mortal eye.

I think I had expected Charlton Heston playing Moses with green radioactive fire flickering around his whiskers and hair.

In person, the Reverend Hinkley looked like a regional sales manager on his day off. He was in his mid-fifties, I guessed, a slightly portly man of medium height with pomaded brown hair that receded in a wave from his wide forehead. He was wearing one of those detachable-collar shirts with the collar missing, his suspenders were hanging from his waistband, and his trousers sagged below his paunch. The most striking feature of his face was moisture—his eyes were filled with liquid and his large lower lip was gleaming. For a moment I wondered if he was going to cry or drool.

"Grace," he said, "what's that man doing in my house?" His voice was flat and menacing with a good-ole-boy accent.

Grace closed her eyes for a moment. "Daddy, Will was just—"

"Will wasn't just anything," Will said. "I'm bringing my friend here to meet Grace, Hinkley, and if you—"

Hinkley had been contemplating him listlessly. "*Reverend* Hinkley to you."

"Hinkley."

"Reverend."

"Hinkley."

"Rev-er-end," Hinkley said as if he were explaining with tried patience to a stupid child.

"I'd *call* you reverend quick enough if anybody could find out which college reverended you." Will put his thumbs in his belt. "Suppose you tell us what college it was, Hinkley."

"Will, please . . ." Grace said.

Hinkley summoned enough inspiration from his cold, gray interior to smile faintly. "Reckon everybody knows which college you went to, Timberlake."

"Sure they do," Will said. "I don't make any secret of mine.

I did time for bouncing around a state trooper. Now, why don't you—"

"Y'all threatening to bounce somebody *else* around, Will? Maybe go after a man with your pickup truck?"

Will stuck his tongue in his cheek, bulging it out, as he glared at Hinkley. His face had flushed to a fire engine red and his eyes looked paler and harder in it. "Don't tempt me, Okie," he replied.

I began to feel alarmed.

The Reverend Hinkley looked at me. "Talks pretty violent, doesn't he?"

I wasn't supposed to answer the question. I didn't want to.

"Daddy," Grace pleaded, "Will—*stop it!* Both of you!"

"You calm down, Grace," Hinkley said without looking at her. "Your daddy doesn't have to be insulted in his own house. Go call the police."

"If you'd just *talk* to him . . ." Grace said, tears coming into her eyes.

"I *am* talking to the jailbird, honey," Hinkley said.

"You're getting close to the edge, preacher man." Will's voice was toneless and tight.

Grace put her arms around him. "Will, hush!"

"You never did have no sense about men, Grace," Hinkley said. "First a no-count garage mechanic, then a jailbird . . ."

"That's not fair!" Grace cried, turning back to her father.

"You talk like that to her again, Hinkley," Will said, "and I'm going to kick your ass right back to Oklahoma."

The Reverend Hinkley turned to look at his daughter. "Haven't you got any *pride?*" he said with dull nastiness. "You had a Christian upbringing, Grace. You haven't got any pride."

Suddenly Grace began to cry.

Will blew. He pushed Grace aside and made a lunge for the Reverend Hinkley, muscles bulging under the tightly rolled sleeves of his khaki shirt.

"*Mr. Eppe!*" Grace screamed.

I was as scared as she was by then, but I was bigger than

Will and had a reasonable amount of muscle of my own. I grabbed Will's arm as he went by me, spun him and pushed him back into a kitchen chair.

He leaped up, swinging the chair over his head. Although I am nonviolent by nature, I am also averse to having my skull caved in by kitchen chairs. I hit Will Timberlake in the mouth.

I was sorry I did it once the emotional air cleared, and I watched Grace bending over Will where he was sprawled out on the kitchen floor. She was sobbing.

I turned to the Reverend Hinkley.

"I saw John Wayne do that one time in a picture show," he said, looking down at Will. "Forget which one it was but this man was going to hit John Wayne with a chair and John just let him have it, like you did with that scum there."

"Sir," I said, "I'm—"

Hinkley turned his watery eyes on me. "You're Mr. Eppe, the television reporter," he said.

I must have looked startled, because I was.

"Your coming was foretold," he said.

Aftertold, I realized instantly. Mrs. Timberlake had obviously telephoned him about me while we were on our way in town.

"I'd like to have a talk with you," I said.

Hinkley looked down at his weeping daughter. "He's a *good* man," Grace sobbed to her father.

"Mr. Eppe," Hinkley said, tepidly but with an undertone of meanness in his voice, "we're just your ordinary American Christian family and we haven't got anything to say to reporters. There's no news about us. Now, you just go back to your television station and tell them that."

On the floor Will was sitting up, testing his front teeth with his thumb and forefinger. "It's okay, honey," he said to Grace. "Bornie's got a pretty good wallop on him."

"Get that man out of my house," Hinkley said.

"Tell him to go shit in his hat," Will said to me. "Time we went along, anyway. I got the milking to attend to."

Will's mention of my wallop reminded me of Art Olsen's instruction that an investigative reporter has to be tough and hard-nosed. "Reverend Hinkley," I said, "I'm going to be around talking to a lot of people about Holier Than Thou. Some of them don't think much of you. I'd like to get your side of the story before I write anything."

Hinkley's face was a study in several different kinds of hesitation for a moment. "Y'all come see me at ten-thirty tomorrow," he said.

His face reassumed its bland, regional-sales-manager expression as he turned and disappeared into the dark passage. It was supposed to be a dignified exit, I think, but the effect was spoiled by the dangling of his suspenders along the floor and the wrinkled sag of his trousers at the rear.

Grace walked with us to the pickup, wiping her eyes on a wadded piece of Kleenex. "Mr. Eppe," she said, "why are you trying to find out things about us? My father's just a man doing God's—"

"It's his job, honey," Will said. "Isn't everybody in the world thinks your old man's God's mouthpiece, you know."

"Oh, Will," she said, "why can't everything be peaceful and just—just *ordinary*?"

"Because your pa won't let it be," Will said. "*He's* the one who won't let you and me—"

"I'm right in the middle," she said. "He's my *father*, Will!"

"And I'm the man who loves you."

"Oh, I know that and count on it, and I love you, too. But I *can't* leave Daddy. I wish you'd try to get along with him . . ."

"I've tried. I can't stand the way he treats you. Someday when that son of a bitch makes you cry I'm going to wrap his ears around his ankles. You've either got to fight back or get out, honey."

"Will, I—"

Will put his arms around her and pressed her head against his chest. "I know you think you're in the middle," he said, "and if I were a praying man, I'd pray for the day when you come to know you don't *have* to hang around here any longer." He grinned suddenly and put his work-hardened hand under her chin. "Trouble is, your old man's giving prayer a bad name."

She pulled away from him and turned to me. "Is that what *you* think, Mr. Eppe? Are you going to say that on television?"

I reminded myself that I was hard-nosed. "I don't know, Grace," I said. "First I want to find out all the facts about Holier Than Thou. Then I'll write the facts."

"I know there are people who think Daddy's a charlatan. Big-city people like yourself who don't believe . . ." She took a deep breath. "If you could just understand . . ."

"Understand what?" I asked.

She leaned against the truck, pressing her hands on the panel door. She looked at the ground. "God chooses particular people and reveals himself to them." She raised her head. "Sometimes the people he chooses seem—*unlikely*, Mr. Eppe . . . people who have led obscure lives, sometimes even sinful lives. But when those people *are* touched by God, they change. They aren't like other people anymore."

From what I had read of Christian history at Craigie Glen I knew what Grace Hinkley was talking about: the ecstatics, men and women driven to unearthly behavior by their glimpses of the divine—John the Baptist howling his prophecies in the wilderness, the other St. John riveted by visions on the island of Patmos and writing them down in the Book of Revelations, Theresa of Avila swooning at the sight of God.

"I know there are people like that," I said.

"You *do* accept it?" Grace asked eagerly.

"I think so."

"I'm going to tell my father that you believe in charismatics," she said. "It will help him to trust you."

"Do *you* believe he's a visionary?"

She either didn't hear me or didn't choose to answer. She and Will made plans to meet that night after Rhett Hinkley had gone to the tabernacle.

We drove back to the farm. The light was fading and the sky

was overcast. The landscape was hushed and empty of birds as the pickup truck bumped along the dirt road. The hills were black. I told Will I was sorry I'd hit him.

"Oh, hell," he said, "that's all right. If you hadn't, I'da hit you and booted Hinkley into the middle of next week. But," he added without changing his manner in the slightest, "don't get in my way if it ever comes to a real showdown between him and me because if you do, I'll kill you, Bornie—unless you kill me first."

It was one of those statements that come across with the flat, chilling ring of true intention. I made a mental note to try to stay out of the way if Will Timberlake ever decided to kill Rhett Hinkley.

"Do people around here usually know when strangers come to town?" I asked.

"It depends," Will said. "We got folks from all over coming in every night to hear Hinkley. Why?"

"There's a private detective looking for me," I said.

Will drove in silence until we'd nearly reached the farm. "I suppose a man like that would be asking questions," he said. "If he did, I'd hear about it. We won't talk about why he's looking for you."

"Thanks," I said.

"Guys like you and me have to stick together," he said. I decided to let him go on thinking I was a guy like him. It was good cover.

As we drove up to the farm we could hear the tractor roaring in the dusk. Hannibal was sitting in its seat gunning the engine.

Will got out of the truck and walked over to him. "I'll be goddamned," he said. "What was wrong with it?"

"Fuel line," Hannibal said, switching off the engine.

"What do I owe you?"

"Nothin'," Hannibal said. "Didn't take much." I will say one thing for him—he wasn't the least bit interested in money or possessions. As far as I know, his inflamed mind never discovered avarice.

"Look," Will said, "the least I can do is offer you guys a place to sleep."

I said we were grateful. I really was, too. With disease seeping through the streets I didn't much feel like staying in Andrewstown.

After we got settled I used the credit card the TV station had given me to call Art Olsen. I told him I'd met Rhett Hinkley and had a few contacts but that I didn't know anything yet.

"Well, do your best as fast as you can, Sherborne," Art said. "How is it out there?"

"Unreal," I said.

Eleven

THE ANDREWSTOWN FOLLIES

FULL EVENING CAME ON and chilled the countryside. While Hannibal watched Will milk the cows in the barn I leaned on a wired-together fence and looked across the Timberlake farm to the broad pasture beyond the road where Charlie, the giddy horse, stood in motionless droop, half asleep; beyond his field a row of hills was just a smudge beneath the first stars.

A vague streak of mist hovered over the field directly in front of me. An apprehension just as vague had begun to seep like fog from the evening recesses of my mind. I was in a territory of American life I had never known before and I felt the unease of the interloper.

I had read about and, I suppose, tried to imagine places like Andrewstown. I had the usual ambivalence about country towns; they are the true America, they are all Winesburgs where, beneath the placid surface, young men lust after their mothers, they are populated by rubes who get euchred by the likes of Rhett Hinkley and enjoy it.

I looked across the dimming landscape and wondered if a

private detective might be out there watching me through binoculars, waiting for me to do something crazy so that he could call up my mother and tell her about it.

I listened to the sounds that the open country made as it settled into nightfall—the distant, sporadic whish of cars on the highway more than a mile away, Will's radio in the barn broadcasting a hillbilly song of lost love and plaint.

When the milking was finished and the cows shooed into the pasture, Will took off for town and Hannibal and I went inside to get changed. While he wrestled with his necktie as if it were a snake I filled him in on the situation that prevailed—Hinkley, Will, Grace and all that.

"Motherfucker!" he roared as the necktie began to strangle him. His mood was fouler than usual.

I got off the bed, pulled his hands away from the tie and unsnarled the mess he had made. "Keep your voice down," I said. "I don't think Mrs. Timberlake holds with swearing, being a religious lady and all."

He pushed me away. "You listen to *me*, Sherbert, and you listen good. *I* don't hold with money preachers like that Hinkle."

"Hinkley," I said. "What the hell are you so upset about?"

"Preacher got all my ma's money," he retorted, glaring at me as if I'd done it.

I sat down on the bed again. It was the first time Hannibal had ever mentioned any part of his history. He was such an immense, contemporary presence in my life that I'd never even thought about his past, much less the possibility he had a mother. "What happened?" I asked.

Hannibal buttoned his suit jacket over the huge escarpment of his chest. "Nemmine what happened, smart-ass," he rumbled. "You just pay attention to what I tell you. Money preachers is a sumbitch."

The point was obviously inarguable. I wondered for a moment whether I ought to take him to Holier Than Thou that evening. But I needed him. He was my only source of transportation.

We put Mrs. Timberlake in the back seat of the Pierce-Arrow. She thanked Jesus for every rut and pothole we lurched through. When we got to the highway there was a bumper-to-bumper line of cars stretching into Andrewstown. For at least a mile across the dark countryside, automobile headlights gleamed like double strings of pearls, looping over the low hills and disappearing into valleys.

Maneuvering the Pierce-Arrow as if it were the Ark of the Covenant on wheels, Hannibal eased into the line and we proceeded in ten-mile-an-hour fits and starts through town to the Jesus Christ Church of Holier Than Thou. Lights from the tabernacle sparkled on the dark surface of the river. Young men with flashlights guided Hannibal to an empty parking space.

Swarms of people were converging on the tabernacle from the parking lot and the lamplit streets surrounding the Jesus Christ Church of Holier Than Thou. Hannibal, Mrs. Timberlake and I were compressed into the crowd moving toward the entrance and I was amazed at the dimension of the Reverend Hinkley's following. When Art first told me about him, I think I imagined Hinkley operating out of a tacky old wooden church with a few hundred of the faithful. If he wasn't the General Motors of the salvation trade, he was the biggest dealer in the tristate area.

As we moved up a carpeted ramp toward the auditorium I saw people of all shapes, sizes and plumage—women in apricot-colored raincoats with gauzy nets covering their teased hair, men in yellow or plaid jackets and string ties clasped at jowly throats by little silver ornaments; high school boys with water-slicked hair held hands with girls, and old people crept up the ramp clutching to a handrail with fingers permanently curved by the years.

There was a look of anxiety on many of the faces around us while others carried an expression of milky blandness. As Mrs. Timberlake smiled and called greetings I could tell the Holier Than Thouers from those who were there because they were scared stiff of the Bug Plague.

The auditorium was curved and sloped down to a stage hidden by a massive red curtain that had a huge cross and HOLIER THAN THOU emblazoned on it in purple sequins. There was a wooden railing dividing the lower part from the upper. "The holy people sit down there, and the invited guests up here," Mrs. Timberlake said. She beamed at us again. "Perhaps you'll make your witness this very evening, Mr. Eppe. You, too, Mr. Hannibal."

Hannibal mumbled a foul and derisory phrase as she went down the aisle to join the other saved souls in the area below the railing. My anxious gloom deepened; I sensed that Mrs. Timberlake was beginning to like me—perhaps, even, seeing me as a pious substitute for Will, who was going to burn in eternal perdition.

As we found seats in the top row the lights began to dim and the auditorium hushed. The organ music stopped.

Solemn silence.

The tabernacle was now dim as smoke. As if from a great distance, I heard a sound like the swarming of bees. After a few seconds I identified it as the first vowel being sung by a large number of people: "Aaaaaa-AAAAAAAAA . . ."

By that time the auditorium was completely dark. I heard a creaking and the swish of heavy fabric, which I took to be the parting of the sequin-splattered curtains. Suddenly the stage was filled with dazzling light. A choir stood before us dressed in white robes and purple capes covered with—you guessed it—sequins.

"Aaaaa-mazing GRACE!" boomed the choir. People in the audience applauded and some sang along as the choir went through "Amazing Grace" with two choruses.

It was a grand opening. It set just the right tone—revivalist reverence with a zingy shot of showbiz thrown in. As the choir sang, its members peeled off in fours and by the time "Amazing Grace" faded away they had all taken their places in the front of the auditorium.

"CHRISTIAN PEOPLE!" bellowed a voice over a loudspeaker system, "you are *welcome in love*! God's love! The love of Our Lord and Saviour Jesus Christ!"

"Amen," murmured voices from the section reserved for the Holier Than Thouers.

"And for those of you who are new here tonight—thirsting for safety and salvation in Jesus Christ—welcome in *special* love! The love of your brothers and sisters who have made their witness, taken Jesus into their lives and who are like the faithful of old—'The people that walked in darkness have seen a great light: they that dwell in the land of the shadow of death, upon them hath the light shined'—Isaiah Nine: Two. The faithful here tonight have got an inoculation! JESUS is the inoculation! And before this evening's over, I know we're going to have *hundreds* of the *new* faithful, hundreds who have renounced sin, fornication, loose living, and have taken Jesus into *their* lives and will never again *have anything to fear*!"

"AAA-men!" shouted somebody.

"Thank you, Jesus!" hollered another.

"We've got a wonderful program this evening," the loudspeaker voice said, "a wonderful, inspirational program that's going to thrill you and bring you to Jesus! Will you welcome, please—Brother Willy and The Messengers!"

The audience blew up into a storm of clapping and whooping as four middle-aged men in red sequined jackets loped out onto the stage, picked up electric guitars and began to play.

Brother Willy and The Messengers were familiar favorites judging from the protracted applause, the yells and nudgings in expectant glee; so was the song they belted out in the twangy, amplified beat of country-and-western. It was the ever-popular "Drop-Kick Me, Jesus, Through the Goal Posts of Life."

"How they make their money?" Hannibal mumbled.

"I don't know yet," I answered.

When The Messengers finished there was wild applause, and then one man whom I took to be Brother Willy stepped forward and held up his hand to make the hoo-rawing in the audience stop. He was tall and broad-shouldered, and his smile was a combination of just folks and the contrived charm of the professional performer.

Brother Willy told us that we were living in a dark and terrible time. The Jesus Christ Church of Holier Than Thou was fighting the greatest battle Reverend Hinkley's ministry had ever undertaken—not against the Bug Plague, because that was the will and work of God like the ten plagues delivered on Egypt that you can read about in Exodus, but against the sin which had upset God and for the salvation that was the Only Way. "Now, this crusade costs a lot of money," Brother Willy said. "It means spreading the gospel message of our Reverend all across Pennsylvania and parts of Maryland where people are losing their hair, going out of their minds and vomiting because of their sins. *And we have to reach these people!*" Brother Willy spread his red-sleeved arms wide, threw back his head and closed his eyes. "We have to get those poor sinners *here!* Where they can find Jesus! Where they can be saved by the truly spoken word!" He dropped his arms to his sides, opened his eyes and assumed a chatty, confidential manner. "Now, we all know that costs money because the word has to be spread on radio stations and in paid newspaper advertisements. And *you* know how much those old radio stations and newspapers charge—what do *they* care? They're just part of the *media*. So we want—JESUS wants—all of you to be part of this great work of salvation with your fives, your tens, your fifties . . ."

"That's how they make money," I muttered to Hannibal.

He grunted in disdain.

When Brother Willy finished the sales pitch he and the other Messengers did one more number and skipped off the stage hollering "God bless you" while the audience stomped and cheered.

"Thank you, Brother Willy and The Messengers," intoned the voice on the loudspeaker as the house lights dimmed again. "Now, witness time is coming soon, and all of you who are wondering about the greatest decision you'll ever make in your life, the decision to *take Jesus into your heart* and be free forever from sin, sickness, *even death*!!! All of you who are going to make that great decision for Christ tonight have a *double opportunity* because you can contribute to the great work of spreading the Reverend Hinkley's personal, God-given word of immunization, healing and salvation out there in that bug-plagued world . . ."

After a few more moments of that, the loudspeaker voice said it was going to introduce someone we all knew and loved and whose life was a real Christian inspiration—*Sister Cornelia!*

A spotlight speared onto the stage. At the rear a curtain covered entirely in silver sequins parted and a woman walked toward a lectern at the side of the stage. She was wearing a white dress; a gold cross glittered at her breast. Her black hair was cut short, her face was fine-boned and handsome. For a moment she gazed at the audience with large, immobile eyes.

When she began to speak I understood her role in the Holier Than Thou carnival; we had had familiar old hymns, country-and-western Jesus whoop from Brother Willy and The Messengers, a few warm-up sales pitches. Now the deeper and more serious stuff was starting. Any good show has to have a transition between the likes of Brother Willy's pranks and the delivering of the True Word. Sister Cornelia was the transition.

Her voice was soft, intense and well-bred as she began with her tale of sin, suffering and salvation. She got the script off to a promising start by telling us about her mother's death, her father's desertion of the family in Detroit, Michigan, about how she and her sister Liz were moved around from orphanages to foster homes. Liz died when a crazed Catholic child molester threw her off a porch.

"I was nineteen years old," Sister Cornelia said. "I had been married twice." She lifted her eyes to the upper tiers, where we unwitnessed sinners were sitting in the peril of our souls. "Twice," she said a second time. "My mother and sister had gone to heaven, my baby girl had died in my arms." She placed both hands on the sides of the lectern and let the enormity of it all sink in for a moment. "My dear little daughter, born out of my own wildness and lust, was taken back by God and I was—all—alone." She looked up again, but this time she wasn't seeing us. She was looking at heaven. "Dear God," she said as if she were about to break down and cry, "I—did—not *know* that you were testing me as you had tested my brother Job before me. I had *no idea*, Lord. So I fled from my misery to the greater misery of *more* sin!" She opened her eyes to give the impression that she was horrified by the story she was telling, as if she had never heard it before. "I tried to disappear! I tried to disappear into the bottle! I craved whiskey! Then gin! When that wasn't enough it was whiskey, gin—and *dope*! I was drugging my body with whiskey—gin—and dope and I was *selling* my body to get it! I had two—five—*ten* men a day! I lost count!"

There were appropriate gasps and murmurs of horror in the auditorium.

"That lady didn't know when she was well off," Hannibal grunted.

Sister Cornelia was getting to the main part now. She was in the hospital and sick. Sick was the big point—her wreckage and what saved her.

"I couldn't stop shaking," she said. "My poor ruined needle-scarred body was drying out. I tried to vomit and I couldn't. I was freezing one minute, boiling hot the next. My eyes blurred, there was a roaring in my ears! I had sores everywhere, blisters that burst, oozing poison all over me, poison that burned my skin, leaving great, raw patches of pus—"

I'll spare you the details. It was pretty hair-raising. Sister Cornelia could get more mileage out of a social disease and dope withdrawal than anybody I've ever heard in my life. It was all the more dramatic for being described in the cultivated tones of a lady who looked as if the worst that had ever happened to her was spilling a teacup in her lap.

"I was dying, and then"—she looked up at us—"and then it happened. God, in his infinite wisdom and mercy, sent his doctor of the soul to save me. One day as I lay alone in that terrible charity ward, through my fever and feeble eyes I saw a hand reach out to me. It was the hand of help. It was the hand of salvation! It was a hand that healed as the balm of Gilead—Jeremiah Eight: Twenty-two." She paused so we could all guess, as if we didn't know already. "It was the blessed hand of the Reverend Rhett Hinkley."

I thought of the watery-eyed man I had saved from being booted into next week by Will Timberlake and wondered if this interesting, histrionic lady and I were acquainted with the same Rhett Hinkley.

"And he took my infected hand in his pure one," Sister Cornelia was saying, "and he led me up the mountain. He bathed me in the healing waters—"

I had a quickie fantasy of the Reverend Hinkley and Sister Cornelia making it in a mountain spring.

"—of the spirit," she said. "And I was cured in body and soul. And I found Jesus, Jesus the healer, Jesus who loves me and waits for me in heaven.

"And I sinned no more. And that good man, that *God-touched man*, our dear Reverend, heard my witness and I was *reborn* in Jesus to a new and radiant life of health and joy!

"And I will bless Reverend Hinkley's name and praise God until the final day," Sister Cornelia went on, her voice soft but ringing. "For if he has taught me to say, 'I am holier than thou,' *he* is truly the holiest of men, for God has given him the miraculous gift of healing." She bowed her head in prayer. "And, Lord, through him I have heard Thee, I am cured—and I believe."

The spotlight went out.

I felt Hannibal squirm beside me. "S'pose *you* think that's a true story."

"Which part?" I whispered.

" 'Bout Hinkley curin' her clap."

"She didn't exactly say *that*."

"Then what *did* he do?"

I was stumped for a moment. "I guess she means he changed her life," I murmured. "He's supposed to be a faith healer."

"How'd she get rid of the clap, then?"

"Maybe she only *thought* she had it. And if he changed her life, she got over the symptoms." For some reason—perhaps it was because of Hannibal's ferocious hatred of money preachers—I was giving Hinkley the momentary benefit of the doubt.

Hannibal glowered at me in disgust.

The choir sang "Rock of Ages" in appropriate tones of reverent melancholy. Nobody was smiling now. The cheery revivalism of Brother Willy and The Messengers had been vaporized by Sister Cornelia's horrible visions of running sores and cold-turkey withdrawal, and that, I supposed, had reimplanted vivid reminders of what the Bug Plague did to you. It also left the indelible imprint of Sister Cornelia's commercial message: you could get immunization by succumbing to the Reverend Hinkley and Jesus and would, thereby, be saved from sin.

Sin is a very handy concept if you can handle it. Almost everybody except the simple-minded and ascetics living on bleak islands in stone huts believes he is guilty of something. There are two ways to rid yourself of guilt: be analyzed or be saved. If you believe in sin, you can be saved in one short jolt, which costs money but is easier on the intellect than analysis—and a lot faster. I don't know if all the newcomers at Holier Than Thou that night fully believed in the concept of sin, but they were at least hedging their bets. The Bug Plague was tearing around the countryside, and the Reverend Hinkley was batting one thousand.

"Rock of Ages" moaned and frittered out to its conclusion.

"That old gospel hymn," said the voice on the loudspeaker, "that fine old gospel hymn which reminds us that the old-time religion is as eternal as the Rock of Ages itself. Yes, indeed."

We all sat in the twilit tabernacle for a few moments supposedly pondering the durability of that old-time religion when our brother on the speaker system got going again. "Brothers and sisters, and all of you who are *going* to be our brothers and sisters in Christ," he intoned, "while the Reverend Hinkley prepares himself in communion with Jesus to bring us his *world-famous* message of hope, inspiration, *health and salvation,* the choir is going to sing 'Resting on the Ever-Lasting Arms' and our young people are going to pass among you, and we *know* that as you open your lives to Christ, you're going to open your hearts to this great ministry . . ."

Fork-out time had come. Even I felt a whiff of obligation. I hadn't had much done for my soul, but if the Reverend Hinkley was going to go to all the trouble of communing with Jesus, arranging for Brother Willy and The Messengers to drop-kick me over the goal posts of life, and have Sister Cornelia escort me into sin's chamber of horrors and out through the great gospel car wash, the least I could do was contribute a few dollars. That's what I was supposed to feel.

Doors opened on either side of the stage and the young people filed out, each one neatly dressed, shiny and meek-looking. As the choir groaned its way through "Resting on the Ever-Loving Arms," imitation gold buckets were passed along each aisle.

Hannibal shoved our bucket at me without putting anything in it. I dropped in five dollars and as I did I saw that the bucket was full of tens, twenties, fifties—and even the corner of a one-hundred-dollar bill peeking out here and there. I made a guess at the number of buckets, how much was in each one, and took into account the fact that the Reverend Hinkley was holding eight services a week. After a quick calculation I decided that he was making enough money to buy ten acres in heaven with all the bowling alleys thrown in.

The last young person disappeared through the doors, staggering under his weight of cash. The choir reached the lachrymose finale of its hymn and the auditorium went suddenly dark— pitch, disorienting black.

For thirty seconds nothing happened. Then I heard a rumbling sound, faint at first, but growing stronger. I don't know if the tabernacle was shaking, but that was the effect. The rumbling was joined by a new set of sounds—the terrifying vocabulary of human suffering; I heard shrieks, groans and wails of lamentation. The awfulness of it was compounded by that total darkness. In my mind I envisioned maimed and tormented souls crawling over a landscape of stone while scaly demons pranced around stabbing them with hot tridents.

Fearful noises from nature gone berserk were added to the human din—cracks of thunder, bashing of waves against rock, the raging of wind and the splitting of the world by earthquakes. I heard people in the auditorium crying out to Jesus and little children screaming in terror as red and white lightning jagged in split-second flashes from one side of the tabernacle to the other. It was an awesome assault on the senses, the kind of show God himself might have put on if he had some strobes and a stereo system.

Suddenly the stage exploded into brilliant light. To my astonishment the Reverend Rhett Hinkley was standing on top of a gleaming white pulpit, looking like Mount Rushmore in a gray suit and diamond stickpin.

I was astonished at the transformation in him. The regional sales manager with a burned-out soul had become the prophet Jeremiah, flushed of face, his whole being drawn together like God's coiled rattlesnake. I knew I was watching a staged and contrived performance, but there was no way that spotlights, taped sound and theatrical trappings could have changed the Rhett Hinkley I knew into the emotionally irradiated creature who now stood before me. Some inspiration had ignited his inner core with a mighty electricity.

Hinkley flung his arms wide. *"Ye winds and waters be still!!!"* he roared.

Instantly the recorded racket and strobe flashes stopped. The shrieking of babies and a few wails of evangelical fervor still echoed in the auditorium.

Slowly, deliberately, Hinkley lowered his arms. Carefully he placed his hands on either side of the pulpit. For a hushed moment his moist gaze moved over his congregation, his eyes creating the illusion that they looked into each pair of the thousands of eyes fixed on him in undivided apprehension or belief.

"Peace," he said.

His voice was low, a full octave deeper and decibels more powerful than when I had first heard it. The word rang across the auditorium, up to the highest balcony, where Hannibal and I were sitting.

" 'Though your sins be as scarlet,' " said the Reverend Rhett Hinkley in the same low, muscular voice, " 'they shall be as white as snow.' "

He perused the tabernacle again, looking from the left, across the gaping faces, to the far right. The hot lights glinted on his pomaded hair and huge wet lower lip. "Isaiah," he said. "One: Eight."

The wailing of children had stopped, the shouts of holy enthusiasm had been hushed by the unspoken order of Hinkley, the archangel of Andrewstown.

" 'Though—your—sins—be—as—scarlet,' " he repeated, " 'they shall be as *white*—as snow.' "

He paused to let us think about that for a moment; a flat Old Testament fact flatly stated.

Hinkley raised his head and peered down at us over his nose and that immense lower lip. "I have been to the mountain," he said, his voice gathering more volume. "Yes, I have been to the mountain and I have seen that white snow shining against God's Heaven! And I have been to the valley," he went on, his voice getting louder as he described his allegorical travels, "and I have seen the Rose of Sharon and the purifying waters. And I have heard the voice of God as the children of Israel heard it in Leviticus Twenty-six: Fifteen and Sixteen—'or if your soul abhor my judgments, so that ye will not do all my commandments, but that ye break my covenant' "—Hinkley's voice was now at pre-boom—" 'I also will do this unto you; I WILL EVEN APPOINT OVER YOU *TERROR, CONSUMPTION AND THE BURNING AGUE, THAT SHALL CONSUME THE EYES AND CAUSE SORROW OF HEART*'!"

He was good, he was very good. He knew how to modulate

his pitch. He obviously had a mind full of biblical quotations and could whip out exactly the right one to suit the occasion.

"Now, that's the Holy Bible," Hinkley said, lapsing back into an ordinary voice of low, stern tones. "God's word. Right there from the witness of Leviticus, that's what God said personal to the children of Israel if they broke his commandments, what he'd *do* to them if they broke his commandments." He drew a piece of paper from the breast pocket of his pearl-gray suit, unfolded it, laid it on the pulpit before him and put on a pair of reading glasses. "Now, this here," he said, "is an announcement put out this afternoon by the United States Public Health Service." Before he read, he glared at us over the tops of his glasses as if the U.S. Public Health Service were all our fault. " 'The symptoms which have appeared in the affected area during the last five weeks have now been definitely diagnosed as chemical, not bacteriological in origin. The source has not yet been identified and a new investigation has begun, based on the conclusion of a chemical origin for the outbreak.' "

Hinkley crumpled up the paper and threw it across the stage with a dramatic gesture that was supposed to indicate contempt. He took off his reading glasses. "The gummint is going to start a new investigation!" he barked. He paused to let the enormity and folly of such a move sink in. "A new investigation to track down a *chemical—a MOLLY-CULE*! The gummint is telling us this pestilence is a *MOLLY-CULE*. And the Holy Bible tells you it's what God *said* he'd do to Moses and the Israelites if they sinned! And who—are—we—going—to—believe? GOD? Or a buncha bureaucrats who say that the pestilence is caused by a MOLLY-CULE but they don't know what it is?"

"God!" a male voice shouted.

"*Thank you, Jesus!*" cried somebody else.

"*We believe God!*" Hinckley roared, his hand flashing up into spotlights, grasping a Bible. "We believe God not just because we're Christian people but because it's *common sense*! We believe that God delivered the plague because he's done it before

—where it says right here *in his holy book!*" He shook the Bible like a weapon. "He did it to Egypt with plagues of locusts, *with the smiting of the first-born!* Exodus! Twelve! Twenty-nine! God did it WITH THE MARK SET UPON CAIN! Genesis! Four! Fifteen! With RIVERS OF BLOOD that are THE WRATH OF GOD!" He waved the Bible again, brandishing it at an invisible army of U.S. Public Health Service bureaucrats and assorted other rationalists and skeptics. "Let the heathen and the non-believers *look it up!*" Hinkley yelled.

"Yes, JESUS!" screamed a female voice.

"We believe God because nothing else makes sense!" Hinkley bellowed. "What kind of MOLLY-CULE are they talking about which afflicts only wives running around with other men, husbands running around with other women and drunks spending their family's bread money, or liars, or Catholics, Methodists and Jews? Yes, my brethren, there's a METHODIST lying close to death from the plague not five miles away from this holy tabernacle! *Close to death* from a terrible pestilence that the *gummint* says is caused by a MOLLY-CULE!!!"

Hinkley put the Bible on the pulpit and smashed his fist on it. His face was purple with his exertions, his wet eyes bulging. "In the *whole history of the world* has there been a molly-cule that crawls into the eyes, brains and stomachs of *fornicators,* SIN-NERS and *UNBELIEVERS only?*"

His voice dropped. He made the good actor's sudden de-crease of volume at just the right moment in the drama. "No, my friends," he said, "there has *never*—been—a molly-cule—like *that.*" He brooded on us from the gleaming height of his pulpit, damp, powerful and stuffed to the gullet with righteousness. "What there *has* been in the whole—history—of—the—world is the wrath of God delivered on the breakers of his covenant—"

"Thank you, Jesus!" somebody cried.

That cry yanked my mind back to Mrs. Timberlake, whose spirit had been ushered into the realms of serenity by this Bar-num of the Bible Belt. I'm not scornful of emotion's power to convey the truth. I heard more real feeling uttered in the rages and despairings of Craigie Glen's unbalanced population than in any of my life's other settings.

But as I sat in the balcony and felt the fever of fear and oratory-ignited belief growing in the people around me, I realized something I had never thought of before: emotion can be contrived and still appear to convey a truth—if you need a truth badly enough. Mrs. Timberlake's loneliness had made her believe that Rhett Hinkley was God's mailman. The frightened and guilty crowd perspiring and leaning forward in eagerness around me needed to believe because the plague was real, their lives were imperfect and Hinkley knew exactly how to connect it all together. That night I discovered demagoguery and it was making me both angry and sorry about Mrs. Timberlake, who was a nice lady and deserved better.

"God's wrath was delivered on the Dark Ages when the Great Plague wiped out the sinners of Europe!" Hinkley bellowed. "Let 'em look *that* up!"

I felt like bellowing back that the seventeenth century wasn't exactly a dark age.

"Let 'em look up what happened in America after our soldier boys came home from the Great War, corrupted by hard liquor and French women!" Hinkley bawled. "There was a MYSTERIOUS PLAGUE that killed *MILLIONS!*"

Mysterious, bullshit! I roared back mentally. It was an epidemic of *flu* in 1919.

"And here it is happening again!" Hinkley yelled. "A plague! A PESTILENCE! *The—wrath—of—God!!*"

"Save us, Jesus!" somebody wailed from the top balcony.

To hell with it, I told myself. I was there as a reporter, not a participant. I decided to just settle back and observe the spectacle.

"The wrath of God," Hinkley was saying, dropping his voice to its low, ominous and warning croak. "And who has earned that wrath?"

The auditorium was silent. I looked around. In the upper

tiers, the unwitnessed wore gloomy and apprehensive expressions. *They* had brought down the wrath of God, they thought; you could imagine their minds compiling lists of sins for which they needed forgiveness in order to be saved from the Bug Plague.

"And who," he cried so suddenly that it made me jump, "who *doesn't* deserve God's wrath? Who *hasn't* had the fever and the terrible torment of invisible demons crawling on his skin, the nightmares, *the burning ague that consumes the eyes, the consumption—WHO?*" His last words slashed through the auditorium in a declamatory yowl: "*WHO?*"

As if by a signal—hell, it *was* a signal—every one of the Holier Than Thouers sitting below the railing rose to his feet.

Up on his pulpit Rhett Hinkley appeared to have gone clean out of his mind. The sight of his rising followers slammed him into high gear. "*The saved are safe!*" He flailed his arms and his greasy hair fell over his forehead.

"Thank you, Jesus!" roared the Holier Than Thouers.

"*The faithful are healthy!*" Hinkley thundered, his ascot askew and his eyes bulging as if holy passion were going to pop them out of his head.

A woman two rows down from me leaped to her feet screaming, "*Save me, Jesus!* Louanne made me do it! I took the whole six hundred dollars! I'm sorry, Jesus, so sorry . . ."

"Bring that woman to me!" Hinkley yelled. "*Bring her to Jesus!*"

"Thaaaaaaank you, Lord!"

More people in the upper section were getting out of their seats and moving into the aisles. A fat man got up, grunting. A woman beside him grabbed his shirt but he wrenched free. "Don't touch me, Angel!" he yelled. He started down the aisle, stumbled into the railing and fell. He began to claw at his garments, screaming that horrible beings were crawling all over him.

"*Bring him down!*" Hinkley bawled. "*He shall be cleaned of sin!!!*"

"Yeeees—Jesus!"

Three Holier Than Thou men had climbed over the railing,

picked up the shrieking fat man and were lugging him down toward the stage. He was ripping his shirt to pieces and tearing out clumps of his hair, trying to rid himself of invisible bugs.

Rhett Hinkley threw his head back, spread his arms and shouted with all his might, "FETCH—THEM—TO ME! BRING 'EM RIGHT DOWN INTO YOUR LOVIN' ARMS— JESUS!"

The crowd in the auditorium swirled like a cattle stampede getting ready to turn on itself. All of them were watching the stage as they pushed and struggled past one another. The three Holier Than Thouers had carted the howling fat man to the white pulpit. They dropped him on the floor, where he rolled around, grabbing at his crotch, clawing his face and forearms, screeching that he was covered with invisible little fiends. His shirt was in tatters and one of his shoes had fallen off.

Rhett Hinkley leaped from the pulpit like the Archangel Michael going for a fifth-round knockout against Satan. He grabbed the fat man beneath the armpits and hauled him to his knees. "*Confess your sin!*" Hinkley roared.

"Get 'em offa me!" the fat man shrieked, flopping and scratching. "GET 'EM OFF!"

"*Confess!*"

"I been fu-fu-fu—"

"*Confess!*"

The fat man looked up into the balcony. "I'm sorry, Angel!" he wailed, tears spurting from his flesh-ringed eyes. "I been cheatin'! I been doin' it—Get 'em offa me, *pleeeeease!*"

"CLEANSE YOUR SOUL!" Hinkley bellowed, shaking him.

"I been doin' it with this other lady—*eeee-YAHK!*"

Hinkley clasped the sweating, tattered mass of hysterical flesh to his waist. "Leave him, Satan," he boomed, "*take him, Jesus!*" He cast his gaze heavenward, closed his eyes and dilated his nostrils. "Forgive his sin, Jesus! See his sorrow, Jesus! *Cast out this man's affliction, Lord!*"

He let go of the fat man, who crashed backward onto the stage.

The noise in the auditorium hushed abruptly. Both the Holier Than Thouers and the unwitnessed held their breaths and watched.

The fat man was sitting like a bear on the stage—legs spread, fleshy arms dangling, rolls of beef bulging beneath his undershirt. His eyes were glazed, perspiration poured in rivulets down his red face as he gasped for breath.

Hinkley got up into his pulpit again. "Be clean!" he commanded.

The fat man raised his head and looked up at the Reverend Rhett. He seemed dazed.

"Say your name," Hinkley ordered.

"Bubba Johnson."

"Jesus has forgiven you, Bubba Johnson! Rise, be clean— *rejoice in Jesus Christ!*"

Bubba Johnson held out his arms and looked at them. He felt his head and ran his hands over his globular, sweaty face.

He looked back up at Hinkley. "They went away," he said in wonder.

"*Rejoice in Jesus Christ!*" Rhett Hinkley bellowed again.

"*Thank you, Jesus!*" whooped the Holier Than Thouers.

"Thank you, Jesus!" Bubba Johnson yelled. He gathered his fat legs under him and stood up, tattered shirt hanging from his upper body, one shoe off, one shoe on.

Hinkley flung his arms wide again. "*Fetch them to me, Jesus!*" he screamed. "*THE WRATH OF GOD PASSES OVER THIS HOUSE! HALLELUJAH!*"

The tabernacle erupted like Old Faithful spouting forth the whole world's guilt. The people in the upper rows who had been mesmerized by the curing of Bubba Johnson burst forward, flinging themselves down the aisles into the smiling, hand-offering upward surge of Holier Than Thouers. I saw old ladies fall, I heard screams of fear and joy. Grown men with tears gushing down their faces belted each other and climbed over the railing as if the devil himself was thundering down from the dark recesses of the balcony and Jesus Christ was waiting beside Rhett Hinkley in the white light below.

The choir began to shout out "The Old Rugged Cross." Holier Than Thouers were reeling back, each clutching the hand of a repentant sinner, and Bubba Johnson was dancing around, hollering "Hallelujah!" High on his pulpit, Rhett Hinkley was still shouting to Jesus. He was livid, wet, disheveled, in an ecstasy of self-exaltation.

The side doors burst open and the shiny young people poured out, each shoving a golden bucket into the mass hurtling and clawing toward the stage and salvation. Money started to fly around, handfuls of coins and crumpled bills showered into the buckets while little children began to shriek in terror.

I couldn't hear Rhett Hinkley's words over the tumult, and if I had, they probably would have made neither sense nor any difference. Hinkley's work was done, he had thrown dusty handfuls of fear and a psychological pseudomiracle across a human acreage that was more than ready to receive them.

I saw Mrs. Timberlake, floating in holy bliss and smiling, working her way up the human-choked center aisle; she was looking straight at me, holding out her hand, coming for me.

I leaped out of my seat and stumbled over an old man who was wiping the steam off his glasses and muttering "Sweet Jesus."

I got to my feet and ran.

For several minutes I stood in the parking lot, dippy with panic, my head full of thoughts about fraudulence and God. The air was cool, the lights of the parking lot gleamed on immobile rows of cars. I was beginning to calm down a little when Hannibal came out of the Jesus Christ Church of Holier Than Thou. He crossed the parking lot and, for once, he seemed almost concerned—that is, the look on his face indicated he'd settle for breaking just one of my legs instead of both of them. "How come you run off?" he demanded.

"I couldn't stand it."

"First sensible thing you said in a week," he grunted. He looked at the tabernacle looming above us. "That's one sumbitch," he said. "Gone stop him dead."

My alarm flared again at the word "dead." "There isn't any way to stop him," I said. "He isn't breaking any laws."

"He's lyin'. Him and that Cornelia woman both."

"There's nothing illegal about lying unless you're under oath."

"So how come you gone put him on the teevee?"

"Because he *is* a son of a bitch," I said. "If I can find out the real truth about him, get a lot of facts and have them broadcast on television, maybe people will stop believing in him."

Hannibal's face resumed its familiar look of murderous contempt. As he glared down at me I couldn't decide whether he was expressing his skepticism about the procedures of democracy or a general disdain for human nature. Maybe both. "Now you bein' a asshole again," he said. "I'm talkin' 'bout stoppin' that Hinkle and *you're* talkin' 'bout *talkin'* 'bout him."

"Hinkley," I retorted. I was beginning to get mad again. "If you do something violent to him, they'll put you in jail and it'll serve you right! Nobody gave you a license—"

"Don't tell me 'bout what I'm gone do," he snarled. "You just go around playin' teevee reporter and *I'll* take care of Mistah Rhett Hinkle!"

I was about to enlighten him as to the rules and regulations against swinging down from the trees and pounding disagreeable people into a bloody pulp when I saw Will Timberlake coming through the rows of cars. "Thought you'd have had a gutful about now," he said.

"It's pretty God-awful," I answered.

"Scared ole Sherbert outa his skin," Hannibal said.

Will spat and grinned. "Didn't convert either one of you guys, huh?"

Hannibal said "Shee-yit."

"I fixed it up for you to see Betty Darius from the bank

tonight," Will said. "And the Public Health Service guy is over at Tom Dawson's house."

"I want to talk to him, too," I said.

"I figured. He's expecting you."

We got into the Pierce-Arrow and drove through the cool, empty streets. The center of town looked like a deserted stage set. It was illuminated by spaced pools of streetlight which softened everything and created the illusion that Andrewstown had fallen asleep long, long ago.

Following Will's instructions, Hannibal turned up a side street and stopped in front of a small Victorian house. We got out, crossed the sidewalk and went up three steps onto the porch. There was a frosted glass panel set in the front door. Will knocked.

The porch light switched on and the door was opened by a tall young guy in a black turtleneck sweater. At first glance he was ominously dramatic—he had crisp black hair, a black beard and gray eyes that seemed intense with either brooding or wrath. But the drama crumbled when he spoke. His voice was low, approaching mumbly-sullen like a punished child's. " 'Lo, Will," he said.

Before Will could answer, a black Labrador retriever hurtled out of the hall, nearly knocking me over. As the dog shot across the porch Hannibal grabbed him by the scruff of the neck and lifted him in the air.

"Nice catch," Will said.

Inside, Hannibal put down the squirming Labrador, and Will introduced us to Tom Dawson. "I'm glad to meet you, Reverend," I said.

"You might as well call me Tom," Dawson answered. "Will says you've been at Holier Than Thou this evening."

"As long as we could stand it," I said.

Dawson gave me a look with those curious eyes and then led us into the living room.

His house was spare, neat and polished. The wood floors

gleamed, the walls were painted stark white; two canvas-backed chairs stood in the living room with an ammunition chest between them as a table. Over the mantel there was a West Point class picture and a photograph of a football team with a black-haired, beardless young player in it who could have been Tom Dawson. Above the pictures I saw the insignia of an Army division. I felt as if I were in a bunker instead of in a parsonage.

A skinny, tired-looking man in rimless glasses stood up. "This is Jerry Moss," Dawson said. "USPHS."

Jerry Moss, USPHS, shook hands and sat down again. "Tom's letting us use his house as a headquarters during the emergency," he said.

The Labrador came ambling in from the hall. "And this is Croaker," Dawson said, more as if he were talking to the dog than to us.

"Hi, Croaker," I said. The Labrador gave a slobbering grunt of delight as I patted his head. "How come he can't go out?"

Tom Dawson sat down on the ammunition chest and looked at his dog. "He's a chaser," he answered. "He chases everything that moves. Dogs, cats, cars, squirrels."

Croaker reared up and put his front paws on Hannibal's stomach. Hannibal rumpled his ears and mumbled something. Croaker groaned in pleasure and lashed his tail back and forth. They were already talking to each other. Maybe, I thought, in the remnant of my peeve at Hannibal, they could go out to the highway and chase cars together.

No such luck. Hannibal pushed Croaker away with an uncharacteristic gentleness and the rest of us sat down. "How're you coming in tracking down the cause of the epidemic?" I asked.

"The goddamn government makes you do everything by the book," Jerry Moss answered. "The first official theory was a bacteriological source, so we followed that track until it petered out. *I've* always thought it was chemical—I've seen symptoms like these before and they're usually associated with DDT. You get them in people who work with pesticides. But you try telling that to the bureaucratic jerks I work for. So *now*, after four weeks of chasing a virus, we're starting all over again looking for a chemical source, which we should have done in the first place."

"Where are you going to begin?" I asked.

"Well, DDT is banned, so we have to find something of a similar chemical configuration," Moss said. "The biggest employer around here is a tire factory about ten miles outside of Andrewstown. A lot of men who work out there have gotten sick. That's where we'll start."

"I guess you've questioned all the victims."

"Well, Christ, of course we have. When we were on the bacteriological track we tried to find something common to all of them, something they'd eaten, water supply, somewhere they'd all been. No dice."

Hannibal was listening with a scrunched-up expression of concentration on his face.

"Are you sure they were leveling with you?" I asked.

"I don't know why the idiots would lie," Moss said. "They were the ones with the biggest stake in finding the cause of this thing. Now we've got to interview all of them all over again and try to dig up something that infects like a pesticide."

"How many people got sick?"

"One hundred and twenty-nine that we know about as of this afternoon."

"Have any recovered?"

"About forty."

Hannibal shifted in his chair, clasped his hands together and scowled at Moss. "There's somethin' them sick folks ain't tellin' you," he grunted.

"If there is," Moss answered, "I can't do a goddamn thing about it. The government can't *make* them talk. They've got their civil rights even if it kills them."

"Maybe the *gummint* can't make 'em talk," Hannibal said.

Moss, Tom, Will and I looked at him. Moss raised an eyebrow.

"You got a list of dudes that got well?" Hannibal asked Moss.

"Just men? Sure. What the hell are you getting at?"

"You'n me gone take a walk around the block," Hannibal said.

"Look, I hate the goddamn rules, but—"

"Ain't no rule 'gainst a man takin' a walk, is there?"

Moss stared at him for a moment. "If there is, I don't want to know about it."

"Shake ass," Hannibal said.

He baffled me. Despite our lengthening association I didn't know all that much about Hannibal except that he could fix cars, hated money preachers and had an antisocial disposition. I was pretty sure, though, that epidemiology wasn't one of the big interests of his life. I wondered what the hell he was up to, and I was pissed off at him all over again for butting into my investigative reporting.

After Hannibal and Moss went out for their walk, Will left to meet his mother at Holier Than Thou. Tom Dawson said he would walk me over to Betty Darius' place. He snapped a chain leash on Croaker's collar and we started off through the shadowy streets to the center of town.

Periodically Croaker made lunges at the dark lawns where, presumably, chaseable creatures were moving about. Each time he did, Dawson wordlessly yanked the leash up short.

He was just as wordless with me for the first block we walked. There was a dark vapor around Tom Dawson's personality that repelled conversation. But I had to talk to him because he was my only real contact. "Do you know Hinkley personally?" I asked as we crossed a street.

Dawson nodded. In the lamplight I could read no expression on his bearded face or in those gray eyes. "He and I can't avoid each other," he said. "This is a small town. We're the only two Protestant clergymen here."

"Do you think he's really an ordained minister?"

"I doubt it."

"Is there anything you can tell me about him?"

We were moving into the shadows of the evening again.

Dawson yanked Croaker back from another leap at a murky lawn. "Nobody knows much about Hinkley," he said. "He came here in 1971 and took out an eight-hundred-dollar mortgage on an old church. Then he moved to that place he's got now in 1977. It was a movie theater. He added on offices."

"So he was making a lot of money by then?"

My question was stupid and answered itself. Tom Dawson didn't bother to reply. I had just asked it to keep the talk going. "Do you know anything about his past? Where he came from?"

"He says he's from Oklahoma. I don't have the time or the means to investigate him."

We were approaching Main Street. "You told Art Olsen that you had some inside information," I said.

Tom Dawson stopped. "I said I thought something was going to happen."

I looked at his face in the half light. I suddenly had the feeling that this man was a damaged piece of clockwork beneath his impressive appearance. The black, square beard became, in my eyes, a disguise; he looked more anxious than wrathful. "What *do* you think is going to happen?"

Dawson looked at me. "Maybe you could find out."

Jesus wept, I told myself; he's my principal source in Andrewstown and he doesn't know a damn thing. "Tom," I said, "what's this inside information you've got?"

He took a deep breath. "I know for a fact that Hinkley made two trips out of town last month. One was to Pittsburgh. I don't know where he went on the other."

"That doesn't prove anything," I said.

"It meant he had to cancel several services," Dawson answered as if he were desperate to persuade me. "Canceling services costs him money."

"Anything else?"

He shook his head.

"Do you know anything about Holier Than Thou's finances?" I asked.

Tom Dawson shook his head again.

Great, I told myself. I've been sent to Andrewstown to whip up this great big exposé of Holier Than Thou, and the only thing my main contact can tell me for sure is that Rhett Hinkley took a trip to Pittsburgh.

"I'm not cooperating with you because Hinkley's an evangelical," Dawson said. "I want you to understand that. I'm an evangelical myself."

"Tom," I said, "why *did* you call Art Olsen?"

"The television station's been watching Hinkley," he said. "They sent a reporter out here last year to look around. It's important to me that they really get the goods on him before it's too late."

"Too late for what? Why are you so anxious to have him investigated?" I asked.

Tom looked toward Main Street. In the soft, reflected light from the center of Andrewstown, the look of desperation on his face was unmistakable. "I want the fear of God thrown into Rhett Hinkley," he said.

So, there it was. The television station and I were being used to run Hinkley out of town, maybe even have him indicted; we were being used by his competition, a second-rate evangelist who was so inept at the trade that he had to drive a milk truck part-time to make his living. "Well, thanks," I said. "I'll be in touch."

"Use my house anytime," he said. We shook hands. "Betty Darius lives over the hardware store. Turn left on Main, two blocks, to number thirty-eight." Dawson pulled Croaker around and walked up the dark residential street.

I made my way to the center of town. I didn't know whether to pity Tom Dawson because he was such a pathetic nerd or be angry because he'd conned Art Olsen into sending me to Andrewstown under false pretenses that served his ambitions. Either way, my hope that Tom would start me on a burrow into the hidden affairs of Rhett Hinkley had just gone bloop. I had nothing to show for my first day's work and I felt sorry for Andrewstown. In matters of religion it was trapped between a bearded dismal and the Greatest Show on Earth.

I walked two blocks up Main Street to number 38 and rang the bell in a narrow doorway. Lights went on over a stairwell inside and the door buzzed. I pushed it open and went up.

A fat lady was standing at the top before the entrance to a small apartment. When I say *fat* I don't mean your ordinary blubber-prone American. This lady was certifiably fat; it drooped from her upper arms, made necklaces of creased flesh at her throat, engulfed her chin, spread her pale-blue slacks to the breaking point across her vast pelvis and created permanent gaps between the strained buttons of her sleeveless blouse. She was holding a beer can. "Hi," she said.

She was so immense that I felt as if I were confronted by somebody with a condition. It tends to inhibit your conversation for a moment.

"You're Will's friend."

"Yes, ma'am," I said. "My name is Sherborne Eppe and I work for the television station in Pittsburgh."

She held out her hand. Mine didn't quite fit all the way around it, but she had a firm, hearty grip. "Come on in," she said. "Want a beer?"

"Yes, please," I said.

I followed her into a small cluttered living room. There was a daybed, an easy chair that looked crushed and defeated, newspapers on the floor, and a TV set, alive but with the sound turned off.

I sat down on the daybed while Betty Darius went into a little kitchen. I heard the refrigerator door whump shut and she reappeared with a beer can. She ripped off the tab top, handed me the can and sat down in the chair. I could almost hear it groan.

"Must be exciting working in television," she said.

"I haven't been doing it for long," I said, taking a large swig of beer. "It's kind of dopey."

"How dopey," she said, leaning forward.

"The people you work for . . ." I shrugged. My inhibitions

were dissipating as I looked across the little room at this fat lady. Incongruously, she was pretty. She had straight white-blond hair cut short. It fell in bangs over her forehead, almost reaching to her sparkling hazel eyes. That round face was bisected by a slender nose with slightly flared nostrils. Her mouth smiled easily, collaborating with her eyes to radiate sensuous good humor.

"Go on," she said, "tell me about the people you work for. I've never heard anything about television—I mean, behind the scenes, as they say."

So I told her all about the collection of zombies and dip sticks who ran the television station—and about Barbara, too. She laughed enormously when I described Big Ned and Carlos, and asked if Barbara was my girl friend.

"No," I said. "We're just friends."

"You're a good-looking guy. How old are you?"

"Twenty-four."

"I'll bet you do have a girl somewhere."

I nodded. "In Rhode Island."

"Go on," she said, "tell me about her."

"You like life stories, don't you?"

She nodded. "Love 'em. Don't you want to talk about your girl?"

"Well, I don't want to disappoint you . . ."

"Aw, that's all right. Listen, are you hungry?"

I hadn't had dinner and I was. I followed her into the kitchen. Her own dinner dishes were drying on a rack beside the sink. She got a platter of salami, sandwich ham, cheese, sausage and pickles out of the refrigerator. She took a loaf of German rye from a tin bread box, found a head of lettuce, mayonnaise, ketchup and mustard and made two huge three-decker sandwiches. She opened two more beers and we went back to the living room.

"Will said you might be able to help me," I told her.

"Maybe."

"You work in the bank, don't you?"

She had a mouthful of sandwich again, so she limited herself to nodding. When her jaw was free, she said, "You know Will long?"

"I just met him today," I said. "His horse fainted in the road, and my friend and I—"

Betty Darius laughed and shook her head. "That horse. Crazy things are always happening to Will Timberlake. Did he tell you about the Model A?"

I shook my head.

"Will was my boyfriend," she said.

"He told me."

She raised her head. "What did he say? I mean, about us— him and me?"

"Just that you were his girl friend when he used to come up here in the summer to visit his uncle."

She smiled slightly—sadly, I thought. "What did he say we were now?"

"Buddies," I said.

She ate the rest of her gargantuan sandwich in silence, fin- ished her beer and wiped her lips with a paper napkin. "That's Will," she said.

"What's Will?" I asked.

"You haven't finished your sandwich," she answered.

"I'm working on it," I said. I had forgotten all about the finances of the Reverend Hinkley for a moment. "I like life stories too," I told her.

She looked up at me and smiled suddenly. "I'll tell you what Will told you. He said, 'I used to screw Betty Darius when we were kids.' " She looked at me. "Isn't that what he said?"

"Something like that," I answered, feeling ashamed for Will, for myself.

"He did screw me," she said. "It was my first sex and the best I've ever had." She took a drag on her cigarette. "You still haven't finished your sandwich. I'll bet you don't like my cook- ing."

"Sure I do. It's just that it's a big sandwich."

"Here," she said, "hand it over."

I passed my plate across to her. She put her cigarette in an ashtray and picked up the remaining half of my sandwich. "My first mistake was really falling for Will," she said, taking a bite. "I mean, I *really* fell for him. I got past the stage—you know, the first skyrockets and falling stars of being in love. I really got to know him and understand him. I *still* loved him. Even more."

"What happened?"

"Then I made my second big mistake. I *told* him I was crazy about him."

The living room was silent. On the television screen a carful of 1938 gangsters was careening silently around a corner; they were firing off revolvers that made no sound.

"What do you want me to do for you?" Betty asked.

I was still back contemplating her lost love. She had either said all there was to say about it or had abruptly decided that she had confessed enough.

"I'm investigating the Reverend Hinkley," I began. "Will said you know about his accounts at the bank where you work."

"I do know," she said. "It's illegal for me to talk to you about it."

I nodded.

She leaned back, arms dangling over the sides of the mortally wounded easy chair, looking at me with the lovely eyes of a girl in the face of a woman who eats too much. "Want a piece of chocolate cake?" she asked. "Fresh. Made it this afternoon."

I was full of beer and sandwich, but I'm also a chocolate junkie. "Thanks," I said. "Yes."

She got out of her chair, went into the kitchen and came back in a few minutes with a tray. On it were two plates holding the two biggest pieces of chocolate cake I've ever seen, and two more cans of beer. I picked up a fork and tasted the cake. It was a chocolate freak's dream.

"Why are you after Hinkley?" Betty asked after she'd resettled herself in her chair.

"My news director thinks he's a crook."

"Sure he's a crook. You don't have to know anything about his bank accounts to see he's a crook. Holier Than Thou—what kind of a name is that for a church?"

Betty finished her cake. "Want another piece?"

Mine was finished too. "I couldn't," I said. "It's terrific. Give me a rain check. I'm so full I don't know if I can even walk."

Betty laughed. It sounded like silver coinage in her fleshy throat. "You know what Will Timberlake needs?"

"Tell me."

"The love of a good woman. I know that sounds corny, but it's true. He needs a woman who can be strong for him." She finished her beer. "Do you know Grace Hinkley?"

"I've met her," I said. I didn't mention that I liked her.

"She's a mouse," Betty said. "A poor little thing. There just isn't much to her."

There didn't seem to be a lot I could say to that. It was Betty's frustrated opinion.

On the television screen a pretty blond woman was feeding a pack of dogs from a huge red bag of some dry food. She was smiling at the dogs, then at the camera.

"When you look like I do," Betty said, "your imagination goes. You can't even have daydreams because you *know* they could never come true, not for a woman who weighs two hundred and eighty pounds." She lit a fresh cigarette. "I've got a boyfriend," she said quietly. "He isn't much. An ugly woman hasn't got much choice. The poor slob thinks he loves me, though." She exhaled. "He's weak, too." She smiled at me. "He was going to come over tonight. That's why I asked Will to send *you* over. I thought that finding me talking to another guy might stir up my boyfriend's life a little. I'm still a woman even though I look like a mountain."

"Do you love your boyfriend?"

She shook her head. "He's better than nobody. Did you know that Will was in the penitentiary?"

I nodded. My mind was drifting back to what I had come for.

"I used to go see him every month. That was ten years after—" She stopped abruptly.

"Betty," I said to fill up the pause that followed her broken sentence, "—is it all right if I call you Betty?"

"Sure it is."

"What can you tell me about Hinkley's money?"

She got up from the chair, put the plates and beer cans on the the tray and took them out to the kitchen. "Want some coffee?" she called.

"No, thanks."

"How about an Alka-Seltzer?"

"Not a bad idea," I answered.

She laughed and came back to the living room with a fresh beer in her hand. She went over to the window and looked down onto the street. I could hear cars moving in a steady stream. The service at Holier Than Thou was over, and the old and new faithful were going home.

"I could tell you things about Hinkley's money," Betty finally said.

I took out my notebook, excited at the prospect of getting my first inside information.

Betty Darius turned around and looked across the room at me. "But I'm not going to," she said.

I was stunned. "Why not?"

"Because if I tell you and you put it on television Hinkley might go to jail. He'd certainly be finished in Andrewstown. Either way, he'd be gone and Will would marry that mouse."

"But—"

"I'm sorry, honey," she said.

I sat listening to the traffic below. I couldn't refute her logic, even though its results made me feel robbed.

"You never told me about the Model A," I said.

She laughed. "It was during the second summer. There was a dirt road that led into the lake through the woods, an old logging road on a hill. Most people didn't know about it. Will and I drove out there after a dance. We went skinny-dipping . . ." She paused and smiled again at the memory of it all. "I weighed a hundred and nine that summer. I was really something. We'd put our clothes in the car and were up in the woods on a place where the pine needles made it like a mattress. Will was just about to come when the brakes let go on the Model A and it went banging down the hill right into the lake." She laughed again. "Bet it's still there."

I got up. I imagine I sighed because she looked at me compassionately. "No hard feelings, kid?"

You couldn't have any hard feelings toward a lady like that. I shook my head. "Thanks for the dinner and the conversation," I said.

I went downstairs and stood for a long time watching the cars file past on their way from the Jesus Christ Church of Holier Than Thou, back to the world as God actually made it.

Twelve

I JUST
MIGHT BE JESUS

ON MY SECOND MORNING at the Timberlake farm I awoke
to the sight of sunshine and the sounds of agriculture. Chickens
were awing and tutting over their new eggs, a rooster periodically crowed as if he'd done the laying; from the barn came the
roar of a generator used to power the milking machines, and an
occasional moo from the milkees. The din of country life and my
disappointment at having discovered exactly nothing about
Rhett Hinkley were so great that I couldn't get back to sleep.

I ran a bath and lay in it for a long time trying to think of
what to do. Sunlight splashed over the wallpaper and shimmered
beneath the water like the ghosts of silvery fish on my legs. I was
getting depressed, my fantasies about becoming a great TV reporter were being successfully assaulted by the undeniable fact
that I knew zilch about how to go about the reporter's trade.

After an hour of cooling water and self-disgust I got dressed
and went downstairs. Mrs. Timberlake and Hannibal sat facing
each other at the kitchen table. It was like finding the Incredible
Hulk and Grandma Moses having morning coffee together.

Forgetting—or maybe not caring—that I had fled from her the night before, Mrs. Timberlake looked up and smiled her mom smile at me. "Good morning, Mr. Eppe. I was just telling Mr. Hannibal about the Rices. They're a Negro family that the Reverend Hinkley witnessed three years ago. They moved to Memphis. The Rice family were nice, clean, respectable colored people and we enjoyed them very much."

"Ain't that somethin'?" Hannibal said.

"That's something," I answered. I felt a special urgency to get us out of there before Hannibal threw the refrigerator through the house wall.

After breakfast he and I went outside. The black-and-white cows were ambling into the pasture behind the barn, lashing flies off their flanks with long swishes of their tails. Will was heaving milk cans onto his pickup truck. The sun was already hot, his face was perspiring and his forearms were knotted with exertion as he lifted the cans. Hannibal went over, picked up a milk can in each hand and put them on the truck.

Will pulled out a blue kerchief and wiped his forehead. "You're a pretty strong fella," he said. "One of these days we'll get drunk and have a fistfight. Bet I could take you."

"Ain't no sense in fistfightin' less you mean it," Hannibal grunted. He pulled a cigar from his shirt pocket, lit it and walked over to the Pierce-Arrow.

"He doesn't like me much," Will said. "Still, I could whip him."

I got into the Pierce-Arrow. Hannibal was sitting behind the wheel, gnawing and puffing on his cigar.

"I didn't know you smoked," I said.

"Lot you don't know," he said, starting the engine, "and when you *do* know something you shoot youself in the foot with it."

"I know you've got a list of men who've recovered from the plague and you're going to threaten information out of them. That's what you and that guy from the Public Health Service are doing."

Hannibal steered the car up onto the grassy edge of the road to avoid a long rut filled with muddy water. "What you *don't* know ain't gone hurt you," he said.

Safety through ignorance, I thought bitterly, he's as bad as Hinkley.

We had no more exchanges until he dropped me off at the top of Main Street. I decided to take one last crack at him. "Who are you going to beat up first, Bubba Johnson?"

"You tend your own business, smart-ass," he said. "When I've a mind I'll tell you *my* business and you can put it on the teevee." He drove off. Big deal. I'd brought him to Andrewstown on my mission to expose Rhett Hinkley, he'd taken over the war against Hinkley with techniques that weren't in the Geneva Convention and he'd relegated me to the status of his chronicler.

I looked at my watch. It was only seven forty-five—I had just under three hours to kill before I was supposed to see the Reverend Rhett. I walked down Main Street toward the river, got myself a newspaper from a vending machine and went into a coffee shop. I read the headlines, glanced at the sports page and had a look at the funnies—but they were as desperate as Spider Man or as somber as Mary Worth and I was feeling dented enough with frustration. I sipped my coffee, put down the newspaper and stared through the plate-glass window. I began to go tingly cold.

Main Street was almost deserted. The only human face in sight was behind the front wheel of a blue Plymouth with a New York State license plate. It was the face of a patient, middle-aged man. He was smoking a cigarette and watching the coffee shop. I was the only person in the coffee shop.

I remembered Beth's warning about a private detective following me. My cold tingles congealed into a small solar plexus–gnaw of alarm. I raised the newspaper.

But I couldn't sit for more than two and a half hours holding a newspaper in front of my face to avoid the gaze of a man in a blue Plymouth. I paid for my coffee and went out into the street. The spring sun was glittering on the breeze-mussed surface of the river. The man in the blue Plymouth had suddenly developed an all-consuming interest in the sky as I looked straight at him; he was peering at it through the windshield of his car.

I began to walk toward the river, my alarm turning into irritation. I felt the way I did during all those years at Craigie Glen, going around trying to act hugely normal—then because the psychiatrists and aides were watching me, now because a man who had probably been hired by my mother was watching me.

My irritation had turned into defiance as I reached the parking lot of the Jesus Christ Church of Holier Than Thou. I stopped. One of the doors to the auditorium was open.

I looked back up the street at the blue Plymouth. I decided to ignore that intrusion from my past and concentrate on the present. I turned around and looked at the open door to Rhett Hinkley's Cash and Christ emporium. If I went in there, poked around and got caught, my mother's detective would have another juicy item for his dossier on my lunacy. If, on the other hand, I went in, found something and *didn't* get caught, I'd be a hard-nosed, tough investigative reporter doing his job.

So be it, I thought. I walked across the empty parking lot toward the open door, tearing a piece of paper from my notebook. I went in. A bony-faced young woman in coveralls was vacuuming the ramp that led up to the auditorium. She switched off the machine. "Whaddya want?"

I looked at my piece of notebook paper. "Man named Hinkley."

"He isn't here."

"I'm from Dashford Sound Systems over in Johnstown," I said. "We got a call about something being wrong with the stereo."

The cleaning woman—who looked as if she hadn't smiled since her fourth birthday—shrugged. "I wouldn't know what that is."

"The sound system," I said. "I'm the guy who installed it."

"Know where it is?"

"Sure," I said. "Backstage."

"Then go fix it," she said. She switched on the vacuum cleaner again.

All you need to gain entrance to anyplace is the appearance of belonging there. Appearing to be a man who could fix stereo systems, I walked past her, entered the upper tier of the auditorium, descended to the stage, crossed it and slipped through the silver-sequined curtain.

It was dark, but after a few seconds my eyes began to adjust to the gloom. I saw a large door with a bar handle at the back of the stage. I walked over and opened it. Dim daylight came down a long carpeted corridor. I stepped into the office section of the Jesus Christ Church of Holier Than Thou and let the door silently close behind me.

I looked at my watch. It was ten past eight. I figured I had twenty minutes before the office staff started coming in.

I walked down the corridor, reading the nameplates on the doors until I found one that proclaimed the office of the Reverend Hinkley.

My heart was pounding as I went in. It was a large office, carpeted wall to wall and done up in that blandness which, I have subsequently learned, is a décor designed for people who want to appear earnest and inoffensive to their visitors—preachers, insurance agents, dentists and the like. The walls of Rhett Hinkley's office were covered with dark-stained imitation pine paneling; at one end the wall was dominated by a life-sized portrait of Hinkley in his regional-sales-manager incarnation. An American flag stood beside the portrait, and at the other end of the office, Hinkley's desk was positioned so that he could spend all day staring at himself and the flag.

I sat down at the desk and looked at my watch. It was eight-seventeen. I tried the drawers on either side of the desk, but they were locked. I wasn't about to push my luck by prying them open. I had a fleeting recollection of the night I tried that at Great Lakes and nearly got my head blown off by Rafe Haddon.

The surface of the desk was almost bare—there was a Bible,

a stack of paper slips and a packet of letters held together by a rubber band. I riffled through the slips. They were receipts from the night before and they amounted to an awful lot of money. But I already knew that. I picked up the packet of letters. In the upper left-hand corner of each envelope the sender had scrawled her name and address in the same crude handwriting: Mrs. T. R. Hinkley, Box 2101, Norman, Oklahoma. What interested me more was the writing in the middle of the envelopes. They were all addressed to Mr. Gerald Luther Hinkley, 43 Perry Street, Andrewstown, Pennsylvania.

I slid one letter out of the packet and read it. It began "Dear Gerry," thanked Hinkley for the check, said that a drunk Indian had gotten run over by a taxi, that Melissa wasn't much better, and it was signed "Ma." I put the letter back and my depression returned. I don't know what I had expected to find—the great criminals of this world usually don't leave evidence of their fiendishness lying around on their desks where investigative re-porters and other breakers-and-enterers can see it. The Reverend Rhett had, as a matter of fact, left evidence of a small virtue—he sent checks to his mother.

Aside from that and the oddities of Hinkley's name, I hadn't found anything of use to me. I picked up a slip of paper from the desk blotter. "Gerry," it read, "Sam Michaelis called. Call him. L.J." I looked at my watch. It was eight twenty-six. I made sure the desk was arranged the way it had been when I got there, walked back down the corridor, across the stage and into the auditorium.

The cleaning woman was vacuuming an aisle. As I climbed up toward the exit, she switched off her machine again. "The whamicam was blown out," I said. "It's okay now. I'll send a bill."

"Don't send it to me," she replied in an endearing snarl.

I walked back to Main Street. The blue Plymouth was gone. I made a bet with myself that it hadn't gone far. I killed an hour wandering around Andrewstown, fifty minutes more drink-ing coffee and thinking unpleasing thoughts about my mother,

Rhett Hinkley, Tom Dawson and other of this world's fanatics, frauds and finks. At ten-twenty I walked over to Perry Street and went up the driveway to the front entrance of the big gloomy Hinkley house.

I mounted the front porch and rang the bell. Through the screen door I could see a dark, wood-paneled hall and staircase; a grandfather clock ticked in the midmorning hush, a Persian rug covered the hall floor.

There was a rustle of white skirt at the top of the stairs. Sister Cornelia came down and crossed the hall. She was wearing the same gold cross at her throat, the same manner of cool sanctity. "What do you want?" she asked through the screen.

"My name is Sherborne Eppe," I said.

"I know who you are," she answered. She gave the impression that knowledge of me was beneath the dignity of somebody like her.

"I have an appointment with the Reverend Hinkley."

"What do you want to see him about?"

I reminded myself to be tough and hard-nosed, which means, among other things, not showing that you feel annoyed. "He told me to come this morning."

Sister Cornelia sized me up for a moment with those large, unblinking eyes. She walked across the hall and disappeared down a passage. If it weren't for her professed history, she could have been Hinkley's vestal virgin. She was certainly his portal keeper. Maybe, I thought, just his keeper. In her offstage manner Sister Cornelia struck me as a very tough cookie.

Sounds of discussion floated from the dark, cool recesses of the house. Once voices were raised. Then Sister Cornelia came back and opened the screen door. "You may have fifteen minutes," she said.

"What if he wants to talk for longer than that?"

"Fifteen minutes," she repeated.

She led me across the hall and down the passage. She opened a tall paneled door to the Reverend Rhett Hinkley's library and skewered me with those eyes as I passed through.

Hinkley sat at a large desk in his collarless shirt with his suspenders hanging down as usual. His eyes were moist and dull, his body slumped back in a posture which told me that his spiritual pilot light had gone out again. He needed a shave. "Mornin', Mr. Eppe."

"Good morning, sir."

He contemplated me for a while. A bumblebee buzzed frantically up and down the dusty windowpane behind him.

"You writ up your TV program yet?"

"Not yet, sir," I said. "I don't know enough about you and Holier Than Thou to start."

"What you want to know?"

He had me at a psychological disadvantage because he was sitting and I was standing before him. I read somewhere that Mussolini used to do that to people he wanted to intimidate.

"I've discovered that you were baptized Gerald Luther Hinkley," I answered, making a conscious effort to take it slowly and calmly. "Now you call yourself Rhett Hinkley." I was trying a little intimidation of my own.

He moved his body forward, stood up and sidled slowly out from behind the desk. He waved me to a sofa covered in cracked red leather. Hinkley sank down in a brown easy chair with a rip on the top of the curved back; bits of hairy stuffing were sticking out.

"You ever see a picture show called *Gone With the Wind*, Mr. Eppe?"

"I've never seen the movie," I said, "but I read the book."

"I saw that picture show twenty-seven times," Hinkley said, never taking his damp eyes from mine. "Clark Gable plays a man named Rhett. God had that picture show made for a purpose." The library was filled with enigma. "Do you know what the purpose was, Mr. Eppe?"

"No, sir."

"To give me my true name."

Time passed. Out in the vast world people were being born

and dying. Hinkley leaned forward, still fixing me with his mud-dull eyes. "God Almighty caused that picture show to be writ up and acted so that it would capture *my mind*, Mr. Eppe. It *did* capture my mind and I *did* understand why Divine Providence had done it. I changed my name to Rhett."

I couldn't think of any answer to that. There wasn't one.

"God's ways are not for ordinary men to know," he said. "Only the holy."

"Do you mind if I take notes?" I asked.

Hinkley leaned back in his chair. The ends of his suspenders were hanging over the cushion; he was wearing carpet slippers. He shook his head.

I got out my notebook and pretended to write. He was putting on a crazy holy-man act and he was doing it because Grace had told him I conceded that the God-touched weren't like other people. Hinkley was protecting himself from my prying into his affairs. "I'd like to talk to you about the finances of Holier Than Thou," I said.

"Names," he said from the depths of his torpor. "God sets great store by names. Look at the vast number of names in the Holy Bible. Why, the begats alone . . ."

"Yes, sir," I said. "Of course, Holier Than Thou doesn't pay any taxes, being a church, but—"

"Take that name," Hinkley mused.

"What name?"

"Holier Than Thou. You'd never guess in a thousand years how God named my church."

"I wouldn't even try," I said.

"Lucy Jo."

"Sir?"

"Lucy Jo," he repeated.

Rhett Hinkley took a deep breath. He wasn't looking at me now. His extinguished eyes were fixed on a point above my head, not seeing the cobwebby junction of the wall and the ceiling, but sometime far gone, someplace far distant. "Lucy Jo Patterson," he said. He glanced back at me. "The ways of God are not for ordinary men to know, Mr. Eppe. You take a woman like Lucy Jo Patterson, *you* look at her and what do you see?"

Since I couldn't see her, I couldn't tell him.

"What *you'd* see," Hinkley went on, "is a good-looking woman with a sharp tongue who wanted more than anything to go to New York. A woman who had her heart and mind set on being an actress." There was a brief light in his mud-bank eyes. "You'd see voluptuousness in Lucy Jo Patterson, Mr. Eppe." His voice became hoarse and low—whether from remembered pleasures or in Calvinistic warning I could not tell. "A woman of such body and guile that a man would go crazy over her."

While female bodies and guile interest me greatly, I was there to pry information out of him—and I was losing. "Reverend Hinkley," I said, "Holier Than Thou is obviously a very prosperous church—"

But he had escaped me. He was looking back at upper space again, remembering times gone and places left behind. "*I* saw different after the miracle that created my ministry," he said. "I saw that Lucy Jo was part of God's great plan for me." He ran his tongue between his gums and upper lip.

"Of course, I didn't know there was *any* meaning when Lucy Jo threw me out of the motel near Tulsa in January nineteen and sixty-two. I'd caught her fooling around with another traveling man." Hinkley glanced back at me for a moment. "I was traveling myself in those days. Men's underwear. 'Don't be so holier than thou!' Lucy Jo hollered at me. She called me a lot of names, but after the miracle, that's what I remembered. 'Don't be so holier than thou!'"

Hinkley reached into his shirt pocket, brought out some small object and picked his teeth with it. He examined what he had extracted, flicked it away and put the small object back in his shirt pocket. "I drove my car in rage and sorrow for two nights and three days," he said. "Right through Oklahoma, Kansas and Missouri. I picked up a hitchhiker outside of Ottumwa, Iowa, and he robbed me. That man took everything I had—car, money, clothes, sample case. I was sitting in a hotel room in Ottumwa on a rainy Saturday night, broke, alone, everything gone—and then the miracle happened."

He shifted in his chair and blinked his wet eyes a couple of times. "I was sitting in my long johns on the side of the bed, Mr. Eppe, when suddenly God guided my hand to the drawer of a little table. There was a Gideon Bible in that drawer and it was open." He shifted in his chair and rubbed the stubble on his neck. "That Bible was lying open at Matthew Sixteen: Twenty-six. Know what that says, Mr. Eppe?"

"No, sir."

Hinkley leaned forward. For a moment some of the drama and intensity I had seen the night before flared in him. " 'For what is a man profited,' " he said, " 'if he shall gain the whole world, and lose his own soul?' Then, Mr. Eppe, I knew who that hitchhiker was."

"Who was the hitchhiker?" I asked.

"Jesus."

For a moment I forgot about finances. I must have looked as surprised as I felt.

"It was Jesus in disguise," Hinkley said, leaning back in his chair and fixing me with his watery eyes. "He'd taken away my worldly goods so that I could find my true calling. He wanted me to establish a church and call it Holier Than Thou. God had put the name in Lucy Jo Patterson's mouth."

"Do you see Jesus often?"

"Two, three times a week. He's always disguised as some mortal and ordinary person who just happens by."

The door opened. "Your fifteen minutes are up," Sister Cornelia said.

"Like the hitchhiker," I said.

Hinkley nodded. "Like the hitchhiker."

Sister Cornelia rustled in impatience. "Mr. Eppe . . ."

"Am I Jesus?" I asked the Reverend Rhett Hinkley.

He studied me for a long time. "Depends on what happens as a result of my encounter with you," he finally said.

When in the Rome of Rhett Hinkley's craziness, I thought, act like a crazy Roman. I stood up. "If I'm Jesus," I said, "I want to know what you've done with all the money you've made in my name."

"Mr. Eppe!" Sister Cornelia snapped.

Rhett Hinkley was sprawled in his chair, hands shoved into his pockets. It was hard to deduce precise expressions on that face of his, bland as it was and damp as a half-drained swamp. But I could have sworn he was smiling the faintest of smiles.

I followed Sister Cornelia down the passage and across the hall. She held open the screen door. "You—are—*not*—Jesus," she hissed, her eyes half closed in protective fury.

"You never know," I answered.

The day was getting hotter. I walked over to Main Street and stopped at the bank. I hadn't given up on Betty Darius yet. I thought I might buy her lunch—a large lunch—and see if I couldn't make her change her mind about talking.

A dark-haired girl was typing a letter as I walked into the bank. She showed no inclination to stop typing. "I'd like to see Betty Darius," I said.

"She's out sick today, Mr. Eppe," the girl said without looking up.

I went back out onto the sidewalk. It's chilly when a total stranger knows your name and signals instant dislike for you.

I looked down the Main Street ending at the river. Holier Than Thou loomed above the trees on one side. The street was almost empty of people. There was no blue Plymouth. But in the midday sun, Andrewstown was taking on a sinister aspect to me.

Across the street I saw a large plate-glass window printed with gold letters:

THE ANDREWSTOWN TELEPHONE
Published Weekly Since 1904

If there was anyplace a reporter could find haven from his queasiness, it was at a newspaper office. Besides, I was feeling that frustration which comes from having great work to do and no means of doing it. Perhaps I could dig up something on Hinkley in the files of the *Andrewstown Telephone*.

The newspaper office was one huge room. A counter ran across the front, the press—a large black and oily-looking piece of machinery—stood at the rear. In between there were two desks, file cabinets and shelves stacked with years and years of Andrewstown history as recorded in its weekly paper.

A tall underweight man in his sixties got up from one of the desks and came over to the counter. He had an Adam's apple as sharply pointed as a cartridge; he was wearing a dull-green shirt and a bow tie—a snap-on if I ever saw one. "You're the television fella, aren't you?" he said.

Christ, I thought, they've even circulated my picture around town.

I nodded. "Are you the editor?"

"Editor, publisher, printer, delivery man, you name it," he said, with a smile that seemed splintery because some of his teeth were out of alignment with the basic design of his upper and lower plates. "Harry Carew," he added without offering to shake hands.

"I was wondering if I could look through some back issues of the paper," I said.

He waved a hand disfigured by arthritis at the shelves of newspapers. "Help yourself. Use that desk over there."

So for the next three hours I pored over copies of the *Andrewstown Telephone* dating from 1971, the year that Rhett Hinkley had come to town.

It was one of those weekly papers that print notices instead of news. There were notices of weddings but never divorces, notices of deaths without saying how they'd occurred, notices of Andrewstown boys and girls going off to college without mentioning anything but their graduations, notices of committees being formed, funds being raised, annual dances being held, with no further illumination as to whether the committee members held together, how the funds were finally spent, who fell in love, picked fights or got drunk at the dances. There were social notices about people's sisters-in-law visiting from Winnetka, other people planning a trip to the Rocky Mountains, the same people showing color slides of their trip to the Rocky Mountains and serving punch on July evenings.

All the references to Rhett Hinkley were also notices—about opening his first church, starting a crusade for school prayer, buying his second church, holding an Americanism Month, the increasing attendance at Holier Than Thou.

Even the Bug Plague was dealt with by notices in recent editions—a notice about Jerry Moss coming in from Philadelphia, summaries of Public Health Service releases for the week.

The only thing that vaguely resembled a news item in the *Andrewstown Telephone* concerned the Reverend Thomas Avery Dawson's arrival to take up a vacant ministry. It started as a notice, mentioning that Tom had graduated from West Point in 1965, was commissioned a second lieutenant and sent to Vietnam. At that point the notice turned into a news item: "After being wounded in Vietnam, the Reverend Dawson returned to the United States, where he studied at Union Theological Seminary in New York."

The *Andrewstown Telephone* was a monument to the impotence of the written word in the right hands. Harry Carew had managed to chronicle the years and lives of his town without conveying the slightest hint that it was a place of human habitation. Only names lived there. Only truncated formal or official events took place there. Nobody slashed his throat in a paroxysm of despair, nobody lusted, nobody even said anything.

I put down the last paper.

Carew was sitting at a desk across the room, fingers drumming on the arm of his chair, watching me. "Didn't find any dirt on the Reverend Hinkley, did you?"

"No," I answered, unable to think of any way of denying

that that's what I was after. Andrewstown seemed to know a lot more about me than I did about it.

"Could have told you you wouldn't," he said.

"You can't win 'em all."

"I don't understand why a young fella couldn't find something better to do with his time than trying to blacken the name of a man like the Reverend Hinkley. Why, he's put Andrewstown on the map."

I wondered why Andrewstown *wanted* to be on the map.

"He's world-famous, you know."

I know, I answered mentally, they fall off their bar stools in Bulgaria every time somebody mentions the name Rhett Hinkley.

"Thanks for letting me read the paper," I said. I got up, walked around the counter and headed for the door.

"Give up," Carew said.

I turned around. "I guess you must be a member of Reverend Hinkley's congregation."

"Me?" Carew looked surprised. "Not me. It just does a lot for Andrewstown to have that man basing his operations here. Give it up, young fella."

And that is how I learned the way you get to be a great man in a small place. Big cities are famous for being famous. Small towns want to be known for something—a local grotto, an annual spitting contest, the red-spotted toad capital of the world. Andrewstown thought it was famous as the home of the Jesus Christ Church of Holier Than Thou, Rhett Hinkley, Prop. He had the place wired up and on his side, he'd passed the word that I was trying to damage his reputation, which meant I was putting dents in Andrewstown's claim to fame.

The shade trees and old houses had lost their charm for me as I walked to Tom Dawson's house. I wondered if people were standing behind big old windows with stained-glass fringes at the top watching me in hostility.

When I got to Tom's I found excitement. Hannibal had apparently just arrived with a plastic bag full of sawdust. He,

Tom and Jerry Moss were in the dining room. Several girls whom I took to be Public Health staff were watching from the sun porch.

Moss held a handful of the sawdust under the hot, direct light of Tom Dawson's reading lamp on the dining-room table. Moss sniffed at the stuff in his palm. "Whew! Where'd you get this?"

"Barney's," Hannibal said.

Moss looked across the table at Tom Dawson.

"It's one of those daytime roadhouses, bar and dance hall," Tom said. "It opens in time to get the first shift of men from the tire factory and closes when the housewives have to go home and feed their kids. It's a terrible place. Half the adultery in the county starts there."

"Sarah," Moss yelled at one of the girls, "get me that list of health-code violators!" He dumped the handful of sawdust back into Hannibal's plastic bag. "Tell me about it."

"That Barney covers the dance floor with fresh sawdust every mornin'," Hannibal said. "Black fella says they sweep it up every night."

"Does Barney tell the black fella to mix anything with the sawdust?"

Hannibal glowered at him. "How come you think the *black* fella does the sweepin'?"

"Because I'm a goddamn racist," Moss snapped. "You guys push the brooms and clean the toilets, and the rednecks screw each other's wives in their campers out behind Barney's. Cut the crap, Hannibal."

"That black fella's a bartender," Hannibal said. "Polack sweeps up."

Moss's thin, tired face assumed an expression of exasperation. *"Do they put anything in the sawdust?"*

Hannibal took a piece of paper from his shirt pocket. "Stuff from a whole bunch bags in the cellar. Here's what's writ on 'em."

Moss held the paper under the lamp's hot light. "Jesus

wept," he said. He took off his glasses. "Gentlemen, I think we've found the source of the Bug Plague."

I walked over to the table. "What is it?"

The girl came in from the sun porch and handed Moss a clipboard. He riffled through the sheets of paper. "Aha," he said softly. "Here it is. Barney's was closed four times last year—lice, cockroaches, vermin. He's been okay since October." He turned to Hannibal. "I suppose you didn't find out when they started mixing that stuff with the sawdust?"

"You s'pose right," Hannibal said.

"It doesn't matter," Moss said. "Here's what I think happened. Barney got sick of being hassled by the health inspectors and didn't want to go to the expense of ripping his kitchen and bar apart and having them really deloused. So he took the cheap way out. Somewhere he found a leftover supply of DDT and two other pesticides that are absolutely lethal if you use them undiluted. Barney mixed that stuff with the sawdust on his dance floor and bar. It got rid of the bugs but it raised dust that hit the lungs, hair and clothes of all the adulterers and a lot of them got sick."

"But children have the Bug Plague too."

"They probably pick up the dust off their parents' hair and clothes," Moss said.

"And Hinkley's congregation didn't get sick because they don't hang around places like Barney's," I said.

"You got it," Moss answered. "We'll run this sample up to the lab in Pittsburgh and tell them to make an overnight check. We ought to have positive confirmation in the morning. But this is it."

"I'd better call the TV station," I said.

"Don't call yet," Moss answered. "We want to be absolutely sure because a lot of things are going to happen if I'm right. Twelve more hours won't make all that much difference."

I said I'd wait.

As we drove home, directly into the flaming orb of the setting sun, I thought I detected in Hannibal the smugness of a gorilla who's just won a chest-pounding contest. "Pretty weird, you finding out about Barney's," I said. "You managed to discover in one day something that had the government baffled for weeks."

"Gummints got rules."

"How many people did you mangle before you saved Andrewstown?"

"Asshole," he grunted.

When we got to the farm and went indoors I found Mrs. Timberlake in the kitchen taking a freshly baked apple crumb cake from the oven. I asked her how she was.

She made no direct reply. She put the cake on the kitchen table and said, "That's for the raffle." I thought she said it with unnatural stiffness.

"What raffle?"

"It's on Tuesday. Reverend Hinkley thought it up personal to raise money for—" She stopped, clasped her hands and lowered her eyes. At first I thought she was praying. Then I knew that she was trying not to look at me. "Mr. Eppe," she said, "I want—" She stopped. I knew something stern was coming and that she was fighting to overcome her naturally sweet disposition so that she could say it.

I sat down on the kitchen stool. "Go ahead and tell me what you want, Mrs. Timberlake," I said. "I'll understand." I already understood, and my disdain for Hinkley as a fraud became an active, personal dislike because of what he had done to this decent and innocent lady.

"I'd like for you and Mr. Hannibal to move out," she said in a voice so crumpled and weak that I could barely hear her words.

"Of course," I said, "we'll go right away."

She came to generous life again. "Oh, I wouldn't *dream* of asking you to go tonight. Now, you just stay until you can find a nice comfortable place. You just stay as long as you have to."

"Mrs. Timberlake," I said, "I don't want to embarrass you and you don't have to tell me if you don't want to . . ."

"What is it, Mr. Eppe?"

"I was wondering what Reverend Hinkley said I have done."

She turned to the stove and lit a burner under a percolator of coffee. Then she opened a drawer in the kitchen table, took out a knife and cut a slice of the apple crumb cake. She put it on a plate and set the plate in front of me.

"But that's for the raffle," I said.

"Oh, fiddle the raffle! I'll bake another one. Now we both need a cup of coffee after a talk like this."

"We haven't finished the talk, Mrs. Timberlake. Or would you rather not tell me what Reverend Hinkley said I've done?"

"You know what you've done, Mr. Eppe. Now we're going to have a cup of coffee and change the subject to something more pleasant."

"I *do* know what I've done," I said. "But I'd like to hear what *he* says I've done."

"Oh, Mr. Eppe, don't make it worse by calling our Reverend a liar. Isn't it enough that you've threatened to go on television and say he's a crazy man unless he tells you what he's done with our money?"

"Do *you* know what he's done with your money, Mrs. Timberlake?"

"We leave that entirely in Reverend's hands," she answered. "Jesus tells him how it's to be spent." She looked at me sorrowfully. "Honestly, you media people. You're always trying to find something bad to put in the news. Look what you did to poor Mr. Nixon."

"I didn't."

"You just eat your cake and drink your coffee," she said. "You're too nice a young man to spend your time looking for bad things to write about, Mr. Eppe. You ought to go into another line of work."

Harry Carew had told me the same thing at the newspaper. Rhett Hinkley's grapevine got the line right and got it all over town fast.

"You mustn't think that because I've asked you to move out—when it's convenient, of course—that the Reverend Hinkley's angry with you," Mrs. Timberlake said. "He's not. He feels sorry for you, Mr. Eppe. When he telephoned me this afternoon he said, 'The poor young fellow doesn't understand that love is the morning and the evening star.' Those were his very words."

I finished my coffee but I couldn't manage the cake. I was full up to my twitching throat with the machinations of Rhett Hinkley. I told Mrs. Timberlake that Hannibal and I would move out tomorrow.

"You just take your time," she said. "It isn't personal, Mr. Eppe, it's just that—"

"I know," I said.

I wandered outside and leaned on the wired-together gate again. The dusk was coming down again, Will's radio was lamenting in the barn again, the mist was on the fields again. All that had changed was the feeling of the air. I knew now there was no plague in it. I breathed deeply and tried to think if there was anything I could do, any fact I could turn around and see differently to nail Hinkley before he got me run out of town altogether. Hannibal and I were already homeless and Tom Dawson was probably the only person in Andrewstown who'd take us in.

I couldn't think of anything. My mind was taken up with feeling sorry for Mrs. Timberlake.

"Goddamn you, Rhett Hinkley," I muttered aloud and immediately felt foolish.

God and Hinkley had a good thing going together.

Thirteen

A DISMAL AND DESERVED FATE

THERE IS, IN THIS LIFE, a difference between screwing up and failing. When you screw up it's because your mind isn't fully on—or your heart isn't fully in—what you're doing. Failure is when you try hard at something you really want to do and fall flat on your face.

You are aware by now that my life has not been without screw-ups. When I was a kid in New England, being thrown out of the best schools because I devoted my mind to fantasy instead of studying, antagonizing my mother by behaving like my father, tossing a Latin American in the swimming pool and even losing nine million four hundred and forty thousand fictional dollars to my grandmother because I was such a hopeless backgammon player, I could have entered every screw-up contest in the country and won first prize.

But now I was at least halfway grownup, I wasn't in New England anymore, my mother was only a threatening wraith in the form of her private detective who was around trying to gather evidence to prove I was a lunatic. I had lost track of my father and grandmother and almost abandoned fantasy because, from Cleveland to Andrewstown, reality had kept me too busy to spend much time in my dream world, where love was perfect and I was a great man. Having settled for reality, I had to revise my mind's workings to accept actual life's imperfections and to decide what I *really* wanted from it. No more king or guerrilla leader for me.

These were my thoughts as I packed my suitcase on my last morning at the Timberlake farm. It was a dark and rumbly morning. The sky was a low, dirty gray; a thunderstorm was far to the west but approaching, clearing its throat as it came. The heat of the previous day still hung in the air—metallic-smelling and motionless.

I folded the few shirts I had on top of my suit. What I wanted most was to go to Rhode Island, meet Beth in the flesh and find out if the lady of braveries, loss and lyrics was what I thought she was or an unwitting new fantasy. I wanted to find my father and I'd start trying as soon as I could figure out a way of making inquiries about him without tipping off my mother where I was. I didn't want her to come whooping back into my life, breaking my psychic china and trying to put me into an insane asylum again. And I still wanted to *be* something, somebody whose life had purposes and consequences.

Those were desires that lay in my middle and farther distances. I pulled on my blue jeans and sneakers and tried to figure out what I wanted right now, this very day.

I'd had two immediate objectives. I wanted to succeed as a television investigative reporter—not because I thought that craft of indignations and finger-pointings would look good in my obituary, but because, if I did succeed at it, I would have a profession. At that time I didn't know enough about anything to be even an amateur.

To establish myself as an investigative reporter I had to find out what Rhett Hinkley had done with the millions of tax-free dollars raked in by Holier Than Thou. I also wanted to nail

Hinkley because he was a trafficker in the piety of people like Mrs. Timberlake, in the fears of a plagued populace.

Those were the two things I really wanted to do. My mind was fully on them, my heart was fully in them—and I'd gotten nowhere. I wasn't screwing up again. I was failing.

Hannibal shoved open the door of my room. "You gone sit there all day 'til that lady has to *kick* us out or you gone come with me and find someplace to live?"

"I think Tom Dawson will let us stay at his house," I said, getting to my feet.

"You *think*," he snorted. "That's your whole trouble, Sherbert, you think too much."

"You ought to try it sometime," I answered, "just for the novelty."

We went downstairs. Mrs. Timberlake had made a huge breakfast for us—fresh orange juice, eggs scrambled with cream and dill, country sausage, waffles, syrup, bacon and mountains of toast, not to mention gallons of coffee. She stood smiling at the dining-room table as we sat down.

That breakfast was an attempt to get out of the conflict Hinkley had created for her. She really liked us because she liked everybody. But her Oklahoma guru had told her to get rid of us and she couldn't resist him. I was even more hostile to Hinkley as I put away the biggest breakfast I've ever eaten in my whole life before or since. By the time I was gorged, cross-eyed and had begun to have a stomachache, I positively hated him.

We thanked Mrs. Timberlake and I asked her if we could leave our bags until we'd relocated ourselves. There was no way to lock anything in the Pierce-Arrow, and considering the way Andrewstown felt about me, I didn't want to unpack that evening and find a rattlesnake in with my underwear.

"Why, of *course* you can," she said. Her eyes were swimming behind her thick glasses and her funny, crooked smile carried the implication of grief. "You do understand, don't you, Mr. Eppe?"

"Certainly I do," I said.

She put her hands on my shoulders—which wasn't easy, me being so tall. "You don't think I'm a mean old woman, do you?"

For a moment I thought *I* was going to cry. "I think you're a wonderful woman, Mrs. Timberlake," I said. "I think you're a—" Words failed me.

"Fine Christian lady," Hannibal grunted.

Mrs. Timberlake put her forehead on my chest. Her hands were still on my shoulders. "Thank you, Jesus," she whispered. She looked up with tears in her eyes and kissed my cheek. She turned. "Mr. Hannibal, would you be offended if . . ."

He reached out one huge paw and took her hand, bending over so that she could kiss him.

"Now, you promise me I'll see you when you come back for your bags," she said.

"We promise," I said.

"You won't come sneaking in or anything?"

"If ole Sherbert come sneakin' in, I'll take him out to the barn and whop him and you'll hear him hollerin'," Hannibal said.

We all laughed. Hannibal and I left her smiling happily on the porch as we got into the Pierce-Arrow.

Neither of us spoke until we reached the highway. Then Hannibal peered out the car window. "Gone rain before evenin'," he said.

"I guess so," I answered. My cold tingles were resuming as we picked up speed, going toward Andrewstown. Maybe the man in the blue Plymouth would be there waiting for me.

For a moment I considered telling Hannibal that I thought a private detective hired by my mother was on my tail. I decided against it. That would involve explaining too much about myself, and besides there wouldn't be anything legal Hannibal could do about the man.

"Where you gone be this mornin', Sherbert?"

"I've got to have another go at that lady in the bank," I said, "the one who knows about Hinkley's money."

"What if she won't talk?"

"Then I'm really stuck."

"I'll wait for you at that Dawson's house."

"If you aren't out beating up the population."

He gave one of his short wheezes that passed for mirth. "Your mouth keep runnin' off and I'm gone fix it so your teeth's growin' out the back of your haid." He was obviously pleased with himself.

I got out at the top of Main Street and looked down at the river. The wind was rising; the surface of the water was irregular and choppy like a moving channel of broken glass. Dark clouds scudded across the town. Thunder rumbled in angry, distant confirmation of my mood. My gods seemed to have deserted me on the road to Andrewstown.

I walked three blocks down to the bank and went in. The same girl was typing at the same desk. I tried standing without saying anything to see if she'd look at me. She didn't. "Miss Darius is still out sick," she said, zipping her fingers over the keyboard of her electric typewriter.

"I have a billion dollars to deposit in your bank," I said.

"We don't want it," she answered.

"Then I'll buy the bank," I said. "Maybe you'd be happier in some other line of work."

Finally she looked up at me. She couldn't have been more than nineteen. She had dark-brown hair cut short and a pretty, compact face. "It isn't my fault," she whispered. "You've made yourself awfully unpopular, Mr. Eppe."

"Is Betty at home?" I whispered back.

The girl glanced around the bank and nodded. "I talked to her this morning. She sounded awful, as if she were all spaced out or something."

"Is there anything I can do?" I asked.

The girl glanced around the bank again. Nobody was paying any attention to us. "She wanted some aspirin. I was going to take it over on my lunch hour."

"I can take her some now."

"You don't look like a Communist to me," the girl murmured, pulling out the top drawer of her desk. "In fact, you're kind of cute."

"Who says I'm a Communist?"

"They do," she said, handing me a set of keys quickly. "Let yourself in if Betty can't come to the door. I go over there and water her plants when she's away. She can bring back the keys."

"When I buy the bank I'll make you president," I said.

The girl giggled and returned to her typing.

I went outside, bought some aspirin at the drugstore and crossed the street. I thought I saw a blue Plymouth parked in the next block. As I passed the offices of the *Andrewstown Telephone*, Harry Carew was looking through the front window. I waved. He grimaced and shook his head as if he'd just seen the village idiot doing something outrageous.

At Betty's house, I unlocked the street door beside the hardware store. A sudden whistle of wind stirred up dust around me. Thunder muttered again, this time closer.

I went upstairs and knocked at the door of her apartment. I could hear something loose on the roof of the building banging in the wind.

A muffled, inconclusive response came from inside the apartment. I waited and knocked again. There was no answer. I unlocked the door and stepped inside.

The shades were drawn. The little apartment was thick with the stale air of illness; clothes, teacups and newspapers were on the floor in that disarray which surrounds the incapacitated.

When my eyes adjusted to the gloom I saw Betty on the daybed, huge, damp and gasping for breath. She was covered by a rumpled sheet; one plump foot stuck out from beneath it. "Is that you, honey?" she whispered, her eyes closed in her sweaty, fevered face.

I went over and squatted next to her. "It's Bornie Eppe, Betty. The reporter who came to see you."

She lay immobile for a full thirty seconds. Her hand moved

up to her head. Feebly, she clawed her plump fingers through her hair. "Damn things all over me," she mumbled. Her fat arms were covered with scratches.

I went into the kitchen and found the telephone. I called Tom Dawson's house and told him to send a doctor and Jerry Moss. "Betty Darius has the Bug Plague," I explained.

"Right away," Dawson said. "The laboratory confirmation's in from Pittsburgh."

"Good," I said. "I'll tell the television station when I'm finished here. Get that doctor—fast."

I found a clean dishtowel and soaked it under the cold-water tap. I went back into the living room and raised the shades. The room filled with dull light; the windows rattled in the wind.

I dragged three pillows from where they had been squished between the bed and the wall, put them under Betty's head and washed her face and arms with the wet towel.

She opened her eyes and looked up at me. She half smiled. "I'll be damned," she said in a whispery voice. "It's Will's friend."

"Just be quiet," I said. "A doctor's coming." I drew a chair over to the bedside and went on mopping her face with the towel. "That feels good," she said. She looked at me again. "I thought it was Bubba when you came in."

For a moment I stopped mopping her. "Who?"

"Bubba Johnson, my boyfriend," she said. "What day is it?"

"Wednesday."

"I've been sick since Monday night. He hasn't come over once." She lay looking at the wall for a moment. "I'm hungry," she said.

"I don't think you ought to eat anything until the doctor sees you," I told her, still trying to absorb the fact that the fat, repentant man I'd watched squealing his confession on the stage at Holier Than Thou was Betty Darius' boyfriend, the man she didn't love but who was better than nothing.

"A cup of tea isn't going to kill me," she said, coming a bit further out of her stupor. "And— What's your name, kid? I forget."

"Bornie."

She raised herself on one fleshy arm. "Bornie, honey, there's a carton of Marlboros on the table behind the TV set. Get me a cigarette, will you?"

I got a cigarette, lit it for her, handed her an ashtray and went out into the kitchen to make her tea. She was better for the moment, but judging by what I'd heard about the Bug Plague from Jerry Moss, she'd soon be off her head and crawling with invisible vermin again. I hoped the doctor would get there before then.

I took the tea in to her. She sipped at it and lay back on the pillows. "Why'd you come over, Bornie?"

"They told me at the bank you were sick. I wanted to see if you were all right."

She turned her head and looked at me. "Aw, that's sweet." She drew on her cigarette. "Wouldn't you think Bubba would've come by at least *once*? Usually it's every afternoon . . ."

"Betty," I said, "I don't think Bubba's going to be around anymore."

"What do you mean, he won't be around anymore?"

"Bubba's got religion. I was at Holier Than Thou the same night I came to see you. He got carried away by Hinkley's preaching. He went up on the stage and confessed in front of everybody that he'd been cheating."

Betty rolled her head back and closed her eyes. "Oh, my God," she said. She lay without moving for a full minute. "Was his wife with him?"

"Yes."

"Did he say it was *me* he was . . ."

"No, he didn't mention any names. At least not in public."

"Thank God for small favors," she muttered. She crushed out her cigarette. "Give me another one, honey."

While I lit her a fresh cigarette she lay with her eyes closed. Finally she said, "That son of a bitch."

"Well, you did say he was weak," I reminded her.

Betty opened her eyes and took the new cigarette. If transfiguration is visible through that much fat and fever, I thought I saw a hard rage in her face and eyes. "I wasn't talking about Bubba. He's just a poor mutt who follows whichever way the wind blows. *I mean Hinkley.*" She fixed me with a look of bitterness. "Where does that sanctimonious bastard come off messing around with other people's lives?"

"Life changing is his business."

"Well, he can goddamn well go practice his business on somebody else's life! First his daughter gets her hooks into my Will, now *he's* taken away Bubba, all I had left." She lay back facing the ceiling and took a savage drag on her cigarette. "What was it you came here for, honey? I can't remember. I'm not thinking too good."

"I was hoping you could tell me about Hinkley's bank accounts."

"That's it. I remember. You're a reporter."

"Would you be willing?"

"I'd be willing to fix Hinkley's wagon," she said, drawing on the cigarette as if she were sucking blood from the Reverend Rhett's jugular. "And I got an idea that *maybe* he's doing things with money he shouldn't."

"Why haven't you told anybody before?"

"It didn't happen at our bank. All I heard was the gossip, but you could check it out. I didn't give a damn before, but now I do."

I got out my notebook and she told me everything she knew. There had been two million four hundred thousand dollars in the Holier Than Thou account at the Andrewstown bank. In February, Hinkley had transferred one million three hundred thousand to a Pittsburgh bank. During a phone chat with Betty, a lady at *that* bank said that Hinkley had been sending big sums to somebody in New York.

"Do you remember who in New York?" I asked.

Betty crushed out her fourth cigarette. She was perspiring again, the psychosomatic vermin picked up from Barney's dance floor, Bubba Johnson's underwear or the wrath of God were crawling again upon her vast body. She was beginning to gasp for air. "Wait a minute . . ." she mumbled.

I went out to the kitchen, soaked the towel and wiped her face. "Gotta remember so you can check it out . . ."

"Don't worry," I said. "Try to rest until the doctor gets here. I can ask the Pittsburgh bank."

Betty shook her burning head. "They won't tell you . . . against the law for you to know. If I didn't hate that son of a bitch— Sanford," she said, heaving her chest in a new struggle to get air, "Sanford and Upson . . ."

I put down the towel and wrote "Sanford and Upson, New York" in my book.

"Fix that bastard, kid," Betty said, her last articulate sentence before the Bug Plague repossessed her. "Where's Bubba?"

She was raving and trying to claw away the pestilence when Jerry Moss, Hannibal and the doctor arrived. Moss looked down at Betty's mountainous writhings. "Classic case," he said. "Is she a friend of yours?"

"Sort of."

"Then you'd better get yourself checked."

"She's not that kind of friend," I answered.

While the doctor was taking Betty's pulse and temperature, Moss looked around the room. "This place ought to be fumigated before she comes back," he said. "The dust's probably in all her clothes."

When the ambulance came to take Betty Darius to the hospital in Johnstown, Jerry Moss got a plastic garbage bag from the kitchen, and using a double-tined cooking fork, dropped her immense slacks, blouse and underwear into the bag. "Those were the last things she had on. They'd better be destroyed," he said.

It was almost noon when Hannibal, Moss and I got back to Tom Dawson's house. The heavy ceiling of sky that covered Andrewstown had built, in the west, to a towering range of black thunderheads. The metallic smell of the approaching storm was strong, and the wind was coming in vicious bursts. I'd picked up the plastic bag of clothes and I burned them in Tom's incinerator. The smoke whirled around me, and when there was nothing left but a pile of fragments and ashes I went indoors. Tom Dawson was sitting in the dining room at a long table covered with papers and books. "I have to make a long-distance telephone call," I said.

He looked at me anxiously. "Could you reverse the charges?"

"I'm trying to confirm something I found out about Hinkley. I'll use the credit card the TV station gave me."

"Something interesting about Hinkley?"

"What Betty Darius told me could finish him."

Dawson's eyes brightened with pleasure. He pushed the telephone across the table and my irritation at him returned.

I dialed New York information and got the number of Sanford and Upson, investment counselors.

Mr. Harold Upson of that firm was haughty at first. In a sub-zero, Ivy League accent he told me that Sanford and Upson *never* discussed clients' affairs with strangers—they never even gave out the names of clients.

I speak Ivy League like a native and I can do frosty indignation pretty well myself, especially when I'm feeling indignant. I told Mr. Upson that he was probably handling money that had been embezzled from a Pennsylvania church. I added that I was a television reporter.

Mr. Upson reacted as if someone had just told him that his daughter was going to marry a Democrat. He said the idea was outrageous and how dare I. At that point I went into my tough, hard-nosed investigative-reporter act. I told Mr. Upson that the client in question was named Hinkley—probably Gerald Luther —and that I was prepared to discuss the whole matter with the Justice Department, the Securities and Exchange Commission, the Governor of New York and maybe the Pope unless we could talk about it right now. So we talked about it. Mr. Upson admitted that his firm had drawn up a portfolio of investments for Mr.

Hinkley and had made a down payment on an apartment in the East Seventies in New York.

"Sir," I said, "have you ever heard of the Jesus Christ Church of Holier Than Thou?"

"The *what*?"

"The Jesus Christ Church of Holier Than Thou."

"Good gracious," Mr. Upson murmured in genteel, Episcopalian surprise.

"So the account is in Mr. Hinkley's name, not the church's?"

"That is correct. Did I understand you to say that you are a television reporter?"

"Yes, sir," I said.

Mr. Upson told me that he didn't see why this whole unpleasant matter couldn't be settled without dragging his firm's name into it. He said he was going to get hold of his attorneys immediately, and I said I thought that was a super idea.

The wind was shaking Tom Dawson's house, and the Public Health girls out on the sun porch began closing windows.

I called the television station and told Art Olsen that the source of the Bug Plague had been discovered and that I had almost enough on Hinkley to start a series on the great Holier Than Thou ripoff. "Good work, Sherborne," he said. "Can you write a piece today?"

"I could do one on the epidemic."

"We'll have a crew out there as fast as we can," Art said. "You can do the piece about discovering the source of the disease for the six o'clock. Then we'll sit down and talk about organizing, checking out and filming a series on Hinkley and Holier Than Thou."

I suddenly blanched, as they say, at the prospect of my journalistic fantasies turning real. "Look, Art," I said, "I've never actually *been* on television . . ."

"I'll come out with the crew and be your producer."

"Art, maybe I ought to tell you how I got the information on Hinkley."

"How a good investigative reporter gets his information isn't important. What's important is that the information is correct. Is yours?"

"I'm pretty sure it is."

"Fine." Art lowered his voice to a whisper. "This is your first series, Sherborne. It has to be *very* good. You know why."

"Yes, I do," I muttered.

Before he hung up, Art told me to put on a suit and tie for the filming.

Tom Dawson had been listening to my telephone conversation. He was leaning back in his chair with a smug and pious look on his face. The television station and I were doing exactly what he wanted done to Hinkley—without his having to dirty his reverend hands.

I got up without saying anything to him and went out on the front porch. Two voices had started an argument inside my head. The first said that I had scored big, that I now had everything I needed to establish myself as a hotshot investigative reporter for television. With my reputation as the man who uncovered the scandals of Rhett Hinkley I could go to Rhode Island, get myself a job with another TV station and live happily ever after with Beth.

There speaks the fantasist, said the second voice, a prudent one implanted in me by my New England ancestors. You aren't an investigative reporter any more than you are a trapeze artist. That was true. What I had discovered about Hinkley I had discovered through dumb luck—and with a little help from my friends. I was to true journalism what Hinkley was to true religion.

I felt an overpowering need to take assertive action, to dig up something using my own intelligence.

I went back into the house and told Dawson I needed to make another telephone call. "It's local," I added.

Behind his black beard there was a big smile beaming at me as if he and I had accomplished a great work together. "Go right ahead," he said, "unless you want to use the extension up in my bedroom."

"Here will be fine," I answered.

I dialed Rhett Hinkley's house and said I wanted to speak to him. A voice like the ice caverns of Siberia which I recognized to be Sister Cornelia's said that the Reverend Hinkley wasn't free to speak to me—any time.

"Tell him I've had a conversation with Sanford and Upson in New York."

There was a momentary silence. "Just a minute," Sister Cornelia said.

It was less than a minute before I had the Reverend Hinkley on the telephone in person. "Now then, Mr. Eppe," he said in his flat, ole-boy drawl, "what's all this 'bout you pokin'—"

"Reverend," I said, "I want to come over and talk to you. I know about your investments and your apartment—"

"Now, looky here—"

"I've got to go out to Mrs. Timberlake's and change my clothes for a television piece I'm doing. It'll be about a half-hour before I get to your house."

He started to say something else, but I hung up. I collected Hannibal from the sun porch, where he was talking to Jerry Moss, and we drove back to the farm.

The wind was bending trees on the landscape and stirring up mini-twisters of dust in the barnyard as Hannibal parked the Pierce-Arrow. The thunderheads were rolling from the west, black breakers on which all the demons of this world could have surfed in the sky. Will waved to us as he crossed from the house to the barn with his jacket collar turned up.

When I got into the house the telephone was ringing. Mrs. Timberlake didn't seem to be anywhere around. The telephone rang again. I went into the dining room and picked it up. "This is the Timberlake—"

"*He hit me!*" Grace Hinkley screamed. "*Will, darling! Please!*" She began to sob.

"Grace!" I said loudly. "This isn't Will, it's Bornie Eppe. What's going on?"

"I don't want to talk to you!" she cried. "I want— He hit me, and he's packing! I want Will!"

"*Who* hit you?"

"My father, you fool! Get Will!"

I put down the telephone, ran outside and over to the barn. "Will!" I yelled. "Grace on the phone. She's in trouble!"

Will had been tossing hay from the loft with a pitchfork. He came down the ladder faster than most men can slide down a firehouse pole, sprinted out of the barn and across the windy yard to the house.

"What's goin' on?" Hannibal said, coming to the barn door.

"I think Hinkley's flipped out. Grace said he hit her, and he's packing his bags."

"Sumbitch gone run away. God*damn*!"

Will came rocketing out of the house without even touching the steps, sprinted across the barnyard and into the barn yelling, "The bastard pulled her away from the phone!" He grabbed his shotgun, which was leaning in a dusty corner with a hoe and some poles. "I'm gonna kill him for sure this time!"

"Will!" I shouted, starting for him. "For Christ's sake—"

He spun around and leveled the shotgun at me. His face was deep purple in color, his eyes had the cold fix of madness, and his chest was heaving. "Get out of my way or I'll blow you in two, Bornie!"

Before either Hannibal or I could move, he turned and made a break for his pickup truck. He had the door open as Hannibal caught up with him. There was a writhing too quick for me to see in the clouds of churning dust. The gun flew through the air and crashed into the barn wall. Will Timberlake grabbed Hannibal around the neck with both hands. Hannibal speared his arms up and broke the grip as if it had been a child trying to strangle him. He swung one mighty arm back and hit Will in the mouth with a walloping smack. Will stumbled back into a row of milk cans that clattered and clanked in all directions. Hannibal reached inside the pickup, pulled out the keys and tossed them across the yard to me. I caught them in one hand. "Hold him!" I yelled above the sound of the gales whipping around the barn. "I've got to call Dawson!"

As I ran inside, Mrs. Timberlake was coming down the stairs in her flowered dress. "Oh, I'm *so* glad I saw you before you—"

As I have told you, I have good manners, but that afternoon I didn't have time for them. I rushed into the dining room and dialed Tom Dawson's house without answering Mrs. Timberlake. "Tom," I said, "Bornie Eppe. Something's happening at Hinkley's house. I think he's trying to leave."

"I'll get right over there," Dawson said and hung up.

I dashed back outside. It had begun to rain. Will was standing in the mess of milk cans. He wiped his hand across his mouth and tested his teeth. A swatch of his oily hair was hanging over his forehead. He glared at Hannibal.

Hannibal was standing loose in the barnyard, rain splattering on him, legs slightly apart, his huge hands hanging at his sides. He looked as looming and lethal as a Minuteman missile. "You want fistfightin' with me," he said to Will, "we'll do fistfightin'. Otherwise you sit down quiet and me'n Sherbert'll take care of Mistah Rhett Hinkle."

"I'll murder the cocksucker!" Will shouted.

"You try murderin' me first, country boy," Hannibal said.

Will made a gurgling sound. He opened his mouth, shut it and then—suddenly—let out a yell like a Comanche on the warpath. He grabbed his shotgun, and before Hannibal could get to him, vaulted over the wired-together gate and ran down the sodden pasture toward the dirt road, howling descriptions of what part of Rhett Hinkley's anatomy he was going to blow off.

Mrs. Timberlake came out on the porch, gathering the front of her dress together against the wind. She peered through the rain. "Jesus has a grip on him," she said, watching Will cross the dirt road and start to chase Charlie the horse around the pasture. "Jesus knows best."

"He's crazy," I said to Hannibal.

"And that Hinkle's gettin' away," he retorted. "You drive the pickup. Shake ass!"

The storm was disgorging its first heavy downpour on the countryside by the time the Pierce-Arrow got to the dirt road with me following in the pickup truck. Through the screen of driving water I could see Will leaping around the pasture, waving his shotgun while Charlie the horse trotted in circles, whinnying with the pleasures of the chase.

The Pierce-Arrow was doing forty as it slithered to a stop at the highway. I hit the brakes on the pickup and nearly crashed into the car. Hannibal pulled out onto the main road. The wheels of the pickup spun in the mud and the Pierce-Arrow was far ahead of me by the time we got to the edge of Andrewstown.

The first explosion of the storm was over. The rain was coming down in a steady staccato as I turned in Hinkley's street. Hannibal was pulling over to the curb in front of the house, and Tom Dawson was running up the sidewalk with Croaker on a leash loping beside him.

I parked behind Hannibal and got out. Tom reached us a few seconds later. He was dripping wet but hardly out of breath at all. "What's going on?" he asked.

"All I know is that Grace said her father hit her and was packing his bags," I said, wiping the rain from my face.

Dawson looked across the lawn at the big gloomy Victorian house, ominous, wet and unlit. "Lord God," he murmured, "make him still be there."

We walked up the driveway. There was no sign of life. A squirrel dashed across the wet gass. Croaker leaped forward, half yanking Tom off balance.

"Gimme that dog," Hannibal said.

Tom handed him the leash. The squirrel changed its mind and scuttled back to its starting place. Croaker lunged again, did a back flip in midair as if his leash were attached to a brick wall. He gagged, looked cross-eyed and settled down to a plodding walk beside Hannibal.

We followed the driveway around to the back of the house.

A car was parked ten feet from the porch. Its trunk was open. Sister Cornelia was putting something into it, and Rhett Hinkley was coming down the back steps with a suitcase in each hand. Sister Cornelia was out of costume. She was wearing slacks, high-heeled shoes and a sweater with a V neck. Her gold cross was missing. Both of them froze when they saw us.

Tom walked forward.

At the foot of the steps Hinkley lowered his suitcases onto the wet gravel drive.

"Taking a trip, Rhett?" Tom asked.

Hinkley stood in the rain gazing at him with tepid hostility. The dimness of his eyes and the sag of his body showed that his inner core was in cold shutdown again. "Don't see that that should concern you, Dawson," he said.

Hannibal and I went over to listen.

"None of your business," Rhett Hinkley added.

"Eppe's been looking into your business," Tom said. "He's been kind enough to share what he's found out with me."

Hinkley looked from Tom to me and back at Tom again. "Now, I don't know what you're talking about, Dawson, and I don't think this *reporter* found out anything worth anybody's time. He's a liar. I had him in here, treated him decent, and the things he went around—"

"Harold Upson confirmed it," Tom said.

Hinkley looked at him dully. "Never heard of the man," he said.

There was a distinct cry from the top of the house. We all looked up in time to see glass bursting from an attic window into the rain. Grace's face appeared. "He's locked me in!" she screamed.

"Family trouble," Hinkley said. "None of your business."

"We've just made it our business," I said, looking up at Grace again. "Where's the attic door?" I called to her.

"On the second floor landing!" she wailed.

Pulling Croaker with him, Hannibal strode up onto the

back porch, pushed open the kitchen door with a crash and disappeared into the house.

Hinkley looked at me with his familiar expression of leaden hatred and intoned, " 'He that spareth his rod hateth his son: but he that loveth his son chasteneth him betimes.' Proverbs Thirteen: Twenty-four."

From the interior of the house came the rending, wood-splintering sounds of a door being ripped off its hinges.

" 'And put a knife to thy throat, if thou be a man given to appetite,' " Tom said. "Proverbs Twenty-three: Two."

"*Now* what're you talking about, Tom?" Hinkley said.

"Reverend Hinkley," I cut in before Dawson could answer, "you transferred over a million dollars of Holier Than Thou funds to a bank in Pittsburgh."

Grace appeared on the back porch followed by Hannibal and Croaker.

"From the Pittsburgh account," I went on, "you started sending checks to Sanford and Upson in New York, the investment counselors. They've put together a portfolio of investments for you and they've bought you an apartment." I wiped the rain dripping from the end of my nose and looked at Sister Cornelia. "I guess the apartment's for you and her."

Grace's face, which was also streaming wet, was expressionless in shock. She came down the back steps and walked over to Sister Cornelia. *"You?"* she asked as a child might ask it. "The woman Daddy saved?"

I decided she might as well know everything. "Your father didn't save her, Grace," I said as gently as I could. "Her name is Lucy Jo Patterson and she wants to go to New York and be an actress."

Sister Cornelia—*née* Lucy Jo Patterson—fixed me with her large hard eyes. "Thank you, Jesus," she said bitterly.

"Don't mention it," I answered.

"Now look here, young fella," Hinkley said, stirring out of his sullen torpor, "I think we got us a little misunderstanding about the money. I can see how you might suspect something fishy was going on." He tried a laugh. It came from him in a staccato cackle as if he were imitating a machine gun. "That's what you TV reporters are *supposed* to do. Find out fishy things that's going on. Attack the gummint, attack the church. That's the way you get people to listen in."

"Are you saying you didn't transfer the money?"

"Well, of *course* I transferred it." Hinkley was wiping his hands down the wet front of his shirt. "Had too much of it in the bank here. It's just a little old bank, you know. I left a *lot* in the bank here. But I needed services, I wanted to *invest* it, make the money grow for the church . . ."

"The account at Sanford and Upson's is in your name," I said. "They've never heard of Holier Than Thou. I imagine that when the investigators look into the Pittsburgh account they'll find that was in your name too."

"*What* investigators?" Hinkley asked, swallowing involuntarily between the two words.

"Internal Revenue . . . the Justice Department . . . Pennsylvania State . . ."

"I can explain about the names," Hinkley said in a voice that let you know he'd have a hard time explaining.

Grace turned to him. She was soaking wet; her blond hair was plastered to her head. "Daddy—for God's sake tell the truth —*please*, Daddy!"

Rhett Hinkley, crucified by discovery and drenched to his skin, suddenly ran out of every resource *except* the truth. His eyes ignited with his pulpit righteousness as he exploded all over his daughter. "*Daddy!*" he roared. He twisted his flabby, wet face into an imitation of Grace's weeping face. His voice became a yowling, nasal echo of hers. "Pleeeee-ase, *Daddy!*" He paused, letting the metronome of drama tick a few beats. "Sure," he spat, dropping his volume, "I'm *your* daddy, Grace, daddy of a selfish bitch who lays with garage mechanics and jailbirds—that's *all* I am! Nothing more! *Just your daddy!*"

Grace put her hand over her mouth. Her eyes widened, her sobbing was coming in wrenching jolts from her. I thought she was going to go into shock. I stepped in front of Hinkley. "I don't think you should talk to her that way, sir."

He ignored me. *"And what is Grace Hinkley's daddy?"* he bellowed. *"Just a daddy? Just a man going into his last, slob years? Just a piece of Grace Hinkley's life and nothing more?*

"No!" he yelled at his daughter. "Your *daddy* is a *whole* man! A whole *other* man! He *wants* like any other man! He's got *rights* like any other man!"

Grace dropped her hand. She stood in the sluicing rain with her head back and her eyes closed.

Hinkley grabbed her by the arm. "LOOK AT ME!" he shouted.

Grace opened her eyes.

Hinkley jerked her around and pointed at Dawson. "Call *him* Daddy!" He spun her around again and pointed at me. "Call *him* Daddy!" He flailed his free hand toward Hannibal on the porch. "CALL THAT NIGGER DADDY!" He seized Grace's other arm. She stared at him in shock. "Have you changed any of those men by calling them Daddy?" Hinkley rasped, his wet hair falling over his forehead, his eyes blazing with guilt and unmanageable fury. "Have you made them something less by calling them *Daddy?*"

Hannibal came down the back steps into the rain, dragging Croaker with him. "You better take your hands off that lady," he rumbled.

Hinkley paid no attention to him. "You're your mother's daughter, Grace," he said, dropping his voice in his dramatic, pulpit style. "I wasn't a man to her—just a *husband.* I was obliged to be a husband like *her* daddy—a poor preacher man! She couldn't imagine *her* daddy ever lovin' up a woman, so *I* wasn't supposed to—"

Hannibal jerked him back with a forceful twist of the arm. Hinkley let go of his daughter and staggered against the car. He glared at Grace with water streaming down his face. "Wonder you ever got born at all."

"Enough, Rhett," Tom said.

"What do you know about it, Dawson?" Hinkley snapped. "You ever been poor?"

Tom had been watching and listening with his hands shoved in the back pockets of his blue jeans, a rapt and attentive expression on his bearded face. He nodded slightly. "You bet I know about being poor, Rhett."

"You deserve it," Hinkley snapped at him. "You're a shit-ass of a preacher. I been poor when I *didn't* deserve it. *And I got sick of it!*" he roared suddenly. "I got sick of scrabbling to make a living like the rest of the poor white trash! I got sick of the God-thanking when there wasn't a goddamn thing to thank God for! I got sick of going to the picture show and seeing how *real* people live, how the *quality* get to live! You know how real people live, Dawson?"

"Tell me about it, Rhett," Tom said softly. He was as tranfixed by Hinkley as the rest of us.

"*Charles Boyer lovin' up Claudette Colbert!*" the Reverend Rhett bellowed.

"CARY GRANT WEARIN' A GOOD SUIT AND RIDIN' AROUND IN A CONVERTIBLE AUTOMOBILE!

"*A POOR MAN LIKE JIMMY STEWART GETTIN' TO GO TO WASHINGTON AND BE A SENATOR!*" Hinkley shrieked to the oily gray skies.

I was afraid he'd come completely unbolted and bite somebody. But that was part of Hinkley's act. Just when you thought he'd gone stark out of his mind in one of his religious or confessional ecstasies, he'd make a dramatic switch back to normality. I'd seen it at Holier Than Thou. I saw it now.

He shrugged. "I got sick of it," he said to Tom. "Sick of going to the picture show, seeing how the quality lived, and coming home Saturday night to a plate of beans and a dried-up woman who was forever quoting scripture *her* daddy taught her, and pushing me over to my own side of the bed."

He turned back on Grace. "Your mother always said I was nothing but a big mouth. Well, they can talk about all that money, *but my mouth made it!* And if *I* want to live like the quality, I got the right, I EARNED the right! I AM quality now! *I* got the money now!"

Grace had herself back under control. She had returned to quiet weeping.

"No good you carrying on and looking like that at me, Grace. You feel let down by your daddy. Well, the rest of me— the part that *isn't* your daddy—got himself out of the hard life, got himself his woman and his money and, yes, his apartment in New York, and that's where I'm going." He ran his paw down his face, wiping off the water. He scowled defiantly at Grace. "You'll be took care of."

Tom Dawson said, "I've been worried about you for quite a while, Rhett."

Hinkley tried a laugh. "You *shoulda* been worried, Dawson. You couldn't draw a crowd if you had Jesus himself reading the lesson."

"Reverend Hinkley," I said, "it looks to me as if you had decided to close Holier Than Thou once they discovered what caused the epidemic and you stopped getting big crowds. That's when you were planning to go to New York, wasn't it?"

Hinkley didn't answer; he just stood there scowling at me. He was beginning to deflate; his fires were guttering out. He was becoming the regional sales manager again.

"They've already discovered the source of the epidemic," I said. "Hannibal found it at Barney's, a roadhouse on Route Thirteen."

"Got nothin' to do with me anymore," Hinkley said.

"You're finished, sir," I said. "You could even be going to prison."

The word "prison" appeared to bring Hinkley totally back to the wet earth and stark reality. He frowned at me, quizzical and afraid. "What d'you mean, *could?*"

Tom Dawson took his hands out of his pockets. "All I have to do is call the police," he said.

"Tom," Hinkley implored, "look here, Tom, I never did you any harm . . ."

"There are people who need Holier Than Thou," Tom said. "They'd be lost—abandoned—if it closed."

Hinkley thought he saw what Tom was driving at. "Tell you what we'll do," he said. "*You* take Holier Than Thou. You're a *real* minister."

I glanced at Tom. Standing in his black turtleneck sweater with raindrops glistening on his curly black hair and beard, he didn't look victorious at all. Grab it, you wimp, I thought bitterly. This is what you set it all up for.

Tom took out a handkerchief and wiped the rain off his face while we all gave him our undivided attention. He stuffed the handkerchief back into his pocket.

"As you say, I'm a real minister, but the truth is—I'm a rotten preacher," he answered in his soft, unemphatic voice. "I'm minister and pastor enough to know that God's intentions are vast and minute, logical but inscrutable." He coughed slightly. "Almighty God selected you for a purpose, Rhett. You have a gift that transforms people's lives and gladdens them; you have been graced with a power that brings souls to their Saviour. It doesn't matter that you don't believe in the purpose of your life—the Lord probably intended that too. And you're going to stay right here in Andrewstown doing what God intends you to do at Holier Than Thou."

A squirrel hopped across the moist grass, poking around, looking for an acorn he'd misplaced somewhere. Croaker, still tethered to Hannibal, gave a small groan of frustration.

"And what if I *don't* stay?" Hinkley asked in a voice so wavery that you knew he already suspected what the answer would be.

"Then I'll personally do everything I can to see that you go to the federal penitentiary," Tom answered. "Bornie's dug up enough evidence to give the prosecutors a good start."

Hinkley turned to me. "I suppose *you* want something out of me, too," he said in a defeated but baleful voice.

"Yes, sir," I said, still trying to recover from my astonishment and chagrin at being so wrong about Tom, "I do."

"All right. Let's hear it."

I was about to tell him when the cavalry arrived.

The line of tall shrubbery at the end of the lawn parted with a crash and a rebel yell. A horse came thundering across the wet lawn straight at us. It was Charlie with Will astride him waving his shotgun and screeching like a fiend with hives.

He reined in Charlie so hard that the swoon-prone horse nearly sat down, his skidding front hooves spraying gravel and water all over me and the car.

Will swung down the gun. "Get the hell out of the way, Bornie!" he yelled.

"Jesus God!" Hinkley hollered, cowering behind me and grabbing me around the waist.

"Will!" Grace screamed.

"Bornie," Will yelled again, "get the goddamn hell out of the way because I'm going to blast that bastard to kingdom come!"

I don't know if you have ever stared into the steel nostrils of a twelve-gauge shotgun held by a temporarily crazed man who, you are certain, will use it. The experience makes everything immediately clear. I didn't hear any explicit orders from the universe, but I knew that Rhett Hinkley was going to go on living and preaching, and if my time had come, that had been decided in some cosmic crap game long before the world began. I wasn't afraid, just curious about what, exactly, a faceful of buckshot feels like.

"No, Will," I said.

Hinkley had scrunched down to the point where his arms

were around my legs now. "Don't let him do it!" he bawled. "Don't move, sonny!"

"I *am* going to kill that son of a bitch," Will said in an eerily calm insane voice.

"All you'll do is kill *me*," I said. "That won't accomplish anything." Out of the corner of my eye I saw Hannibal make a quick movement.

"I got two barrels," Will said, cocking his head and baring his teeth. "I'll let you have the first one, Bornie, so help me God I will."

Croaker bounded forward with a joyous Labrador woof and streaked across the driveway at the horse.

Charlie reared, whinnied in fear and then toppled over on his side in a dead faint. Going down with him, Will shot off both barrels. Bits of twig and leaf came pelting down with the rain.

Grace ran over and threw her arms around my neck. "Oh, Lord, save us!" she cried. "He wouldn't really have done it, Mr. Eppe! *He really wouldn't!*" Her father was still clutching me around the knees, blubbering and quaking. I was soaking wet and draped with Hinkleys.

Out on the lawn Croaker was cavorting around the unconscious horse, barking his head off and wagging his tail in rapturous triumph. In his entire career as a chaser, Croaker had never brought down anything that big.

From somewhere beneath Charlie, Will Timberlake was shouting "Goddamn!" and "Son of a bitch!" It was a shouting sort of afternoon all the way around as I look back on it. After beseeching the Lord to save us a few more times, Grace ran across the grass. Hannibal went into the kitchen, got a bucket of water and dumped it all over Charlie's head. He took a powerful grip on the horse's neck, making him get up slowly and carefully.

I walked across the lawn while Will was separated out from beneath Charlie. He wasn't hurt, Grace was swarming all over him and I thought I'd better get up close in case Will decided to have another crack at killing Hinkley.

Will tested both legs to make sure they weren't broken and then looked at me. "I don't blame you for hating me," he said.

"I don't hate you," I answered. "In fact, I like you quite a lot, but I'll hit you in the mouth again if you move."

Will glanced down at Grace. "He has a pretty good wallop, honey."

"I remember," Grace said, clinging to him.

I looked across the lawn at the Reverend Hinkley. "We were just talking about what I wanted from you to keep my mouth shut," I said.

The Reverend Rhett was rain-soaked, disgraced and miserable.

"First, I want the same thing Tom does," I said. "Give the money back and stay here in Andrewstown."

Hinkley's dull eyes stared at me.

"Second," I said, "let Grace go if she wants to. I think she could civilize Will."

"He couldn't stop me from going," Grace said. "Not now."

"Third," I said to Hinkley, "I want you to call Mrs. Timberlake and tell her it was all a misunderstanding between you and me."

Hinkley still didn't say anything. I have seen two water-logged men in my life. One was Raoul. The other was Rhett Hinkley that afternoon. He was waterlogged inside and out, in spirit and in body.

"Is it a deal?" I asked.

Hinkley—slumped and extinguished—thought before answering. Perhaps he was trying to come to terms with the obliteration of his fantasies and choose between the ignomies facing him. "It's a deal," he finally said. He turned to the former Sister Cornelia. "You'n me better go inside and unpack."

Lucy Jo Patterson tilted her head back, giving a graceful arch to her long neck. Her large eyes and aristocratic features were as composed as they had been on the first night I saw her at Holier Than Thou. "Go screw yourself, Gerry," she said in her cultivated voice. "You can get somebody else to charge your battery." She picked up a suitcase. "Do any of you gentlemen know when the next bus leaves for anywhere?"

Thus was sealed the dismal and—I guess—deserved fate of Rhett Hinkley.

It rained until five o'clock that afternoon. The storm held up Art Olsen's arrival with the camera crew, but it didn't matter. My adventures with the Jesus Christ Church of Holier Than Thou and my career as an investigative reporter were over.

Art sat on the edge of Tom Dawson's symmetrically made bed looking like a bewildered undertaker when I said I couldn't tell him—or write about—the chicaneries of the Reverend Hinkley. "Besides," I said. "It's finished. It isn't news anymore."

"But he *was* doing something crooked," Art said.

"Planning to. But the money's going to come back to the bank in Andrewstown."

Art leaned forward. He folded his hands between the drooping folds of his raincoat and looked solemn. "Reporters are supposed to *tell* what they know, not hide it, Sherborne."

"I know," I said.

"I'm not sure I can protect you from Ned Plotkin when I go back and try to explain this," he said, fixing me with his small, earnest eyes.

"You shouldn't try," I said. "I don't really think I'm cut out for this line of work, Art. I'd rather be fired by you than by Ned."

He made a sort of scowl of anguish because I was putting him in a hard position. Art Olsen wasn't one of this world's belligerents; he didn't enjoy fighting with or firing people. "Sherborne," he said, "did you become a *part* of this story?"

"I'm afraid I did."

"That wasn't what we sent you here to do."

I looked out of the window. In the wet dusk every tree dripped and the black tar street gleamed. "I know," I said. "I couldn't help getting involved."

So he fired me and was sorrowful about it. But I was relieved. My immediate ambitions were disposed of—Rhett Hinkley had been nailed in a way I never could have foreseen, and if I had struck out as an investigative reporter, I had at least learned that I wasn't going to do *that* with my life.

Tom, Hannibal and I went out for dinner at a steakhouse on the edge of Andrewstown. Tom said we could stay at his place that night if we didn't mind sharing a bedroom, and Hannibal went off to the Timberlake farm to collect our bags.

I went up to Tom's room, closed the door and dialed Warwick, Rhode Island.

"Hello?" said the voice like a cello.

"Beth," I said, "it's Bornie."

"Hold it a sec," she replied, "I have to go to another phone." I heard her footsteps walking away. I envisioned a vast, dark-stained, hardwood floor and a little knot began to draw tight beneath my breastbone. She could at least have given a murmur of pleasure at hearing from me.

She picked up the other telephone. "Okay, I have it," she said. The first phone went dead as someone put it back on the receiver. "Hey, listen," Beth said, "I'm sorry, but—"

"Beth," I said, "use my name."

"Come again?"

"Speak my name," I said.

There was a silence in Warwick. I wondered if it had been raining there, too.

"Bornie," she said. "Sherborne Eppe."

"I wasn't sure you knew who I was."

"Of *course* I knew it was you."

"Maybe I wasn't sure you *wanted* to use my name."

She didn't say anything for a moment. "Well, if we throw out all those niceties," she finally answered, "there might be something to that."

One of my character flaws is a naïveté about time and human nature. I keep expecting people to remain unchanged—forgetting that *I* change moods all the time. Since my last conversation with Beth I had drawn all my happiness from two of her final phrases—"Don't give me up, Bornie" and "Good night, dear friend."

Now I had intimations of something dire, of an impending and catastrophic disappointment.

"What's happened?" I asked.

"*Please* don't sound so truculent . . . Bornie."

"It's because I'm scared," I answered. "Something's changed and I guess I'm trying to protect myself."

"And *please* stop telling the truth like that. It unnerves me."

"You still haven't told me what's happened."

"I—" She paused. "Um, well—Bornie, you can't call me here anymore. I'll give you my office number at the university."

"Why not, Beth?"

"I can't tell you."

"I don't get it. I haven't done anything. The last time we talked—"

"I know," she said. "But something *has* happened, the thing I can't tell you. Besides, I've been thinking."

"About what?" I was tense and my heartbeat had gone up considerably.

"Bornie," she said, "listen to me. I'm going to tell the truth too. From that first morning you called me by mistake, this has been a—wonderful, a *whole* experience. I met you when I needed you, we had a big misunderstanding and got through it, I met your mother, we saw pictures of each other, you read my poems, I got an insight into your life . . ."

I waited. I looked through the window. A street lamp in front of Tom's house was spreading its nimbus of light on the half-dried street. "But it's all unreal," I said.

"*No*," she answered sharply. "Don't finish sentences and make up thoughts for me. It *hasn't* been unreal! It's been one of the realest things, one of the most moving encounters of my whole life. It's taken me into all sorts of feelings because it *has* been so real."

"Have you written any poems about us?"

"Yes."

"How many?"

"Six. You mustn't ask about my writing. It's a private room, Bornie—no entry, all that."

"What's this thing you've been thinking, Beth?"

"The last time we talked you said you'd conjured up a big fantasy about me. You'd fallen in love with the way I speak."

"That's right," I said.

There was another pause at her end of the line. "I bet it's a fantasy about a polished, pristine young poet with a low voice."

"That's what you are."

"That's the part of me you know now. There's a lot more of me you *don't* know."

In the midst of my tension I was feeling surprisingly confident. Although Beth had shaken me with her mysteries and half-uttered reservations, my brain hadn't switched off to an unfathomable numbness in which I could find neither words nor thoughts.

"Listen," I said, "neither of us is a calculating machine. You detected something in *me* the first time we talked, something hopeful and promising. You went to Cambridge to check me out, you saw my picture. We're just beginning, Beth. Everybody who meets anybody has to start somewhere. What are you afraid of?"

"I'm afraid of what happens if reality doesn't live up to your fantasy," she said. "I feel this *pressure* . . ."

Goddamn that Manfred, I swore to myself, if I ever catch up with him I'll kill him—right in the head. Aloud I said, "That's your ancient history speaking. You wrote about it in a Manfred poem, 'The Grammarian's Complaint.' 'Past imperfect'—"

" 'Present tense'—"

" 'Future perfect,' " I quoted. " 'Your regret and fantasy are too immense . . .' Beth, I'm not Manfred and I don't feel like taking his rap. I'm me, a whole new ball game—and you got into the game voluntarily."

"All right, all right, all right," she said, "I *concede* there's this chemistry between us. But it can't come to anything if we have to perform. You've got to be what you really are, I've got to be what I really am, even all the things I hate in myself."

"Which scares you the most?" I asked. "Me finding out what you're really like or you finding out what I'm really like?"

Pause. "Um—that's not the question."

"It's the one I'm asking," I said. "Look, there's only one way to solve this. I'm leaving for Rhode Island in the morning."

"No, Bornie, not yet. You *mustn't* come here." She was talking in a voice on the edge of panic. "Not now. I'll tell you when."

"That may not be until Manfred's dead and buried in your memory. I'm not willing to wait that long."

"It hasn't anything to do with Manfred!" she cried. "If you come now *I'll* be responsible for what happens to you!"

"Beth," I said, "what the hell's going on? If you're talking about that private detective who's after me, I think I've spotted him and I can shake him."

"It's not that! I *promised* I wouldn't—"

"Listen, Beth—"

"Bornie, where are you calling from?"

"I won't tell you."

"Bornie, I'm frightened for you."

"I think I'm in love with you," I replied and hung up before she could give voice to all the shock, doubt, qualifications, perturbation and unadmittable delight that such a statement would arouse in a pristine, polished young poet when uttered by a man with whom she has an inexplicable chemistry and only a tentative beginning.

I was feeling pleased with myself. As you may have gathered I am not one of this world's assertive types, yet that day I had stood up to death by shotgun blast and the protests of a lady whose affections I was trying to win.

I lay on one of the twin beds in Tom's spare room, alternately reading a book I borrowed from him and trying to figure out what peril could possibly await me in Warwick, Rhode Island. Nothing gory or menacing suggested itself, so I turned back to the book. It was Byron's "Manfred," a dramatic poem concerning a man who hates himself because he has committed a terrible crime. I was just reading the part where Manfred is trying to decide to chuck himself off a cliff because he can't love the day, the mountains or art, the part where he says,

> There is a power upon me which withholds,
> And makes it my fatality to live—

when the living fatality of *my* life walked in and dumped our suitcases on the floor.

He sat down on the opposite bed. "That farm lady say Hinkle called her 'bout you."

"That's good," I said.

Hannibal looked at me as if I were a newly discovered object. "Sorry they ain't gone put you on the teevee."

I was touched. "It doesn't matter," I said.

"Ain't no laughs on the teevee news," he said. He started to wheeze and jiggle in his unsmiling humor.

"They could always try you reciting the multiplication table," I said.

When he had finished indulging his brutish mirth he said, "What you gone do now?"

"A couple of things," I answered. "Sometime soon I'm going to start looking seriously for my father."

"Where you lose him?"

"We lost each other," I said. "My mother pried us apart. I haven't seen him for eight years."

"What she want to do that for?"

"She doesn't like either of us very much."

Hannibal snorted. "If your mama don't like either you or your daddy, why don't she just go off and tend her business and leave you be?"

"It's a long story. My mother's a little crazy. Anyway, tomorrow I'm going to Rhode Island."

"What for?"

"To see a girl."

"You mean to tell me you goin' all the way to *Rhode Island* on account of some fox?"

"Girl," I said. "You know what girls are. A lot of them have bumps in front."

"Nemmine what I know or don't know," he said. "You sittin' there tellin' me I got to carry you to *Rhode Island* just so you can—"

"I don't want to hear about it. Besides, nobody's asking you to come along."

"If I don't come," he said, "you gone start for *Rhode Island* all by youself and you gone end up in Alaska because you the biggest asshole that ever lived."

My cup ranneth over.

Fourteen

AN EARLY DINNER

MY GODS HAD CAUGHT UP with me in Andrewstown and suddenly all was right with the world—at least the part of it I was inhabiting.

I was alive and unmaimed. My confrontations with death and Beth's will had tightened the rivets around my self-esteem. While I didn't exactly think of myself as combining the best traits of Wyatt Earp and Johann Sebastian Bach, I *was* reveling in a growing confidence that I could proceed through life without stepping on the third rail.

After Hannibal and I said our goodbyes to Tom, the Timberlakes, Grace and the girl at the bank, we started across Pennsylvania toward Rhode Island in the Pierce-Arrow. I was prudent enough to remind myself that even though meeting me over the telephone had been one of the more moving experiences of Beth's life, she wasn't going to greet me with shrieks of glee when we actually came face to face. There was some mystery about her—but I couldn't focus my mind to think about it.

Spring was in full whoop. The bright morning sun had

baked away the dampness left over from the storm, the hills were green and the farm land a loamy brown. We had put the top down and were on a broad highway where Hannibal could cruise at a steady fifty-five miles an hour.

I don't know about your gods. Mine specialize in *almost*. The condition of my life at Craigie Glen had been almost hopeless—but fate had mitigated it with little glops of redemption like Dusty, the psychiatric aide who brought me candy bars, and Mr. Fletcher, the mystic junkie from New Jersey. At other times —like that morning we left God's proving ground in Andrewstown—my life was *almost* perfect except for one thing: I couldn't wake up.

It was as if everything I felt existed one layer down in me. On my surface, an opaque film of lethargy hung between me and the world. I decided that I was worn out from all the turmoil of the day before. I told Hannibal that we were heading for the house of a Mr. Harold Watts in Warwick, Rhode Island, and I crawled into the back seat. I had barely a moment to breathe the comforting aroma of the red leather and feel its cool against my cheek before I fell into a dark, senseless slumber that was beyond dream or remembrance.

The next thing I knew, Hannibal was shaking me. "You all right?" he rumbled.

"Of course I'm all right," I said. "I've just been taking a nap."

"Some nap," he grunted. "You been nappin' through Pennsylvania, New Jersey, New York, Connecticut and Rhode Island. Thought you'd gone and died."

"I'm not dead."

"Man lyin' in a car with his eyes closed *looks* daid."

I opened my eyes. The bright morning of Pennsylvania had dissolved into early dusk. There was a tang of salt in the air and a whiff of kelp.

Hannibal was standing by the open back door of the Pierce-Arrow. "You *still* look daid. You able to stand up?"

"Sure I can stand up," I said, rolling off the back seat onto the floor and crawling out of the car, over the running board and onto the gravelly edge of a tar road. I lay there watching the stalks of brittle grass that were moving slightly in the evening breeze close to my face. "Just give me a minute."

Towering above me, Hannibal said, "I think you one sick man, Sherbert. In fact, I *know* you a sick man."

"Sand fleas," I said.

"What you talkin' about now?"

"We're near the shore. This place is full of sand fleas. I have them inside my clothes. I can feel them." I began to clutch at my armpits and crotch where the sand fleas were at their busiest.

"Godamighty," Hannibal muttered, looking down at me.

In the midst of my scratchings I fell asleep again. Hannibal woke me up by shaking me. "Why did we stop here?" I asked.

He held out his hand. I grasped it and he pulled me to my feet. The salty breeze was refreshing and good, the twilight was deepening. "I must be clean outa my mind," Hannibal said, "cartin' you around the country when you oughta be sickabed. Shoulda known when you slept so long."

"Why did we stop here?" I asked again.

Hannibal pointed across the road at a large white house with a widow's walk on top, a screened-in porch, wings sticking out in several directions, and an old white barn in the rear with a weather vane on the roof. This handsome establishment was set back on a wide lawn among large trees whose shapes were blurring in the smoky dusk.

"Man in town told me that there's the Watts place," Hannibal said.

"Something's burning somewhere," I said. "It's all smoky."

Hannibal stared at me with the closest approximation to anxiety I had ever seen on his face. "Godamighty," he muttered again, "you most likely breathed in the dust when you were burnin' that fat lady's clothes."

Disconnected as I felt from the whole world, I heard his words and they made sense in the senseless oatmeal of my brain.

My trouble wasn't fatigue and sand fleas. I looked back at the Watts place and thought I saw a gazebo on the far lawn, among the trees. But the light was dimming and I knew I was off my head from the Bug Plague.

"You gone stand there dyin' on your feet or you gone go in and say howdy so we can fetch you to the doctor?" Hannibal demanded.

There was a gravel driveway and a gravel path leading to the front door. The windows were bright squares of orange light, and a voice—not Beth's—was calling to me from inside the house, betting me I couldn't walk a straight line up the gravel path and ring the doorbell. I'm fond of games like that, so I tried. I didn't do badly, either. I only hit the driveway twice and a tree once on my way to the front door. I didn't do as well ringing the doorbell. It kept jumping around so that I mashed my thumb against hard wood about four times. Finally Hannibal rang the bell.

A long, long time passed—it could have been several years—before a maid in a black dress and a dainty white apron opened the door.

"Good evening," I said. "I think I've sprained my thumb."

The maid looked up at me. She appeared perplexed. I realized I had begun all wrong. "Good evening," I said. "My name is Sherborne Eppe. I've come to see Miss Elizabeth Watts."

"Please to come in," the maid said. "I call Mister."

We were standing in a front hallway. The house was so old, serene and settled that it acted as a tranquilizer on me, bringing the scattered portions of my brain back together and reducing my surroundings to an ordered proportion for the moment. My excited anticipation began to seep through the Grand Banks fog of my mind. I had arrived, at long last; I had come to the place, girl, voice and fulfillment toward which my adventures had been pointing me with this life's usual zigzags and subtleties.

The floorboards of the hall were wide and dark-stained, as I had imagined them during one telephone call to Beth. There was an antique sideboard with a small silver tray on it; above the sideboard an ancestral portrait hung in an ornate gold frame. It was a portrait of an eighteenth-century-looking man, high-collared shirt, black coat, a sharp-nosed face with ruddy cheeks and highlights glinting from his eyes. He could have been an Eppe or Sherborne ancestor; New England forebears run to a certain type—the weather burns their faces, the glint in the eyes comes from a mixture of pride in literacy, Congregationalist guilt and satisfaction with the profits from the molasses and slave trade.

A staircase ascended to the shadows of the second floor. Somewhere up there Beth was being told that I was waiting. I imagined the combination of alarm and excitement in her heart as she combed her hair and tried to compose herself before coming downstairs. The bugs were dancing a Virginia reel up and down my legs, but it didn't matter.

I heard footsteps crossing a room directly above the hall. My heart began to beat faster because now I would see in the flesh the girl I had imagined. I was in a half delirium from either the Bug Plague or the imminence of one of my life's great moments.

She came down the stairs.

She was bald.

"I'm Harold Watts," said a man of medium size with an instant, welcoming grin. The madness began to overcome me as he held out his hand. He was a youngish man, as the fathers of my generation go; he was wearing a pale-green sweater, shorts and sneakers.

Numbly I shook his hand. "This is Hannibal," I said.

Mr. Watts shook hands with Hannibal. "Glad to meet you." He looked down at his clothes. "Sorry I haven't changed. We were racing at the Saunderstown Yacht Club today and the wind died on the way home. I've just gotten back." He turned to me. "Elizabeth said you were on your way."

"I was hoping she'd be here," I said.

"How did you guys come?" Mr. Watts asked.

"Drove," Hannibal said. "Car's out on the road."

"Have you had dinner yet?"

"This man," Hannibal said, gesturing toward me, "is sick."

Harold Watts looked at me. It was one of those looks that convey the looker's understanding that you aren't yourself. I was somebody else, I don't know quite who, but Mr. Watts' glance told me that he instantly grasped the situation. "Look, pull your car into the driveway. I'll call a doctor and we'll have Sherborne looked at."

"Bornie," I said. "Even Beth calls me Bornie."

Mr. Watts smiled again, a grin that implied he found life full of things that amused him. "She mentioned that. Come on, I'll show you where you can clean up before dinner."

I wanted to know where Beth was. I wanted to see her. But as I have told you on more than one occasion, I was raised to good manners, and sick as I was, I caught on that Mr. Watts didn't want to talk about Beth. There was another mystery going on. The best thing to do with mysteries is wait them out, no matter how anxious they make you. Besides, the plague was coming back full blast, the bugs were swarming all over my body and I couldn't think of any more adroit ways to force the issue of Beth. My mind was beginning to fling out hallucinations. The ruddy-faced Watts ancestor on the wall winked at me, the antique sideboard was shuffling its feet preparatory to running the Boston marathon, and my first imperative was to work hard at acting as rational as I could around Mr. Watts.

I followed him upstairs to a bedroom with a painted dresser and a window that looked out across the dark water to lights glittering in a low strip upon a distant shore. Gauzy curtains wafted away from the sill and returned in the soft breeze. I tried to be polite, acknowledged my understanding that they'd get the doctor to come as soon as he could and that we'd be having an early dinner. Swordfish, I think Mr. Watts said. I stumbled onto a low bed with a striped spread covering it, I scratched and ripped at the bugs while I raced a swordfish around the third curve of the world.

Hannibal came up and looked at me. "Doctor's gone be a few hours," he said. "You feel like eatin'?"

"Sure," I said. If you can't beat a swordfish, eat him.

The attack was passing. I was beginning to come back to hard ground for a moment.

I got up and went into the bathroom. I looked at myself in the mirror. I was pale and horrible. My face had a streak of dirt on the left side—presumably from lying on the road. I was ashamed that Mr. Watts had seen me in such a condition. I was grateful that Beth hadn't.

I washed my face, combed my hair and went back to the bedroom. Hannibal was sitting in a chair watching me with a broody stare of helpless concern. "How long have we been here?" I asked.

" 'Bout a half-hour."

"Have you seen a girl around anywhere? She's blond and looks like—"

He shook his head. "I ain't seen no girl. Ain't nobody here 'cept that man and the maid."

Hannibal cleaned up and we went downstairs. Mr. Watts, who had changed into slacks and a seersucker jacket, was in a small cozy room off the hall having a drink with a young man.

Now, this was a manufactured young man. I knew, in the depths of my fever-induced genius, that he had been stamped out in an East Heidelberg factory where they produce psychiatric aides, Texas insurance agents of the sort I'd seen in TV commercials, and middle managers. He had ordinary brown hair and an unastonishing face, was wearing a lightweight suit, a drip-dry shirt and was short. Mr. Watts introduced him as Mr. Finch. I knew I already knew his name. In that factory they produce hundreds of Mr. Finches, and once in a while a Mr. Wilson.

"Do you feel up to a drink?" Mr. Watts asked me.

The big carousel of the world was beginning its slow turn around the place where I was standing and I wanted to listen to the music. If I had a drink, the clinking of the ice cubes might be out of tune. "I'd better not," I said, shrewdly declining to explain my reasons.

"I think you're right," Mr. Watts said. "You'd better wait until the doctor has a look at you."

That, precisely, had been my reason for refusing a drink.

"What about eating?" he asked me.

I was eager to do that because of my fierce competition with the swordfish. "I do feel hungry," I said. "I'll be all right."

We went out onto a screened porch where a white wrought-iron table had been set for four. My addled senses took in the silver, china plates gleaming in the light of a large candle set in a hurricane lamp, the crystal glasses and green napkins folded beside each place.

Beyond the porch, fireflies were switching themselves on and off across the rolling lawn, among the trees. Twilight was about to give up and let darkness have the world for a while. I tried to eat the cold soup that was set before me. But sights and sounds, enlarged and menacing, held my attention. The distant beepings of cars on the shore road where Beth's cat had died long, long before were really tiny trumpet flourishes calling together the legions of bugs waiting among the lilac bushes on the far side of the lawn; the big blobs of white lilac visible in the last light were bug regimental banners, and I knew what those fireflies were doing—they were casting their beacons around, looking for me, the enemy, and illuminating the grassy route along which the bugs would march for their final attack upon my itching, burning body.

"It's a painful subject," Mr. Watts was saying as the maid in the black dress and dainty white apron passed the swordfish, "but I guess it can't wait any longer."

"Yes, sir," I said, wondering what he was talking about.

"I'm not too worried about Elizabeth," Mr. Watts said as he began to eat his dinner. "I imagine she's gone to stay with one of her friends."

"I hope it isn't Manfred," I said.

Mr. Watts put down his fork, looked at me for a moment and then laughed.

"I'm going to really fix him when I catch up with him," I went on.

"You don't know Elizabeth very well," Mr. Watts said.

He began to tell me about polished, pristine young poets, the life of the imagination, poetic reality which is different from true reality because it *is* rooted in the imagination.

But I couldn't focus on what he was saying. The trumpet blasts were growing louder, the hot beacon of searchlights was sweeping across my face, the tiny bug officers were piping commands and I was distracted by the sound of the orders being repeated and relayed by tiny bug sergeants. The attack was about to begin. It would take them a while to march across the lawn by firefly light. Mine was a madness that knew it was mad; it recognized another world of rational events and conversations of the kind Mr. Watts was trying to have with me. The repeated mentions of Beth's name finally yanked my focus back from the imminence of bug wars to a summer night where four men were having dinner together as the last light fell and the stars rose.

". . . and perhaps she didn't want you to know that," Mr. Watts said. "Elizabeth is a very unusual girl. She may seem fragile and a little fey on the outside, but she's strong and persistent where it counts, in her creative life. Maybe she thought you wouldn't understand."

I understood. The only trouble was that I didn't know what I was supposed to understand. The firefly lights were becoming brighter, flares bursting over the lawn as attack sounded on the bug trumpets. I fought for time, trying to ignore the great impending battle in which zillions of bugs were going to swarm all over me, gnawing and slicing me down to a zillion bug-sized fragments. I was terrified, but what Mr. Watts was saying was more important than my fear because it had to do with Beth.

"A lot of people have blamed me for overprotecting her," he continued, "and I guess, in a way, there's something to that criticism. But you can't make final judgments unless you take all the circumstances and human foibles into account. Elizabeth is an only child, her mother died when she was seven, which is a bad enough experience for any child of that age, but when it hits a gifted, sensitive child like Elizabeth . . ."

The white light of the flares was bursting over the lawn;

hidden from normal view—but not mine—the bug legions were marching toward the house, clarions of trumpet call steering them around trees and roots. The bug commanders were shrewd; they'd left their regimental banners behind. A normal eye could see the white smears of lilac blossom in the last light. Only I knew that the enemy was coming by the millions, each bug rasping its pincers and sharpening its teeth in preparation for my flesh.

". . . which I'm sure you can understand, Bornie."

"I'm sorry," I said. "I wasn't listening for a moment."

Harold Watts leaned back in his chair. Finch, Hannibal and I were all watching him. "I said I've been a prosecutor and a U.S. Attorney for nineteen years," he said. "In that kind of work you see human nature at its worst—and maybe that made me neurotic about shielding Elizabeth from the rawer side of life—especially among the young."

Cars honked on the distant road, the trumpets were louder and closer to the porch. I switched back to a desperate strategic assessment of the enemy; they would come at me from three sides, I thought, ripping through the screens. If I ran into the house, slamming doors behind me, it would slow down the bugs. I could get out through the kitchen, run down the driveway and escape in the Pierce-Arrow. But Hannibal had the keys, and besides, if I did that, Mr. Watts would think I was crazy and wouldn't let me near his overly protected daughter.

"I don't question Elizabeth's fascination with you," he was saying, "nor yours with her—even though you've never physically met." He smiled that friendly yet cautionary smile at me. He was about to say "but." "That's why I'm telling you all this. But I can't let it go any further."

The World War of the Bugs paused and throbbed in the gloom. "Why not?" I asked. "I don't understand."

"I've checked on your family," Harold Watts said. "They're fine people. I know your cousin, Percy Sherborne, the Suffolk County District Attorney up in Massachusetts. That's why I'm doubly surprised and sorry about you."

Lightning bolts of apprehension and bewilderment were flickering across the dark fevered sky of my mind.

"What about me?" I asked. "I'm just an ordinary—"

Mr. Watts drew an envelope from his jacket pocket. He held it in his hands looking down at it with a sorrowful expression on his amiable face. In my growing panic I had the fleeting thought that maybe he really *was* sorry for whatever it was he was going to do to me.

"A grand jury has convened," he said. "You've been indicted for conspiracy and for the interstate sale of stolen merchandise." Sadly, reluctantly, he handed the envelope to me. "This is a copy of the indictment. You'd better get an attorney, Bornie, and arrange for bail. I wish—well, I wish this didn't have to happen, for Elizabeth's sake especially. She did try to warn you not to come here."

I took the envelope. It was like taking the first artillery round of the Bug Plague war. It made me cringe.

Mr. Finch stirred and crushed out the cigarette he'd been smoking. He fired round two. "Mr. Eppe, I'm from the Providence office of the FBI. You're under arrest."

I couldn't think of anything to say. I looked out at the dark lawn. I heard a tiny, shrill command. The attack was about to begin.

"You jes hold it right there," Hannibal rumbled. "I was with this man in Cleveland at that auto-parts racket, I been with him ever since and I can tell you—"

Finch looked at him in the candlelight and said, "Who are you?"

Hannibal squirmed his huge body around and pulled his wallet from his hip pocket. He flipped it open and handed it to Finch.

The FBI agent looked at a card in the wallet and turned to Mr. Watts. "He's a private investigator," he said; "license issued by the state of Ohio."

I was having shocks on top of my shocks, astonishments were coming faster than I could absorb them. Hannibal was still a huge creature of implied wrath, but he was someone I had never seen before.

"Who's your client?" Harold Watts asked.

"This man's mother," Hannibal said. "Lady named Eppe in Cambridge, Massachusetts."

I fainted.

As my face mashed into my dinner I thought how ironic it was that the swordfish had gotten me before the bugs did. Then my madness conceded that it was mad and I knew the truth. My own follies had done me in—follies which, if seen by a baleful eye, could be construed as a madness which conceded nothing at all.

Just before I surrendered to the summer night and the battlefield of the Bug Plague I saw a new beacon brighter than ten thousand flares and fireflies. It was aimed directly at me. It was Hannibal's eye.

Fifteen

THE GIRL
IN THE GAZEBO

SUMMER COMES TO NARRAGANSETT BAY with sea winds
bellying out spinnakers in the afternoon sun, wet sneakers
lying on the porch, and as the shadows lengthen, elderly gentlemen drinking martinis on the lawn. The hot nights blaze with
light and party babble, pop music is heard across the water while
on beaches and flat rock promontories, in bushes and in cars,
young men try to interest young women in the propagation of
the species. Or so it was during the summers of my early adolescence at Narragansett Bay.

But as the July of my twenty-fourth year began, I neither
saw nor heard such pleasures. Instead, what I saw were fragments
of reality, perceived between ravings, retchings, itchy torments,
fevers and agues beyond chronicling. In the exhausted intermis-
sions when the Bug Plague took time off, I saw the mud-yellow
walls of a hospital room and a lot of chrome-and-glass equipment. I saw faces—a nurse with freckles, and legions of young
residents who would come in and peer at me, thrilled by my

unusual disease. I saw a familiar black face which I knew, by some demented instinct or memory, that I must now hate and fear. Once or twice I saw the bald-topped face of Mr. Watts, who seemed to be trying to praise and reassure me about something. One face hovering before me seemed special—it was composed of large eyes and delicate features framed by blond hair. Sometimes the person to whom it belonged would sit on the far side of the room with her chin propped on her fist. It looked as if she was brooding upon me, as if she was trying to figure out if I was real.

Time had no meaning for me, nor did day and night. I madly measured my existence by the attacks and remissions of my affliction. Gradually the symptoms decreased in ferocity and the pauses between attacks grew longer. I lay speechless and worn out, unable to do much more than exist. Then one afternoon I really knew I was better when I awakened from an untormented sleep, saw a black man looking at me and sat bolt upright with a yell of fury.

"Not bad," he said.

I took a second look at him. He was wearing a white coat and had a stethoscope dangling from his neck. "I'm sorry," I said, "I thought you were somebody else." The room swayed and tilted a bit.

"Let's get you back down before you decide to jog around the parking lot," he said, putting his arm across my shoulders and easing me onto the pillows. He sat on the edge of my bed. "Remember me?"

He was a guy in his forties with tortoise-shell granny glasses. "I'm sorry," I said, "but I don't."

"Well, there's no reason you should. You've been one sick cookie." He held out his hand. "Eric Huxley's the name. I'm the doctor who's in charge of you."

I shook hands with him. "How long have I been sick?"

He took a pencil-sized case from his pocket, unscrewed its cap and popped a thermometer into my mouth. "You're still sick," he said. "They brought you in here"—he turned over some sheets on a clipboard—"five weeks ago tomorrow."

"Jesus," I mumbled.

"Shut up," Dr. Huxley said. "Do you remember a man named Jerry Moss?"

I nodded.

"He put us onto the doctors at a hospital in Johnstown, Pennsylvania, who've been dealing with this thing. That's how we knew what to do for you." He took the thermometer out of my mouth and looked at it.

"How did you hear about Jerry Moss?" I asked.

"That friend of yours told us. The black guy."

That was damn decent of him, I thought bitterly. Hannibal, the bounty hunter, didn't want his prey dying before he could collect his reward.

"Good man," Dr. Huxley said. "Your temperature's almost back to normal." He smiled at me again. "I think we can get you out of here in ten days or two weeks if you keep on the way you're going. But you'll have to take it easy for a while."

"Who's been to see me?" I asked. "Everything's mixed up."

"Your friend. Oh, and the U.S. Attorney for Rhode Island."

"I'll bet," I said. "Are there cops guarding my room to keep me from escaping?"

Dr. Huxley laughed. "No. Harold Watts's daughter's been in almost every day. Nice-looking girl." He glanced at his wrist watch. "In fact, I'll be calling her in about a half-hour. They'll be glad to know you're lucid."

"You mean the Wattses are in charge of me?" I was beginning to feel woozy again.

Dr. Huxley nodded and got up from the bed.

"Not my mother?"

"We didn't know about your mother. Want me to call her for you?"

"Don't bother."

"Do you play backgammon?"

"Badly," I murmured as I slithered into an exhausted stupor.

"Me, too," I heard him say. "We'll have a game sometime soon."

I slept.

I slept away the ensuing days. When I wasn't sleeping, I ate meals of increasing solidity with growing relish. In between meals I was still hungry. The nurse with freckles brought me hamburgers when she came on duty at four o'clock. Her name was Judy and she was engaged to a lieutenant in the Navy.

Between sleeping, eating and feeling better I tried to think. That kept me from feeling *too* much better. My future was bleak. I was going to end up either in prison or in another lunatic asylum. I figured that Hannibal had given my mother a complete fill-in on everything I'd done since he first met me in Cleveland. How I was discerned would depend on who was doing the telling and to what end the listener was listening. Between my mother and Hannibal, her creature, I could be portrayed as a seller of stolen merchandise, a forger of federal tax forms, a riot-starter; they would take note of my mercurial swings of mood after telephone calls to Rhode Island, the fact that I had quit a promising career in television news for no apparent or good reason, that I had been crazy enough to stand up to an equally crazy man with a shotgun. While I still hadn't the wildest idea why my mother wanted me committed again, I had no doubt she'd give it her best shot.

At the same time the federal government wanted to throw me in a penitentiary. The coming battle between my mother and the feds would be of morbid interest to me. All that Washington had on its side was a good case against me: the law, the evidence, the Justice Department, the U.S. Criminal Code, the FBI and the Marine Corps. On her side, my mother could marshal her inexhaustible determination to have her own way, the greatest one-track mind of modern history and that brazen courage which comes from not being bright enough to know what you're up against in a fight. Considering the balance of forces in the struggle to determine who was going to do vile things to me, the smart money had to be on my mother.

On top of all that, the mystery of Beth was deepening and making me even more depressed. She had come to see me almost every day during the five weeks I was off my head with the Bug Plague. But now that I was becoming my old self again—which she knew because Dr. Huxley had told her—she hadn't visited me once, nor had she called. I could have telephoned her but I didn't. As my body recovered, my soul began to sicken with something I'd never experienced before—deep wrath.

I'd gotten angry in my life, but I had never really gotten angry at life itself. Once I started to do that during those early summer weeks I couldn't stop; general fury was a whole new fantasy experience: I invented scenes of telling off my mother. I had fantasies of being cold and righteous as Beth pleaded with me to forgive her capriciousness toward me. My most voluptuously satisfying fantasy was one in which I called Hannibal a double-crossing son of a bitch. I saw fear in his eyes as he recognized the truth and power of my indignation, and then I beat him to a bloody pulp in a fair fight.

One afternoon I was sitting in bed looking through the window at the trees, a church spire, the tops of old factories, and a distant strip of Narragansett Bay with sun sparkling on the water. I was having the Hannibal fantasy in a form so powerful that I physically acted it out.

I jabbed my right hand into his stomach and he doubled over. I nailed him in the mouth with a left hook that sent him reeling backward. He crawled away from me in the dust, pleading, "Please, Sherbert, don't hit me no more, I know I done you wrong . . ." I kicked at him so hard that the covers pulled loose on my bed. "I haven't even begun on you, you bastard!" I yelled mentally. "I'll teach you to betray me!" I kicked again, and my foot flew up and hit a tabletop stretched across my bed. A bottle of medicine crashed to the floor.

"Bornie!"

I looked up. Judy, the freckled nurse, was standing in the door staring at me with astonishment on her face. "What *are* you doing thrashing around like that?"

I came all over hot with embarrassment. "Exercising," I said.

I was getting stronger physically—even though I was a far cry from the Volkswagen-lifting man I had been. One day when I was walking the corridors a nurse told me I had a visitor. I stopped by the men's room, combed my hair and tightened the belt of my bathrobe. I was tensing with anticipation, sure Beth had come at last. I checked myself, remembering my fantasy of being cold and reproachful. I was still trying to decide whether to be the offended me or the delighted me when I pushed open the door of my room and saw Mr. Watts looking out the window.

He turned around and gave me his amiable grin. "For a guy who nearly died you look pretty good," he said.

I reluctantly shook hands with the man who was going to send me to the penitentiary, and sat down on the edge of the bed. I decided I could use my huffy act on *him*.

He took a chair on the other side of the room. "How's it going?"

I nodded. Nice touch. Noncommittal, signaling resentment.

He opened a briefcase and took out a paper. "I've brought something for you to sign. It's just a—"

"I'm not signing anything until I've talked to a lawyer," I said.

He looked puzzled. "It's just a technicality, Bornie, an evidence release form. You don't want to take back the evidence, do you?"

It was my turn to be puzzled, but I wasn't about to abandon the pleasures of fury. "What evidence are we talking about, Mr. Watts?"

"Boy, your illness must really have screwed up your memory," he said. "I'm talking about the reason you came to Rhode

Island—to give me the list of all of Great Lakes Discount Auto Parts dealers in the country."

I pretended recollection even as I experienced further bewilderment. "Oh, that," I said. "I didn't know it was important."

"*Important?* Bornie, before you brought me that list, all the Justice Department had as suspect dealers was the one here in Rhode Island and one in Iowa. When we subpoenaed Great Lakes' records the most important thing was missing—the list of their nationwide network. You've provided it."

"Then how come I'm being indicted?" I asked.

Mr. Watts' forehead wrinkled right up to the southern border of his bald head. "I guess none of us knew how sick you were. Don't you remember my coming in here and telling you the charges against you had been dropped?"

"I don't remember much of anything," I said. "I don't even remember giving you the list. I was pretty sick that night."

"After Hannibal came back from taking you to the hospital he told me I'd find it in your suitcase," Mr. Watts said. "He also told us you only worked at Great Lakes for three weeks. We checked that out with a Mr."—he fished around in his briefcase, brought out another batch of papers and leafed through them— "Herbert Hyman of Cleveland. Do you remember *him?*"

Hebba. I nodded.

"Mr. Hyman told us you'd gone to work at Great Lakes in response to a classified newspaper ad. Hannibal also told us about your breaking into the office to get the list. That was after you'd met Beth accidentally on the telephone and knew that her father—I—was a federal law enforcement official. That's right, isn't it?"

It had apparently been Hannibal's story, and if I didn't have it in me to confirm and embellish that version of what happened, I wasn't stupid enough to deny it, either. "Mr. Watts," I said, "why hasn't Beth been to see me lately?"

He unscrewed the cap from a fountain pen and handed the pen and the release form to me. "Sign this thing, will you?"

I took the paper and signed it without even reading it. Relief was beginning to seep into me. If I wasn't going to be indicted, what I signed didn't matter.

He put the document in his briefcase and screwed the cap back on his pen. "Bornie," he finally said, "you know that Beth is a very serious writer, don't you?"

"Yes, sir."

"Her poetry imposes some very special demands on her," he said. He smiled at me. "I don't pretend to understand how that part of her works. I just try to help create the climate and way of life she seems to need."

"But—"

He smiled again. "Beth's a grown woman, Bornie. She moves at her own speed. I think you and she had better talk it out."

He knew something about me and Beth, but he wasn't willing to say it and there was no point in pushing him. "Any idea where Hannibal is?" I asked.

"He was staying with us until we got word that you were over the worst of it. Then he left."

"Do you know where he went?"

Mr. Watts shook his head. "We'll want you as a witness when the Justice Department takes the Great Lakes Discount Auto Parts company to trial."

"I'll be there," I promised.

After he'd gone I sat looking around my empty room. I was hugely relieved to know I wasn't going to prison. But I had no illusions about how I had escaped *that* fate: Hannibal had snatched me from the federal clutches so that my mother could have an unimpeded crack at committing me to a mental hospital. He was still a son of a bitch, and whatever my future plans, I had to get far, far away from him.

But my first order of business when they sprang me from the hospital was to see Beth. I now understood one reason why she didn't want me to come to Rhode Island—she knew I'd been indicted even though she couldn't tell me so out of loyalty to her father. But even with that cleared up, some other mystery still stood between us.

That afternoon Dr. Huxley came in and checked me over with a bunch of interns and residents who seemed to be disappointed that I'd recovered. They would have liked me to stay there forever, raving and tearing at imaginary bugs while medical students watched and took notes.

"How do you feel?" Dr. Huxley asked me.

"Pretty good."

"Tired?"

"A little. Kind of weak."

"Well," Huxley said, "I think we can let you go tomorrow. I suppose you'll be staying at the Wattses'."

"That'll be my first stop," I said.

"Just be easy on yourself," he cautioned.

Judy came in early the next morning to say goodbye. She gave me a big kiss on the cheek and volunteered to take me downstairs in a wheel chair. For some reason hospitals pronounce you cured and then refuse to let you walk out. Dr. Huxley said goodbye to me at the elevator. He was a fine man and I knew I was going to miss him.

On the way downstairs I had a sudden panic. "I haven't any money to pay the bill," I said to Judy.

"It's been taken care of."

"By whom?"

"Your family," she answered. "Oh, and they've sent a man to get you. Bornie, that's some car."

Jesus God, I thought, going as cold as Cleveland in February. My mother had paid the hospital bill, and Hannibal, her muscle man, was waiting to deliver me to Cambridge. I cursed the illness that had left me so weak that I couldn't even try to fight my way free of Hannibal.

I saw him leaning against the Pierce-Arrow in the sunlight as Judy wheeled me through the cool, dark lobby of the hospital. Hannibal pushed open the glass doors and walked toward us, and my panic went up to eight on the Richter scale. I looked wildly around for an escape route. The lobby was full of visitors and nurses, and people looking at the plastic offerings of the gift shop. I grabbed the arms of the wheel chair and was about to propel myself out of it and make a mad dash for anywhere when the chair stopped rolling. I looked up.

Hannibal looked down. "Mo'nin', Mistah Sherbert, sah," he said, his big face and red-rimmed eyes radiating innocence.

I didn't answer.

"He's all yours," Judy said, "all nice and well again."

"I sho' am grateful to hear *dat*," Hannibal answered with an ingratiating smile.

He was shrewd. He was playing the faithful family retainer, and if I made an uproar about being taken away by him, it would be further proof of my looniness.

Hannibal took my shaving kit off my lap and grasped my left arm. "Now you jes' move slow an easy, Mistah Sherbert," he said, pulling me to my feet as if I were a rabbit being picked up by the ears. "You let Hannibal he'p you to the car and you gone have a *nice ride* home!"

I shot Judy an imploring look.

" 'Bye, sweetie," she said. "Come back and see us."

Hannibal propelled me out the front door. "Cut the Old Black Joe crap," I snarled between gritted teeth, "and let go of my arm!"

"Shut up 'less you want it busted, smart-ass," he rumbled in reply. We were out in the sunlight by then. Two cops were standing near the entrance. "Yes, *sah*," Hannibal said loudly, "the home folks gone be *mighty glad* to see you, Mistah Sherbert."

He shoved me across the pavement, opened the front door of the Pierce-Arrow and helped me into the front seat with all the gentleness of a meat worker in a cold-storage warehouse. "You make one move," he muttered hoarsely, "and all them doctors in that whole hospital ain't gone be able to put you back together again. You hear me?"

"I hear you," I answered in helpless fury.

He circled around the front of the car, watching me through the windshield, got in and started the engine.

He guided the Pierce-Arrow out the hospital drive and onto a road that led to the main highway. The morning was hot. No wind blew. My doom was sealed and I knew it, but I'd be eternally goddamned if I'd surrender to my mother before solving the most pressing mystery of my immediate life.

There was a tool pocket in the door beside me. I slid my hand into it, felt a rag, some loose bolts, an object I couldn't identify. Then my fingers closed around the handle of a screwdriver.

I yanked it out and pressed the steel tip into my stomach as Hannibal braked to a stop at the highway. He glared at me. "What you doin' now?"

"I'm going to stab myself to death," I said, glaring back.

He started to take his hands from the steering wheel. I shoved the screwdriver harder and winced. I felt it break the skin, but I kept on glaring.

"You aren't being paid to deliver me dead, you son of a bitch," I said.

He grunted. "You gettin' blood on your shirt, smart-ass."

"That's your problem."

He shook his head. "Shee-yit," he muttered. "You're *some kinda* crazy man, Sherbert."

"Tell it to the judge," I retorted. "If you turn left on this highway, you're heading for Cambridge, Massachusetts."

"I know that, asshole. I come from there last week."

"If you turn right," I said, "you get to Warwick. *That's* where you're taking me. To the Watts house. If you don't, I'll stab myself to death right here, all over your fucking car. Then you won't get your money."

He shook his head in a gesture of disdain again, slid the Pierce-Arrow into gear and turned right onto the highway.

"Keep both hands on the wheel," I said. I pretended to give the screwdriver another shove, but I didn't really. The little cut on my stomach was hurting enough as it was. I glanced down. My white shirt *was* stained with a small patch of blood.

Neither of us spoke for a couple of miles. Hannibal's face was a study in unexploded rage mixed with a surly petulance which made him even scarier. Since he was a professional detective, I assumed he had a certain talent for strategy. He'd just been outmaneuvered and he didn't like it one damn bit. That realization was one of the few things that comforted me on what I was sure was my last day out in the free world.

"Your mama's—"

"I don't want to hear about it."

"Dumb sumbitch," he grunted.

"Just keep driving," I told him.

He turned the Pierce-Arrow onto the shore road leading to the Watts house. As I looked out over the bay seagulls were wheeling and screaming against the cloudless summer sky. I offered up an anxious prayer to my gods, beseeching them to fix things so that Beth would be home. The prayer, I realized, might be in vain; the unpredictable switch-throwers of my fate hadn't done very well by me that morning. Still, it never hurts to try.

Hannibal braked the Pierce-Arrow to a stop. "Watts house," he said.

"I know it, stupid," I said. "Now listen. Take out the ignition keys and toss them in my lap. Keep your hands on your side of the car. Try anything and I'll spill my guts."

He mumbled an obscenity and did what I'd told him. I put the keys in my pocket. "I'm going to get out of this car," I said, "and I'm going to keep the screwdriver right where it is. After I talk to Beth I'm going to try to get away from you. I'm going to do my damnedest. Got that?"

"Crazy man," he said.

I got out and slammed the door. Hannibal didn't move. I walked up the gravel path to the front door of the Watts house holding the screwdriver to my stomach. I rang the bell.

I heard footsteps on the hardwood floor. The maid came to the door and peered through the screen at me. She looked at my face. She looked at the screwdriver shoved into my gut, then back at my face again. The last time she saw me at that door I was off my head with the Bug Plague and complaining about a sprained thumb.

"I've come to see Elizabeth," I said. "Is she here?"

The maid looked at my face again. "In back," she said and walked away toward the kitchen—rapidly, I thought.

I put the screwdriver in my hip pocket, opened the door, walked down the hall and came to another screen door. Through it I could see the back lawn. My first, addled perception of that house in the summer dusk hadn't been wrong; there *was* a gazebo among great spreading trees. Elizabeth Watts was sitting in it wearing a man's shirt and girl's shorts, her blond hair glowing in the sun as she bent over a card table covered with papers.

I opened the screen door, stepped outside and let the door slam softly behind me.

Beth looked up. Then she put her pen on the table and stood up.

My heart was doing a triphammer number as I crossed the lawn to the gazebo.

In the big movie of my reveries this was the ultimate scene— Beth dropping whatever she was doing, flying across the floor, the lawn, the beach or wherever our first physical encounter took place, flinging herself into my arms while I braced my legs and lifted her as she kissed me all over the face and neck, half crying, half laughing with unrestrainable rapture because we were to-gether at last.

"Hello, Bornie," she said. Her finely wrought features and large eyes were devoid of any expression at all.

She wasn't playing it right. "Hello," I said for lack of a more dramatic opening line.

"You've got blood on your shirt."

"It's just a nick," I said. "Something happened in the car on the way over here."

She was smaller than I had imagined her to be, a perfectly proportioned miniature of the picture I had been carrying in my mind since that afternoon in the Pittsburgh book shop. Her father had been wrong when he said Beth was a grownup. She was a golden-haired girl-woman.

She gestured with her left hand toward the gazebo bench opposite the place she was standing. "Why don't you sit down?"

Something was restraining her, something, I sensed, she had decided but didn't know how to utter. This wasn't the way I had imagined our first face-to-face meeting at all. I felt as if I were there for a job interview.

I squeezed myself between the card table and the bench and sat down. "How about some coffee?" Beth asked. Her voice echoed my own uncertainty.

"No, thank you."

She sat down and began turning the papers on the table face down.

"I just got out of the hospital an hour ago," I said.

"I know," she said, still turning the papers over. "Dr. Huxley called me."

The shirt she was wearing was vintage Brooks Brothers—blue-striped and white-collared; it was several sizes too big for her, the sleeves were folded back to the middle of her forearms. I was filled with sudden eruptions of love. She was even more beautiful than her photograph. I had to bulldoze a path through her reserve and hesitancies.

"Then I didn't take you by surprise coming here," I said.

She looked up and smiled prettily. "Nope. I imagined you would."

"Didn't you *know* I'd come, Beth?"

She thought, arched her eyebrows, made a clownish grimace with her mouth and cocked her head to one side. "Mm, yes, uh huh, sure—I guess I knew you'd come."

"Are you glad I did?"

"Ouch! Don't hit me with the hard ones right off, not yet, let's lead up to—"

"You're always telling me 'not yet.' "

"I guess I do say that a lot."

"When does 'yet' get here?"

She put the long fingers of her right hand against her cheek, looked down at the table and laughed. Then she raised her eyes to me. "Are you sure you wouldn't like some coffee? Anna could—"

I shook my head. "Speak my name, Beth."

"I *did*. When you walked out of that door over there."

"Say it again."

Suddenly her child's buoyancy seemed to drain away. "Okay, Bornie, I guess 'yet' had better be now. I've been circling your fort, shooting arrows into the logs because I can't find the right words to explain—and me a writer."

"Just tell it any old way."

Above the gazebo, huge tree branches stirred in a breeze that was passing through from the bay. Beth cupped her hand under her delicate jaw and tapped her fountain pen on the table. She was looking off into the distance.

"Are you scared of me?" I asked.

"No. No. Scared is definitely not it."

"Everything was fine as long as I was somewhere else talking to you on the telephone," I said, "or off my head and helpless in the hospital."

Beth glanced at me. She nodded.

"Then isn't it fine when I'm here?"

She leaned her arms on the table and clasped her hands together. A lock of blond hair blew across her forehead. She looked into my eyes. "I write poetry, right?"

"Right."

"Bornie, poets are radios, they're receiving sets. They write about themselves, their own impressions and feelings."

"I'm with you so far."

"You make poems out of the feelings you get from experience," she said, "from the way atmospheres and scenes strike you."

"Okay," I said.

"So," she said, fiddling with her pen, "poets don't see the world and other people in quite the same way that—um"—she raised her eyes to me again—"non-poets do. That's why poetry is a selfish calling, Bornie. You take all sorts of things from life and you don't give them back. You give them to poems."

"What have you taken from me?"

"Delight was the first thing I took when you called me last February. Then I took anguish when you didn't call back, then anger at you. I met your gargoyle of a mother—oh, that was *something*! I had this whole big conundrum to unravel—whether you were as brave and open as you sounded to me, or whether that woman had turned you into a monster underneath." Her eyes brightened with excitement. "That was terrific because I'd fallen in love with you over the telephone and I could fantasize spending my life with you—that gave me anxiety and passion mixed. I wrote a poem called 'Tightrope Walker' about it."

"I fell in love with you, too," I said.

She didn't seem to hear me at all.

"I got so much emotion and thought for poems from you. And they're pretty good. They're *our* poems. You inspired them; I wrote down the words."

"That's great."

Beth nodded. "The *Atlantic Monthly*'s going to publish 'Tightrope Walker' in December."

"Super," I said.

She nodded again and clasped her hands again.

"We don't have to love each other over the telephone anymore," I said. "I'm here."

"You're here, you're here, you're here," she mumbled, looking down at the table. "That's the problem, Bornie."

"I don't understand."

Beth raised her eyes. "Can't you see? When you were a distant, half-imagined man you were the stuff of poems and I didn't have to give too much back. Just some telephone jabber once in a while. Now that you're here you have to be *dealt with,* Bornie—responded to, quarreled with. You take up space where my poems live."

Crazy, I thought, she can only love me if I'm living in Outer Mongolia and gnashing my teeth over my mother.

"Having you here is like being in a room that's too brightly lit," she said. "I can't see anything."

She was so innocent in her self-absorption that I couldn't get angry at her. I'd read some about creative geniuses. At least Beth wasn't as dirty and grouchy as Beethoven. She had both ears, which is more than Vincent Van Gogh could say for himself. She wasn't a neurotic drunk like Poe. The fact that she was a genius who was also a beautiful girl capable of coherent conversation made my hurt all the worse.

She reached out and took my hand. "Bornie, dear Bornie, this is why people who write and paint pictures and stuff like that feel so guilty about their relationships."

"Are you going to feel guilty about ours?"

"Uh huh. After you've gone."

There wasn't any answer to that. The romantic scenario of Elizabeth Watts and Sherborne Eppe that had been so vivid in my imagination had just been carted off to the Warwick town dump.

Beth looked past me. "Hey," she said, "there's Hannibal!"

I turned around. He was standing on the lawn, several stories tall and half a football field wide, legs spread and arms folded, glowering at me.

"What's he doing here?" Beth asked.

"We're going on a trip together," I answered.

She squeezed my hand and looked at me in delight. "You mean you were planning to leave, anyway?"

If I couldn't get angry at her, I was becoming furious with myself for being so romantic an idiot as to assume a future with Beth before I really knew her. And I hurt badly. Still, she needed to be let off the hook.

I nodded.

"Well, then," she said, releasing my hand and leaning back against the gazebo, "it's all worked out beautifully, hasn't it?"

"Beth," I said, "there's something I have to know. Was Manfred real?"

Her pretty face frowned. "Um, well, I ran into this man named Edward Karnow at a symposium. We wrote letters back and forth and then he sailed his boat down here from Prince Edward Island. He did it in January. Big *macho* stuff . . ."

"You mean you didn't meet him on a railroad platform in Westchester County?"

"No, but I've *been* on a railroad platform in Westchester County."

"And he didn't abandon you on Martha's Vineyard?"

She shook her head. "Three years ago when I was staying there with my aunt, I woke up on this rainy spring morning—"

"Was this guy Karnow like Byron's Manfred?" I asked. "Self-loathing? Difficult?"

She brushed the blond wisp of hair back from her forehead. "Edward? Oh, no—he was kind of—well, he could be nice. I mean, we all have our flaws. He was a natural-born sea captain, so he liked to boss people around." She tucked her chin down into her neck and started barking orders. " 'Beth! Grab that goddamn sheet! Not next week—*now*, goddamn it! Keelhaul the tiller'—" She broke off and grinned. "Or whatever they do in boats."

"But you liked him."

"I was crazy about him."

"Until he got too close."

She nodded glumly. "You see how it is, Bornie."

I saw how it was; the great love of *my* life had just been grist for *her* poetry—and not even whole grist. I was a series of suggestions to her; wisps of me would be stitched together with train stations, clock towers and bad weather to make poems about events that never really happened.

There was no way I could lash out at that as unjust. Nor could I be happy about it. I just had to accept it.

"I can hardly wait for the December edition of the *Atlantic Monthly*." I stood up. "I've kept Hannibal standing around too long."

"Bornie . . ."

"So long, Beth," I said. I leaned across the card table, kissed her cheek and stepped out of the gazebo.

As I walked toward Hannibal he unfolded his arms. "Thought you was gone try runnin' away."

"Shut the hell up," I snapped.

I kept going past him, past the lilac bushes and around the porch of the Watts house without looking back.

I was already in the front seat of the Pierce-Arrow when Hannibal caught up with me. He climbed in behind the wheel and looked at me.

"Let's get going," I said. "We can beat the rush-hour traffic in Cambridge."

"You got the keys," he said.

I took them out of my pocket and handed them to him. I didn't even care anymore that he was about to dangle me before the fangs of my mother. I was tired and I felt weak again. That was all right because it was just the aftermath of the Bug Plague and it would pass. The emptiness inside me was worse. I had spent so long steering my life toward Beth, filling my imagination with her, planning my life in terms of her—and now it had all crumbled. I may be a romantic, but I don't comfort myself with hopes and dreams that can't come true. There was a huge empty space in me where Beth had been until an hour before. It was a space of dusk, silence and no anticipation; I had reached my evening of the spirit and I didn't believe I'd ever see morning again. The madhouse would be an appropriate place for me.

"Trouble with you," Hannibal said as he drove toward the main highway, "is that you too dumb to know who's on you own side."

"I don't want to hear any crap about how my mother's trying to do what's best for me," I said.

He didn't say anything more until we reached the highway

and he'd braked the Pierce-Arrow to a stop. "Which way to Cambridge, smart-ass?" he snarled.

"We're on a different side of the highway from the hospital, stupid. From here you turn *right* to get to Cambridge."

He grunted, shifted the car into low gear, waited for two trucks to roar by and turned left.

"I said *right!*" I yelled in a sudden overflow of all my furies and despair.

He shifted into second. The car accelerated. He shifted into third.

To hell with him, I thought. I put my head back on the leather seat and shut my eyes. I was too agitated to really sleep. I dozed, feeling the warm air rush over me, seeing the summer light as an orange glow on my closed eyelids.

I was in a semistupor when I felt the car slowing down and turning.

I opened my eyes. Hannibal was heading us down a road that led to a bridge connecting the mainland to Jamestown, the island where, you will recall, my grandfather the bishop has his summer house. "What the hell are you doing?" I demanded.

"Jes' tend your own business," he grunted.

We crossed the bridge. The panoramic views on either side did not thrill me, nor did the prospect of returning to a place I had loved as a child. I wasn't capable of loving anything anymore. I never would be again. Maybe, I thought, my mother had instructed Hannibal to take me to Jamestown and throw me off the sea cliff at Beavertail. I couldn't have cared less.

We hit the island, drove by a clutter of motels and up a hill past the graveyard. The great skeleton of the bridge leading over to Newport loomed ahead. It occurred to me that Hannibal wasn't going to throw me off a cliff. Perhaps they were going to commit me in Newport—perhaps, I thought, it was easier to certify a nut like me in Rhode Island than it was in Massachusetts.

But Hannibal didn't head for the bridge. He stopped at the Jamestown east-shore road and motioned to a Volkswagen that was waiting to turn. I got a glimpse of the driver as the Volkswagen moved past us—a dark-haired girl wearing a yellow-and-black striped rugby shirt. She was handsome but looked as glum as I felt, another lost soul.

Hannibal turned right and drove along beside an inlet called Potter's Cove. He pulled the Pierce-Arrow over to the side of the road and switched off the ignition.

"Okay, you double-crossing bastard," I said, "what happens now? The tide's too low to drown me."

"You get your ass out, thass what happens," he rumbled.

I got out and followed him through a stand of coarse grass onto the beach.

It wasn't much of a beach—just a curved strip of sand ending in a scatter of big rocks. A pickup truck with some kind of hoist device attached to it was parked halfway into the water by the rocks. A man wearing baggy pants and a khaki undershirt was standing thigh-deep in the water near the back of the truck. He was bent over in a mighty struggle with something underwater, wrenching and jerking a crowbar up and down.

As we approached I could hear him grunting and talking out loud as if someone were with him. Suddenly he straightened up, flung the crowbar into the rear of the truck and howled in frustration. With his back to us, he shook his fist at the sky. "Hold back the tide so I can root it out!" he screamed. "Can't you cooperate just *once*?" His balding head and bare shoulders were blistered and sunburned. "Imbecile!" he shouted at the sky. "Incompetent!"

Hannibal stopped at the edge of the water, put two fingers in his mouth and let loose with an ear-shattering whistle.

The man stopped his fist-shaking and name-calling. He turned around, shielded his eyes with his hand and peered at us. "Got him?" he yelled.

"Got him!" Hannibal bellowed.

I barely heard that bellow. I was riveted by the wet, raving, weather-scorched man in the water.

It was my father.

Sixteen

❦

MORNING AGAIN

I AM ABSOLUTELY NO GOOD at unexpected events. Start a war near me, drop a piano from the third floor or run the Indianapolis 500 through a glass factory in my vicinity and I'll stand there mute as a cigar-store Indian.

I stood mute as a cigar-store Indian on the beach at Potter's Cove while my father sloshed ashore, grinning all over his face. That was a big change in him. During my childhood he was a man given to restrained or obligatory smiles.

Hannibal waded out and drove the pickup truck to the road while my father and I went through the first embracings, back-thumpings and exclamations over each other.

I was still stunned and trying to reconcile this man with the father of careful tailoring, neatly parted blond hair and hands like a concert pianist's whom I had lost long, long ago.

He was the same size and shape, of course; he had even retained some of his familiar mannerisms. His vowel-flattening Boston accent hadn't changed, but what he said and the vernacular he used to say it in were radically different. He seemed to have broken out of the armature of reserve that constricts most male Eppes. I have already mentioned that he was sun- and wind-burned. His hair was almost gone except for disorderly patches and tufts. His eyes, once pale-blue, now had a kind of manic glitter.

"What were you doing in the water?" I asked.

He put his dirty, calloused hands on his hips and gazed across the cove. "I've been trying to dig out a boulder. The sand's only dry enough to work on it three hours between tides."

"This island's loaded with boulders," I said.

My father squinted in the sunlight. "I know, but that son of a bitch out there's just the right shape, size and weight. It's exactly what I need."

"For what?"

"My tower," he said. "Come on, let's go home."

Amazing. When I was growing up he eschewed all forms of exercise except for walking away from my mother; he was strictly a cerebral, indoor type. Now he was slamming around in a truck, prying up rocks with a crowbar, using sinewy muscles and swearing. The years alone couldn't have wrought such changes in him. It had to be his long search for the meaning of life. I wondered if he was still at it.

As we drove down the east-shore road with Hannibal following in the Pierce-Arrow, the questions that had been teeming in my mind began to line up in order. The first and biggest question was about my grandmother.

"Jesus wept," my father said. "Didn't your mother tell you?"

I shook my head. "Gran's dead, isn't she?"

"She's dead," he said.

"What did she die of?"

"It was very interesting," he answered. "She just decided that she'd lived long enough. She went to bed in the Beacon Hill house, paid her bills, called in her lawyers, spent six months writing letters and some sort of memoir. Then your cousin Percy sent word to me that she was getting weaker by the day. I flew home from England but saw her only once before she went." His eyes fixed themselves on something that was not in the land- and water-scape around us. "She was my mother-in-law," he said, "but I loved her more than my own parents or that benighted daughter of hers."

"Did she say anything about me?" I asked as a new sadness joined the heavy one I was carrying over Beth.

"She gave me a letter for you," he answered. "I asked her that last day what was the matter with her. She said the god- damnedest thing. 'Life has begun to bore me. Screw it.' Where do you suppose she picked up an expression like that?"

"From her chauffeur," I said. "He was modernizing her vocabulary."

The big questions were obviously coming to the forefront of my father's mind, too. "I visited or called every mental hospital on the East Coast," he said. "Where did your mother put you?"

"It was in Ohio. A place called Craigie Glen. Didn't she let you know?"

She hadn't. As we drove through the waterfront part of the village of Jamestown, my father regaled me with an account of the screechings and legal skirmishings that took place after my incarceration in Craigie Glen. My mother got her cousins—that headmaster at St. Stephen's and the psychiatrist who first ex- amined me—to tell a court that my father was the source of my mental disorder. The judge ordered him to neither see nor com- municate with me. My father countersued, trying to have my mother declared unfit for parenthood or anything else that re- quired elementary thought or walking on her hind legs. He lost. As he told me these things I had the strange sensation that I was something like Jerusalem—an object fought over by some who loved me and others who wanted to possess me for dark and obscure reasons.

My father glanced at me as we left the village behind us. "What *was* your problem, by the way?"

"It took them seven years and four months to find out I

didn't have one," I said. "Are you still looking for the meaning of life?"

"Still looking for it." His blistered lips tightened and his face became grim. "Seven years and four months in an insane asylum. My God, Bornie, you poor bastard. Are you okay?"

"They never laid a glove on me," I said, which was more reassurance than truth.

"I couldn't have survived it," he said. "You're a better man than I am. If the karma is right, that mother of yours is going to spend her next life as a wharf rat."

"How's Clarissa?" I asked. (You will recall that when he left my mother he took our English maid with him.)

"We went our separate ways about four years ago," he said. "I was too eccentric for her, she was too pigheaded for me."

The road curved away from the shore and up a hill past 1920-vintage summer houses. Summer, as a matter of fact, used to be a big industry for the year-round populace of Jamestown. The farther south you go along the island, the larger the vacation houses get. At the end, where Narragansett Bay joins the ocean, there are big estates laid out among juttings of rock and low, scrubby brush.

My father's house was at the junction of two roads. It was screened from them by twenty-foot-high hedges. As we turned into the driveway I recognized the place—it used to belong to a family named Guest and I'd gone to parties there when I was a kid.

The property was laid out on a couple of acres. There was a wide lawn, gardens in the back, two garages and a three-story gray-shingled house trimmed in green with a large front porch.

But that conventional Rhode Island summer setting was embellished and disrupted by some very strange objects. There was a nine-foot-tall pyramid on the front lawn. Near the stone wall that separated the grounds from a forest of brush I saw a circle of large rocks fitted together with great ingenuity. That, I decided, must be the base of my father's tower.

As he parked the truck and Hannibal pulled in the Pierce-Arrow beside it, I saw that the side of one garage had been cut away and a huge wooden machine with a cylindrical drum and a platform had been shoved up against the opening.

I got out of the truck and walked over to this apparatus. "What is it?" I asked.

"A replica of the air conditioner that Leonardo da Vinci designed for the Duchess of Milan," my father said, gazing with satisfaction at the weather-grayed contraption.

"Air conditioner?" I exclaimed in astonishment. "In the sixteenth century?"

He nodded. "The idea of air conditioning was unheard of. Leonardo conceived of it through pure intuition. That's what I'm studying now."

"Does it work?" I asked.

He shook his head. "No. I ran out of money before I could have it finished. But that isn't the point. How intuition operates is a mystery. The mind suddenly knows something it has no way of knowing." His face became bright and eager. "I've got this theory, Bornie. When a man like Leonardo had one of his intuitive bursts, it was in response to a problem—in this case Beatrice of Milan was probably bitching about the heat and Leonardo was struck by the concept of air conditioning. *My* theory is that the intuitive signal carries more than just the solution to specific problems. *I* think it also carries hints about its own mystery, its origins."

"So you're trying to relive Leonardo da Vinci's mental life?"

My father nodded. "If the intuitive leap comes to me, I'll be listening for the mystery, not the solution of the problem." Suddenly he grinned. "I'm also reinventing calculus to get at Sir Isaac Newton's mind."

" 'Scuse me," Hannibal said. "This man jes' left the hospital, he's already had a big day and he's s'posed to take himself easy."

"Oh, hell," I said, "I'm okay." I wanted to hear more about intuition and sixteenth-century air conditioners.

"You gone rest," Hannibal rumbled.

Once we were inside the house, a tall handsome woman came out of the kitchen. She was about sixty; her features were swarthy and her hair was pulled back in a bun. "Look at that man," she said to and about my father, "always coming home wet."

"This is Anna, who takes care of me," my father said. "Anna, this is my son, Sherborne."

We shook hands. Her strong face lit up in a smile that could have warmed three winter months. "Maybe now that you're here," she said, "your father will behave himself, hah?" She turned back to him. "Give me those trousers. I'll put them in the machine."

My father unzipped his fly, unbuckled his belt, pulled off his trousers and handed them to Anna.

"A man your age out digging up stones," she said. "You'll have a heart attack."

"I'm not that old," he retorted. He scratched his behind through his undershorts. When I knew him last he wouldn't have blown his nose in mixed company.

I left them to their bickering and followed Hannibal upstairs to the third floor. There were two bedrooms and he'd already moved himself into one of them. My suitcase was on a rack in the other. "How long have you been here?" I asked.

"Jes' found your daddy yesterday."

"How many of my mother's fingers did you have to break before she told you where he was?"

He grunted. "You tend your own business and I'll go 'bout mine."

I went into his room and sat down on the bed. "I'm sorry about all the names I called you. I just didn't know . . ." Words failed me.

He was leaning against the wall, his huge hands stuffed in his pockets, looking through the small windows at Newport across the bay. A salt-flavored draft was stirring the curtains. "Man's got to go on what he thinks," he said.

"You tried to tell me you were on my side."

Hannibal glanced at me, and for a moment I thought he was actually going to smile at me. But he managed to catch himself just in time. "You ain't one to listen when you don't want to hear."

"I know," I said. "When did you stop being my mother's detective?"

He looked out the window again. "Pittsburgh. 'Bout the time the old man died. Called her up and said you ain't crazy, least not crazy-house crazy."

"But why didn't you tell me *then?*"

"What you don't know ain't gone hurt you."

"But you told Mr. Watts you were working for my mother."

"Listen, smart-ass," he rumbled. "There was a *F-B-I* arrestin' you for stolen auto parts. Best witness you could get is a licensed 'vestigator who was on the inside. Licensed 'vestigator ain't got no business bein' inside nowhere less he's got a client."

"I think she hired another detective after you quit. There was a guy in a blue Plymouth in Andrewstown. He was watching me."

Hannibal grunted again. "That man had hisself a whole mess of car trouble jes' as we was leavin' town."

I considered it all for a moment. "I hope you'll accept my apology," I said.

He looked back at me. "I don't need no 'pology from you. What I need is for you to get on that bed and sleep some so I don't have to fetch you back to the hospital."

"I tell you, I'm all right."

"You get on that bed 'less you want to wear your ass for a hat!" he roared. *"You hear me?"*

I went into my own room, closed the door and unpacked my bag. Holding my grandmother's letter in my hand, I looked down at the replica of Leonardo da Vinci's air conditioner. When I first saw it I wondered if my father hadn't gone a little soft in the head. But once he'd explained the machine to me and his reasons for building it, I knew he had been possessed by a timeless and honorable mystery. He was in good company. If Clarissa thought my father was eccentric, she should have tried a weekend with Socrates.

I sat down on the bed and read my grandmother's letter. It was dated Nobember 9, 1972, and it was typical of her—straight to the point.

Dear Bornie:

When I have finished this note to you I am going to die. I have lived for a long time, there is nothing new to be learned. I am more interested in what happens next.

At the time your mother put you in that absurd institution your backgammon debt to me was, according to my accounts, nine million four hundred and forty-four thousand dollars.

Someday you will be released from that place because you have character. It is illogical to assume that men of character can be kept indefinitely in hospitals dedicated to the practice of immodest and disagreeable Austrian medical theories.

No young man should begin his life knowing that he is burdened by debt. I have, therefore, deposited nine million four hundred and forty-four thousand dollars in a trust fund for you at the First National Bank of Boston. Your obligation to me will be unpayable. Do as you see fit with your money.

I have appointed your mother as trustee until you manage to get out of that place. Since she is greedy, it is my conviction that she will enlarge your inheritance. As trustee she will receive a fee every time she withdraws and reinvests your money. I am told that her current inamorata is a stockbroker with good financial sense and none whatsoever when it comes to women.

My only advice to you as you progress through life is to resist the temptation to throw greaseballs into swimming pools. I have been fonder of you than most people I have known.

Hang in there.

Gran

I lay down on my bed and looked at the avenue of brilliant summer light slanting across the ceiling. I couldn't do anything about the powerful sadness surging through me, so I tried to think about the facts instead.

The fact that I was a millionaire didn't add anything to my perception of myself and my life, but now I knew why my mother had been trying so hard to have me recommitted to a mental hospital. As long as I was legally insane she could go on horsing around with my money to her own profit. My mother already had a lot of money, but she is one of those people who have never worked out their personal definition of enough.

Suddenly a peculiar thing began to happen to me. I was filled with sorrow over my mother. She had been born stunted in the spirit. No one, not even my grandmother, had ever really loved her, as far as I knew; she had never really loved anyone.

I put my grandmother's letter on the bedside table, turned my face into the pillow and wept. I did not know whether I was grieving for my mother, my grandmother or Beth. Loss weighs a lot.

It was dusk when I awoke. I heard a voice shouting out on the grounds. I recognized it as my father's, but I couldn't make out the words he was yelling.

I went down to the kitchen, where Anna was cooking dinner. I asked her what my father had been upset about.

"He was hollering at God," she said, laughing. "There's fog coming in and your father wanted you to have nice weather on your first night home."

I wandered into the library, a large room bare of all furniture except four immense tables covered with papers, books and scientific instruments. Hannibal and my father were studying a photographic blowup of a drawing.

"Four hundred years ago," Hannibal was saying.

My father nodded. "No electricity, no gasoline engines, no steam power."

Hannibal put both huge hands on the table and scowled

down at the drawing. "Only couple ways you could make that motherfucker go, then. Put a man inside here"—he pointed to the cylinder in Da Vinci's drawing—"and make him run his ass off . . ."

"Or?"

"Water power."

My father looked at him with a mixture of pride and anticipation. "That's exactly what Leonardo thought! How did you get the idea?"

"Jes' come to me," Hannibal grunted.

"Anything else come to you at the same time?" my father asked.

I went out onto the porch. It was almost totally dark, a moist, sea-smelling dark. The street lamp on the corner beyond the hedge was a smear of light through the mist. The top of the pyramid on the front lawn was barely visible in the diffused reflection. I could hear the distant Beavertail foghorn moaning at precisely spaced intervals, another one across the bay intoning like some prehistoric creature answering the call of its own kind.

My father came out with a drink in his hand and stood beside me. "Sorry about the weather," he said.

"I like fog," I said. "What's the pyramid for?"

"It's a scale replica of the one Cheops built in 2680 B.C. I did a lot of work on nonmagnetic, unmeasurable currents. There's a theory that Cheops' geometric design gave off a life force. That's why I had mine constructed to exact specifications."

"Does it really give off a life force?"

"I'll tell you something," my father answered. "You know those plastic razors you buy and throw away when they get dull?"

I nodded.

"Every time my plastic razor gets dull I leave it overnight inside the pyramid," he said, "right at the point where the diameter lines are bisected by the vertex."

"And?"

"I've been shaving with that razor for over seven months and I haven't cut myself once."

"I'll be damned."

"Your friend Hannibal's a very interesting man," my father said.

"Do you really think he's another Leonardo da Vinci?"

My father chortled. "You never know."

"You told me you ran out of money before you could have the air conditioner finished," I said. "Are you broke?"

"I'm considerably reduced," he said. "I can afford the mortage, Anna, food and fuel and the pickup truck. That's about it."

"But what happened to all your money?"

He grinned at me. "It costs a lot to divorce your mother."

"I'll bet," I said.

"Clarissa took a one-shot settlement when she divorced *me*. One million, as a matter of fact." He looked out at the fog drifting past the street lamp. "And then there was the guru."

"What guru?"

"A Kashmiri. He was a very interesting man. I was his disciple for a while. He told me to renounce all my worldly goods."

"Did you?"

"I was half seeker in those days," he said, "and the other half of me was still a Boston banker. I renounced sixty percent of my worldly goods." He sipped at his drink. "The money that didn't go for divorces and renunciation was spent in one way or another. Pyramids . . . I financed a project—this would have interested you, Bornie, if it had worked. I financed the translation of Homer into a particular Eskimo dialect." He leaned forward, that intense, eager light in his eyes. "I was working on myths at the time. I wanted to see how those Eskimos would react to the *Iliad* and the *Odyssey*, you get the idea—whether they could see a kinship with their own myths."

"How did they like Homer?"

He laughed suddenly. "They used the books I gave them for toilet paper."

It was good to be home.

I'd never been home before.

The tragic life can be very satisfying. Literature is full of young men who brood, pine and starve to death over unrequited love while everybody stands around watching in helpless anguish.

The trouble with my tragic life that summer was that nobody paid any attention to it. Anna kept stuffing food into me; my father patted me on the back and told me that he'd been in love lots of times and had survived all of them.

There were a good many handsome girls around Jamestown that year, but I wasn't interested. I was stricken with the image of Beth sitting in the gazebo with light on her golden hair, concocting poetic drama based on a few telephone calls from me. As well as suffering acutely from rejection by the only woman I would ever love, I felt humiliated and used.

In contrast to me, Hannibal was having a marvelous summer. My father thought he was an authentic, primitive genius and kept following him around with a notebook, waiting to write down all of his utterances. I could have told him he was wasting his time; uttering was, to Hannibal, what kettle-drum playing is to orchestral music—an undertone which accompanies the main theme.

My father's place was full of machinery which also kept Hannibal satisfied and occupied—he was supervising the drilling of an artesian well out by the garage; if they hit water underneath the rock shelf below the lawn, its power would be used to drive the sixteenth-century air conditioner. Hannibal had figured out a way. Also, he was able to work off his crude energies by helping my father dig up rocks and fit them into the base of the tower.

But the greatest pleasure of Hannibal's life, it seemed to me, lay in the fact that I had been sick. It gave him an excuse to boss me around more than usual—and usual was already too much. He would yell at me to rest and then go out and set up a horrible racket with the well-drilling equipment, which, at that point, was gnashing and howling its way into solid rock. Not even Lazarus could have slept through it.

In a way, that drilling and the other rackety, frenzied activities that broke out at my father's place were all my fault. After I found out that he was nearly broke I made my first trip to Boston in nearly eight years.

It was the hub of my earliest memories, not all of them cheerful, but I was there on money business, not for recollection. The day was warm, the newspaper headlines proclaimed the latest racial tensions and Red Sox loss, the traffic crawled and jammed around State Street and environs.

I found a parking space and went to the bank where my fortune was being held in trust for me. When I told them who I was they trotted out a vice president especially to deal with me. Nine million four hundred and forty-four thousand dollars gives you a lot of status in a bank. My personal vice president was a grave man with heavy eyebrows that were useful for frowning, thus heightening his general appearance of gravity. The first thing he told me was that I was now worth about twelve million dollars due to my mother's maneuverings, compounding and other matters of disinterest to me. It was all just numbers. I told him I wanted to finance my father's research.

He did his frown. "What sort of research is your father engaged in, Mr. Eppe?"

"He's trying to find the meaning of life," I said.

"I see."

Some time passed. Letting time pass is a Boston banker's way of expressing shock, contempt or disapproval.

"And you want to give your father a million dollars to go on with—*that*?" he asked.

I nodded. "And another million if one isn't enough."

The vice president gazed out his office window for a few moments. "Well," he said, "it's your money. I'm not sure your grandmother intended—"

"You didn't know my grandmother as well as I did," I cut

in. "The important thing is that my father mustn't realize the money is coming from me."

And that—after some hemming, hawing and telephone calls to lawyers—is how the Anne Lowell Sherborne Foundation for Higher Metaphysics came into being. It was named for my grandmother, who had supplied the money in the first place; the bank got some tame philosophy professors to serve on its board; the foundation's sole purpose was to give salaries to my father and his assistant. My father is no fool—I think he knew that I'd arranged the foundation, since it started operating a few weeks after I'd re-entered his life. And I think he understood that this was my discreet way of providing happiness for him and for Hannibal, who were my two best friends in this world. They were all I had, now that Beth was lost to me forever.

As I have said, the great tragedy of my life that summer had to be a solo act. Nobody else took it seriously. The only person in Jamestown who even *reflected* my mood of loss, inner emptiness and future desolation was the girl in the Volkswagen we had passed on the day we arrived.

I saw a lot of her—you see a lot of anybody who attracts your interest when you live on an island—sometimes driving around, sometimes sitting on the wide beach at Mackerel Cove, her knees drawn up, her arms resting on them as she stared out to sea, solitary and unapproachable.

I tried approach, anyway. After I'd rebelled and shouted that nobody would let me do anything because I was a recuperating invalid, Hannibal and Anna relented a little and said I could handle the food shopping.

One day in the supermarket I saw a familiar yellow-and-black striped rugby shirt going around a corner into an aisle. I pushed my shopping cart around the same corner. The girl was picking canned goods off the shelves. I wheeled my cart slowly toward her, casually looking her over. She was as striking as my first glimpse of her had promised she would be: tall and slender, with brown hair pulled back and flowing down from a point at the nape of her neck where it was held together by a rubber band. I thought I saw some unfathomable sadness expressed in her eyes.

"Excuse me," I said, stopping beside her. "I'm looking for chives. Do you know where they are?"

She raised her head, glanced around the store and then pointed at the freezer. "Over there," she said. "I don't think they sell fresh ones." Her voice was soft and her manner polite but expressionless.

I thanked her. She signaled no interest in further conversation, so I moved on and picked up a packet of frozen chives that I didn't need. Something ventured, nothing gained.

That evening while my father, Hannibal and I were sitting on the porch before dinner I described the girl in the red Volkswagen and asked my father if he knew who she was.

"Sounds like Debbie Huntington," he said. "Rob Huntington's daughter. Nice girl. I think I heard she's just broken up with her young man and is taking it pretty hard."

I went to bed right after dinner that evening and tried to read. But I couldn't keep my mind on it. A girl who had been a mere reflection of my own bereft state had now assumed a voice, situation and name.

Tragedy not only enjoys itself, it is interested in other tragedies: grief calling to grief across the barren tundra and all that. In my imaginings Debbie Huntington and I were walking side by side around Beavertail as the suicide-tempting surf thundered below us and the sea wind tossed her long brown hair. With gentle patience I got her to tell me about her shattered life.

I, of course, would be reticent about the story of my own betrayal and lost love. The new me would be a man who didn't talk about himself much at all. I would convey an aura of having been bruised, of having endured and survived by my manner and appearance: the calm understanding radiating from my eyes, the way I puffed on a pipe and nodded slightly as I listened, my tastefully rugged outfit—corduroy jacket, black sweater, trappings of leather and brass. It would help a lot if I could achieve my father's weather-hardened appearance—in a younger, handsomer form, of course. Finally, one autumn evening Debbie and I would be having dinner together in Newport, and she would smile, for the first time. I would actually make her laugh.

The pivotal moment in my fantasy was that first smile I coaxed from Debbie Huntington. It would be the sunup of a new morning in my life, a beginning in mutual consolation with a beautiful girl. I fell asleep.

The next day I went over to Newport and bought myself two corduroy jackets, four black sweaters, work shirts, elegant blue jeans, highly polished boots, belts with large brass buckles on them, several bottles of brisk, masculine shaving lotion, two pipes and some tobacco.

That afternoon I tried pipe smoking in my room. It tasted awful. I decided to hell with it and went downstairs to find Hannibal. I told him I was going out to dig up a boulder for my father the next morning and that he could come along and help if he wanted.

"Come 'long and pick up the pieces, most likely," he said.

"Don't kid yourself," I told him. "I've been doing push-ups, sit-ups and body bends every morning for weeks. I feel great."

"Now you listen, Sherbert—"

"If you try to stop me tomorrow," I said, "I'll rip out every banister in the house with my bare hands."

Hannibal glared at me. "Asshole."

"Asshole yourself," I shot back. I was secretly pleased. He was off my back. Now I could start on my weather-beaten look by doing some hard work outdoors.

When I woke up the next morning I was disappointed. There was no sun to burn me. A pall of fog hung over the island and the bay. Newport was invisible from our house. The Beavertail foghorn was moaning like a cow with a bellyache.

After breakfast Hannibal got the drilling crew started on the noisy search for water while I threw chains, the block and tackle, tools and some planks into the back of the pickup truck. Hannibal and I pulled on heavy boots. "S'pose you want to drive," he said.

"You drive," I answered. "The strain of putting on the brakes might make me faint and we'd have an accident. The world can't afford to lose you."

He circled the truck and got in behind the wheel. We drove across the island, past Mackerel Cove beach and onto a dirt road that led to a farm overlooking the west channel. About halfway up that road Hannibal turned off. The pickup bumped and jolted down a pasture toward a muddy strip of salt marsh at the edge of the water. We stopped and got out.

"Which rock does my father want?" I asked.

He pointed at a black boulder protruding from the wet, soft ground at the edge of the marsh. "She's a sumbitch," he said.

"If we pry it loose, we could get the truck close enough to winch it out."

Hannibal stomped on the ground with the heel of one boot. "Too soft."

"I brought some planks," I said.

He looked at me. "Knew if I waited long 'nough, you'd do something smart," he said.

Coming from him, that was tantamount to winning a prize for exceptional brilliance. I laid the planks on the ground to a point about three feet from the rock. Hannibal carefully backed the pickup, set the emergency brake and switched the engine over to the winch.

For the next hour we labored at the rock, ramming iron bars under it, grunting and straining to make it move. We were working against its weight and the suction of the mud it rested in. I was pouring sweat by the time we got the first length of chain looped under it, but the exertion exhilarated me. I could feel my whole body coming alive and responding to the demands I was making on it.

The fog had lifted a little by the time we had a second strand of chain under the rock. Hannibal straightened up, breathing heavily. "You sure you all right?"

"I'm great," I said. I had been working so hard and with such concentration I'd even forgotten all about being tragic.

We connected the chain ends together and attached them to the cable that led over the hoist. Hannibal climbed into the pickup, started the engine, gunned it and put the winch in gear as I bore down with all my strength on an iron bar inserted beneath the rock. It moved, it rolled slightly and then slurped out of the ground. Hannibal backed the pickup a few more feet and we winched the rock onto its bed.

"Jesus," I gasped, wiping the perspiration from my forehead, "what do you suppose that thing weighs?"

Hannibal was leaning on a shovel, looking at our prize in the back of the truck. "She's jes' a little one," he said. "Maybe three quarters a ton."

"Big deal," I said.

He looked at me. "You done all you gone do for the day. You hear me?"

I heard him but I wasn't about to admit it. I felt too good. I got into the truck, we drove back up the pasture and onto the dirt road.

As we were heading down toward Mackerel Cove I suddenly saw a yellow-and-black striped rugby shirt on the beach. A red Volkswagen was parked on the edge of the road. "Stop at that car," I told Hannibal.

"What am I gone stop at that car for?" he demanded.

"Just do it," I said.

He mumbled one of his indecipherable obscenities and slipped the pickup into second gear. When we got to the place where Debbie Huntington was sitting on an empty stretch of sand staring out at the fog, Hannibal stopped the pickup and switched off the engine. "This won't take long," I said.

I got out on my side; he got out on his, slamming the door. "Sherbert," he said, "you listen to me . . ."

Hearing the door slam and the sound of Hannibal's voice, Debbie turned around and looked at us.

I walked the ten feet to the front of her car, took a deep breath and offered up a little prayer to my gods. Debbie was staring at me with an expression of perplexity on her unhappy face.

I bent my legs, grasped the bumper of the Volkswagen and offered a second, hasty prayer that she didn't have the front compartment filled with gold bars or rocks.

I strained with all my might and felt the body move on the chassis. Then, as I gritted my teeth and lifted with every muscle I had, the wheels raised a few inches off the ground.

I glanced at Debbie with my heart pounding—but whether that was more from strain or hope I cannot say.

She stared in astonishment as I held her car's front end off the ground. Then she smiled. Then, suddenly, she laughed and the first glimmer of sun announced a new morning in my life.

Behind me, I heard Hannibal snorting in contempt.

"Smart-ass," he said.

RODERICK MACLEISH is a novelist and journalist who has worked in the United States, Europe, the Middle East and Southeast Asia.

Mr. MacLeish divides his time between Washington and London. *The First Book of Eppe* is his third novel and sixth book.

THE BOOZE BATTLE

THE BOOZE BATTLE

Ruth Maxwell

A FRANK E. TAYLOR BOOK

Praeger Publishers · New York

Published in the United States of America in 1976
by Praeger Publishers, Inc.
111 Fourth Avenue, New York, N.Y. 10003

© 1976 by Praeger Publishers, Inc.

**Library of Congress Cataloging in Publication
Data**
Maxwell, Ruth Elaine.
    The booze battle.

    "A Frank E. Taylor book."

    1. Alcoholism. 2. Alcoholism—Treatment. 3.
Alcoholics—Family relationships. 4. Alcoholism
and employment. I. Title. [DNLM: 1.
Alcoholism—Rehabilitation—Popular works.
WM274 M465b] HV5035.M39 362.2' 92
ISBN 0-275-22910-6   75-36859

Printed in the United States of America

For Judy, Rachel, and Dan

CONTENTS

1 ME SICK?   **3**

I believe you are *not* crazy—if you know what to
do, you are apt to do it.

2 SALLY   **9**

She seeks help even before she is sure her husband
is an alcoholic, and calls his hand at every turn.

3 ELLEN   **27**

She copes with her husband's drinking by herself.
Out of a family of three, one never learns to cope,
one ceases to cope and one ceases to live.

4 WIVES OF ALCOHOLICS   **43**

Their reactions help to bring about the very situations they dread the most.

5 KEN   **59**

He could not make his wife stop drinking, so he
took the children and left her to do as she pleased.

6 HUSBANDS OF ALCOHOLICS   71
They do not like their wives to be lushes, and
punish and abandon them when they are.

**7 THE ALCOHOLIC—
HOW THE WORLD VIEWS HIM   83**

**8 THE ALCOHOLIC—
HOW HE VIEWS THE WORLD   101**

9 INTERVENTION   121
Can the alcoholic be forced to stop drinking? It's
amazing how willing he becomes when he finds no
other choice.

10 EMPLOYERS   135
How to reduce your costs while saving lives.

11 FAMILIES AND FRIENDS   157
How to make a natural law operate for you, instead
of against you.

12 FREEDOM   175
Guaranteed Rx for recovery.

ACKNOWLEDGMENTS

I am deeply indebted to my good friend and colleague Robert deVeer, who heads the Smithers Alcoholism Rehabilitation Center of Roosevelt Hospital. Not only was he a constant source of encouragement, but much of what I have said has come from him. I am equally indebted to Rod Elden, president of Rodney Elden Associates, who sponsored *The Booze Battle*. Without the expert services of his staff, particularly Marilyn Trice and Kathy Bradley, his research techniques so freely taught, and his ideas and enthusiasm, the book would be but a dream.

There are many others, but I am especially indebted to Ross Von Wiegand, director of Labor-Management Services at the National Council on Alcoholism, Adolf "Sully" Sullivan, coordinator of Special Health Services, Standard Oil Company of

California, and John Williams, director of Special Health Services, Morgan Guaranty Trust Company, for their assistance in the chapter for employers. Special gratitude is also due the Reverend Joseph Kellerman, executive director of the Charlotte, North Carolina, Council on Alcoholism. Not only did he devote many hours to the entire manuscript, but my thoughts in the final two chapters for families were inspired in part by two of his pamphlets, *The Merry-Go-Round Named Denial* and *AA—A Family Affair.* Vernon Johnson, director of the Johnson Institute in Minneapolis, and the author of the book *I'll Quit Tomorrow,* was also most helpful, especially with the chapter on intervention. Dr. Frank Seixas, medical director of the National Council on Alcoholism, edited the entire manuscript, paying particular attention to the medical data.

The publications of the following were helpful as well: Dr. Richard Heilman's pamphlet, *Early Recognition of Alcoholism & Other Drug Dependence;* Edmond Habib Lahage's pamphlet, *Precipitating a Family Crisis in Alcoholism;* Joan Jackson's paper in the Rutgers December 1954 *Quarterly Journal of Studies on Alcohol,* "The Adjustment of the Family to the Crisis of Alcoholism"; Nada J. Estes' article in the July 1974 *American Journal of Nursing,* "Counseling the Wife of an Alcoholic Spouse"; and Betty Reddy's pamphlet, *Alcoholism: A Family Illness.* Although I have borrowed ideas from far and wide, the concept of a direct public presentation and the words are mine, and because they are, they do not necessarily reflect the views of those from whom I have borrowed.

There would be no book without all the alcoholics and their families who have shared moments of their lives with me at the Smithers Alcoholism Treatment and Training Center of Roosevelt Hospital. I am most grateful to them, as well as to R. Brinkley Smithers, for making that possible. And there would be no book without the incentive and enthusiasm of my children, Judy, Rachel, and Dan, who also assumed the task of renaming the persons whose stories I have presented.

THE BOOZE BATTLE

There must be something the matter with him
because he would not be acting as he does
unless there was
therefore he is acting the way he is
because there is something the matter with him

He does not think there is anything the matter
with him because
one of the things that is
the matter with him
is that he does not think there is anything
the matter with him

Therefore
We have to help him realize that
the fact that he does not think there is anything
the matter with him
is one of the things that is
the matter with him.

R. D. Laing

1
ME SICK?

Soon after I began counseling alcoholics and their families in an alcoholic rehabilitation center, I realized that although there is a great deal of literature available to professionals in the field of alcoholism, very little is available to the people who live or work with alcoholics. The professionals know what should be done, but the people responsible for the doing are left in the dark. Time after time I heard the words "But I have read everything I could get my hands on and I still didn't realize . . ." and "If only I could have known years ago . . ." Believing at first that what I was hearing from these people involved with alcoholics had more to do with their own denial processes than with reality, I nevertheless scoured the bookstores and li-

3

braries. They were right. Many books have been written on alcoholism which are available to the public, but none meets the need these people have for specific guidance in the pretreatment phase of alcoholism—the most important phase of all. The people most in need of specific information were actually the people with access to the least. This book addressed to families, friends, and employers of alcoholics is my attempt to correct this tragic situation.

Before I go farther, I will interrupt the train of thought to tell you about a problem I have encountered and try to resolve it so we do not have to deal with it throughout the rest of the book. I have not known what to do with genders. There is no way I can say he (she) and vice versa. We will be hiccoughing throughout the book, those of us who stick it out. One gender or the other has to be chosen. So the masculine pronouns will be used for the alcoholics, while the feminine pronouns will be used for the wives of alcoholics. This will be done throughout the book except where I speak directly about female alcoholics and husbands of alcoholic wives. I can assure you this is purely a grammatical constraint and has no relationship to the relative proportion of male and female alcoholics among the general population. The genders can almost always be transposed in reading without altering the validity of the statement or example, and I must ask each reader to do the transposing according to need.

The pretreatment phase of alcoholism is crucial because it is the phase that causes the most difficulty for the people involved with alcoholics. It is also the phase when, if the alcoholic is approached constructively, he can be reached earlier in his disease process when his chances for recovery are the greatest. Consequently this book is devoted almost exclusively to the pretreatment phase of alcoholism. I do not discuss in detail the actual treatment of alcoholics: Vernon Johnson covers this topic very well in his book *I'll Quit Tomorrow*. Nor will I discuss the recovery phase of alcoholism. If you start doing things differently during the pretreatment phase, I can assure you, you will be prepared for the alcoholic's recovery. You will, you see, have already entered your own recovery period.

I hear you asking, "Me recover? From what? He's the one who's drinking. He's sick, not me! After all, I'm the one who's held things together all these years." Right you are, but you have paid a price.

Alcoholism is a rough disease. Without fail it causes the alcoholic to act in ways that hurt, which in turn cause you to react by hurting yourself—unless, of course, you are already receiving help. The destruction is subtle in the beginning and always insidious, ever occurring. Most likely you will not realize what is happening or even that anything is happening to you until the time comes when you find yourself screaming at the kids when you are not even angry with them, or crying a lot, or very nervous, or preparing for drastic action which you do not want to take, or feeling just nothing, day after day.

Are you crazy? No, I do not believe you are. I have only met one spouse of an alcoholic who in any way fitted the mold of what we would generally consider insane. All the others had simply attempted to adjust to the unadjustable. That wreaks havoc in the best of us, and it is this havoc, this destruction, that I will speak of; why and how it comes about, and what it is like. I will also tell you why the alcoholic close to you behaves the way he does, what is taking place within him, and how his unpredictability is so predictable. I will also describe new ways for you to respond to him. Not only will you then be better able to help him, but you can end your own destruction and begin the mending of whatever damage has already occurred. Alcoholism is too big for anyone to deal with alone. Without guidance no one can know how to react constructively, because the natural responses we use in other crises do not work in alcoholism. It is as simple as that. I have never met anyone involved with an alcoholic who has not been traumatized to some degree. On the other hand, some of the healthiest people I have ever met are people once caught in the destruction of alcoholism who have gone on to find new responses to living.

I am writing this book because I believe you are *not* crazy. I believe in your basic core of health and that if you know what to do, you are apt to do it. Many of you have given me reason for my beliefs. You have allowed yourselves to be receptive to new views and new responses. You are very different people today.

I am writing this book, also, not only to give you information about the disease, knowing that knowledge is power, but to tell you of people who can help you, for there is no need for you to be alone. There are at least 36 million people like you involved with alcoholics in the United States. Thousands of you are seeking help and helping each other right this minute; some are in your own community.

Not only can you get well, or protect your present health, by getting help; your alcoholic can be helped as well. Alcoholism is a highly treatable disease, and alcoholics can be forced to an earlier recognition of their condition than they will reach if left alone. They can be forced to earlier "bottoms," but only by certain people. Alcoholics grant that kind of power to but a few—their families (as well as lovers, sometimes close friends) and employers. Because most alcoholics have families and/or are employed, most alcoholics can be forced into treatment by the leverage these people have against them.

Pressure is required. The nature of the alcoholic's disease is such that he perceives neither his sickness nor his need for help. I will describe not only actions for families but actions for employers as well, all of which put pressure on the alcoholic to perceive reality better. None of these actions is particularly drastic in and of itself; all of them or several of them, however, can have an enormous impact upon the alcoholic. None of them is complicated, although few are easy. All are possible, and all help to strengthen the person performing them while creating the climate and the pressure for change in the alcoholic.

I will tell you about some of the people I have known who have been involved with alcoholism. Their names have been changed, but their experiences are real. Sally is the only atypical person in the book, and she is atypical only because she received guidance before she was even sure of her husband's alcoholism. She did all the right things. She is real, but few people identify with her. Ellen and Ken reacted to their spouses' alcoholism in a lot of self-destructive ways, using natural responses which are more typical for most of us. And you will meet others as well, whom I have selected to write about because they too are not unusual. They describe fairly accurately what takes place in alcoholism. If it seems grim, remember that it need not be.

2
SALLY

  Sally was nineteen when she married her high school sweetheart, Tom, who was twenty. She was exceptionally attractive, full of energy, and well liked. Tom made friends easily, was a natural athlete, and, along with Sally, eagerly assumed responsibilities in community and church affairs. After one year in college, Tom went to work for his uncle and, having the gregarious charm of the born salesman, was able to help expand the business. Sally was a secretary for a local law firm and enjoyed it enough to continue on a part-time basis after the birth of their children. There was no reason in those early years for either of them to suspect that anything could go wrong in their lives.

  But by the time Sally was twenty-six and the

mother of two small children, Tom was a full-blown alcoholic. He did not drink daily, performed well in his work, never drank in the morning, and never even had the shakes. However, he did drink heavily nearly every weekend and occasionally on a week night when out with the boys. He drove while intoxicated and had been involved in at least one accident that Sally knew of. She was beginning to live in dread of Tom's killing himself or others. She pleaded, scolded, and occasionally screamed, but to no avail.

When intoxicated, Tom was often insulting to those he was with, including Sally. She and their friends were on guard when Tom drank, for he was becoming increasingly erratic. More and more often he got drunk when he drank. More and more often he became belligerent when he became drunk. Not only was he no longer pleasant to be with on social occasions, he was actually frightening. Several times he had to be restrained from physically assaulting people who inadvertently crossed him. It was not long before friends no longer invited them out.

Following some of his heavy drinking bouts, Tom would be full of remorse and promises for better conduct and less drinking in the future. Occasionally he would feel sick enough the next morning to promise not to drink at all the next time. Sally accepted his promises eagerly and suffered pangs of guilt thinking she had overreacted and should not have said all those things to him.

They would make up and Tom would improve for a while, but eventually he always returned to his pattern of excessive drinking and inappropriate behavior.

At work one morning Sally burst into tears. She could no longer contain her despair, her fear, her anger. She felt that Tom's drinking was destroying her marriage and her sense of well-being, yet Tom was not effectively altering the pattern of his drinking. Things were just getting worse. She blurted the whole story out to her boss, who told her then that he was a recovered alcoholic. He suggested the possibility of Tom's being an alcoholic and invited Sally to attend an Alcoholics Anonymous meeting with him.

That meeting was a turning point in Sally's life. Although she couldn't really believe that Tom was an alcoholic, she heard enough to make her wonder. Sally's boss was extremely patient and understanding. He stressed her need for information so she could determine what she was up against. He encouraged her to continue going to AA meetings and to keep an open mind. He also suggested that she go to Al-Anon, which is for families of alcoholics. He said that if Tom was an alcoholic then Sally would be in need of sustained help, both to maintain her own emotional health and to learn the best approaches to the disease. She attended meeting after meeting of AA and Al-Anon and gradually reached some understanding of the disease.

It was helpful for Sally to learn about the loss

of control which is the hallmark of alcoholism. She learned that it did not matter how much Tom drank—or when or what. What *did* matter was whether he had control of his drinking or not. Although Sally could see that Tom was very different from most of the people she heard speak at AA meetings, she could also see that these people were very different from one another. Some had drunk around the clock; others had not. Some had suffered physical complications; others had not. Some had hit skid row; others had never lost a job. While some had drunk for years before problems arose, others had had very rapid progressions. Some had been nasty drinkers, others friendly. Some were fat, some skinny. Some rich, some poor. Some educated, some not. No two people seemed alike in any way except for one thing they all shared: a loss of control over their drinking.

Although it was difficult for Sally to accept, she finally acknowledged that Tom, too, had lost his control. She knew he was unable to always predict when he was going to drink, or where or how much. He did not drink during the day or every evening, but he was unable to consistently predict how much he was going to drink when he did drink. Time after time he promised he would have only one or two, yet ended up having his usual amount or more. Occasionally he promised he would not drink at all at a particular event, yet drank anyway. And Tom could not always control his behavior once he started drinking. Although there were lulls in his drinking and the resulting asocial behavior, he could not maintain them or stay stopped. Eventually all his promises and good intentions went by the wayside as he drank when he intended not to, drank more than he intended to, or did things while drinking that he did not intend. Tom was hooked and Sally realized it. He was an alcoholic!

The moment Sally accepted that fact, she accepted as well that it was all beyond Tom. Compared to the force of his addiction he was a dwarf. She no longer believed that Tom could cut down or stop if only he wanted to, if only he loved her enough, if only he tried harder. She knew he needed help.

With her knowledge, her hope, and the help she received from recovered alcoholics and their mates, Sally set upon a course of action that not only got Tom to the treatment he needed, but, just as important, a course that allowed her to cope effectively during a demanding and painful period of her life. She grew as a person. She did not succumb to the circumstances surrounding her because she stopped involving herself in self-defeating actions. Sally now knew that alcoholism is a treatable disease. Her employer was an alcoholic, yet alcohol no longer interfered with his life. She had met scores of alcoholics in AA who, with the help they received, were able to stop drinking. She had every hope that Tom too could be treated.

Sally was one in a million. Instead of falling

into a pattern of destructive responses to her husband's drinking, she took constructive action almost from the beginning, and she was able to do it because she had help.

Sally had revealed her problems to a knowledgeable person early in the progression of Tom's disease. Her boss was able to give her constructive assistance and lead her to sources of information and help. She was fortunate to have selected a knowledgeable person, because more often than not the people selected as confidants are not informed and cannot give the help so desperately needed. Even more frequently there is a reluctance to discuss the problem at all until several years of ever deepening destruction occurs. One recent study indicates that wives wait about *seven years* from the time they first become aware of the alcohol problem to the first time they seek outside help. By then the marriage, if it still exists, can be beyond repair and all the family members so severely traumatized that treatment may not be effective.

Sally was unique on another count. She decided she was not going to wait for Tom to realize he needed help. She feared that if she waited for Tom to have any spontaneous insight of his own, she was in for a long wait. She decided to intervene in the progression of his disease by letting Tom experience his own sickness every way she could.

She had become intrigued with the concept of *hitting bottom*, which she heard mentioned so often in AA and Al-Anon. People reached their bottom, then reached for help. Sally wanted desperately for Tom to reach his bottom, but everyone's bottom seemed to be different and it also appeared to be a mental state rather than a physical condition or set of circumstances. Sally once heard it called *that moment of truth* the alcoholic reaches from a pit of utter despair, when he perceives clearly the futility of his position, the futility of his very being. With that moment of truth the alcoholic will reach out for help if he has hope that help exists and that he is worthy of help. Those without hope are apt to kill themselves. That's how clearly they see their futility and how acutely they feel their despair. This explanation clicked with Sally because it fitted so well with everything else she was hearing in AA and Al-Anon. Sally knew Tom had to feel the pain of despair and futility. She loved him dearly but she knew he would have to perceive his sickness before he would pursue treatment. She was determined to allow him to feel the pain caused by his drinking. She could then offer the hope and help she knew existed.

Meanwhile, Tom did not admit that he even had a problem. But Sally was prepared for this because she heard over and over in AA about the alcoholic's unique ability to deny. She knew that alcoholics could fall flat on their faces, pick themselves up, and claim they had never fallen. What drinking and resulting behavior Tom would admit to he blamed on others: "those nuts she was hanging around with at her meetings," his uncle, her mother, the kids, and anyone else handy. Sally was, as well, hearing ever more frequently that it was her fault. But she did not buy any of this anymore. She knew that blaming outside people and events was but another symptom of the disease.

The alcoholic has to deny, excuse, and accuse in order to continue his drinking. By her attendance at meetings Sally was able to reinforce these facts in her mind. Otherwise she feels she would just have given in, as it would have been so much easier to forget the whole thing and go along with Tom. When he was not belligerent and threatening, he was extremely charming and persuasive. And Tom insisted he had a right to drink; after all, he was working, providing a style of living for his family that allowed for many luxuries, and was entitled to drink when he wished along with all his friends. Sally's response never wavered. She said he had a right to do anything he wished as long as it did not interfere with her life or that of their children. Sally felt acutely that her needs, those of the children, and of the marriage itself were not being met. So much attention was diverted to Tom's drinking—before, during, and after—that the ongoing problems of living were not being coped with effectively. Tom did not have a right to interfere in these vital areas of their lives and none of his protests convinced Sally otherwise.

She stood up for her rights and acted in ways

to meet her own needs and those of their children while letting Tom feel his sickness. She refused to compromise because she was determined not to let his alcoholism destroy her, the children, or Tom, if she could help it. She knew the progressive nature of the disease was such that if it were not arrested everything ultimately would be lost; consequently she was able to take some very courageous actions.

Today Sally and Tom are in their forties. Tom has been sober nearly eighteen years. Both are vital and appealing people and Tom laughs when he recalls Sally's actions. At that time, however, she was driving him right up the wall: "I couldn't come out winning no matter what I did." Sally today says she really did not feel all that strong much of the time. "The only reason I could do it was because of the help I got. My friends in AA and Al-Anon gave me enormous support in many ways but mostly by constantly confirming that what I was doing was right. Much of it seemed so wrong."

What Sally did was to take her focus off Tom's drinking. She no longer extracted promises, knowing they were just going to be broken eventually. She no longer threatened, realizing that Tom did not go by her words. *He listened to action only.* Up until that time her actions had not matched her threatening words. She began to formulate a plan of action that she was prepared to follow through on if Tom refused treatment. She took her attention off his drinking and focused on his inappropriate behavior and need for treatment.

Sally started seeing their friends and family by herself, breaking her own social isolation. She reasoned that because Tom was acting in an unhealthy manner did not mean that she had to, even though she felt awkward at first. She did not look to her friends or family for advice (she knew they didn't have it to give) but calmly stated that Tom had a drinking problem (they all knew it anyway) and that she was taking steps to help him. She carefully stopped her explanations at that point except to add that one way to help him was to remain healthy herself and that she was so grateful they were helping her do this by including her in some of their activities. Sally reports that her friends and family readily accepted her on those terms. Many times she enjoyed herself, although often she would go when she really would have preferred staying at home. Sally forced herself to go because she always felt better about herself for having gone and because her going might allow Tom to compare his abnormal social activities with the more normal behavior of others. She was not only insuring her own emotional health, thereby removing some of Tom's control over her, but was enabling Tom to see some of his own sickness. She could socialize; he could not! *On some level* he was being forced to look at that.

Sally was always aboveboard in her activities, telling Tom about them both in advance and af-

terwards. Neither her words nor her actions gave
him reason to be suspicious. She always made it
clear that she wished he were able to join her but
the problems related to his drinking made that
impossible at the present time. She avoided arguments on this point and remained resolute no
matter how angry or contrite or drunk Tom became. After all, Sally reasoned, all he had to do to
be with her was to see someone about his drinking problems. Since he was not willing to do that,
she was not willing to adjust to the unhealthy social isolation his drinking demanded.

Sally gave up all her attempts to control Tom's
drinking. She kept out enough money for the
household needs and did not nag Tom about the
rest. She hoped the money would not always be
squandered on alcohol but was prepared for that
to happen and accepted it when it did. Sally also
stopped trying to control the alcohol in the
house. It was always replaced anyway, and only
served to give Tom valid reasons to be angry with
her. She no longer hid the liquor or threw it
away. In effect, she allowed him to drink any old
way he chose, as he had always done even with
her struggles and manipulations. She worried
about him when he drank away from home, but
accepted the fact that she had no control there
either. She says, "Many times my prayers were
my only comfort."

Sally went further still, taking steps that went
directly against everything she had been taught
about being a wife and a loving person. She

began to let Tom suffer the consequences of his drinking behavior. He had started to become very abusive toward her and on one occasion assaulted her physically. When he could not remember his behavior the next day Sally reviewed it for him, pointing out that such behavior indicated a need for help on his part. When Tom denied both the behavior and the need, Sally told him that if he assaulted her again she would call the police. The next time he started throwing things about the house and it appeared she might be next, she did call the police. When Tom was sober the next day she again reviewed his behavior of the night before for him. Tom remembered the police but flatly refused to speak to anyone about his drinking problem. Sally then said she would have to go to court to get an Order of Protection out against him to protect herself in the future. Tom still refused help and Sally proceeded with her court action. Once again Tom was being offered the opportunity to see that his behavior called for action that does not occur in healthy families.

By providing protection against violence for herself and the children Sally was once again refusing to accept a sick situation as if it were normal. Aside from any physical trauma, Sally had learned at Al-Anon that it would be extremely damaging to her sense of self-worth to allow herself or her children to be physically abused. The positive aspects of calling the police and going to court were far more important to Sally than protecting herself from the shame and embarrassment of seeking such assistance.

Tom's assaultive behavior at home stopped after Sally went to court, but his already excessive drinking increased. He now began to suffer hangovers so severe that he was occasionally unable to go to work. He begged Sally to call his office for him to say he had the flu and would be in tomorrow. Sally flatly refused to do this under Tom's conditions. She said she knew he was sick and that he needed help: Did he wish it? If he agreed to make an appointment that day with a physician who could help him (she had the name of one knowledgeable about alcoholism) then she would call the office explaining that he was sick and she was taking him to the doctor. Otherwise Tom would be responsible for making his own call.

Sally did not give Tom the angry, silent treatment during these hangovers, but she did not baby him either: she accepted them as inevitable. She simply reinforced her attitude of "Yes, I know you are sick and there is help available." Tom always refused help and Sally allowed him to suffer through his hangovers and to make or not make his own phone calls. Although she was fearful of Tom's job being affected by his drinking, she knew very well that the progression of the disease was such that if he did not get help the job would be lost anyway. Therefore she focused only on Tom's need for treatment, rather than covering for him out of fears of her own.

Sally stopped assuming responsibility for other consequences of Tom's drinking. Whenever his drinking caused him to do things that required picking up the pieces afterwards, Sally allowed Tom to do the picking up, even if the picking up was of Tom himself.

Several times Tom made it home safely after a night's drinking but ran out of steam before making it to bed. Sally let him sleep it off wherever he plopped. She would actually walk over and around him the next morning making her usual amount of noise with the pots and pans and the vacuum cleaner. When Tom came to he would stumble off on his own, but he had to look from whence he picked himself up. *On some level* he was once again being forced to look at where his drinking was taking him.

Sally explained everything she knew about Tom's illness to the children, even though she was not sure they were old enough to understand. She encouraged their normal activities but did not hide Tom's drunken stupors from them. She did shepherd them out of the room when Tom seemed especially aggressive and near violence. At those times she stayed with the children, giving them support at least with her presence.

Once Tom parked his car on his neighbor's front lawn in the middle of the night. When Sally spotted it her immediate temptation was to move it before the whole neighborhood knew. But she asked herself, "Which is most important? Protecting my pride or letting Tom see the result of his

drinking?" Sally reasoned correctly that Tom
could not perceive the futility of his ways if he did
not see his ways. Therefore, when Tom came
downstairs at noon, Sally said, "Tom, you parked
your car on Ben's front lawn when you came
home last night." After an immediate denial from
Tom she added, "It's still on Ben's front lawn,
and I'm sure he would like you to move it." It's
not impossible, but it is more difficult for an alcoholic to deny concrete evidence. Once again
Tom had to suffer the consequences of his own
behavior.

Sally stopped her efforts to control the environment so life would be easier for Tom. She did
not accept his excuses for drinking; that it was
the kids' noise, his boss, the neighbors, her
mother, or anything she or anyone else did. She
knew the problem was within Tom, not in his
outside world. Sally reasoned that everyone had
problems to cope with but not everyone used alcohol as the method of coping. She stopped all
efforts to ease situations in the hope of reducing
Tom's need for drinking. She had learned that if
she took care of one of his pet annoyances, he
would just replace it with another. More than anything he needed his reasons for drinking to continue drinking.

Sally stopped minimizing Tom's behavior. Previously, she had made much of it while he was
drinking but little of it when he was sober. Many
wives fall into this trap because they are fearful of
upsetting the apple cart while peace reigns. Sally

correctly assumed that the very time to point out his behavior was when they had a moment of peace. Whenever she attempted to do this when he was drinking she lost her cool, and anyway Tom could not absorb reality and the next day frequently had little or no memory of what had been said the night before. Knowing that Tom always had some guilt and remorse the next day even if he tried not to show it, Sally decided to use it constructively. He would get angry at something sooner or later anyway, and it was important that he become aware of his behavior. She became an expert at nonchalantly reporting the events of the night before. One of her typical reports: "Billy was very disappointed when you didn't show up for his Little League game yesterday. He made a home run and came running over to tell you, but you weren't there. He didn't cry but he wouldn't come down for supper even though I made pizza for him. The manager said it's the first home run he's ever made in a big game."

Now it was Tom who had to live with his own behavior and his guilt, shame, embarrassment, and consequences. He often reacted with anger, but was still being faced over and over again with his own behavior. Sally was no longer as emotionally vulnerable. She still felt hurt very often, especially when the children were involved, but for the most part she was able to recognize his behavior as symptomatic of his disease, thus eliminating a good deal of the pain.

Sally constantly provided opportunities for Tom to see that his behavior was really not normal and that help was available. She removed herself from his drinking and irrational behavior as much as possible. She no longer covered up for him or assumed responsibility for the consequences of his behavior. She no longer tried to control his drinking or his environment. She let him drink, see what he had done, and cover his own tracks, while she went about meeting her needs and responsibilities.

Tom says today, "Nothing was working any more. I was constantly frustrated and I couldn't take it out on Sally. She just wouldn't be my target." By allowing Tom to make his own bed and sleep in it, she was removing herself from Tom's blame and letting his anxieties increase. Tom was feeling sicker quicker and Sally was accomplishing what she had set out to do.

One particularly bad Monday morning Sally offered to call AA and Tom, for once, agreed. He listened, started going to AA and did stop drinking. However, after a few weeks he reasoned that he was too young to be an alcoholic and had just gone about his drinking the wrong way. He started drinking again and soon became worse than he had ever been. Sally told Tom, in one of his sober moments, that if he wished to drink he must do it from another base; she just did not have the strength to put up with any more. That afternoon, when Tom left with the obvious intent of drinking, Sally put her plans into action. She

installed new locks on the doors, had her Order
of Protection ready in case the police had to be
called, packed a suitcase for Tom, and left it outside the door. She settled down to wait for his
reaction, fearing the worst.

Tom came out of a blackout (temporary amnesia) fumbling with the lock and trying to get his
key to work. He says, "Even though I was drunk I
knew this was it. I knew she had changed the
locks and the ball game was over. Sally always did
what she said she would." As he turned to leave
he stumbled over his suitcase and any doubts
were removed. He was in an absolute panic because he knew there was nothing he could do to
change her mind. He picked himself up along
with his suitcase and made it to a motel, where he
promptly passed out. The next morning he had
trouble remembering what had happened, but it
slowly came back to him. He knew his only option
was to get sober. He was not even sure sobriety
would get him back to Sally, but perceived that he
needed it anyway. Tom showered and then
opened his suitcase. It was packed with dirty
underwear. Tom says he just started to cry. "I
couldn't even get angry with her. I couldn't
blame her any more for anything. It was *me* that
got *me* to a strange motel all alone with only dirty
underwear, and I knew it." Tom has been sober
ever since. He returned to live with Sally and the
children when both he and she were comfortable
with his sobriety, and then "Our marriage finally
began, with all its troubles, all its joys."

3
ELLEN

An alarming phone call from a total stranger with news of her son finally forced Ellen to seek help. There were many things that Ellen had not faced over the years, but one was the gradual retreat of her son into a world of his own. Now she was shocked into action. For several months ten-year-old Steven had been getting on his bike every Saturday and Sunday and riding off for the day. Ellen never knew where he was going, but hoped it was to be with friends—even though she was not sure he had any friends.

On this particular Saturday, Ellen heard that Steven had been riding out to the local airport, where he sat without moving, talking, or apparently seeing. Every Saturday and Sunday he sat and stared from early morning to late afternoon seemingly unaware of either the people or the planes. The stranger on the phone, an employee at the airport, said he often spoke to the boy but never received an answer. Today his concern had mounted when he discovered Steven sitting on his customary bench, unmoving, during a violent thunderstorm. As if in a trance, Steven had followed the employee inside and given, simply , the phone number he was now calling.

Ellen had witnessed Steven's retreat into his own world for a little more than a year. She was aware of his prolonged silences, periodic violent outbursts, poor school grades, and lack of friends, but had not taken action. Now, with the stranger's report on top of everything else, Ellen was desperate. She was facing more than she could handle and more than she could any longer overlook.

The psychiatrist she found for Steven told her the entire family needed treatment. He recognized alcoholism as the problem immediately after talking with Ellen and Steven, and directed both Ellen and her husband, Michael, to the help they each required while he began treating Steven. Michael refused to work with a counselor but Ellen had reached such a point of despair that she was willing to do anything to get help, even if it meant displeasing Michael. She was no longer willing to live the life she had been living, even if it meant that Michael would leave her, which he threatened to do. Ellen today says that it seems as if all their life together she was waiting for the right conditions in order to be happy. "I know now that I was always off in the future. When Steve got so sick, I was finally forced to deal with the present. I couldn't deny it anymore and I couldn't afford to wait for the future."

Her life up until that point had been one of waiting. When she and Michael met and fell in love they were both in college. They could not get married at that time and Ellen envisioned her happiness forthcoming in the future, when they were married. When at last they did marry, Michael was in law school and Ellen was working in a publishing house, patiently awaiting the day when they could afford their own home and children. She had all the dreams: "White picket fences, lots of kids and dogs running around and, me, the supermom."

Ellen had the home soon enough, but eight years passed and several miscarriages occurred before she gave birth to Steven. By that time, although she was overjoyed with the baby and relished motherhood, she harbored a gnawing worry about Michael. His drinking had become a source of contention between them.

On many evenings in the past few years Michael had missed dinner and arrived home drunk. When he was at home for dinner he frequently passed out in the early evening and Ellen had to help him to bed. At social gatherings he became a source of humiliation for her. He was never deliberately rude but he had begun to repeat himself and slur his words; occasionally friends had to help her get Michael home. Twice in the past year he had actually fallen off his chair while eating, once at a wedding and once at a formal dinner party with several of his business associates.

Ellen became a shrew about his behavior. "I nagged him constantly until I finally extracted a promise. He absolutely refused to discuss the episodes and it seemed the only thing I could do was to get a promise for the future." When Michael modified his drinking for certain periods, so that his behavior was socially acceptable, Ellen felt she had exaggerated and was remorseful about her own behavior.

In the first years of their marriage Ellen had not minded Michael's drinking, or if she did, had not complained. She knew his job was very demanding and all the men they knew seemed to drink a lot. Michael was always considerate of her, loved the baby, and had even made their home his hobby. He enjoyed working with his hands and had become a skilled craftsman. To Ellen's delight she did not have to depend on local plumbers and carpenters, for Michael made all the necessary repairs and improvements.

The changes in Michael were gradual, but they were drastic. By the time Steven was four, Michael was having ever more frequent occurrences of inappropriate drinking behavior at social gatherings. He was also taking less interest in the house and their family life and increasingly withdrawing into himself and his alcohol. Ellen says, "He was leaving much of Steve's care and entertainment up to me. He just didn't seem to be interested in anything anymore if drinking was not involved.He had spurts of enthusiasm but rarely followed through."

They started to avoid facing the many problems of living. "When we were making up to each other, I didn't want to talk about the budget, cracked tiles, Steven's lisp, or anything else. And when I was involved in a disturbing situation brought about by his drinking, I was concerned solely with that situation. I was afraid to bring problems in because I felt they would just upset Michael and cause him to drink even more." Ellen and Michael continued to avoid reality for several years to come.

Ellen's concern mounted. Nothing she was doing seemed effective and Michael's drinking was getting worse. She expressed her worries to members of her family and close friends. Several felt that Michael was drinking heavily but most felt she was exaggerating, that it was a rough time in Michael's life and things would get better. Many offered advice for handling specific crises as they arose and it all was conflicting. "I was either to make threats or to be reassuring, to not speak to Michael at all or to talk it all out with him, to ignore him completely or to give him more attention. I just became more confused and felt, somehow, I just had not stumbled on the right approach yet." Ellen's feelings of guilt increased whenever she spoke to anyone. She didn't seem to be helping Michael at all, yet others seemed to feel that if she would do things differently she could help him. She began to feel that perhaps she was actually the cause of Michael's drinking.

When Ellen spoke to the family doctor about Michael's drinking, he agreed to see Michael and to speak to him. He discovered that Michael had an enlarged liver due to alcohol. Michael was told to stop drinking and actually did stop for six months, when a second examination revealed that his liver had returned to normal. Michael was then told he could have an occasional drink, but not to overdo it. Within a very short time, Michael's drinking was right where he had left off six months earlier if not worse. He flatly refused to see the physician again, saying, "He told me I could have an occasional drink and that's all I'm having."

Ellen next spoke to the priest at their church, who suggested a need on both their parts for counseling and recommended a psychiatrist well known for his work with couples involved in alcoholic marriages. Michael adamantly refused. Not only was he angry with Ellen for talking to outsiders, he was also angry at the outsiders for their "meddling" in his affairs. He stopped all his church activities and insisted that Ellen keep her problems to herself. Instead of pursuing counseling for herself, Ellen went along with Michael, who flatly refused to acknowledge any need for any help whatsoever.

Michael also started using her "disloyalty" as another excuse to increase his drinking. By this time anything Ellen did had become reason for his drinking. Even Steven became a reason, and, of course, there was always his job, which had pressures he felt Ellen added to. Without realizing it, Ellen gradually accepted this burden of guilt.

Ellen and Michael gradually entered an almost total social isolation. Ellen is not sure exactly where or how it started, but feels she began to withdraw about the same time that friends and family began to exclude them. "I think I was beginning to see the handwriting on the wall and I wanted to erase it before anyone else saw it. I was scared. I still thought the drinking could be controlled, but I knew there was something very wrong with Michael's drinking. I was ashamed and afraid to have anyone else see the extent of it. I was afraid we'd be ostracized, so I gradually refused invitations and stopped entertaining so people wouldn't know how bad it really was." Ellen also believed Michael when he blamed his upsets on what others said or did, so she withdrew as a way of removing Michael's reasons for drinking as well. "It didn't work and I can see how the isolation hurt us even more."

When there were virtually no other people around them, Ellen and Michael each became even more dependent upon the other's behavior, and they both sank more deeply into the mire of active alcoholism. The isolation reinforced

Michael's sense of control over his environment. Now he had only Ellen to contend with and she was becoming increasingly unsure of herself. Michael's need to control his environment was increasing in direct proportion to his loss of control over his drinking. The more he felt the need to drink the more he needed an environment that allowed it.

Because Michael was now almost her only adult contact, Ellen was even more deeply threatened by his inappropriate drinking behavior. She therefore became almost totally preoccupied with Michael's drinking and tried harder and harder to control it. She always failed. When she hid or threw liquor away, Michael became angry and replaced it, or drank away from home. He always had a supply. Ellen threatened to leave him or to lock him out, but she never did, and Michael knew she never would. She babied him, berated him, refused to cook for him, made his favorite dishes, slept in the guest room, slept in his bed with sexy new negligees, ignored him, attended to him solely, wept and laughed. And Michael continued to drink. There was nothing Ellen could find to do that was effective in getting him to modify his drinking, while Michael used everything she did as a reason to drink further.

Ellen was fearful that Michael might lose his job and was terrified at the thought of having anyone in his firm know the extent of the problem. Therefore she never hesitated to cover Michael's tracks any way she could. She was quick to make Michael's excuses for him and on several occasions called his office with detailed descriptions of Michael's "flu" or new case of "intestinal upset."

Ellen also kept Michael from seeing much of his own behavior. She knew that he could not always remember everything from the day or evening before and she did not remind him. She feared that being made aware of either his behavior or memory losses would be upsetting and cause further drinking. She found herself living for those rare moments of peace, hoping each time that then Michael could gain control of his drinking. Consequently she lived from crisis to crisis, soft-pedaling each, vainly waiting and hoping that somehow, someday Michael would be able to get on top of it all.

With every crisis, each found reason to be resentful of the other—Michael because she added to his troubles and didn't understand him, Ellen because she was mistreated and knew it but could not stop it. With each crisis their resentments mounted until that seemed to be the all-pervasive feeling between them. Usually they kept it buried, but occasionally each exploded and when they did, they violently attacked one another both physically and verbally. After a time they accepted physical violence as normal behavior.

Ellen had rages in which she was beyond control, "Once I ran after him with a butcher knife and when I couldn't catch him I just threw it at him. I missed, but only just." She was terrified of her own behavior because she was having feelings and losses of control that she had never dreamed were possible. "I hated myself, but I couldn't stop myself. I would just freak out completely."

It never occurred to Ellen to call the police when Michael, once so considerate of her, became violent. "I would not have done so even if I had thought of it. Police are just not called to settle domestic problems in my town. Besides, I had my own behavior to look at and I was feeling too inadequate to do anything but accept what Michael doled out. What I felt mostly was that I was losing my mind—that I was going crazy."

Ellen spent many years performing actions designed either to control Michael's drinking or to eliminate the reasons for it and every action failed. Each was guaranteed to fail since Ellen never had any more control over Michael's drinking than Michael himself. Each failure eroded Ellen's sense of self-worth. Her self-esteem went down a notch each time until she came to view herself as inadequate, and she became capable of living in a way she would formerly have considered abnormal. She had adjusted to a sick situation and in accepting it as normal came to think of herself as crazy.

Except for short periods when Michael went on the wagon and treated her as he once had, Ellen felt little if any love for him. She had not reached the point of giving up on Michael and feeling predominantly pity—which many wives eventually reach—but she was consumed by feelings of anger, fear, and frustration. She often thought of leaving Michael but never did.

Michael was still working, and in fact his income increased in spite of the extent of his drinking. Ellen had not worked in years and compared her present financial security against slim chances of being able to support herself and take care of Steven alone. Whenever she threatened to leave Michael, Michael threatened to withhold any support from her. He painted vivid pictures of her and Steven living in a cold-water fourth floor walkup. Ellen believed Michael. She had lost all faith in herself. Because she felt guilty for Michael's drinking, Ellen did not feel she had a right to walk out on him, but most of all she feared being alone, so she could not admit failure. "I just would not or could not accept that Michael's drinking was beyond me. We had had so much together at one time and I was sure we could someday return to that. Because he was still working I thought he could also get the rest of his life put together. I really believed that if he loved me enough, if we both tried harder, he could drink normally and then everything would be all right."

Michael's periodic abstinences and occasions of acceptable drinking behavior also kept Ellen from making any kind of stable adjustment. Her hopes and positive feelings for Michael were rekindled each time. Though her hopes were unjustified, they kept her from facing Michael's inability to control his drinking. Instead, she kept trying to pursue the reasons for his drinking and to find ways to control it, all the time feeling more and more a failure as a wife and, in time, as a mother.

Her son got Ellen to the help she so desperately needed. While both Ellen and Michael suffered immeasurable agonies, Steven certainly suffered as much if not more. He changed from an open, alert, affectionate toddler to a ten-year-old so turned in upon himself that several years of psychiatric treatment were necessary before he could cope effectively with his world.

For one thing, Steven did not know how he should behave. He was often rewarded for reasons he could not understand and as often punished for no apparent reason. Steve could not know that his mother was really angry at the father when she struck out against the son, and was therefore guilty and inappropriate in her rewards to him. Nor could he understand his father's withdrawals and silences and then overabundant affections. Steve did not know what to expect or when to expect it, nor did he know what was expected of him.

Steve was raised in a household where inconsistency was his only constant. He knew early that there was something very wrong, but he could not know what. He knew early that his family was different, but not why. His questions were asked but never answered. After all, his parents knew little more than he and were ashamed to speak of what little they did know. Steven knew he could not ask others because "it" was something to be kept secret. It was not long before Steve, turning his feelings of being different into feelings of being ashamed, reduced his own contacts with the outside world.

He felt "it" was his fault, whatever the "it" was. Ellen had herded him to bed "before your father gets home," had requested his silence "so your father won't be upset," and had stifled activities "because Daddy won't like it" so often that Steven grew to believe there was something very wrong with him and he was riddled with guilt.

Steven lived in a cruel world caused and compounded by parents who were not offering healthy modes of coping with life situations. He retreated ever deeper into his own world of fantasies. It was more tolerable there.

The psychiatrist who treated Steven encouraged Ellen to receive counseling at the alcoholism service at their local hospital, even though Michael refused to admit to a drinking problem. Ellen not only learned about the disease, she also learned a great deal about herself and why so much of what she had been doing was destructive—to herself as well as to Steven and Michael. With continued therapy plus Al-Anon meetings, she slowly started the upward path to health. She was able in time to recognize many of her real needs and to assume the responsibility for meeting them. Consequently she was able to bring about new directions to her own life. She did not, however, reach help in time to have any influence in interrupting the progression of Michael's disease. He died before Ellen reached the point where she felt capable of confronting him directly and unequivocally with his need for treatment.

During the year before his death, when Ellen and Steven were in therapy, Michael's world was rapidly falling apart. His addiction was robbing him of the resources which at one time could have been motivating forces for treatment and recovery. In that year Michael was hospitalized twice with pancreatitis, a condition brought on by alcohol. After each hospitalization Michael stopped drinking for a time but refused to seek any help to stay sober. His doctors suggested AA but Michael still flatly refused to believe he was an alcoholic. He was willing to admit to a drinking problem but refused AA because he did not feel he was as bad as all that. He felt that because he was still working he could not be an alcoholic.

And then he was no longer working. A few weeks after his second hospitalization, Michael lost his job. Ellen later learned that Michael had been warned about his drinking on several occasions and was finally forced to resign when he did not comply with the firm's warnings. His employers, as uninformed about the disease as Ellen, reacted to it as if Michael had control over his drinking. They did not recognize his need for treatment and, consequently, did not use all the power at their disposal to get him to the help he so desperately needed.

After his forced resignation Michael started drinking more heavily than ever. While driving home from a bar, where he had been drinking most of the day and evening, Michael started vomiting large amounts of bright red blood. He was hemorrhaging from ruptured blood vessels which had become enlarged in his throat, a condition secondary to the liver damage of alcoholism. He was found in a pool of blood in his car alongside the road by an early morning passer-by. He had been dead for hours.

Ellen was not the cause of Michael's alcoholism. She and their child were, in fact, nearly destroyed because of it. But all the destruction and Michael's wasted life were needless. *Alcoholism is a treatable disease!*

4
WIVES OF ALCOHOLICS

The wife of an actively drinking alcoholic who responds to the disease by herself, without either knowledge or help from knowledgeable people, can only lose. So does her husband and do so her children. Her actions are such that she actually helps her husband to drink. Her actions are such that she herself becomes emotionally unstable and raises emotionally crippled children. She is in desperate need of help, but puts it off until *she* perceives *no other choice*.

There must be something within all of us that allows us to sit back without constructive action until the moment is at hand when we are finally forced to move. Why else are we suddenly sitting on top of the energy crisis volcano? We have known for years that it was coming. Fifteen years ago I spent a semester studying about the impending ravages of the population explosion. The notes I took at that time outline events that would occur if corrective measures were not taken; shocking events which today are occurring. Is there anything I could have done? I don't know. The point is that I, along with many, did nothing. Constructive action often brings momentary discomfort which we will pay almost any price to avoid. Perhaps it is part of being human to take constructive action only when there is finally *no other choice*.

As people in general cannot afford to wait, the wife of an alcoholic especially cannot afford it, for alcoholism is as progressive and clearly predictable as the energy crisis or the population explosion. Effective measures for halting its destruction demand that the wife rise above herself, above her humanness. A tall order indeed, yet that is what is asked of her.

As if that alone were not enough, the wife has other hurdles before her. Traditionally our society has placed women in a dependent position. Although this is changing today as women redefine themselves, for the most part the status of the wife is still based on what her husband does and how well he does it. Consequently she feels in immediate danger if her husband's performance is in any way adversely effected. Her natural survival reaction is to make things all right. She urgently feels the need to control her husband, to manipulate him, to get his performance back up to snuff and keep it that way, and to cover poor performances any way she can. In doing what comes naturally, she provides the ideal environment for her husband to drink further, ensuring the very thing she is most fearful of: a worsening of the situation.

And it does not stop there. The wife is further impelled by old tapes programmed since infancy, which she has whirling around inside her telling her how to be a good wife. And that involves, so her tapes tell her, nurturing, caring for, a little nursing and doctoring now and then, being kind, sympathetic, understanding, and responsive to her husband's wishes. She is programmed to do all this and the better she does it, the better wife she is. And the sicker her alcoholic husband becomes! Natural "wifely" responses that a traditional marriage calls for only further the progression of alcoholism.

Constructive approaches to alcoholism require the wife to go beyond herself. She must be willing to forgo her desires for immediate comfort, because to effectively interrupt the progression of alcoholism and its destruction she must face and cope constructively with each crisis as it arises, hoping that something good can come of it but without specific guarantees. Whenever she feels compelled to cover her husband's tracks or to rescue him from a situation out of her own feelings of shame, embarrassment, or fear, she will have to face these feelings and take actions not necessarily designed to reduce or alleviate them.

She will have to embark upon new behavior designed instead to interrupt the course of her husband's alcoholism. She must be willing to adopt the all-abiding faith that if she is doing the right things for the right reasons, good will come of it. Exactly *what* that good will be, or *when*, is out of her hands. She must let go of the results and concentrate on the necessary constructive action at hand. To discover her best options and act on them, she will need help.

The wife of an alcoholic must become willing to let go of the idea that she has any control over her husband's drinking. Each time she manipulates or controls in any way, she fails. That's a guarantee. No matter how determined, attractive, clever, knowledgeable, strong, or sly she is, she cannot overcome the force of her addicted husband's need for his fix. A modern-day Cleopatra would not have that much power. The most any wife should hope and strive for is emotional health for herself and treatment for her husband.

Every attempt at controlling either her husband or his environment will backfire, and her husband will gain the further control which he needs in order to continue drinking—to satisfy the compulsion of his addiction. When she feels the urge to control, she will instead have to face her own fear, anger, and anxiety. She will have to substitute constructive actions, for only then does she stand a chance of getting her husband to treatment and of keeping her own emotional health.

She will have to give up for the time being some of her preconceived ideas of what a loving wife is. What her alcoholic husband needs is described by some in the field of alcoholism treatment as "tough love," which requires that she act in ways that go against what she and society conceive her role to be. Her behavior may seem callous to the casual observer but it is based on a love that has the husband's vital interests at heart, a love that grants him the opportunity to feel his own sickness and to get treatment. This is not the kind of love that caters to his expressed wishes and demands, no matter how persuasive or threatening he becomes.

What wife is prepared for these measures? Few are! Few are until they perceive they have *no other choice*. By then it may be too late.

There are some wives who are no longer waiting, who have gone out to seek knowledge and help for themselves so they may better respond to their husband's disease. These women are not counting on Sally's luck in finding the right help by confiding in the first person who comes along. They are seeking out alcoholism services and specialists. Like Sally, however, they are discovering new ways of approaching the disease and are redirecting their lives instead of adjusting themselves to the sick situation of alcoholism.

Unfortunately, Ellen is far more typical. Like her, most women are still waiting years after they are aware of their husband's drinking problem before they reach out for help. Like Ellen, they do not confront the disease early, when there are fewer problems and less trauma. They allow the disease to progress to the point where an outsider looking into their lives would ask, "What could be worse? Why doesn't she do something?" The answer this outsider would get would be, "But I've tried everything and nothing works." In reality she's only tried all the "home remedies" and, true, they don't work. The next question would be,"Why does she put up with it?" The answer, "Because I perceive something even worse." Being alone and on their own is so terrifying to some women that they are willing to put up with what others would consider a shocking existence. No matter what their present pain is, it does not appear to them as horrifying as the circumstances which change might bring about. No price is too high as long as a person is determined to pursue a desire for comfort by escaping projected fantasies of pain. Wives of alcoholics pursue this desire for comfort as if it were a need, when, in fact, facing pain is their need. It is the only way for them to reach healthy resolutions or to obtain the emotional strength to cope with the recurring crises of active alcoholism.

I am not recommending pain for pain's sake, but if it is present it provides an opportunity to build emotional muscle, to acquire greater personal strength and tolerance for life's discomforts. The wife of an alcoholic does not have to look for pain: it is dropped in her lap by the never ending crises caused by her husband's drinking. When stressful situations are met and coped with constructively, the wife gains in her sense of self-worth. She feels stronger and better prepared to deal with further crises in the future. She gains personal power. When she either flees stressful situations or does not cope with them constructively she robs herself of personal power; her feelings of inadequacy increase and she is more poorly prepared for future crises. What the wife does, then, with the crises presented by her husband's drinking will either make or break her.

Ellen ran from the pain of facing her worries about Michael's drinking. When the priest she consulted suggested that Michael might be an alcoholic and recommended counseling for her, Ellen chose instead to listen to the family physician, who recommended simply that Michael cut down. She chose to believe that Michael could cut down rather than face the pain of exploring the possibility that Michael was an alcoholic. She chose a route that was the most comfortable for her at the moment and as a result entered a denial of the disease that complemented Michael's own. Unfortunately, this is the typical pattern. Rather than face the possibility of alcoholism, wives of alcoholics are as inclined as the alcoholics themselves to examine definitions of alcoholism and pick the one that does *not* apply rather than explore the ones that do.

Sally, too, felt pain when her boss suggested that Tom might be an alcoholic. She was very upset and became even more so when she started investigating the disease and could not convince herself that Tom was not an alcoholic. She says she became more anxious every day. "I was so afraid of what I heard at those meetings that I actually got sick. I had such nausea that I couldn't eat on the days I had to go to a meeting. I used to hope the sitter wouldn't show up so I could stay home." She finally felt better when she found out enough to know beyond any doubt that Tom was an alcoholic. When she accepted his disease and no longer struggled to deny it, she felt quite hopeful and at peace with herself for the first time in years. It also gave her new strength: "From then on, every time I faced a situation and handled it well I felt strong enough to handle the next one."

Far too many women become defeated before they start because they opt for action that will bring them immediate comfort rather than action that has a chance of being effective and therefore strengthening to them. Not only do they enable the disease to progress, they become less adequately equipped to cope with it as it worsens. By avoiding pain, they are ensuring their greater pain.

A woman who is married to someone whose drinking is in some way hurting her should ride with her anxiety long enough to find out what she's up against. If her husband is only a heavy drinker and is able to modify his drinking so as to no longer hurt her, then she has gained a lot and lost nothing. Certainly if her husband is not dependent upon alcohol, the chances are he will not object to her quests for knowledge since he will not feel threatened. She can feel proud of herself for demonstrating the willingness to explore any avenue for guidance in strengthening herself and their marriage.

If the quest for information ends with the conclusion that her husband is an alcoholic, she is then in a position to get the help she will need. She will not have to stumble along the destructive route and she will not be alone. With knowledge and help she will be able to take constructive action to maintain her own emotional health. In so doing she may be able to interrupt the progression of her husband's fatal disease.

Virtually every wife who is responding to the disease of alcoholism by herself is guided by two specific principles that set the tone for all her actions and that ultimately guide her toward her own destruction. First, she attempts to control her husband's drinking, and second, she concentrates on his reasons for drinking and attempts to eliminate them.

The fact that her husband cannot control his drinking is the problem, not the solution. This simple fact eludes her for years. She explores virtually every way she can dream up to get him to drink less or not at all. If he had control, there would be no problem and no solution would be necessary. All her attempts to get her husband to control his drinking are futile, since that inability is his very problem. She wastes herself, and precious time, in attempting to instill such control in her husband.

She threatens, but he drinks anyway. She screams, cries, and wheedles promises, yet he continues to drink. She hides the alcohol or throws it away, so he drinks outside the home or brings more in. She becomes tender, loving, and yielding, but although he may enjoy her more, he still drinks. She drinks to become drunk with him, often going on to alcoholism herself, yet he continues to drink. She takes his money, but he borrows or charges. She removes herself physically from her husband—"no sex with booze"—so he chooses the booze. She could stand on her head and spit pennies in an attempt to control her husband's drinking, and he would still drink.

With every attempt at controlling her husband's drinking, the wife creates new sources of anger for her husband to use against her and as reasons for further drinking. He has but another complaint to lay before his favorite psychiatrist, the local bartender. By attempting to control her husband she is setting herself up as a target for his frustrations and is granting him the very justifications for drinking that he is looking for.

Further, with every attempt at control of her husband, and the failure that results from each attempt, the wife comes to feel less and less adequate as a person. She always fails and she thinks of herself as a failure. Soon she feels insecure in every sphere of her life. She becomes more easily manipulated and controlled; she abdicates power to her husband, who increases his control over her. Thus it becomes increasingly easy for him to drink the way he wants to without outside interference. By attempting to control her husband, the wife is actually granting him the dream of every alcoholic: the freedom to drink the way he wishes. In every way it is dangerous for the wife, for her sake and her husband's, to attempt to control his drinking.

A wife will often believe she must control her husband's drinking for his sake—that he will be killed in an accident if he does not stop! True, he might be. Alcoholics are not known to die peacefully of old age; most of them die violent deaths at relatively early ages and most have people around them still vainly trying to instill controls in them. The wife must accept the fact that there are certain things she cannot control, and one of them is her husband's drinking. She must give up and accept the fact that she is not God. Only then can she apply her energies to those things she can change, so that she does not adjust to a sick situation as if it were normal.

Another fact the wife overlooks is that her husband drinks the way he does because he is addicted. He has, for whatever reasons, learned to cope with life through the use and abuse of alcohol. He is trapped in a maladaptive response to living that will kill him unless he is treated. He has developed a psychic dependence which, unless he receives treatment, will go on to a physiological dependence and premature death.

During the active addiction it is virtually impossible to discover the reasons why he chose this way of living in the first place. But, even more important, if the reasons could be discovered he would still be left with the addictive drinking itself. Before an alcoholic can explore and learn new modes for coping he must first give up the chemical one he is using, and for that he requires special treatment.

Wives of alcoholics spend an inordinate amount of time and energy trying to discover the reasons, past and present, for their husbands' drinking. They become preoccupied with events, circumstances, people, places, and things in their husbands' lives. They believe it is forces in this outside world that are somehow causing it all, and, sadly, they often assign themselves first place among these causes. They do not see the addiction that has to be fed at *any* cost, no matter what is or was taking place in the life of the alcoholic.

Any time a wife concerns herself with what might or might not affect her husband's drinking, she is out of touch with the addiction, the only factor which is going to affect his drinking in any way. Whenever a wife tampers with the environment of her husband in an effort to reduce his reasons for drinking, she is treading upon dangerous ground, because the end result will serve only to allow her husband to drink further.

First, because of her concern that the environment remain or become comfortable in order to eliminate reasons for her husband to drink, the wife is forced to withdraw them both from social contact. She believes that other people are upsetting her husband and causing him to drink; after all, he tells her that often enough. She is very fearful that people will say or do something that will set her husband off and running into yet another drinking spree. She therefore manipulates their lives so that normal social contact with family and friends either does not occur at all or does so very tenuously; contacts are nervous and brief. She then hangs on to her husband's not being able to socialize as an excuse to curtail her own involvement with the world, for she believes that if she has contact with others without her husband he will become upset and drink even more. He, of course, will! He *will* become more upset and *will* have another excuse for drinking. What the wife does not realize is that *he will become upset and find an excuse no matter what she does*. She also does not realize that as her social isolation increases, she becomes more dependent upon what her husband does. By increasing the isolation, she is setting up a cycle whereby she keeps losing power to her husband, who keeps gaining further control over his drinking environment.

When the husband is virtually the only contact a wife has, she is increasingly influenced by him. Isolation increases her dependence and she becomes even more eager and willing to grant his requests and respond to his threats. "Maybe then he'll stop!" She willingly, even desperately, makes calls, apologies, excuses, and reparations, hoping everyone, especially the boss, will forgive, not notice, or offer another chance. As her husband gets worse she feels further threatened and increasingly compelled to reduce his reasons to drink. She tries even harder to eliminate all possible reasons within their world for him to drink. This works just as disastrously as throwing his booze away; as soon as one reason is eliminated, he finds another, and his control over her is increased with her every failure. When she amasses enough failures she will begin to question her own sanity.

Second, in an attempt to reduce reasons for drinking the wife will hide her husband's own behavior from him if she can. She does not want him to suffer the consequences of his drinking because she reasons this would be so upsetting to him that he would then have further justifications to drink. She is quick to pick up the pieces after her husband in order to reduce his need to drink. He has her exactly where he wants her. As he drowns his pains in alcohol, she surrounds him with a blanket of comfortable unreality. Instead of making it increasingly difficult for the husband to accept his own behavior and be that much closer to treatment, she makes his drinking increasingly easy for him to tolerate.

While the wife is busy making changes in her husband's environment to reduce his reasons for drinking, she eliminates his incentive to make the *one* change that is needed, *treatment for his addic-*

tion. As with her attempts at controlling her husband's drinking, her attempts to alter his environment to reduce his reasons to drink serve only to enhance his ability to drink further without interference.

Today thousands of wives are learning how to approach their alcoholic husbands differently. They are stopping the old actions which abetted their husbands' drinking, and which increased their own misery. They are substituting new actions which make it increasingly difficult for their husbands to continue drinking. In the process the wives are regaining their sense of self-worth and their freedom. *They are no longer puppets to their alcoholic husbands, therefore their husbands are forced to change; many are getting sober!*

5

KEN

Ken made up his mind on the 8:37 to New York. He'd leave and take the kids. Barbara could have the house. "She's got her car and I'll send her money for food." He'd done everything he could. "She wasn't even up this morning for Chrissake!" He'd gotten the girls up and given them breakfast. He'd even brushed their hair before sending them to school. "Jesus, she just lies there stinking up the whole room . . . a good lay turned into a reeking, stinking mess!" And now he had to go to Europe. "That's Barbara's fault too. If I didn't have to worry about her and the kids all the time, I wouldn't have made that mistake in the contract in the first place. Now I'll be lucky if I'm able to salvage any profit. . . . Mother will take them. She said she would—at least till I get back."

Ken didn't know where it all started or how. Everyone had wanted Barbara, but she married him. Ken felt lucky and proud. Barbara could do anything and she was always fun to be with. "Jesus, the house is a showplace. She finds these kooky things and turns them into eyestoppers. . . . She's an eyestopper. Two kids and she still fills a bikini better than anyone else. Why the hell is she drinking like this? Why is she so jumpy? . . . God, I wish she'd take care of the kids better."

Ken was afraid and confused. He couldn't figure it out. "She just started drinking a little like the other wives and the next thing you know she's drinking all the time." He didn't remember her drinking much when the kids were little—just before dinner and at parties. "She didn't even get tipsy . . . Christ, she was the one who drove us home . . . and now I never know what she's going to do."

According to Ken, Barbara had reached the point where she was drunk most of the time. Usually she got up before everyone else, but by the time she was getting the girls off to school she was already slurring her words and speaking louder than normal. "And she'd be full of energy and great plans for her day, but the girls would find her asleep and still in her robe in the afternoon when they returned from school." Barbara would drink until she passed out and never did anything until late in the day, at which time she would pull herself together enough to get the marketing done and the house picked up. But it would be a miserable time for Jodi and Suzanne because Barbara would be very pressured and irritable. Anything they did irritated her further and she invariably ended up screaming at them—most particularly at Jodi, who was nine, and whom Barbara found more irritating than Suzanne, who was eight.

By the time Ken arrived home for dinner, the girls were often crying and sometimes even barricaded in their room. They were afraid of Barbara, who would occasionally slap them to get them out of the way. And dinner would be a mess before it even started. Parts of the meal would be burned, parts nearly raw. The girls would be silent, either weepy or sullen with anger, and Barbara would start drinking again and stagger, sashay, slur, and sleep her way through the rest of the evening. Ken would be beside himself, but he was usually able to control his temper till the girls had done their homework and gone to bed.

He tried everything he could think of. He warned and threatened, but was never heeded for long. He took long walks to keep himself from hitting her. He hid the booze and restricted her money. He hired housekeepers to help with the girls and to relieve her of her household chores, but they never stayed long. Barbara was intolerable; each complained bitterly to Ken about Barbara's demands and incessant criticisms before they stalked angrily off. He took the girls out for dinner in the evenings—sometimes en-

couraging and helping Barbara pull herself together enough to join them, sometimes without
inviting her at all. He found a psychiatrist for
her, but after a few sessions Barbara called him
stupid and refused to return. He appealed to his
family and to hers. One group encouraged divorce, the other group blamed him for causing
Barbara to drink, for not understanding her.
Neither was able to offer any advice Ken found
helpful. Ken didn't want a divorce, he just
wanted Barbara to stop drinking and be the way
she used to be. He knew he worked hard and
kept long hours, often traveling for two or three
weeks at a time, but "Christ, I was bringing in the
bread. There was nothing I wouldn't give her."
Yes, he did have an occasional fling, "but nothing
that amounted to anything. Barbara refused to
sleep with me or would be so drunk I wouldn't
want her. I had to do something or I'd have
blown my top. What made her a lush? That's
what I can't understand."

Barbara had been an honor student, editor of
the college newspaper, and homecoming queen.
She was vivacious, pretty, talented, and bright.
What went wrong? She had worshiped Ken. She
loved his strength and good looks. She knew he
was a winner, which he was right from the beginning. She took to their surburban community like
a duck takes to water. She kaffeeklatsched, com-
mitteed, and chauffered school car pools along
with everyone else. Just last year she had headed
a fund-raising committee that brought in more

than they projected. She did get drunk at one of the luncheons, but only that one time. "And now she's dead. God, what could I have done? I never should have left her like that."

Ken returned from his salvaging trip to Europe three weeks later than he expected. It had taken him six weeks to get his business in order. Jodi and Suzanne were with his mother and had adjusted well to their new school. They seemed more relaxed, but Ken worried when they said they wanted to stay with their grandmother. Barbara had been making frequent phone calls to them, always drunk and often threatening and pleading at the same time. The girls seemed even more frightened of Barbara now than they had been before moving in with their grandmother. Ken's mother also expressed her worry and anger. She felt strongly that Barbara was ruining the children and should not be allowed to have them, and she was more than willing to raise them herself, especially because she still had her large home and a doting housekeeper to help her. She knew it would be better if their own mother raised them but Barbara would have to pull herself together first.

Worried and anxious, Ken drove to his home. The scene he encountered was worse than anything he could have imagined. With the girls and Ken away, Barbara had no longer needed to control herself; she could drink as often and as much as she pleased. Every light in the house was on. Furniture was turned over and upside down, curtains were pulled from the windows, every mirror was smashed; every dish, cup, and glass had been bashed into the walls. Porcelain and glass chips were scattered over everything. The refrigerator door was open; burned food was on the stove—it looked weeks old. The heat was turned off and the house temperature was near freezing. Empty vodka bottles were everywhere. When Ken went upstairs Barbara awoke from a drunken stupor and fell into his arms. She clung to him desperately, sobbing convulsively. She was frail—she had lost nearly twenty pounds. He retched at the sight and smell of her. Barbara pleaded with him not to leave her. She promised she would never take another drink as long as she lived if only he'd stay.

Ken stayed and Barbara did stop drinking. A housecleaning service was hired and the house was put in order; china and dishes were replaced. Barbara soon felt strong enough for the girls to return—that seemed to be the only thing she wanted. Ken says everything was great for a while, or almost great; Barbara was nervous and didn't laugh as readily as she once had, but outside of that everything was good. "I was sure she had it made. She started seeing her friends again and we even had people over for dinner. Barbara served them drinks without touching any herself." Ken never thought she'd start drinking again after the mess she had gotten into, but he was wrong.

Barbara picked up a Bloody Mary at a luncheon with friends and within two weeks she was drinking around the clock. Jodi and Suzanne were pleading to return to their grandmother's and Barbara was vicious with Ken. She maintained that she could stop drinking anytime she wished. The girls could go to their grandmother's—Ken's mother had already ruined them and "She might as well finish the job—that will make her happy." Barbara was sure everyone was against her.

A friend of Ken's had told him about AA, but when he mentioned it to Barbara she flew into a rage and started accusing him of not caring for her. She told him that it was all his fault, he was never home and she was sure he loved another woman. She also called him sick and told him he should see a psychiatrist. She demanded that he leave along with the girls; she would be better off without them, since none of them cared for her anyway. And with that she stormed off, locking herself in her room refusing to come out until they left the house.

Ken felt it would be best to take the girls to his mother's and then return to appeal to Barbara to stop drinking again. "I had never seen her in a rage like that. I knew I had to protect the girls. I couldn't do anything with them around. They were scared to death.

"When I got back she was drunker than ever and she had put on one of those sexy negligees. She was slinking around like Marilyn Monroe for Chrissakes. And she picked me apart. She told me she had never loved me, that I was lousy in bed and that other men satisfied her but I never had. When I asked her what other men, she told me about her daily affairs with delivery boys, repairmen, and even the mailman. She didn't spare me the details either. Jesus, she even told how she got on the kitchen table and let them do it to her there. I thought I was going to kill her. I fled when I found myself with my hands around her throat. I must have driven all night. I washed up in a gas station and drove to my office. When I got there, Barbara called saying the telephone repairman was on his way and would I like to learn how a man makes love. Jesus, I couldn't go home—not even when she called later in the day to say it was a lie, there had never been any men. I didn't know what to believe, but I felt she was capable of anything."

Barbara telephoned several times, pleading with Ken to return and promising to do anything if only he would. Ken said he would have to think about it. He was not at all sure he wanted to return to Barbara. He certainly didn't want to touch her. He didn't know whether he could ever trust her again. He was deeply hurt and full of anger. Finally he promised to visit over the weekend.

Barbara looked pretty good for the visit but Ken could smell alcohol on her breath. At first she was casual and businesslike. She promised she would stop drinking if he returned and they could then work everything out together. She said it had all been her fault and she loved him very much. She asked him to please forgive her, she hadn't meant any of the things she had said. She wanted another chance; she was willing to do anything he said.

Ken was undecided and, sensing rejection, Barbara reacted quickly. She accused him of not loving her, of never having loved her, of having another woman, and of wanting to take her daughters from her. When he protested, she started attacking him, calling him a mother's boy, a rotten husband and lover, and screaming for him to get out of the house, which he did.

Ken sent her money regularly. On occasions when he accepted her phone calls he said that he would see her only when she had stopped drinking, and that he couldn't promise he would return to live with her even then. Since she always sounded as if she had been drinking, he didn't see her again until he was called to identify the body.

Barbara had run out of booze late one snowy evening. Because the liquor stores were no longer delivering, she was forced to leave the house to get some more. She left with just a raincoat covering her nightgown and only sandals on her feet. No hat, no gloves, no stockings, no boots. She was on her way to her car, parked in front of the house, when she slipped on the ice. The fall did not kill her, but it knocked her unconscious. The freezing temperature killed her. She froze to death in a blanket of snow.

Although Barbara's alcoholic progression was fairly rapid, her story is by no means unique. She desperately needed help, but the personality changes brought about by alcohol, plus Ken's lack of knowledge about the disease, made it impossible for him to get her to treatment. Because he was uninformed he was unable to remove himself emotionally in order to see her needs. Instead he was shocked by her behavior and believed the things she said. He despised her and at the same time yearned for what had once been.

Ken believed that she was deliberately destroying herself and was deliberately trying to destroy him and the girls. He hated her for making him feel cheap. He hated her for not being a good wife and mother. Instead of seeing her behavior as symptomatic of her disease, he believed and was crushed by her words. He felt he had given Barbara everything a woman could ask for. She had complained because he was always working, but "she liked the clothes and the house and everything. I even got her a convertible when they weren't making convertibles. I was working hard for *her*, for Chrissake. Why did she have to ruin it all?"

Ken is only now beginning to get an understanding of the events that changed his life. It will be some time yet before he works through the residue of his anger and his enormous guilt to a point where he can return to his former level of functioning. At present Ken admits that he is afraid of women, that he doesn't want to get close to them and often uses them cruelly in desperate attempts "to feel like a man."

Although Barbara's progression was rapid, it nevertheless seriously traumatized her husband. Jodi and Suzanne are also in therapy. They are having a difficult time thinking of themselves as worthy. They too feel that if they had stayed home and acted differently their mother would still be alive.

Barbara could have received treatment. Several times she reached a point of being willing to do anything to get Ken back—perfect opportunities to offer and insist upon treatment, if only Ken had known how to deal with her disease.

Alcoholism is deadly! It kills and destroys those not prepared to cope with it.

6
HUSBANDS OF ALCOHOLICS

It is manly to drink! Two-fisted male drinkers are our heroes, and have been since before the days of the Wild West. Little boys should grow up and learn how to drink like them. In our society the male drinking myth is so strong it is considered *unmanly* not to drink!

Society's attitude toward female drinkers is somewhat different, in fact it is often the opposite. If a woman must drink, she should drink like a lady. She is not generally required to drink, but she may on occasion, if she has only a little. She may *not* become unladylike with her drinking or she will be considered a lush.

Society says it's O.K. for a man to get sloshed. It's expected occasionally. It's even funny—some of our most popular cartoons are built on just that theme. Not so for women. Society expects them to control themselves—to *not* get sloshed. If they do, it's by no means funny, it's disgusting! Even though the drunken behavior of women differs little from the drunken behavior of men, drunken women are considered disgraceful. They are lowered a considerable number of pegs in the esteem of others as well as themselves. Men can get sloshed without the same lowering of esteem.

The different attitude we have about female drinkers has an enormous effect on our approach to the female alcoholics in our midst. They are not as acceptable as male alcoholics because they have overstepped the boundaries allowed by society for female drinking. Consequently they are not considered deserving of help. Society does not make the same allowance for their alcoholic drinking as it does for men. A recent article in the London *Times* points this out in reporting the results of a random sampling of people's reactions to alcoholics. The most common view of the male alcoholic was, "The poor soul! His wife drove him to it!" and of the female alcoholic, "The poor husband. He deserves better than that!"

Traditionally women have been placed, or have allowed themselves to be placed, in a dependent position in relationship to men. Women, especially wives, are expected to cater to their men and to their men's careers. Their role in traditional marriages calls for them to care for their husbands, their children, and their homes, placing those interests before their own. This role does not call for drinking, though it is allowed at certain specified times. If the wife consumes alcohol other than at these allowed times, she is considered self-indulgent and irresponsible in her performance of her role. If she becomes an alcoholic, people are shocked. She has very definitely overstepped her boundaries. She has obviously been drinking more than she was expected to. She is found socially unacceptable by the very society which is so tolerant of the man who cannot hold or handle his liquor.

The woman alcoholic is a victim of the double standard existing for men and women. There is a greater stigma attached to her disease than to the same disease in her male counterpart. Instead of being considered sick, she is considered wanton and selfish for drinking the way she does, and even more shame is felt in the families of female alcoholics than in those of male alcoholics. There is a greater tendency to blame the female alcoholic than to understand her when she does not adequately perform her role as wife, mother, and housekeeper.

Our society finds many reasons why a man may drink more than he should. There's his high-pressure job, tense working conditions, monotonous routine, combined business-martini lunches, commuting, demanding wife, unpaid bills. What reasons can a woman have? It's difficult to find any. She's not supposed to be drinking in the first place. Usually husbands and children think her drinking is due to some family problem that will be solved in time. Meantime, however, she should cut or stop her drinking, and she is to blame if she doesn't.

Husbands and children overlook alcoholism as the problem. They do not want to believe their wives and mothers are alcoholics. The idea is very difficult for them to acknowledge and accept even if they suspect it, and they will help her hide her drinking to escape discovery and disgrace. They will exert great efforts to keep her and her problem hidden as long as they can.

The alcoholic wife and mother also suffers acute feelings of shame concerning her drinking. She knows well how society views her. Like her family members she will blame herself, until eventually self-blame and self-recrimination cause a deeper surrender to her addiction. She will keep her drinking a secret for as long as she is able. She will drink quietly and alone; and she will hide it until it can no longer be hidden.

Many wives hide their drinking so well in their early years of alcoholism that when it is finally uncovered it is a genuine shock for the husbands and children. Although it seemed to Ken that Barbara became an alcoholic overnight, the nature and progression of the disease are such that considerable drinking before her last few months was indicated. Upon questioning, Ken could remember behavior indicating that Barbara had been sneaking drinks for several years. Many times Ken had noticed that the bar supply was either lower than it should be or different. Bottles were nearly empty that should have been full; others had obviously been replaced, and some bottles were missing altogether. When questioned Barbara blamed it on the maids or the women who had come to lunch. Ken also remembered that Barbara had stopped drinking at parties or when out to dinner, the only times she had used to drink. Yet she would have alcohol on her breath before going out and frequently appeared tipsy soon after returning home. Barbara no doubt knew she might get drunk, so exerted all her energies toward not drinking in public to escape humiliation and disgrace.

Ken, like most husbands, accepted her explanations even though he did not always believe her. He wanted to believe her. It was too difficult for him to do otherwise. Nor could Barbara do otherwise. Her drinking was as unacceptable to her as to those around her. She was powerless to stop herself, and too ashamed to ask for help.

Nor was there anyone else to help her. Like most alcoholic wives, Barbara did not work outside the home. Although industry and labor have initiated programs to detect and treat alcoholism among their employees and executives, few of these programs cover the housewives as well. They remain isolated in their homes desperately and usually successfully hiding their drinking from the outside world. So they go on unrecognized and untreated.

Husbands do not seem to react in the same ways toward their alcoholic wives as the wives of alcoholic husbands do. They not only have a greater reluctance to accept the idea of alcoholism, but they seem, as well, to have less patience with their alcoholic wives than the wives of alcoholic husbands. This does not mean, unfortunately, they are any more effective in getting their wives to treatment than the wives of alcoholic husbands.

Profiles have been drawn on the responses of wives of alcoholics, and typically most wives respond to alcoholism in their husbands in a way similar to Ellen's. They seem to put up with a lot, at great cost to themselves and to their husbands. Their patience and tolerance, as applied, serve only to prolong the disease and its destruction. Patience and tolerance are certainly laudable virtues to have and are needed in alcoholism, but are of little value unless constructively directed.

Profiles of typical responses of husbands of alcoholics have not yet been clearly established. There is evidence that many husbands act very much like Ellen, putting up with a lot while avoiding treatment for themselves or their mates. Frequently these husbands simply allow their alcoholic wives to live in the house, with little expected of them other than to leave everybody alone. Either the husband assumes the role of mother to his children (along with his role of provider-father) or the role is assumed by an older child. The alcoholic wife and mother is tolerated, but that is all. She is not granted her former roles. Her inability to function has forced others to assume her duties. She is not forced into treatment for her disease, for she is not considered sick or worthy of help, especially if any attempts have been made in the past which proved unsuccessful.

There are indications, however, that most husbands of alcoholic wives do not respond in this manner. More often they abandon their wives. Many will take their children to relatives as Ken did, leaving the wives in the house or in cheaper lodgings. Others will ask the wife to leave and will force her out of the house. And some will desert the entire family, leaving their children to the care of their alcoholic wives and leaving the wives to fend for themselves.

When the husband leaves his family the burden of maintaining the home usually falls upon the older children, who are then deprived of their childhood. Sometimes the husband sends money for their support; frequently he doesn't, or it isn't enough, and the family is forced to appeal for public assistance. The children are usually isolated and ashamed and are fearful of having their peers discover either their mother's drinking or their father's abandonment. They miss school or drop out because they must take care of their mother or because they can't afford the school supplies or because they don't have winter coats. These children may very well carry the impact of the disease of alcoholism on into the next generation, and the next.

Before abandoning their wives, most husbands, like Ken, attempt to control their wives' drinking. They threaten, hide and throw liquor away, withhold money, and a few even resort to abuse. But they have no better luck than the wives who attempt to control their husbands' drinking. Many husbands reduce their wives' work loads and make fewer demands of any kind, in an attempt to eliminate the reasons for drinking. But like their male counterparts, alcoholic wives drink anyway. Many husbands send their wives to psychiatrists, yet the wives continue to drink. Feeling put upon and telling themselves that they've done everything possible—"more than most men would do"—they then feel justified in deserting their wives. On the surface, at least, they seem to feel less responsibility toward their wives and families than do the wives of alcoholic husbands.

When left to their own resources, husbands of alcoholic wives are no more effective in getting them to treatment than are the wives of alcoholic husbands. Society's attitude toward the female alcoholic is a significant factor in preventing her husband from being both more responsible and more effective. Society offers no excuses for her alcoholism. She has not been forced into it by all the extenuating circumstances which society uses as contributing factors for the male alcoholic. If she becomes an alcoholic, it is because she has *chosen* to break a tribal taboo. Therefore she is not considered sick or worthy of help; in fact, she deserves to be punished by abandonment.

This attitude permeates our culture and the husband usually encounters it if he confides in others. Even if he hasn't already crystallized the attitude in his mind, he soon will. He, unlike the wife of an alcoholic husband, encounters very little conflicting advice from families and friends. When the wife of an alcoholic appeals for help, she is given all sorts of opinions and suggestions for dealing with her husband. Some say she should leave him, some encourage her to stay; and all proceed to tell her how to do both differently. Not so with the husband of an alcoholic. He is told, in pretty short order, and almost exclusively (except perhaps by her family) to get out, to get *her* out, to find another wife, to get a mother for his kids who can take care of them properly, she's not worth your worry, and so on. Society, if it doesn't actually support the husband in his desertion of his alcoholic wife, does little in the way of helping him do anything else.

Another factor that contributes to the husband's ineffectiveness in dealing with his alcoholic wife is the fact that most men in our culture place their highest value on their productivity. It is a tragic commentary on our times that most men place more value on their work, their earning capacity and their production, than they do on themselves, their wives, or their children. Most men (and women) do not even question this hierarchy of priorities. Thus, to say the least, husbands do not have as their first priority meeting the needs of their alcoholic wives. The number-one priority lies elsewhere and consumes most of their time and energy. There is very little left at the end of the day to devote to discovering the needs of the drinking wife. Alcoholism is insidious and baffling; it requires considerable time and effort to respond to it effectively. Husbands have more important things to do, or so they think.

Because the husband holds his productivity in such high esteem, he can tolerate very little interference in this sphere, especially when the interference is coming from the person whose duty it is to assist him in his endeavors. No one has a right to interfere in this area of his life, much less his wife. Many husbands very quickly abandon their alcoholic wives when it looks as if the inappropriate drinking might place their work in jeopardy. Their economic security is, in their minds, enhanced by desertion. The number-one priority rigidly remains number-one; the wife must go.

Husbands are not economically dependent upon their wives. They can afford to leave. They are not locked into their marriages to the same degree that wives of alcoholic husbands are. The wife's need for economic security from her alcoholic husband no doubt makes her appear to be more responsible because she does not desert as readily as she might if she were self-supporting. Either way, economically dependent or independent, husbands and wives are not seeking the help they need and are not responding effectively to the alcoholism of their partners. In that sense, neither group is responsible, and the fact remains: because husbands are financially independent from their alcoholic wives, they are able to effect earlier departures. Abandonment is possible for husbands; it's the easiest out for them and the most expedient. It's also, in human terms, the most costly.

There are many other factors which inhibit the husband's effectiveness in dealing with his alcoholic spouse; mostly they have to do with the nature of the disease itself, and here the husbands are not alone. Alcoholism is difficult for all who are involved with it. When it rains it rains on everyone. But with knowledge and help, it is far from hopeless.

Even though there are many factors working against the husbands (the wife of an alcoholic encounters as many), they are for the most part controllable. The husband can alter the inhibiting factors. It is within his domain to change them if he wishes. By gaining knowledge and assistance he can effectively respond to his wife's disease, just as certainly as if she had TB or diabetes. He can be helped to intervene in her illness, thereby initiating her recovery to the world of health. He can change old approaches and substitute new, constructive ones, thereby avoiding further destruction to himself, his children, and his wife; and he can do it without consuming any more time than he is taking with destructive approaches.

Many husbands have sought knowledge and assistance in approaching the disease of alcoholism, and wives are alive and healthy today because of their efforts. All studies indicate that alcoholic women have as good a chance for recovery as do alcoholic men, once they get to treatment. Female alcoholics get just as well as do their male counterparts, but they have to be reached first.

Husbands! Only you can do it. She has no employer to reach her. She *cannot* reach herself. You are her *only* meaningful contact with the outside world and she desperately needs you to initiate her recovery. *She has a disease—a treatable disease.*

7
THE ALCOHOLIC — HOW THE WORLD VIEWS HIM

When the word alcoholic is mentioned, most people quickly draw an image in their mind of the sort of person they think he is; what he looks like, what he does and where he is. He, first of all, is a he! And quite clearly a shiftless character who cares for neither himself nor the world around him. Every part of him that we can see above, below, and through the tears in his black-brown rags is caked with dirt and old blood; we shudder to think what else might be lurking there unexposed. We find him on doorsteps, blanketed from the winter's cold with newspapers covering his bones, and we think he must not feel in the same way we do. We find him on park benches and in alleyways and skid rows across the country. He shuffles out with an impossibly soiled cloth to wipe our windows for a quarter as we stop for a red light. He seems to have been there always, as if he sprouted forth into this world in exactly that condition.

This is pretty much the preconceived image most of us have of the alcoholic. It is such a strong image that not only do we believe it to be true, it deludes us into thinking we know something about alcoholism. This image convinces us we know who is an alcoholic and who is not, what alcoholic behavior is like and what it is not like, what an alcoholic's values are and what they are not. We hold to this image with a certainty that makes us blind to who and what an alcoholic actually is.

Only 3 percent of the alcoholics in this country are in the skid rows, and of the people in the skid rows only a small percentage are alcoholics. Our preconceived image of what we are convinced is an alcoholic is perhaps not even based on an alcoholic in the first place. Yet our distorted conception influences our feelings and behavior toward the alcoholics in our midst. It does not allow us to recognize them when we see them or to get them to treatment when we do finally recognize them.

We do not consider the possibility of someone's being an alcoholic if he works, he is young, has never missed a day at work, drinks only beer, makes more money than ever before, does not drink in the morning, drinks only on weekends, goes for weeks and months without drinking at all, or still has his family. If the problem drinker does not fit our preconceived ideas of what an alcoholic is like, then to us he is not an alcoholic.

Unfortunately for the alcoholic and his family, it is not just a small or isolated segment of society that has misconceptions about alcoholism. Almost everyone does, including the doctors, clergy, families, and friends we turn to for help. Even if we expand our own image of alcoholism, we have difficulty finding someone to help us who also has a clear view. Their guidance often reinforces our original misconceived image because others repeat what we already believe. We are not brought any closer to recognizing the problem and finding the solution.

In our minds alcoholism is a moral issue instead of a disease, and as such it carries a stigma which keeps us from recognizing and obtaining help. We are ashamed. Rather than recognizing the alcoholic's need for treatment, we see his behavior as something he could control if he would. We wonder why he doesn't watch himself more closely. We feel it is a matter of willpower and the inappropriate drinker just isn't applying enough determination. We believe he is weak-willed or lacking in determination. We pass moral judgments and find him wanting. Soon we choose not to be associated with this person or to keep him and his problem hidden.

The alcoholic's behavior helps along the whole process of stigmatizing and moralizing. Alcohol reduces normal inhibitions and allows people to act in ways they otherwise would not—in ways others find acutely embarrassing, disgusting, and even shameful when carried to extremes. And the alcoholic carries to extremes! Under the influence of alcohol he will often do the very things which society deems 'most improper, thereby seemingly asking for society's value judgments.

He frequently fails to meet either his own expectations or those of others. He makes appointments which he does not keep, he makes promises which he quickly breaks, he starts jobs which he does not finish, his work is excellent one day and shoddy the next, he is tardy and sometimes absent altogether. People regard his behavior as willful irresponsibility instead of seeing it as symptomatic of his disease. They assume he is behaving the way he is because he wants to; they do not see that he has *no other choice*. They believe he should straighten himself up; they do not see him as sick and in need of treatment. The alcoholic cannot be helped when he is approached as a moral issue, yet his very behavior seems to invite that approach. His actions perpetuate the moral stance already in existence.

Although changes are taking place, society has not presented opportunities for families to become aware of the true nature of alcoholism. It is difficult for individuals to move out of their own misconceptions when the society they live in offers them no unbiased information. Families continue to hide their shameful secret, destroying

their chances for getting the help they so desperately need, treating the alcoholic with "home
remedies" and going it alone.

Society encourages families to act as a unit in
managing their own affairs and coping with their
own problems. Families are not encouraged to
take their problems outside the family unit except as a last resort. Consequently, when the
spouses of alcoholics do finally seek help, it is
done with reluctance and most likely from other
relatives in the larger family unit. They are thus
turning to people without the knowledge or skills
to help them. Some of the relatives may not want
to be involved while others will not hesitate to
offer their own "home remedies." As one "home
remedy" after another fails, the people who have
suggested them very often give up in disgust—
often attaching blame to the spouse for not having done "it" right. The spouse then feels guilty,
confused, and even more alone.

Frequently the family members to whom the
spouse turns feel threatened. They may fear that
they will end up with more mouths to feed, going
to police stations, or worse, and do not want to be
involved any further. After initially trying to help
they encourage the spouse to "hang in there and
not give up," with assurances that the alcoholic
will shape up as soon as the present difficulties
are over; or they will advise the spouse to get out
altogether. What these friends and relatives are
really saying is, "You've made your bed, now
sleep in it. It's not my problem, so handle it the

best way you can without involving me." Going to friends and family members for help, whether they become threatened or not, serves only to further encase the spouses in the task of dealing with alcoholism all by themselves while adding to their guilt, confusion, and loneliness.

Very few people are knowledgeable about alcoholism. Although the American Medical Association proclaimed it a disease as far back as 1956, many medical schools still do not include it in their curriculum. No schools at all taught alcoholism comprehensively until recently, and many only touch on it today. Some that cover it thoroughly offer the course as an elective only. Yet alcoholism is the third-largest killer in the United States after heart disease and cancer, and there is no doubt that it would be considered the number-one killer if traffic fatalities were taken into consideration or if the correct diagnosis were given on death certificates. The stigma associated with alcoholism is still very powerful indeed.

Although many doctors are knowledgeable about the disease and are very effective in the field of alcoholism, most are still unprepared to deal with it. Many physicians will admit that they are not prepared to treat the alcoholic and will send him to those who are, but unfortunately, there are many who feel prepared even though they have no specialized education in the disease. Alcoholics can drink to their deaths under the care of these doctors because they rarely receive the treatment their disease requires.

With the rapid acceleration in the acquisition of knowledge in almost all the sciences, we have been forced into an era of specialization. There is virtually no profession today which can be mastered in its totality by one individual—each is too vast. The individual must specialize in some very restricted part or area of the larger field—be he a physician, lawyer, or student of literature. As there are specialists for eyes, lungs, nerves, intestines, neuroses, skin rashes, and heart disease, there are specialists for alcoholism. As with any other disease, it is only within the specialization that one can realistically expect to receive the best possible treatment. Putting the treatment of alcoholism under the aegis of one not specialized to treat it will more often than not serve only to prolong the disease and its destruction.

There are many clergymen across the country knowledgeable about alcoholism and involved with its treatment—individually and collectively, from within and from without their discipline. And recently the Catholic Church stopped granting pledges to people with drinking problems. Since the same people were taking the same pledges over and over, the Church realized that the pledges were abetting alcoholism rather than interrupting it. Today it offers Last Rites, the Sacrament of the Sick, instead of pledges to alcoholics.

The fact remains that organized religion, so frequently turned to by alcoholics and their families, for the most part remains unknowledgeable and unprepared to respond effectively. Most churches have been slow to either initiate alcoholism counseling services of their own or refer their troubled parishioners to alcoholism treatment services in their communities. Organized religion, like the rest of society, has been more apt to offer moral advice, which does nothing to interrupt the progression of the disease.

An alcoholic, being addicted, does not respond to exhortations, nor does he respond favorably to the usual psychiatric approaches, although he is far from sane. If the alcoholic agrees to undergo psychiatric treatment, he is not amenable to it unless he stops drinking, and psychiatrists and other mental health therapists report little success in getting their patients to stop. Therefore, many either do not take them on as patients or refuse to continue treatment if the patient does not stop drinking. Many, however, are truly fooled by the alcoholic who keeps his drinking problem a secret.

Rita's case is not unusual. She started seeing a psychiatrist because she was experiencing an ever increasing state of anxiety. She saw him three times a week for two years before alcohol was even mentioned. "Alcohol was the last thing I wanted to discuss. I didn't know I was an alcoholic, but I was afraid if I told him about my drinking that he would tell me to stop, and I couldn't perceive living without it at that point. So for two years we talked about everything but alcohol; how my cradle was rocked all the way up to my views on Queen Anne chairs." Rita did not really know what she expected from her psychiatrist except that perhaps by some kind of magic the anxiety would disappear with analysis. She also thought he might supply enough pills to reduce the anxiety enough so that she, on her own, could reduce the alcohol which she knew she was abusing. It was not until she finally reached AA that she discovered it was the alcohol which was causing the anxiety in the first place. But until that time she made early morning appointments with her psychiatrist, doused her breath with mouth sprays, and unwittingly demonstrated symptoms of nearly every psychiatric condition ranging from paranoia to phobias, to manic-depressive psychoses, to neurotic character disorders. "As time went by the anxiety increased, the drinking increased, the pills increased, and the symptoms became even more bizarre. Finally, my husband called my psychiatrist to ask what was being done about my alcoholism. My psychiatrist wasted very little time from then on. He told me either to go to AA and stop drinking or to find another psychiatrist. I went to AA, stopped the booze and pills, and all my crazy symptoms and anxieties disappeared. I then started to learn how to live without chemicals."

Like Rita's psychiatrist, many therapists will refuse to treat a person once alcoholism is suspected unless the patient stops drinking, for it is only then that psychiatry can be effective in assisting the patient toward a better understanding of himself and toward a more effective response to living. Many psychiatrists who treat alcoholics recommend that their patients attend AA as well and work in conjunction with that program. Others, unfortunately, do not insist that their patients stop drinking. Although they search energetically for unconscious forces causing their patients to drink inappropriately, in time they are stymied by the drinking itself. As long as they treat alcoholism as a symptom of another disorder, the progression of alcoholism is not interrupted. Little or no help can be offered as long as the patient continues to drink. Analyzing the possible motivating forces underlying the drinking does not seem to help the patient to stop drinking, and the total disease progresses.

Many psychiatrists and other physicians prescribe sedatives and minor tranquilizers in order to reduce a patient's alcohol intake. As a result of the addition of new drugs, the alcoholic has yet another chemical with which to feed his addiction and stands a good chance of becoming addicted to the pills as well. The patient also stands a good chance of inadvertently overdosing either by drinking alcohol on top of the pills or by taking the pills while in an intoxicated state.

Therapists who prescribe minor tranquilizers or sedatives or who allow their patients to drink while undergoing therapy are allowing the disease of alcoholism to progress and are thus performing a disservice to the alcoholic and his family.

A non-mood-altering drug frequently used in the treatment of alcoholics is Antabuse (Disulfiram). Although it is not a treatment in itself, Antabuse definitely has its uses. Normally, when alcohol is consumed it is broken down by the body into acetaldehyde, which in turn is rapidly destroyed before it has a chance to accumulate. When Antabuse is taken, the normal breakdown does not occur and acetaldehyde is allowed to accumulate. Antabuse has no effect upon the body if alcohol is not added, but for three or four days following the ingestion of Antabuse even a minute amount of alcohol will cause an immediate buildup of acetaldehyde—and then the alcoholic is in trouble. He immediately experiences a flushing of the face, neck, and chest, which rapidly turns to a deep red and even purple coloring. With the flushing he experiences a sensation of great heat in the area. This is quickly followed by a pounding headache, which becomes very severe. His blood pressure will rise suddenly, then drop precipitously, producing dizziness, faintness, and acute nausea, sometimes followed by violent vomiting. With all these symptoms the alcoholic will experience a sense of impending death.

Obviously Antabuse is not a drug to be slipped into the alcoholic's coffee. Before Antabuse is prescribed, the alcoholic must be made very aware of the consequences if he should drink. (In fact, the alcoholic who is taking Antabuse should carry a card with him indicating that fact so that in case of an accident sympathetic bystanders will not give him alcohol.) When the alcoholic is made aware of the effect of Antabuse, it can act as a "chemical fence" between the alcoholic and alcohol. He is deterred from drinking because he knows Antabuse is in his system.

Alcoholics who want to stay sober but do not feel confident about their ability to do so are excellent candidates for Antabuse. Antabuse alone will not bring about the changes a stable sobriety requires, but it can be an important adjunct to the psychotherapy the alcoholic chooses to undertake. Just staying sober—with or without Antabuse—is not enough. If the alcoholic is not committed to making changes in himself, which he cannot do alone, he will sooner or later lose his sobriety, which is dependent ultimately on change.

At the same time, Antabuse is not an effective deterrent unless the alcoholic is himself motivated to stay sober. Spouses usually cannot bring about that motivation by dispensing Antabuse to the alcoholic every morning or by reminding him daily to take it. If the alcoholic wants to stay sober, has hope that he can, yet feels a need for added protection, he will take it. If he wants to drink, he will not take it, will "palm" it if it is dispensed to him, or will drink on top of it.

For those alcoholics motivated to stay sober, but unsure of themselves in the face of crises, Antabuse can bring a freedom from anxieties about drinking. Their decision not to drink is made when they take their morning dose; they can then use their energies constructively rather than wasting them on whether they will or will not drink. On the other hand, many alcoholics are so desirous of staying sober "no matter what" that they feel no need for Antabuse. In the final analysis, motivation is at the heart of the matter.

Very often the need family members have for treatment is overlooked by both the family members themselves and the healing professions to whom they turn for help for the alcoholic. Their problems are overlooked in favor of what appears to be the more serious problem, the alcoholic. A general feeling exists that if the alcoholic gets well, then everyone will be well, but such is not the case. Spouses and children have a desperate need for help, not because they are causing the alcoholism, but because they are in some measure destroyed by it. They need help to regain and maintain their own emotional health, whether the alcoholic is helped or not. By helping themselves they often are directly or indirectly responsible for getting their alcoholic mates to the treatment they need. Yet the tendency exists to overlook the spouses's need for treatment and to concentrate on the alcoholic's need instead; meanwhile everyone becomes increasingly distraught and traumatized.

The stigma and misconceptions associated with alcoholism which so adversely affect our attitudes and approaches to it can be eliminated in time with acquisition of knowledge of the disease based on facts. But that will not be enough. Before society can effectively respond to the alcoholics in its midst, it will have to define more clearly its stance vis-à-vis alcohol usage. Society now responds to alcoholism from within a schism of unreality viewing alcohol as a social substance but using it as a drug.

Alcohol is an extremely potent drug, affecting the way we think, feel, and act, and that is why it is used. The effect of the drug helps us to relax after a hard day at the office, allows us to be more at ease at a party or intimate dinner or during a sales pitch. Alcohol is consumed to enhance appetites, to reduce appetites, to give us energy, to help us sleep and to perk us up. One glance at a few advertisements in virtually any magazine we pick up shows clearly what effect can be derived from this drug. Virtually any mood is sufficient cause for using alcohol, and that is why we use it—to alter our mood.

Society thinks of alcohol as a harmless social substance, yet uses it and "pushes" it as the potent mood-altering drug it really is. As long as such a schism between ideas and actions exists, there can be no guides or standards for its safe usage. Confusion about what is appropriate and what is inappropriate usage exists, thus confusion about what constitutes an alcoholic and how he should be approached also exists. *Alcoholism is nothing more and nothing less than a drug addiction.* When society does not acknowledge consumption of alcohol as drug usage, the drug dependent person and his family are confronted by naïve thinking and moral judgments. "Why doesn't he drink like other people?" or "Why don't you cut down?" or "I don't get drunk, why do you?" When people deny that alcohol is a drug, they are blind both to its potentially addictive nature and to the actual addiction of the alcoholic. They respond to the alcoholic as if he had control, when in fact he has lost it.

Everyone drinks in our society, or so it seems, and this has an enormous effect upon our attitudes toward the alcoholic. Most adults in the United States drink. Most adults drink safely. The immediate attitude stemming from these facts is that if most people can drink safely, then the alcoholic is going about his drinking wrong. This attitude once again misses the point of the addiction. Once a person has become dependent, and *one out of ten drinkers will*, he can no longer effectively modify his drinking. Once addicted, he no longer has the necessary control to drink safely and must, to save his life, give up drinking alcohol altogether.

The only treatment for alcoholism is abstinence, and people within our drinking society do not look lightly upon abstaining from alcohol. Most drinkers would not want abstinence for themselves and many would even be repelled by the idea. How then can they feel free to advise it for another or to even accept that abstinence is what is needed? Alcohol is readily accessible, its usage is commonplace and causes pleasurable feelings; it is deemed desirable. To recommend its total abstinence one must assume the role of being a depriving person, while not depriving oneself, which is an unpalatable task for most people. It is far easier to shy away from either the need for abstinence or confronting the alcoholic with that need. Thus people tend to adhere to the moral stance and pass out advice for controlled drinking. While overlooking abstinence, the only effective treatment for his disease, the alcoholic will be exhorted on to bigger and better exertions of the will simply because people in our drinking society are uncomfortable with the idea of total abstinence from alcohol.

The spouses are left alone—ashamed and embarrassed to ask for help; rejected, overlooked, further confused, or not helped when they do seek it. They are forced to cope alone and without established guidelines to follow. If it were a crisis such as a divorce to be coped with, or a death, or a heart attack or a multiple birth or a house to be built, one could go running right out to the local bookstore to buy anywhere from five to ten "how to do it" books. One also could turn freely and without shame to others for guidance and inspiration. Alcoholism, however, is a crisis which neither receives the same attention in the media nor invites open discussion on a personal level. Even if we know someone who has had an alcoholic wife or husband, the chances are that their way of coping involved such destruction that we cannot find anything we wish to follow. Instead of being inspired by those who have gone before us, we perceive futility. Spouses are left to work it out alone without precedents of a constructive nature, without guidelines, and without readily available inspiration and expertise from others.

Alcoholism is an unending series of crises. Divorces end, deaths end, heart attacks end one way or another, houses get built, twins get easier, but the crises of alcoholism go on for years. The never ending crises sap our energies and spirits. We respond to them in ways that erode our self-esteem. The very people who need to be healthy to cope effectively with the crises become sick themselves. Moreover, the sickness that invades the people around the alcoholic is so insidious that the people involved do not even know they're becoming sick. Not only is their own emotional heatlh being undermined, they must respond to a sick person who denies that he is sick and who resists the help being offered. They must somehow, if the alcoholic is to get well, permit him to see and feel his sickness, a task that takes a great deal of emotional strength which the spouse is losing with each passing day. It becomes a case of the blind leading the blind, except that in this case neither party recognizes his own blindness or even that of his partner.

Finally, the alcoholic does not respond to reason. He cannot be reached by appeals to his rational nature, whether one is in evidence or not. People surrounding the alcoholic are robbed of one of man's most effective tools, the ability to apply reason. The alcoholic has one all-compelling need, the urge to repeat the experience of "getting high," which does not respond to reason.

Alcoholics suffer unbelievable tortures—hallucinations, shakes, depression, anxiety, public humiliation, convulsions, and racking dry heaves, to mention but a few—yet they continue to drink undaunted by the very pain their drinking brings about. If the alcoholic had the ability to apply reason, he would certainly profit from his past experiences. If he had the ability to apply reason, he would certainly heed the advice of others who forewarn him of future predictable results of continued drinking. But he is both deaf and blind. The urge to "get high" does not allow him to see the past or listen to the future. The urge to "get high" is stronger than *any* of his senses. Such being the case, he is totally irrational.

In every way alcoholism baffles the imagination and confuses the mind. It breaks hearts and buries spirits. Yet the results of treatment are remarkably good when the alcoholic is treated by knowledgeable and skilled people who are prepared to deal with someone who is sick but thinks he is well; with someone who neither feels a need for treatment nor voluntarily seeks it.

8

THE ALCOHOLIC — HOW HE VIEWS THE WORLD

"That's sick! Just look at him!" Peggy remarked as she and her husband lay in bed watching Jack Lemmon dig up his bottle on the grounds of the greenhouse in the movie, *Days of Wine and Roses,* being replayed on TV. She then went to check on the baby, but detoured into the kitchen where she reached for her giant box of laundry suds on the cupboard shelf. Digging into it she got out a quart of vodka, gulped down a few slugs, recapped the bottle, replaced it in the suds, put the suds back in the cupboard, and returned to her husband with more murmurs of disgust for the TV alcoholic's behavior. It never occurred to her that she was doing exactly the same thing.

John began each day by framing his head with

the toilet bowl. Before he could get a drink to stay down he was forced to vomit the two or three he had just gulped. The various physicians he consulted could not find evidence of the "postnasal drip" that John was convinced was the source of his problems. Therefore, while complaining about the incompetency of the medical profession, he continued gulping and vomiting and remained preoccupied with his nonexistent "postnasal drip." It never occurred to him to consider the inappropriateness of his early morning drinking. To John that was not at all unnatural.

Alcoholics do not see things the same way nonalcoholics do. All sorts of different kinds of people become addicted to alcohol, but once the addiction sets in, it is as if these very different people all put on glasses of the same tint and prescription. They all start seeing in a like manner, but in a manner very different from the way the rest of the world sees; and they are all convinced that it is their vision which is true.

The hallmark of alcoholism is loss of control: the alcohol-dependent person's drinking and behavior is frequently different from the way he or she intends it to be. He either drinks more than he intends to, drinks when he intends not to, or behaves while drinking in a manner which he does not intend. He does not have the ability to put his intentions about drinking or behaving into action on a consistent basis. *The chief symptom of alcoholism is denial of the condition.* The alcoholic either accepts as real that which is unreal or rejects as unreal that which is real. Denial in alcoholism is an almost incredible phenomenon. It transforms the alcoholic into a Mad Hatter. He's O.K., everything is under control; its Alice who's acting a bit strangely.

It all begins at that point when an individual has a drink of alcohol which has a *profound* effect upon him—so profound that he feels a vastly exaggerated sense of gratification. That drink of alcohol becomes a memorable experience of the highest magnitude. The drinker is not an alcoholic yet, but he is a setup for it if he continues to drink. How profound an effect alcohol has upon a person appears to be a strong factor, if not the strongest, in determining whether one becomes addicted or not.

When the individual returns to alcohol he finds his next drink to be as immensely gratifying as the first. He is just as profoundly affected this time and will be as greatly rewarded the next time and the time following that. It is not long before our drinker learns that he will *always*, each time, feel an enormous gratification from drinking alcohol. He begins to feel a pull toward it and returns to it increasingly. Soon our drinker develops a very unique relationship with alcohol; a relationship of implicit trust. He comes to believe in it completely. It always works! *Each* time it has a greatly exaggerated but welcome effect upon him.

Not only does he find that alcohol always works, he also discovers it works the way he wants it to. While he is becoming a slave to alcohol he feels very much its master. He can direct it to do as he wishes. What he can get from one drink he can get more of from two, and more from three. He learns that alcohol can always be relied upon to alter his mood, no matter what it is, to one of being "high" or exceptionally gratified. Our drinker learns well that he can depend upon alcohol; and he soon does.

Each experience of being immensely gratified or of "getting high" solidifies the experiences before it and establishes the groundwork for the ones to follow. As the repeated experiences are reinforced, they are incorporated as a permanent engraving in the drinker's mind. For the rest of his life he will have as part of him a craving to repeat the experience of "getting high." Whenever this craving manifests itself, the drinker will respond to it over food, sex, or even survival.

The alcoholic first receives an immense gratification from alcohol. Why the effect of alcohol is so profound for some drinkers and not others is as yet unknown. The alcoholic, for any number of reasons—not the least of which is the profound effect itself—next seeks that effect. With continued seeking and finding, the alcoholic comes to need the effect. He learns to live with it and in so doing becomes unable to live without it. He will need ever increasing amounts of the drug in order to continue coping, and will ultimately be destroyed by its continued usage. He develops a psychic dependence upon alcohol and a resulting maladaptive response to living. From this point on the course of his life is clearly predictable. If he continues to use alcohol, he will need to keep increasing its usage. It may take many years, but he will ultimately suffer social, marital, emotional, physical, economic, and vocational complications before meeting an untimely death. Once the drinker has developed a psychic dependence, he cannot alter the progression of his disease because he cannot consistently modify his drinking no matter how or what he tries. Total abstinence is his only recourse.

But the early alcoholic or physically dependent person looks O.K. in the beginning years. He remains an accepted member of our drinking culture and drinks within the bounds of what is considered acceptable by his peers. Like them, he seeks his mood swings in more or less appropriate ways, and hides from them any drinking he fears they might consider inappropriate. He is not easily detected at this point, but changes in his drinking are occurring and can be discerned upon scrutiny.

Every drinker, perhaps without even being aware of it, has his own set of rules for drinking which he accepts as being appropriate. When a psychic dependence sets in, the original rules must be changed to accommodate larger amounts and more frequent ingestions of alcohol. Where once our drinker just anticipated times for drinking, now there is an actual preoccupation or urgency to the anticipation, and the alcoholic becomes quite adept at accommodating this urgency. He will break his original ground rules and will do so without a second thought; there is always good reason for it.

"Never in the morning" is a common rule among drinkers. Our drinker has this rule as one of his own and follows it for a time, but then comes the morning his boss suggests slipping out for a "quickie" before the sales conference begins. Our drinker doesn't blink an eye. Without a second thought he follows in the wake of his boss. He does not hesitate at all before breaking his own rule. Following that experience some interesting churning takes place in our drinker's mind: "He drinks in the morning! Where have I been? If he can do it, so can I." Very soon he is faced with another uptight morning situation and recalls his other morning drink. "That drink really helped me out then, I think I'll slip out for one right now." It is not long before he is slipping out for a "quickie" every morning, telling himself, "Everybody does it! One drink certainly isn't going to hurt anybody." He easily breaks his original rule, is not concerned that it has been broken, and perhaps will establish a new rule in its place; "never before ten", for instance.

"Never alone," "never before five," "never on weekends," "never during the week," "only after eating," "never after eating," "never straight," "never mixed" are some other often used rules which drinkers deem acceptable and impose upon themselves. The alcoholic will break such self-imposed restrictions with relative ease and will not bother to re-establish them once he does break them. The new drinking rules that he substitutes are just as acceptable to him as his first set of rules. Nevertheless, they are different from the rules he established originally and are just as easily broken; and in time they will be broken until few rules exist at all.

As his need for alcohol increases there is greater urgency to his anticipation of a drink; he becomes preoccupied with alcohol and develops a rigidity about his usage of it. He becomes progressively less casual about his drinking. Oh, he may act nonchalant enough, but watch his resistance to having a regular drinking time interfered with. Someone who is urgently anticipating a drink does not take lightly any interference with his obtaining that drink. In his early years our drinker could have made the adjustment from planning to have a drink to not being able to have it without distress. Maybe some displeasure would have resulted but not the acute agitation which he feels today when such situations occur. Now the distress is so great our drinker will go to any lengths to avoid it. As it becomes increasingly difficult for him to tolerate any interference with his drinking, he becomes exceedingly cunning in manipulating or controlling his environment to accommodate his growing needs. He becomes as ingenious at manipulating his environment as he is with breaking his own rules so that he may satisfy his growing need for alcohol.

For example, he may now refuse any event or activity that does not include drinking. Since he cannot give that as his excuse, however, he will come up with a whole assortment of explanations: he now finds he's too emotional at weddings (those without alcohol), or "the Joneses never have anything to say"; he "can't stand crowds," or "her cooking is too much to ask of anybody."

When he is unable to dodge a nondrinking or light-drinking situation, the alcoholic loads up with a "few under his belt" before leaving home and, if worst comes to worst, will find a reason for an early departure. Usually, however, he maneuvers extra drinks for himself without detection. A favorite peregrination is to fix drinks for others, thereby gaining a chance for nips or loaded drinks for himself while acting the helpful, friendly guest. Another common maneuver in public places is to feign an "inflamed bladder" or some such condition, thereby getting a stab at the bar for a fast one while supposedly going to the rest room.

The alcoholic sneaks drinks, gulps them down quickly, drinks alone and before or after social engagements, and stops attending functions or gatherings where he knows it will be impossible for him to drink the way he wishes. Before making virtually any decision—be it a new wife, divorcing of an old wife, new client, new town, new job, another baby, new friend, dinner invitation, luncheon meeting, or which flight to catch—he will first ask himself, "What will the drinking be like?" and will then make his decision accordingly.

As his behavior begins to deteriorate with his increased consumption of alcohol, he will be subjected to criticism and attempts at control from others. Instead of reducing his intake of alcohol, he responds by going underground to secrete his supply. Because he feels that his life depends upon getting that drink, he is exceedingly devious and cunning about making sure it will be there. He is able to outmaneuver the most compulsive and thorough of searchers. He hides his supply in every imaginable nook, cranny, and container in all the places where he does his drinking—home, office, or car. The idea of not having alcohol available for any given period of time becomes increasingly alarming to him.

The social drinker crosses the line from social drinking to addicted drinking without being aware of it. He does not perceive the line. The undertow is very gentle in the beginning and our drinker, thinking of himself as a strong swimmer, is not concerned with changes in the current when he does detect them. He has gone from wanting the mood change which alcohol brings about to needing that mood change. He now *must* have the drink at any cost, but he will think of this urge or compulsion for the drink as being the same as in the old days when he only wanted it. He will not recognize the shift from wanting to needing.

Now alcohol has him. He has used it to alter his moods. He has returned to it ever increasingly for the mood alterations and in time his ability to cope has become dependent upon having the mood alterations which only alcohol brings about for him. The more he sought the mood alterations, the more he wanted them; the more he experienced them, the less capable he was of functioning without them. The less capable he was of functioning, the more he came to depend upon alcohol and the resulting mood swing. (At first glance it seems as if a vicious circle has been established, but that is not the case, for it is actually a more ominous downward spiral leading ultimately to the alcoholic's untimely death.)

With increased usage of alcohol there is a price the alcoholic must pay and he will do so willingly, for he cannot perceive living without the effects he gets from alcohol. For example, the alcoholic now sometimes loses control of some of his behavior. He becomes intoxicated or behaves in ways he knows are inappropriate. He feels humiliation, shame, embarrassment—all powerful feelings, indeed, and very uncomfortable for him to tolerate. He can look at these feelings and the behavior that caused them and if he were not addicted he could say, "Hey, I really blew it last night," make a few phone calls to apologize, and make and follow resolutions for acceptable behavior in the future. He could look at the facts, accept his own blame, and take steps to improve. He would remain in touch with reality while dealing with his painful feelings. Such a method doesn't work very well for the alcoholic for long. He is forever "blowing it" and must find different ways of coping with his pain.

Essentially he has two defenses. Both take him out of touch with reality. First, he can repress the whole business. Since recalling it is painful, he doesn't recall it. He tunes it out and thinks of something more pleasant instead. Soon he forgets it entirely and acts as if nothing had happened. People around him can't believe their senses and begin to wonder if maybe they are crazy. Because the alcohol-dependent person represses a great deal, he becomes an expert at just shoving things aside or down. With enough practice he very successfully removes himself in his own mind from those unpleasant experiences his drinking caused. Since he actually *believes* they never happened in the first place, he certainly is not willing to discuss them or to apply anyone else's reason to them. To him they do not exist and he wonders why everyone is making a big fuss over nothing. While people close to him are ready to tear out their hair, our dependent drinker goes merrily on his way.

The second defense the alcoholic has at his disposal and which he *routinely* uses is to rationalize his behavior. If he can say the painful results of his drinking are caused by events or other people's actions, then he can feel better. He does not have to look at his own behavior. His need for alcohol and the effect derived from it do not now permit him to examine his own behavior. To do so might mean giving up drinking and his need to drink is too strong for that. Therefore he applies his intellect, against all reason, to put the blame elsewhere, anywhere but on his own drinking. The more he applies his intellect to accommodate ever increasing suffering, the more out of touch with reality he becomes. His rationalizations bury his own feelings and he will come to be entirely alienated from them. His rationalizations distort reality and carry him further into an area of misperception. By being out of touch with his own feelings and by misperceiving his world he develops a deluded or impaired judgment, which he naturally does not recognize.

Healthy people also rationalize on occasions, but unless they are overdefended, they have the ability to retrace their own actions back to the original point and assume their own blame. Even little children have this ability. One of my eight-year-old daughters recently messed up on a section of a rug she was laboriously hooking. "You made me do that, Mommy!" was her immediate reaction. When I asked in what way I, sitting across the room, had that kind of power over her, she was able to slowly but surely take her "boo-boos" back to the fact that perhaps she was concentrating on talking rather than hooking. She concluded, "I like to do both. Maybe when I get better at this rug, I'll be able to talk at the same time." Healthy people, big and small, can examine reality and accept it. They are able to profit from their own mistakes.

Alcoholics can neither examine nor accept reality; it is too threatening to them. If they took a look at reality it would mean only one thing: no alcohol. A greater threat does not exist for alcoholics. Their addiction forces them to make and believe their own rationalizations for what is happening to them. The more they rationalize, the more defended they become from the onslaughts of reality, and the more out of touch they are with the world as it exists.

Another price the alcoholic must pay as he progresses in his addiction is a waning of ego strength, or sense of self-worth. This is more ominous than the pain immediately following drinking episodes because it is a pain that never leaves the alcoholic unless he is "high" from alcohol. As his increased consumption of alcohol causes him to be less effective in the various spheres of his life, he develops a nagging but deep sense of inadequacy. With repeated drinking experiences and the resulting inadequate functioning or inappropriate behavior, the feelings of inadequacy mount until they become a chronic self-loathing.

When the alcoholic begins to hate himself, to feel a self-loathing and to sense his own inadequacy, he puts these painful feelings onto others. What he really feels about himself, he will now project onto others. He does this unconsciously, but does it to relieve himself. Now others are "hateful," "mean," "destestable," "slobs," "garbage dumps," "mediocrity," "against me," "spiteful," "disgusting," to list but a few attributes the alcoholic now sees in others as his own ego strength fades. His attitude often becomes one of being superior to all he encounters. He will act as if the world is responsible for behaving toward him in the ways he considers desirable. As his sense of self-worth is sapped, the alcoholic develops a hostile aura and will frequently show his anger toward the people closest to him: the people he is most dependent upon and consequently the ones toward whom he feels the most anger. Because his hostility is often frightening, the people around the alcoholic will frequently assume the burden of guilt dumped on them by the alcoholic.

Barbara was clearly projecting her own feelings onto Ken when she attacked him in her drunken rages. By blaming him, cutting him apart, and accusing him (and everyone else) of being against her she was actually giving vent to her own feelings of self-loathing. She masked her self-hatred by grandiose and defiant attacks on her family. Feeling hate for herself, she felt hate in others. She could not tolerate, even for a moment, Ken's indecisiveness about returning to her. Feeling worthless, she sensed rejection before it was there. Her immediate defense was to project her own hateful feelings about herself onto Ken, as if they were his.

Such feelings of self-loathing are too much for

the alcoholic to live with. He gets rid of as many of them as he can by dumping them on others. He gets rid of more of them by creating and believing in an image of himself that is not based on reality. He actually comes to believe he is the person he dreams he is. He does not base his opinion of himself on his actions, but on his thoughts of himself.

Perceiving the self-image of an alcoholic can be an astounding experience when the alcoholic's view of himself is compared to the reality of his present condition. When a patient recently complained about President Ford's pardoning of Nixon, I suggested that it sounded as if the patient would like to be President. Without a pause he then described what aspects of the presidency would have to be changed before he would consider it. In fact, the patient had not worked in three years and had worked only intermittently the two years prior to that, because he was forever being fired for being drunk on the job. His addiction had rendered him unemployable; it had also forced him to think in a delusional manner. Rather than being able to perceive the facts of his existence, he believed himself to be excellent presidential material. Images based on ideas about himself rather than on the reality of his behavior are more tolerable for the alcoholic; so he builds his sand castles and lives in them without being aware that anything is amiss.

Still, the alcoholic cannot get rid of all his pain. Self-loathing still persists within him, causing great discomfort and even stronger urges to drink. Where at one time he used to drink to feel better than good, he now has to drink to feel just good. Without alcohol he never feels good any more. His massive negative feelings about himself are too great. They cause a constant pain which he can relieve only by drinking.

The alcoholic never feels good for another reason as well, and this one is physiological rather than psychological, but the end results are the same. There is a rebound effect caused by consuming alcohol. The drinker drinks to go up in his mood and goes up because the alcohol he is drinking depresses or puts down certain activities within his brain. After repeated usage over a period of time there exists a heightened agitation level following the depression. What was put down bounces back higher than the original starting point. The alcoholic does not return to a normal physiological agitation level after repeated depressions ("highs" to him) of his brain. He instead bounces back beyond the normal to a level of increased agitation or anxiety; and he *stays* there. When other depressants, sedatives or minor tranquilizers, are used by the alcoholic, they also act to increase the agitation level following the initial depressant action. The very substances the alcoholic uses to reduce his anxious or agitated state serve only to increase it, thereby putting increased demands on him to use them in greater quantitites, and as he does so he is forced to employ even more arduously the pain-reducing defenses which take him ever further from reality.

Alcohol also causes brain functioning impairment with resulting physiological memory losses and distortions, which also serve to remove the alcoholic from reality. Periods of temporary amnesia, blackouts, are common to alcoholics. Peggy, the woman with her vodka tucked away in the laundry suds, recalls her first blackout and her reaction. Both are typical. She remembers having a drink while sitting at her desk making out a grocery list for a dinner party she was giving the following evening. She next remembers opening the door to the boy from the store delivering her groceries. Among the bundles was her shopping list with each item crossed off in her green ink as it had been selected. Peggy says "Nothing was missing! I had bought everything on my list, paid for it, wrote out my address for the delivery, and came home to await its arrival. Little more than an hour had passed, but it had been a busy hour and I couldn't remember any part of it. I was momentarily shocked, but I didn't want to think about it, so I didn't. I thought instead that it was a neat way to accomplish an unpleasant task."

Blackouts can range anywhere from a few minutes to hours and even days. Anything can happen during a blackout. Our jails are full of prisoners serving time for crimes of which they have no memory. Blackouts are frightening to alcoholics and the first thing many of them do is to check for evidence from the night before. When they finally find their cars they examine the fenders to see if they've been in an accident, they check whose bed they are in, they make frantic phone calls to room clerks for delivery of local papers to discover the dates and cities they are in, they search thoroughly for notes they may have written about phone conversations they may have had. Still, they somehow do not perceive anything unusual about their behavior. Because they have blackouts, they assume anyone who drinks beyond an aperitif has them as well. Some alcoholics do not even let themselves become aware of their blackouts. Although they may not always remember getting to bed the night before, where they have put things, or what they have said specifically in conversations, they simply consider these memory lapses normal and will vehemently deny ever having experienced a blackout.

If someone does not remember segments of his life, he does not have to deal with them, unless of course he is involved in an accident or some other crisis. Blackouts serve as an additional buffer between the alcoholic and reality.

Alcohol also causes perception distortions which further impair the alcoholic's ability to see reality. The alcoholic can go to a party, slur his words, stumble about, burn cigarette holes in carpets, spill drinks, repeat stories, pass out, and wake up the next morning thinking of himself as the life of the party. What to others is embarrassing, boring, and dangerous is seen as hilarious, scintillating, and daring to the alcoholic. His perception and recall of the drinking episode is impaired by the effect alcohol has upon his brain. When it is suggested that he not drive home, he feels perfectly capable of driving even though he is unable to walk without staggering. What he remembers the next day is what he felt the evening before, that he was perfectly capable of driving and that everyone had made a big to-do over nothing. The effect alcohol has on his brain impairs how he perceives himself while under its influence and how he recalls the experience when sober. Such impaired brain functioning is yet another factor that takes the alcoholic away from reality and into a world of his own.

The end result of all the defenses, distortions, and memory impairments is a massive denial by the alcoholic of his condition. He is rendered incapable of evaluating himself with any degree of accuracy. No wonder it is so difficult to talk about drinking problems to the problem drinker. He can't even relate to the simplest questions about how much or when he drinks. He can only reply by wondering why the question is asked. He feels that surely there is something more important to talk about. Even though the alcoholic's denial is understandable and even expected, I still find myself amazed at its openness. One simple question asked of new patients is, "How old were you when you were drunk for the first time?" and a typical reply is, "I have *never* been drunk!" Quite an incredible response when we consider that the patient is where he is because of excessive drinking and inappropriate behavior.

The alcoholic is drowning, but does not even know he is in the water. He is very sick, but thinks there is something very wrong with the world. He is very scared, but believes he has everything under control, or soon will have. He is in a state of chemical insanity, but because he does not fit the mold of what is generally considered "insane," he is not thought of as such by others.

He is totally irrational and will not get well by any magnificent spontaneous insight of his own. His wall of denial keeps him from that. He will have to be made ready for that insight, and he often can be by skillful handling of the crises his drinking creates.

9
INTERVENTION

Without a message from reality the alcoholic has *no other choice* but to continue drinking. As long as he believes he *can* drink, he *cannot stop drinking*. He cannot stop drinking until he perceives that he has *no other choice* but to stop. For that perception he will have to be confronted with the reality of his condition; otherwise he will not be able to see it. His defenses are too massive and his denial too great for his disease to be interrupted by any spontaneous insight of his own.

As deluded as the alcoholic is, it is possible for him to receive a message from reality telling him that his present line of action cannot continue, that his world is not exactly as he has been seeing it. The message, specially worded and specially delivered by people meaningful to the alcoholic, intervenes in the progression of his disease. The message enables the alcoholic to perceive his sickness; only then is he willing to pursue and accept treatment.

Actually the alcoholic is presented with a message from reality every time his drinking is inappropriate and causing trouble for himself or others in any way. Each crisis, brought about by his drinking and inappropriate behavior, is a message from reality saying "This is what your drinking is causing." Unfortunately, the nature of the disease is such that the alcoholic does not experience the full impact of his own crises, and it is therefore difficult for him to receive the message from reality contained within them. The defenses of the alcoholic create a wall between him and the world that makes penetration by reality practically impossible. Unfortunately too, the nature of the disease is such that people around the alcoholic keep him from experiencing his own crises fully. They do not allow the alcoholic to participate fully in the very crises he creates; instead, they rescue him. Family members feel compelled to intercede by assuming responsibility for accepting the consequences of the crises. And so usually do employers, colleagues, and even the law enforcement officers who let the intoxicated driver "get away with it."

Sally did not. She allowed Tom to experience his crises. By forcing him to move his own car, pick himself up, cover his own tracks, face being jailed, make his own excuses, she was refusing to rescue him. Since Tom was unable to escape the consequences of his own drinking, he was forced to experience his crises and he was, therefore, in a better position to receive the message of reality which each crisis contained.

The message is there. But every time the alcoholic is rescued from a crisis of his own making, the delivery of the message is intercepted. *Before the alcoholic can receive the message, the message must be delivered.* Family members who seek knowledge and counseling for themselves, and who achieve a stabilization of their own emotional health, are better able to allow the alcoholic to experience his own crises, and be that much closer to treatment. By helping themselves, they are able to help the alcoholic.

Without outside intervention, most alcoholics die of their disease. Their shield against reality is so great that they are *unable* to perceive their own sickness. Some alcoholics seek help after many years of destructive drinking and it is often thought that these people have in some way experienced a spontaneous insight into their condition. Such is not the case. Rather, they have experienced years of barrages of reality in the form of the crises resulting from their drinking. Crises make attacks on the alcoholic's defensive wall; they do not support it. It is possible, therefore, that enough years of crises will weaken the armor of the alcoholic; then finally a crisis comes along that breaks through it. Very often it is one of the least significant crises which at last brings home the truth to the alcoholic.

But it is dangerous to leave the alcoholic to his

own devices, for he is more apt to die than to crack under the burden of his crises, and if he does finally crack it may be too late for treatment to be effective. If the people surrounding the alcoholic take an active stand and do not leave the alcoholic to his own devices, years of suffering, destruction, and an untimely death can in most cases be avoided.

Spouses and other family members who get help in regaining their own emotional health often precipitate crises for the alcoholic without being aware of it. Besides the fact that they no longer rescue him from his crises, their new attitudes and behavior put additional pressure upon the alcoholic. In effect, *their health makes his drinking too uncomfortable for him*. Alcoholics who have sobered up often report that their families' detachment from their drinking made them seek help. They felt so threatened by the loss of control or possible abandonment the detachment signified, that their very fear allowed them to perceive enough reality to feel their need for treatment. Other alcoholics report feeling threatened because their families were living a full life and they could not stand the feeling of being left out.

When an alcoholic recovers as a result of his family's getting help, it is probably a combination of many behavioral and attitudinal changes on their part which finally allows the alcoholic to receive the message from reality. Whatever the reasons, countless numbers of alcoholics are getting well simply because their family members started getting well themselves.

Besides allowing the alcoholic to experience the crises he creates, another effective course of action is to precipitate new crises for him. A new crisis, not of his own making, but a result of all the ones he has created, can force the alcoholic into a corner which has only one door out, and that door opens into treatment. Some families choose to precipitate a new crisis by confronting the alcoholic directly with the facts of his condition, thus indicating his need for treatment and their desire that he seek it.

A skillful confrontation requires knowledge of the disease and some emotional stability on the part of the confronter. It also requires a presentation of facts about the alcoholic's drinking which are concrete and specific. Generalizations will not do in a confrontation; the alcoholic can worm his way right out of them. Judgments and opinions also will not do; the deluded alcoholic is not concerned with that you think; he has opinions of his own that he believes can match yours any day. And if he feels he is being judged, he will immediately become defensive and even less receptive to what you have to say.

If the alcoholic listens during the confrontation, it will be the presented *facts* which catch his ear. The more facts presented, the broader the view of himself he can see and the better the chance for cracking his armor. If the alcoholic listens to the facts, it will be because he feels that the people who are confronting him also care about him, that even though they are saying things that hurt, they are doing it out of concern and not malice. If he listens to the facts it will also be because he does not feel his dignity of being human is under attack, but the acts which he has performed. When the specific acts are criticized, but not his being, the confronting attitude is, "Even though we feel hurt by or don't like certain actions, we care for you." It is under these conditions that the alcoholic will be the most receptive to the message of the reality of his condition.

However, even with knowledge, health, and an appropriate use of the material, confrontations are likely to be most successful if done by more than one person. The alcoholic's defenses are so massive and his resistance to change so great that he may well be able to outmaneuver one person. He will laugh if one person tells him he has a tail. If three people tell him, he may turn around to look.

Ronnie, an attractive, soft-spoken woman in her mid-forties, had reached the point of feeling she could take no more of her husband's drinking. She had attended Al-Anon regularly for over a year and was being counseled at an alcoholism treatment center. Although she felt she had changed enormously, John, her husband, had made no moves toward sobriety, and Ronnie decided she no longer wished to live in an active drinking situation. Her biggest temptation was to pack her daughter and herself and "just leave."

Their son was no longer living at home and Ronnie felt she was capable of such a move. Her counselor, while respecting Ronnie's right to leave and her feelings about wanting to escape a dreadful situation, knew she would suffer a great deal of guilt if she made the move without confronting John directly with his need for treatment. The counselor suggested that Ronnie, her daughter, and her son confront John with the facts of his drinking behavior and their desire that he have treatment. If, after the presentation of the facts, John chose not to get help, they could then tell him of their plans for departure.

Although she was afraid of such a confrontation, Ronnie said she would do it. The counselor met with Ronnie's son and daughter to explain the need and the methods for the confrontation. All three agreed to make a list of things that had happened to each of them as a result of John's drinking. They were cautioned to keep the list specific to John's drinking behavior, his actions while drunk. The counselor further suggested, since they were all fearful of John's wrath, that a different person take over immediately with facts from his list whenever John became angry with any one of them. In that way they could more easily avoid succumbing to his belligerence and letting him off the hook.

Ronnie and her children met with John in just the manner suggested, and he did become angry as they all feared he might. But something else happened as well. Halfway through their lists

John stopped them by saying, "Please, I can't listen to any more. I'm just no good! I'll leave. You'll all be better off without me." Ronnie's son, recognizing this as one of John's self-pitying moves which he had used in the past to escape painful situations, said calmly, "Dad, this time we want you to hear us out. Kathy has some more on her list and so do I and so does Mom." Ronnie then finished her list and Kathy began again. She described an incident of a month before when a date brought her home and was insulted and berated by her father. She finished by saying, "Dad, he is the valedictorian of his class and you were so drunk you fell onto the end table and knocked it over. I liked him, Dad, and he never called me after that night." John sank back into his chair and doubled over with deep, racking sobs. After a few moments, tearful himself, the son asked in a quiet but firm voice, "We love you, Dad. Will you go for help?" John continued sobbing but nodded and said softly, "Yes, I'll do anything you wish. I never knew it was so bad." The change was dramatic. Where but a few moments earlier he had been in a rage, albeit a silent rage, he now felt and expressed gratitude for their concern. The various options open to him were discussed and John, preferring not to go to a hospital, elected to attend AA. The family accepted this choice with the understanding that he would go to a hospital for detoxification and rehabilitation if he should start drinking again. As it turned out he received all the help he needed in AA and never required additional treatment.

By being forced into a corner where he had to look at the reality of his drinking behavior, John perceived his need for treatment and became willing to pursue it. A friend of mine went through a similar experience with her husband, but under different circumstances as she had no children to help her. Margaret's husband, Gary, who had tried AA, would stay sober a few weeks and then go off on a bender whenever he was away on business. After a particularly bad binge she received a long-distance call from Gary asking her to call AA in the city he was in to help him get on a plane so he could get home. Margaret did so and then asked a local AA friend of Gary's to help her confront Gary with his need for hospitalization. Upon his arrival, Gary promised he would do it AA's way this time and if that did not work he would go to a hospital. Within weeks, however, the incident was repeated, and this time Margaret reserved beds in both the detoxification and rehabilitation units of an alcoholism treatment center. When she and the same AA friend met Gary at the airport, Gary was again sure he could do it with AA. "I know what I did wrong," he said. "Now I know what to do. The next time I have to travel I'll contact AA out there in advance." Margaret and the AA'er shook their heads and said, "You had your chance to do it your way, Gary. We're now going to let you keep the promise you made to us last month." They then drove an angry and protesting Gary right to the hospital from the airport.

Gary says it took him about two weeks to appreciate their action and to see how much he needed the treatment he was getting. He has been sober for over a year now and has become active in getting other alcoholics to treatment. In his turn he was recently asked to meet a drunk falling off an airplane. "The guy chose AA, but you can be sure if he drinks again we'll be at the airport to meet him and hold him to his promise of going to the hospital. It saved my life, maybe it will save his."

Richard, a dignified banker in his fifties, went to a lawyer to start divorce proceedings after nearly twenty-five years of marriage. The lawyer heard Richard out and then asked permission for an interview with Kay, Richard's wife. After his meeting with Kay he spoke to Richard of her apparent alcoholism and need for treatment. He suggested that Richard set up a meeting for both of them as soon as possible with an alcoholism counselor. The counselor struck at Kay's alcoholism and left it to her to decide what was to be done about her illness. Three choices were presented: treatment at one of several hospitals, joining Alcoholics Anonymous, or denying the problem and having the marriage end in divorce. Kay chose to attend AA with the understanding that if this was not successful she would submit herself for hospitalization. In the meantime it was suggested that Richard attend Al-Anon. They have since begun to rebuild a marriage that would have been destroyed had they not encountered a lawyer both knowledgeable about alcoholism and committed to its treatment.

Parents also can be effective in getting help for their children by boxing them in a corner where treatment is offered as the only acceptable way out. Ginny was twenty years old, a former heroin addict and now an alcoholic. Because she was having trouble making a go of it by herself she moved back to her parents' house, causing enormous disruptions and worry for her family. When they sought counseling it was suggested they not condone Ginny's drinking by allowing her to live with them if she continued to drink. Ginny's parents told her they wanted to help her and would pay for her hospitalization, but if she continued drinking and chose not to go to the hospital she could no longer live at home. Ginny angrily stormed out of the house with a few choice words for how she felt about her parents. Two days later she returned, bruised and sick. She agreed to go to the hospital when it was offered again and was admitted that day. Upon completing treatment at an alcoholic rehabilitation center, she went to a facility for extended care, where she plans to stay for a year or longer. While receiving treatment she is completing her high school education and is making arrangements to enter college in the fall. Her parents' firm stand gave her no real choice but to accept treatment. She now has another chance at life.

Employers can often be even more effective in intervening in the progression of alcoholism than family members can. Quite simply, the alcoholic grants his employer more power than he grants his family. Alcoholics, like so many others in our society, place a higher value on their productivity than they do on themselves or their family. Consequently the alcoholic feels threatened at the thought of losing his job and will muster all his will to control his drinking in that particular sphere of his life. But sooner or later he loses his control and his performance on the job will begin to suffer. He can then be detected and motivated to go for treatment.

Employers are not as reluctant to take constructive action as are family members. Being less involved emotionally, they can respond with more objectivity. And because the alcoholic grants them more power, they have the most leverage over him. Thus, although they are usually the last to know, informed employers are often the first to take constructive steps to intervene in the alcoholic's disease.

The most meaningful people to the alcoholic are his immediate family members and his employer. They are usually the only people who have sufficient concrete, factual, and specific data for effective confrontations. They are also the only people who exert enough leverage over the alcoholic to get him to treatment. The greatest service these meaningful people can do for the alcoholic is to force him to go for treatment. Anything else is cruel and unjust.

Many people will say it isn't fair to force a person to go for treatment, and furthermore "it won't work that way." Yet we do not let these arguments stop us if a relative or employee is hemorrhaging, has TB, or has a ruptured appendix and is reluctant to go to a hospital. We cart him off regardless of what he wants, and he gets treated in spite of himself. The same can hold true for alcoholism. *Alcoholics who are forced into treatment against their will have as good a chance at recovery as those who go more willingly.* Further, the recovery rate for alcoholism is exceedingly high when compared to the rates for other chronic physical or mental conditions.

10
EMPLOYERS

Companies, both large and small, unwittingly have an unwritten policy on alcoholism. It is the result of the effects of the social and moral stigma associated with alcoholism on the attitudes and customs of most company personnel. If written in typical company language, it would read something like this: "This company will award cash and other economic premiums to any employee who can successfully conceal his alcoholism from the attention of management. Such premiums will include sick-leave pay, job security, fringe benefits, and promotional opportunities. When the employee can no longer conceal his alcoholism, his employment will be terminated." This unwritten policy, of course, does not solve the problem. Yet all companies are guided by it and will continue to be until they replace the unwritten policy with a separate written policy statement on alcoholism that does work. Until that time, everyone loses. Business and industry lose an estimated $15 billion annually. Unions lose through disgruntled membership, increased grievance disputes, lengthy arbitrations, and loss of members who become unemployable. Alcoholic employees lose their opportunity for a meaningful existence, and ultimately, they lose their lives.

Beyond that, the unwritten policy is terribly uncomfortable to execute. Under it, supervisors (and managers) are forced to warn and threaten, deny and conceal, plead and cajole, feel embarrassed and ashamed, and endure one broken promise after another. They are thus degraded and quite naturally develop resentments and frustrations that in turn affect their own job performances.

Michael's superiors were at a loss. Nothing they were doing with Michael was working, yet they felt they were doing everything they could. Later, when Michael died during a hemorrhaging episode not long after his forced resignation, the officers of his firm were saddened but at the same time felt, because they had not been successful, that Michael had been a hopeless case. Actually it was the actions dictated by their unwritten policy on alcoholism that were hopeless.

Michael was considered a brilliant lawyer and his firm did not want to lose him. For many years it was fairly easy to ignore Michael's downhill progression. There were several times when his judgment was poor, his behavior inappropriate, and his time unaccounted for, but this seemed insignificant when contrasted to his still brilliant resolution of so many cases. Also, no one knew how else to deal with him. For the most part his colleagues and senior officers were embarrassed, even ashamed, to speak to Michael about his drinking problem, so they overlooked as much as possible. When they could not ignore Michael's inappropriate behavior and were forced to speak to him, Michael either insisted that drinking had nothing to do with what was going on or else pointed to his successes as if they somehow made up for his inadequate performances. He made direct confrontations very difficult and members of his firm would back off for the moment, remembering his assets and forgetting his liabilities.

As time passed and his alcoholism progressed, Michael could no longer insist as adamantly that his drinking had nothing to do with his difficulties, nor did he have as many successes to point to. He would try to put the blame elsewhere, on his family or clients or office staff, but would ultimately promise to "cut down" and to "pull myself together," ending each time with the assurance, "I'll be all right."

Of course he was never able to pull himself together. His senior partners, guided by the unwritten policy and thinking they had done more than their share with all the "chances" they had given Michael, eventually reached their limit and asked him to resign. Although suggestions to seek treatment were made on several occasions, treatment was never offered as a firm alternative to the disciplinary action warranted by his unsatisfactory performance.

Alcoholism is not new; it has been around since the cave man first discovered the fermented apple. Effective approaches to alcoholism, however, are new. Attempts to help alcoholic employees originated in the 1940s, when a few employers started offering treatment to those alcoholics they could easily spot. Right from the beginning, the alcoholics thus referred to treatment responded to the treatment received; 60 to 80 percent achieved long-term, stable recoveries—an incredibly high percentage for a chronic and fatal disease. Treatment was never a problem, nor is it today. Detection and motivation are the problems, and in these two areas the industrial alcoholism programs begun in the forties fell short. They neither discovered nor motivated to treatment the vast majority of their employed alcoholics.

To be detected is the last thing an alcoholic wants; therefore he uses enormous energies to conceal his abnormal drinking. He will go on with his act of "drinking like everyone else" even when he can no longer hide his shakes, sweats, flushed face, bloodshot eyes, and staggering gait. By then he is easily detected by anyone; but then he is in the final phase of his illness. Right through the 1940s, 1950s and into the 1960s, alcoholism was not considered a disease in industry any more than it was in the rest of society. Alcoholism was thought of, rather as a self-inflicted condition and a moral problem, and no one in those years was considered an alcoholic unless he came close to the skid-row stereotype. It was therefore these late-stage alcoholics, no longer able to hide their advanced symptoms, who were being reached by the early industrial alcoholism programs. The alcoholics who were not yet in their late stages were remaining successfully hidden in the general employee population.

Awareness of the two problems, identification and motivation, intensified in the mid-1960s, when extensive in-plant industrial studies were undertaken over a five-year period by the National Council on Alcoholism in several large multiplant corporations. Among other things, the thick personnel files were examined, and what a story they told! One such employee's files revealed the following signs of failing job performance over and over for the last fifteen years of his employment: absent, late, warned; sick with "flu," absent, late, warned; vacation days taken individually and without prior notice; sick with "the virus," late, warned. And still it went on—not getting along with fellow workers, spurious and suspicious excuses for poor workmanship, warned; "frozen toes," hospitalization for amputation of toes; alcohol on breath, suspension; transfer to new department; extended lunch hour, asleep on job, terminated; reinstated; late, hospitalization for "high blood pressure," poor workmanship, warned; staggering gait, final termination. File after file, year after year, the same symptoms. This survey led, in the late 1960s, to industrial alcoholism programs that concentrated on the signs of job deterioration rather than those of alcoholism.

Roger was the beneficiary of one of these new and more effective programs. Being a chemist and loving his chosen work, Roger began his career with high hopes. His achievements were great in his early years; then he changed, slowly but surely. Where at one time he was popular with his colleagues, Roger became argumentative and easily slighted. As the people around him withdrew, he became suspicious, thinking others were talking about him and deliberately making his work more difficult. In time Roger became increasingly irritable during the morning hours, barely speaking to anyone, yet unexpectedly voluble and jolly in the afternoons, ever eager for an ear to bend. This change in sociability did not bring about friendship with his colleagues, however. Although jolly, he was boring, often repeating himself. His co-workers considered this behavior no more desirable than his icy morning withdrawals. Nor did his work improve. In fact, it became hazardous to work in the same laboratory with Roger. Both states, the morning irritability and the afternoon sloppiness, caused Roger to break equipment, spill chemicals, and bump into ongoing experiments.

Previously the supervisor in such a situation was placed in a difficult spot. Not only was he told to diagnose people unwilling to be diagnosed, using a grossly incomplete symptomatology chart as his guide, he was also told to "do something" about the alcoholic—to counsel him—once he made his diagnosis. Alcoholics are difficult to deal with, even by those with special training. They are accomplished manipulators. They are forced to be; their addiction must be fed. The average supervisor, well prepared to be both "firm and frank" and "sympathetic and understanding," was soon outmatched. He found himself accepting the alcoholic's convincing tale of woe. His resulting attitude was often one of sympathy— "My God, I might drink too, under those circumstances"—and the resulting action, granting "one more chance," was far from being firm. The alcoholic won another round, the supervisor suffered nagging feelings of having been used (he had been, of course), the illness progressed, the job problems continued, and the problems of early identification and motivation to treatment were not met.

Today's effective industrial alcoholism programs do not impose the role of diagnostician and counselor upon the supervisor. Today he does what he is trained to do in the first place: monitor the job performance of those under him.

Roger's department head had concrete factual data about Roger's substandard performance. In his meeting with Roger he listed the examples of Roger's poor interpersonal relationships (all very different from the way he once was); the instances of errors, spillage, breakage; and the abrupt personality change that occurred each afternoon. When Roger attempted to rationalize his unsatisfactory job performance, his supervisor kindly but firmly stated that he was only interested in restoring performance to an acceptable level, but that if Roger wished help for whatever it was that was causing him difficulty, he could in complete confidence seek help from the counseling, diagnostic, and treatment services offered by the company. Roger refused to accept this service, saying he could handle it alone. The supervisor said, "Fine, I hope you can, because we are concerned. We expect your performance to return to its former acceptable, in fact excellent, status."

And Roger did bring his performance up to par. He was not exactly the friendliest chemist around, but he worked competently and less garrulously for a while. Then his performance took an abrupt change for the worse and Roger returned to his former state, in which his colleagues again considered it hazardous to work with him. This time Roger's supervisor approached him differently. The examples of his poor workmanship were again described but Roger was told that he must now make a choice between either the

professional help offered or the disciplinary action appropriate to his unsatisfactory performance. He was reminded, "You were given the
offer of help before, which you refused on the
premise that you could do it yourself. That has
not worked out. This time we again offer you
help and, if you accept, your job will not be in
jeopardy. However, if you elect to refuse this
offer of help we will then take the appropriate
disciplinary action in response to your recent inadequate performance pattern." Roger was furious but he had no real choice. His only viable option was to agree to seek the help offered.

The system is simple. When an employee's performance drops below acceptable standards, and
when regular corrective procedures fail to restore acceptable performance, he is referred to
professional diagnostic and counseling services
for identification of the problem, followed by
treatment appropriate to whatever the problem
is.

Naturally, not all substandard work performances are due to alcoholism, but usually 60 percent or more of the cases are. Alcoholism alone is
accountable for more impaired job performances
than all the other medical-behavioral problems
combined. Sooner or later the alcoholic's addiction interferes with his ability to produce on the
job, thus all alcoholics suffer impaired job performance as their disease progresses. When all
employees with deteriorating work records are
referred to diagnostic and counseling services,

the alcoholics are identified and treated in the early or middle phases of the illness, before it becomes more costly to themselves, their families, and their employers. At the same time, the non-alcohol-related problem cases are served as well. And supervisors no longer have to get involved in the diagnostic and counseling functions. This is left up to those trained to do it, the professionals operating the company's alcoholism program. Members of management have to do only with what is the proper and legitimate concern of management.

Supervisors often wonder what the real difference is, because they realize they still have to confront the alcoholic. The vital difference is that now all the supervisor has to discuss with the employee is the fact that his performance is substandard. Like Roger's supervisor, he simply describes specifically how the performance is substandard and then offers the employee the opportunity to seek confidential help from the company's program director or an out-of-company resource, without jeopardizing his job, in case a problem of any kind is bothering him. The supervisor does not have to talk about causative factors at all. He does not have to discuss alcoholism. He does not even have to know what the problem is. He simply offers help in case it's needed and at the same time asks that the employee bring his job performance back up to standard. It is not his concern whether the employee seeks the assistance offered or not.

At the second or third corrective interview,

however, it becomes his concern. Now, like Roger, the employee no longer has a choice. He must accept either the original offer of help or the consequences established by the company for unsatisfactory performance. Usually this means his job is on the line, through either suspension or discharge.

At this point, thinking that this is the kind of interview they could happily do without, supervisors often ask, "What if he refuses? How do I get him to go for help?" The answer is, "You don't! He gets himself to go." The choice is clearly his. It is not in any way up to the supervisor to talk him into going by either salesmanship or pleading. The supervisor simply presents the choice as Roger's supervisor did and then sits quietly back. He lets the employee feel the impact of the "treatment or else" offer. He does not dilute it with words and, above all, he does not enter any discussion with the employee about the causes of the poor job performance. He announces that the employee's job performance is not acceptable and that now he must either get help or accept the consequences of refusing help. (Nonalcoholic troubled employees would long ago have accepted the offer of assistance.) The interview is then quickly and quietly concluded by setting a time for the employee's consultation with the professional diagnostician-counselor. This second or third interview, frequently the one most dreaded in the beginning, is very often the easiest and most satisfying one of all.

But, as with Roger, things are not so quiet

within the alcoholic. He is very angry, although afraid to express it, and he begins immediately to plan how to con the professional consultant until the heat is off. Once in consultation, he is out-matched. None of his manipulations will work and he will be directed to the treatment appropriate to his needs, *and all because he wants to keep his job*.

The same desire will motivate him to continue treatment. Once treated and once the recovery process begins, the alcoholic's hostile attitudes are replaced with attitudes more conducive to harmonious relationships. Almost without exception, treated alcoholics return to work with feelings of gratitude toward the very persons they once so deeply resented for forcing them to treatment in the first place. This is truly a rewarding and meaningful experience for both the supervisor and the employee.

Roger effected drastic changes very quickly. Because of his enormous denial and resistance to recognizing his need for help, the program director recommended that Roger be hospitalized. Once again Roger knew he could not refuse because to do so would mean losing his job. Once in treatment he was confronted heavily with the reality factors of his alcoholic existence. The defenses that kept him out of touch with reality were described and new methods of coping were developed. At the same time he was subjected to an intensive didactic education on his disease. Within two weeks, Roger gave up. He recognized the totality of his condition and accepted it. He then could and did begin to assume responsibility for his own recovery. When he was discharged from the hospital, he joined his company's after-care program and became an active member of AA. Once again he was a responsible employee, very grateful for the opportunity given to him by his company.

If the alcoholic chooses to refuse the help offered to him by his employer—only about one out of a hundred will refuse—the interview is still the same. His choice to be fired is quietly accepted without any attempt to make him change his mind, and he is referred either to personnel or whoever handles the next action or it is handled by the person doing the confronting, whichever is standard company practice. Even this choice, and the employer's follow-through on it, may save the alcoholic's life. Now he has no job. He can no longer tell himself, "I'm not an alcoholic! I'm still working." This is frequently the last defense for alcoholics, and its removal allows many to seek help for their disease. Meanwhile the best interests of the company are served as well.

The "treatment or else" choice is extremely effective. It is, in fact, the strongest motivating factor that exists. When confronted with it, alcoholics elect treatment. They elect treatment for all the wrong reasons, but nevertheless they elect treatment. Alcoholics can be helped whether they want help or not, once in treatment. Out of every ten alcoholics referred to treatment with the "treatment or else" choice, six to eight return to their jobs with successful long-term recoveries.

Not all alcoholics make it the first time around, as Roger did, although most do. Some, like Walter, start drinking again. Walter worked as a mechanic in a unionized plant. Like Roger, he accepted (reluctantly) the services offered, which in his case consisted of counseling within his company by the program personnel and AA in his community. It was decided that he did not require hospitalization. Walter responded to treatment for five months, but only five months. After four months he dropped out of his counseling sessions and presumably out of AA, and soon after that his performance on the job fell back below standard.

He was then confronted by both the shop steward and his supervisor. The examples of his poor job performance were described and Walter was asked to take a one-month leave of absence without pay. The shop steward told him his job could not be protected since he was not cooperating with treatment. (Naturally, it would not have mattered at all whether Walter cooperated with treatment if his job performance had not suffered.) Both interviewers told him that if he got back into treatment his job would be there for him in one month.

Walter returned to treatment and then to his job, and made a stable recovery. The lines were clearly drawn for him. He knew very well that if he drank again and his work suffered (as he knew it would if he drank) he would then get a three-month leave without pay, and after that, if he still did not effect a recovery, he would be out of a job. His one-month leave of absence had already told him his company and his union meant business and could not be manipulated. He too was forced to get well.

This is the way successful industrial alcoholism programs work. Alcoholics are both identified and motivated to treatment earlier in their disease process. But there are not nearly enough such programs. Industries, because they control the two most effective motivating tools available, the paycheck and education, are in a unique position to reach millions of alcoholics. The National Council on Alcoholism reports, however, that of the 1,600,000 American corporations now in existence, only about 600 to 700 have adopted some form of alcoholism program. Of these existing programs, which cover only a small portion of the employed alcoholic population, only a small percentage utilize the modern approach and methods just described, and no more than 25 to 30 of these are achieving anything near their potential in terms of early identification and successful motivation to treatment.

As more is known about how costly alcoholism really is to industry, and how easily, inexpensively, and successfully it can be combated, alcoholism progams should begin to proliferate. For example, a recent study undertaken by the National Council on Alcoholism has found that the job performance of employees who are not themselves alcoholics, but who have an alcoholic in their home, suffers as greatly as if these employees were themselves alcoholics. This study contributes significantly to the realization that alcoholism is costing industry even more than previously estimated. The study also indicates that any successful industrial alcoholism program has to be available to family members as well. Thus, industry's potential impact on alcoholism detection and motivation to treatment, already great, becomes even greater.

The best alcoholism programs are available not only to family members but to any employee who wishes to seek help on a voluntary basis. Family members and employees can refer themselves for any problem, and when they do, it is a purely private matter between them and the program personnel. No one in the company is notified that the employee or family member has sought help. (When the employee is referred by a supervisor, the supervisor is then told whether or not the employee has kept his appointment and whether or not he is cooperating with treatment. Beyond that, the utmost confidentiality is maintained in these cases as well.) Consultations and treatment are confidential, unless, of course, hospitalization is needed which is to be covered by the company's insurance plan. If sick time is required, the immediate supervisor is notified, but is not told of either the diagnosis or the treatment unless the employee chooses to give out that information himself.

A successful alcoholism program establishes itself, in time, not only as an effective source for help but also as a "safe" source. When programs start, most referrals are from supervisors. As time passes the proportion of self-referrals increases, often by more than five percent a year. Employees who have been helped spread the word. Others begin to realize that they too may be able to be helped, and they appeal to the same "safe" source that has helped their co-workers. The supervisor of an assisted employee often joins the employee in becoming one of the program's best salesmen.

Within every company there is always a certain number of employees who are not closely monitored. Often these employees are members of top management, who, though they escape a direct type of supervision, do not escape alcoholism. Frequently too, these people are surrounded by colleagues who, for reasons of their own, "cover" for them. Intervention is not as easily made available to employees who hold positions of power and are not closely monitored. When company alcoholism programs are considered both "safe" and effective, many of these alcoholics will seek help on their own.

Alcoholism programs will not be successful without the active involvement of any existing unions. Some companies wanting an alcoholism program are unable to establish one because of union opposition. On the other hand, some companies have alcoholism programs simply because unions insisted upon them as part of their collective-bargaining package.

In the words of Leo Perlis, AFL-CIO community services director, "Alcoholism programs are neither pro-management nor pro-labor, but pro-people." A sound alcoholism program benefits both labor and mangement. Unions reduce the number of grievances and arbitration proceedings and management reduces its costs. Unions protect the true job security of their members and management regains effective employees. Both save lives. Wider acceptance of alcoholism programs among unions is expected as they become more aware of the benefits they stand to gain as well as the crucial role they can play in serving their membership.

When a company is establishing an alcoholism program, it is important to remember the need for a separate written policy statement on alcoholism. Although alcoholism is the most serious health problem any company has, it has routinely been left out of company health benefits. The only way to counteract the stigma of alcoholism is to attack it head on, to call it what it is, a disease, and treat it with the respect it deserves. A separate, written policy statement is the beginning. The joint Union-Management Committee of the National Council on Alcoholism, co-chaired by James M. Roche, recently retired chairman of General Motors Corporation, and George Meany, president of the AFL-CIO, has established a comprehensive guideline that reflects the broad principles of a successful alcoholism program. Obtainable from the National Council's New York headquarters, this guideline

stresses the need to recognize alcoholism as a
disease and to have top-level joint union-
management involvement, with a joint union-
management written policy statement on alcoholism. It discusses, as well, the principles for
inclusion in the written policy statement and the
principles for implementing the policy.

The basic unit, employer-employee, is the
same for any successful alcoholism program,
whether the business is very large or very small or
in between. A successful program is feasible for
any size as long as the basic unit of employer-
employee exists.

Having been on the receiving end, so to speak,
of many industrial alcoholism programs whose
employees I have treated, I take this opportunity
to share my experiences with all of you, but most
especially with those of you who are employers,
supervisors, members of top management, shop
stewards, and union officials. We in the treatment
services take up where you leave off. We get your
employee with his enormous resentment for
being forced into treatment. But because he is
determined to manipulate us as he tried to manipulate you, and to put in his time and then "get
the hell out," he either keeps a very low profile or
volubly describes how much he wants and needs
treatment, which he then proceeds to "prove" by
speaking of his "voluntary" admission, as if he
had about ten other viable options. What he does
not realize is that before he is admitted we establish from the referring person just exactly where

this patient stands vis-á-vis his job. When we know his job is unequivocally on the line, we can attack this denial system immediately and he can then begin to engage himself actively in the treatment process. As a result, we can usually send back to you a "grateful to be alive and sober" alcoholic prepared to begin assuming his share of responsibilities. On the other hand, if the patient's job is not on the line, he is more resistant to engaging himself in the treatment process. These patients are usually very cooperative and comply with the program, but they do little else. They often resemble the student observers who pass through as part of their education. They do not feel compelled to be patients. The energies they could be using on self-examination are used instead on maintaining this "passing-through observer" role. Quite simply, they know they can drink again and "get away with it." And when an alcoholic believes that, he feels little need to take his treatment seriously.

I treated eight patients in the past year from one company whose policy seems to be to transfer the alcoholic to another department (sometimes up) when his performance once again deteriorates following treatment, which in treatment language is when he drinks again. Seven out of eight of those ex-patients are still drinking, their disease is progressing, and they are all still employed at the same company, albeit in ever rotating departments. Some of them may die before their job is put on the line.

This kind of paternalism or protectiveness, either inherent in the company or imposed on management by labor, though well meant, definitely falls into the realm of "killing with kindness." A hard-line approach is necessary in alcoholism. The sooner management and labor recognize this need, the sooner lives will be saved, costs reduced, and jobs protected. Alcoholics can be helped, and aside from humanitarian reasons, it is just plain good business to do so.

11
FAMILIES AND FRIENDS

A natural law exists in all close relationships: *If one partner makes a change, the other partner must accommodate to that change with changes of his own to balance the relationship, else it ceases to exist.*

When a change is made by one of the partners in a relationship, the change is either helpful or not. If it is helpful it serves the person well, and holds the potential for serving the partner well, depending on the partner's reaction to that change. If the change is harmful, it hurts the person effecting the change and is potentially damaging to the partner, depending on the partner's reaction to that change.

In alcoholism the natural law of relationships has a good and a bad aspect. *Alcoholics make changes that are destructive. Partners of alcoholics also make changes that are destructive* in their attempts to restore the physical, emotional, and spiritual norms of the relationship. In so doing they become as much a part of the maladjustment of alcoholism as the alcoholic. They often suffer as acutely as the alcoholic. Partners of alcoholics have a choice, but are rarely aware of it.

Alcoholics change as their disease progresses, slowly, subtly, inexorably and eventually drastically—and *the changes are always harmful*. The changes the alcoholic makes hurt him. The changes hold the potential for hurting his partner, depending on her reaction. Whether the partner gets hurt or not will depend upon whether her reactions are constructive or not; whether they serve her well or whether they don't.

If the partner's reactions serve her well by meeting her rational self-interests, they increase her sense of self-worth and effectively counter the alcoholic's original harmful actions. If the partner's reactions are destructive, they do not meet her own needs, and thus allow the alcoholic's actions to be hurtful.

Contrary to what the spouse thinks, the alcoholic cannot hurt her unless she allows it. But the spouse (male or female) would have to be superhuman not to fall into the trap of responding negatively to destructive changes in the alcoholic. Without knowledge of the disease it is virtually impossible to do anything else.

Alcoholism is baffling, spouses don't know what they're dealing with; it's threatening, they never know what to expect except that it will probably be bad; it's ugly and shameful, they cannot deal with it openly. Spouses respond, therefore, the best way they can, in ways that have worked before and that are natural to them. But with alcoholism, they find they are all alone in a strange, inhospitable land where their old ways do not work. Not having received training in ways that do work, they continue with the old and succumb to the disease.

The spouse responds to harmful changes in the alcoholic with harmful changes of her own which hurt her and which are, in turn, potentially damaging to the alcoholic. Being maladaptive, the alcoholic responds negatively thereby increasing his own destruction and providing more potential for the spouse's destruction.

The responses of Ken and Barbara are an example of destruction feeding upon destruction. As Barbara's drinking increased, she was unable to perform adequately as a wife and mother. The changes she was making were certainly harmful. Ken, being uninformed, felt her changes were deliberate and responded negatively by temporarily abandoning her. His reactions did not make him feel good about himself, nor did they meet his rational self-interests. His negative reactions did not effectively counter hers, and he suffered because of it. Barbara responded to Ken's reactions with increased drinking, which led to increased destruction and severe personality changes resulting in vicious attacks on Ken. Feeling personally attacked—it certainly looked like that on the surface—he reacted destructively by deserting Barbara completely, except for weekly stipends which she used to buy booze, which led to her premature death.

Destruction breeds destruction. It's a whirlpool—a deadly one, wide and relatively gentle at the top and narrow and vicious at the bottom. The harmful changes and negative responses gather momentum, causing both partners to suffer a gradually narrowed range of options until both are acting out of compulsion rather than choice. They come to know and have at hand only negative options. They approach the bottom of the whirlpool with no choice but continued destruction.

Alcoholism, for the alcoholic, is a *learned response* to living which is maladaptive. As the disease progresses, the alcoholic becomes increasingly maladaptive. He becomes less and less well equipped to employ options that work. Alcoholism, for the person involved with an alcoholic, is also a *learned response* to living which also becomes maladaptive. The more the spouse responds destructively, the more she is forced to. Both respond and resespond with continued and ever increasing harmful actions. Most spouses of alcoholics enter marriages as healthy as other people. They cannot stay that way, however, by adjusting to their partner's alcoholism. *Adjusting to alcoholism is maladaptive. It doesn't work!*

Now for the good side. *If one partner makes a change, the other partner must accommodate to that change with changes of his own to balance the relationship, else it ceases to exist.* That's the nature of relationships. With help from outside the whirlpool, either partner can stop the destruction for himself. When he does, his partner is going to have to accommodate to that change to restore the balance of the relationship, or it will cease to exist. Either way, the partner reaching outside the whirlpool of alcoholism for help cannot lose. At the very least she stops her own destruction, at the most she makes it possible for her partner to stop his as well.

In alcoholic marriages it is only when one of the partners reaches for help that both can be helped. When one of the partners starts to replace negative actions with positive actions, the climate is set for constructive changes in the other partner. *Every positive change made by the partner reaching for help contains the potential for positive responses from the other.*

Had Ken sought help for himself, he could have recognized Barbara's failing performance and angry attacks as symptoms of alcoholism. Instead of feeling personally used and abused, he could have seen her need for treatment and, in her contrite moments, could have offered and insisted upon it. By responding positively to Barbara's harmful acts, Ken could have avoided pain for himself while providing the opportunity for Barbara to end her own destruction by accepting the treatment she so desperately needed.

Alcoholics will sometimes have their fill of destruction and will make the positive change of getting sober; then the nonalcoholic partner has to make changes, or the relationship will cease to exist. But it's risky business waiting for the alcoholic to have his fill. It's far better business for the alcoholic's partner to get help, for, not being addicted, the nonalcoholic can be reached earlier. Not being addicted, the nonalcoholic is more amenable to rational thinking and can see the whirlpool and the helping hand better than the alcoholic, who is in the throes of *chemical insanity*. For these reasons, I have addressed this book to you—spouse, partner, employer, friend, child or parent—rather than to the alcoholic.

By seeking knowledge about the disease and by restoring your own emotional security, you will be forcing the alcoholic into a position where demands for change are placed upon him. The chances are good that he too will recover. By seeking help you will also be able to bring new directions and meaning to your own life, regardless of how the alcoholic chooses to respond. That's guaranteed! If you do not choose to get help for yourself, you will be faced, after further pain, with desertion, divorce, or the premature death of your spouse. Aside from recovery, these are the only avenues out of alcoholism. There is help available to you, both nonprofessional and professional. You begin to redirect your life the moment you reach for help.

Alcoholics Anonymous, Al-Anon, and Alateen are nonprofessional organizations which help alcoholics and their families and friends. Alcoholics Anonymous is primarily for alcoholics, but many of its meetings are open to anyone interested or involved with the disease. Al-Anon is for the adult family members and friends of alcoholics, whether the alcoholics are drinking or not. Alateen is for the children, relatives or friends of alcoholics who are under twenty-one and over eleven. (Sometimes younger children attend Alateen and fit very nicely into the program.) All the meetings are free unless you care to chip in for the coffee, and none have any other requirements. You need not even give your name unless you choose to.

Alcoholics Anonymous is the largest, most successful self-help group the world has ever known. Forty years ago, one alcoholic who couldn't stay sober, named Bill W., met another alcoholic, Dr. Bob, who couldn't get sober. Together they got and stayed sober, and then they told other alcoholics how they did it and invited them along. One by one other alcoholics joined them and they got and stayed sober too. History was made! For the first time alcoholics, once considered totally hopeless, were recovering in large numbers. They were even staying recovered and they were doing it with the help they received in

Alcoholics Anonymous, the organization that came into being when those first two alcoholics were joined by a third.

Today AA is worldwide and totals over 800,000 members who have gained their sobriety and entrance back into the world by following the AA program. Alcoholics Anonymous is listed in the telephone directories of virtually every city and village throughout the United States and Canada. For those interested or involved in the disease, AA meetings are educational and offer a tremendous source of hope and inspiration. Living, laughing, friendly, grateful evidence that recovery is possible exists and is demonstrated at every open AA meeting.

But the primary source of nonprofessional help for adult family members or friends of alcoholics resides in the Al-Anon Family Group meetings. When that first alcoholic sobered up, his wife, Lois, met other wives and then other relatives and friends who were eager to help and eager to change. Thus Al-Anon came into being and has continued to grow until it too has spread around the world. Al-Anon is not as large an organization as AA, which it is modeled after but separate from, so it is not always available in every community. Still, in North America it is within the reach of most people and like AA is listed in the local telephone directories under Al-Anon Family Groups. If Al-Anon is not available in a particular area, open AA meetings provide an opportunity to meet other wives, husbands, and friends of alcoholics. It takes only two or three to form an Al-Anon group.

Alateen members meet to exchange experiences and to gain knowledge. Like their Al-Anon parent, teenagers benefit *beyond* an understanding of the disease and how to respond to it. They become enlightened about themselves and through Alateen they learn to guide their own lives more meaningfully. Like their Al-Anon parents, they find inspiration and strength in the group.

Al-Anon is a powerful self-help group that is very effective in helping its members gain an understanding of themselves as well as the disease. Al-Anon is well aware that it is the spouse's own actions and reactions that will make or break her. Thus, it emphasizes the necessity of meeting one's own needs through constructive actions, doing what is right for one's self, knowing that only then do others stand to profit. Al-Anon helps the spouses make the natural law of relationships work for instead of against them. It knows that when the spouse begins to make constructive changes in her own behavior, the alcoholic is then pressured to make changes in return, and that those changes are often constructive. Spouses can rest assured that they are no longer contributing to the progression of the disease. They also can enjoy, perhaps for the first time in years, a resurgence of their own self-esteem and productivity.

Spouses often change enormously, only to find

that their alcoholics are still ensnared in active alcoholism. Al-Anon does not then necessarily assist the spouse in taking definitive action to intervene more actively in the alcoholic's disease because it does not direct itself to the treatment needs of the alcoholic. Often the spouse will feel a need for further guidance in instances where the alcoholic remains recalcitrant, feeling that there is more she could be doing now that she has regained her strength. She may encounter the attitude often expressed by members of AA and Al-Anon that "You can't help an alcoholic until he wants it," but she should proceed past that attitude, because more is known about alcoholism today.

The assumption that "You can't help an alcoholic until he wants it" is erroneous and *is not inherent* in the program or philosophy of AA on which Al-Anon is based. AA holds simply that *AA* cannot help the alcoholic until he wants help. AA *does not* say, "He can't be helped until he wants help" but *does* admit, "He can't be helped *by us* until he wants help."

There are millions of alcoholics in need of help. Less than 5 percent of them are in AA. Yet there is no other organization or treatment modality which even begins to approach the number AA reaches. Obviously there are a lot of alcoholics at large not wanting help. That does not mean they cannot be reached and helped. It does mean, however, that if left to their own devices, at least 95 percent of all alcoholics and their families are destined for continued destruction and the premature death of the alcoholic. We cannot afford to let this happen. Alcoholism is ever on the increase. This year there are an estimated 9 million alcoholics in the United States alone who directly affect more than 36 million family members, employers, and friends. Next year there will be more. Alcoholism is increasing rapidly. The annual cost to the nation's economy has been estimated at $15 billion. Approximately 55% of all traffic fatalities are related to alcohol abuse. The cost in human misery is beyond measure. We cannot afford to take a passive stand.

AA has a marvelous way of expanding as is needed and can easily accommodate itself to tremendous growth. AA cannot, however, go out and drag those millions of alcoholics into its church basements, homes, club houses, and meeting halls. AA'ers are practical. They have learned to face reality. They know they do not have any leverage over the alcoholic who has not come to them for help. Only families and employers have that kind of leverage.

AA has as its First Step the alcoholic's admission of powerlessness over alcohol and the unmanageability of his life. With that admission, the alcoholic can then go on and get well with the rest of AA's program. Family members and employers make possible that admission when they stop the destructive actions of rewarding the alcoholic for drinking and start letting him suffer the consequences of his drinking. The alcoholic cannot make that admission— he cannot come to that awareness and acceptance of powerlessness and unmanageability—when families and employers help him to manage and to feel O.K. again after each drinking crisis. With so many people around picking up the pieces, the alcoholic cannot see his powerlessness or how unmanageable his life has become. AA can help the alcoholic, but only when families and employers stop helping him with his drinking. When they do, they make his recovery possible. If only by restraint, he is *forced* to face the reality of his condition.

We no longer need to be afraid of the words "force," "coercion," "leverage," "intervention," or "influence." Most alcoholics will not get well unless pressured to do so by others. Coercion, force, leverage, intervention, and influence are simply means by which the people around the alcoholic make it possible for him to "reach bottom," the prerequisite for recovery. Our knowledge of alcoholism has expanded enormously in recent years. Thanks to AA, which proved once and for all that alcoholism was treatable, the disease has been studied and researched, and our knowledge of it has expanded enormously in recent years. Although much is still not known, we do know today that alcoholics can be made to want help. They can be brought to an earlier recognition of their condition and their need to change than is possible if they are left alone.

Al-Anon does this indirectly but very effectively. By concentrating on the treatment of the family members, pressures to change are placed on the alcoholics by healthy actions of the family. And the climate for change is also provided as the family members refrain from actions which hurt the alcoholic by helping him to drink. Thousands of alcoholics are sober today simply because their families got well, thus forcing their alcoholics to an earlier bottom and treatment.

Thousands more are sober today because family members, particularly but not exclusively spouses, are directly intervening in the alcoholic's disease. Ronnie is typical of these spouses. She changed enormously through Al-Anon, but John continued to drink anyway. Ronnie knew the marriage could not go on much longer as it was, so she sought counseling. Al-Anon met her needs for gaining emotional health but could not help her meet John's special needs. With counseling she learned the dynamics and techniques of direct confrontation and received, as well, assistance and guidance specific to her needs. She and her children were then able to intervene effectively in John's disease.

Margaret, too, received counseling and says she could not have forced Gary to treatment without it. Margaret role-played with her counselor the interchange they both knew would take place at the airport. "My counselor played Gary and I played myself. I knew exactly where my weaknesses were before I met Gary and was able to deal with them. I also had come to the point in Al-Anon where I knew my strengths and that I could rely upon them."

Neither Ronnie nor Margaret felt that their counseling and their Al-Anon involvement conflicted with each other. Both felt a need to do more—if more was possible—for their recalcitrant husbands as their own health improved, although both admitted that when they first attended Al-Anon they didn't want to "waste time" on themselves and were concerned only that something should be done with their husbands. They soon recognized their own needs, however, and went about meeting them before attempting more than they could handle with their husbands' disease.

Margaret sought counseling soon after joining Al-Anon. Gary's drinking was such that he frequently presented situations that seemed to call for direct confrontations. Margaret wanted to intervene at these times but did not know what to do specifically and was aware that she might "botch it" without assistance. John was just always quietly drunk, or so it seemed to Ronnie. She didn't feel as if he presented crises she could get her hands on, yet she wanted to do something. With counseling and increased emotional security, she was able to use John's minor but frequent crises accumulatively in a direct confrontation. Both Gary and John required more than health on the part of their spouses. Margaret and Ronnie received additional help and were thus able to meet their husbands' needs. Because they did Gary and John were able to begin their recoveries.

Some alcoholics do need more than others! The fact that they are not responding to what is being done does not mean there is nothing more to do. Yet one has to know how far one can go. No one can be asked to sacrifice himself to save the alcoholic. Ronnie had reached the point of knowing she was no longer willing to continue the marriage if John refused treatment. She wanted to do what she could but was prepared to move on in case she was not successful.

Most alcoholics are married and/or employed. Only families (or close friends) and employers can reach the 90 percent or more still untreated. Al-Anon is the largest and best resource available to family members. When family members are helped to change themselves, at least 50 percent of their alcoholics recover as well, and AA can grow to accommodate all those who wish to join its ranks. The emotional security achieved by the family members through Al-Anon may, as well, lead to more definitive action, which can then help even more alcoholics, who will also be cheerfully accommodated by AA if they so choose.

Professional counseling is available for the family member who needs more in the way of help either in gaining emotional security or in being more direct in the intervention process. Counseling can do some things that Al-Anon cannot do. Al-Anon is the best medium for reaching the millions of suffering people who are involved with an alcoholic, but it cannot meet all the needs of some of them. Both Al-Anon and professional counseling help family members in gaining an understanding of themselves and the disease. Both help family members to refrain from harmful actions and to take constructive action, and they help the family members to recognize and meet their own needs. When Al-Anon and counseling are combined, the process of recovery is probably faster. Professional counselors are more aware of the specific needs of both the spouse and the alcoholic. While helping the family member restore her emotional security, they can help her to take more definitive action with the alcoholic when and if she feels ready and if it is needed. But counseling alone can never provide the friendship, love, inspiration, and hope to be found in Al-Anon. Counseling services also can never, no matter how much they expand, be available for all the people suffering from their involvement with alcoholism. Al-Anon, which has the same ability to expand as has AA, can be available to all.

Alcoholics Anonymous and Al-Anon Family Groups are listed in local telephone directories. For further information write to AA World Services, Inc., P. O. Box 459, Grand Central Station, New York City, New York 10017, and to Al-Anon Family Group Headquarters, P.O. Box 182, Madison Square Station, New York City, New York 10010.

Sources of information about alcoholism counseling resources available in your community include:

1. Hospitals in your area. Telephone to find out which ones treat alcoholism and which ones have alcoholism counseling services.
2. National Council on Alcoholism local affiliate. If it is not listed in your telephone directory, write to the National Council on Alcoholism, 2 Park Avenue, New York, New York l00l6. Many local affiliates of the National Council maintain information centers where you can seek information or treatment facilities for yourself as well as the alcoholic. Often they have names of physicians knowledgeable about alcoholism as well as hospitals, clinics, rehabilitation centers, and counseling services.
3. Alcohol and Drug Problems Association of North America, 1130 Seventeenth Street, N.W., Washington, D.C. 20036. The association has a *Directory of Alcoholism Treatment Facilities* which lists more than 2,565 centers in the United States and Canada, some of which have counseling services for family members. Include the cost of $7.50 plus $.50 postage.

You do not have to wait to seek help. You do not need to know "for sure" that your spouse is an alcoholic. The time to go for help is when you have any questions at all about his drinking. That's what Sally did. She knew only that somehow Tom's drinking was interfering with her life. By seeking help early she was able to discover the true nature of the problem, and thus was able to respond to it constructively almost from the beginning. And Tom was forced very early in his disease to accept the help he needed.

Find out about the disease and whether alcoholism is in fact your problem. There is no harm in seeking information; rather, it is a sign of health. There is no such thing as a stupid question in either Al-Anon, AA, or counseling. Keep going and keep asking until your questions are answered to your satisfaction. Bear in mind that earlier detection will result in less destruction to you and yours. Bear in mind as well that the recovery rate is higher for alcoholics who are treated before they have lost their families and jobs.

The sooner you seek help, the sooner you can respond appropriately. Like Sally, you can learn early to use the natural law which exists in relationships by responding constructively, thereby enriching your own life while creating the potential for constructive changes in your partner, whether his alcoholism has been determined yet or not.

12
FREEDOM

Alcoholics are dependent people. They are psychologically and eventually physically dependent upon alcohol, and they are emotionally dependent upon people close to them. This is true in spite of the alcoholic's behavior, which frequently appears to be quite independent, especially when he blusters, berates, abuses, threatens, and leaves home for periods of time. Because of the alcoholic's dependent nature, spouses, parents, partners, children, and even siblings are in an important position to apply leverage in obtaining help for the alcoholic, even when he doesn't want it.

Alcoholics cannot stand alone. Out of their needs they grant power to the people closest to them. Therefore the meaningful people in the lives of alcoholics can either perpetuate the disease or initiate recovery.

It is not easy to be involved with an alcoholic. Perpetuating the disease spells destruction for all involved. Taking steps to initiate recovery is also painful for all involved, yet it is the only route which holds promise for something better, and it is a route made infinitely easier once the person involved with the alcoholic accepts the alcoholism as an established and undeniable fact. Only then is that person in a position to switch from abetting the progression of the disease to initiating the alcoholic's recovery. Acceptance frees you! It keeps you from misdirected action and wasted energy.

If you wish the alcoholic to recover, you have no real choice but to change your ways: you have no real choice but to start assuming attitudes and performing actions which hold promise and to stop the ones which guarantee disaster. You are no longer compelled to do all those things which you never wanted to do in the first place. Your alcoholic cannot force you to do them unless you allow him to. The choice is yours. No one can tell you what to do. You should be told, however, what *won't* work and what *might* work.

The following annotated prescription for recovery shows the usual actions of those involved with alcoholics, how these responses are destructive, and what can be done instead. Because the usual responses to alcoholism are so natural as to be universal, they are presented as assumed actions which you no longer have to do. Because the constructive responses to alcoholism are so rarely used, they are presented as new actions which should be *started*.

The new actions to be started are all constructive in nature; as such, they *guarantee* positive results. They will enable you to regain and maintain your own emotional health. They will keep you from being destroyed by the disease. They will allow you to bring new directions to your life which are in your best interests. They also offer the chance for initiating your alcoholic's recovery; and the chance is a good one, because each constructive response forces the alcoholic *on some level, to some degree*, to see the reality of his condition. Only then can he see his need to change.

You no longer have to run from the disease.
START learning the facts about alcoholism.

● Find out once and for all if alcoholism is the problem; if it is, give up and accept it. Only then will you be able to change the things that can be changed.
● As long as alcoholism is denied, it will progress and so will your suffering. Struggling against acceptance will cause your actions to be misdirected and your energies to be wasted.
● Start attending Al-Anon meetings and open AA meetings. Read the literature.
● Knowledge is power, you will need it.

You no longer have to blame the alcoholic.
START concentrating on your own actions — they are
what will make or break you.

• Let go of what the alcoholic is doing. Stop
blaming him for everything. It is your actions
and reactions that will make or break you, not
what the alcoholic does.

• Examine your feelings and actions. What are
your means of coping? How well do you really
feel about yourself? Would you like to feel better?
Are your actions helping the alcoholic? Or are
you helping to make his life more manageable?
Are you letting him see that he is powerless over
alcohol? While continuing at Al-Anon, seek professional counseling if you feel a need for more.
Go to any lengths to gain the knowledge, insight,
and strength necessary for you to cope with alcoholism in a manner healthy to you and to the
alcoholic.

You no longer have to control the alcoholic's drink-
ing.
START concentrating on his need for treatment and
START offering treatment.

• Let him drink as much and as often as he
pleases whenever he pleases. He's going to anyway! Any of your attempts to stop him or to control him will fail. You cannot afford to fail! Your
attempts at control will grant him the "justification" he's looking for to continue drinking.

• Each time he drinks to excess, causing suffering to himself or others, indicates his need for treatment. Offer treatment at these times, but do it when he's sober. If he's drunk he will not listen. Offer treatment when he's hurting; do not offer treatment when he has himself all put together again. That's too late.

• Whenever he either agrees to treatment or asks for it, get him to it immediately. Given any time at all, he'll talk himself and you right out of it.

• Have AA phone numbers to call; have at hand numbers of alcoholism counseling services, alcoholism counselors, and physicians knowledgeable about alcoholism; and know of local hospitals that treat alcoholics. Get your alcoholic to the place and people that seem most appropriate to you at the time.

You no longer have to rescue the alcoholic.
START letting him suffer and assume responsibility for each and every consequence of his drinking.

• Every crisis caused by his drinking is an opportunity for him to receive the message from reality telling him, "Your drinking is out of control. Your life is unmanageable." He cannot get well until he receives that message. You intercept delivery of that message every time you rescue the alcoholic in *any* way. If you want him to get the message, stop intercepting it; stop rescuing!

• Whenever you bail him out of jail, call his boss with an excuse for his absence, make good his bad checks, tell lies to cover for him, locate his lost car, nurse his hangover, pick him up off the floor, or in any other way protect him from the consequences of his drinking, you are making his drinking more tolerable. You are making his life more manageable. You are keeping him from knowing how bad it really is.

• Without messages from reality in the form of crises caused by his drinking, he cannot stop drinking; he won't be able to see that he has to.

• Let your attitude be, "You did it, you are responsible." Let your words tell that you are willing to get him to treatment, that his behavior indicates a need for treatment, a need he has to at least talk to someone about his drinking. Show your willingness to do anything to help him get well. Show your unwillingness to do anything to lighten his drinking burdens. After all, if he is willing to drink even though his drinking causes problems, then he should be willing to assume the responsibility for the consequences of those problems. Let him!

• The times it will be most difficult for you to refuse to rescue him will be when his earning powers are in any way threatened. You will urgently feel the need at these times to make excuses and to tell lies to cover him—to pull him out of "just this scrape"—so that his job will not be jeopardized. *DON'T*. If you do, you will only prolong his drinking and the job will be lost anyway. You might tell his employer the truth. Maybe he

can help you get your alcoholic to treatment;
many do.

*You no longer have to be concerned with the al-
coholic's reasons for drinking.*
START resuming a normal living pattern.

• There aren't any! Reasons are only excuses for
the alcoholic; he needs them to continue drinking. Everyone has problems, but not everyone
uses alcohol as a means for coping with them. So
stop living your life as if you were walking on
eggs; stomp a little bit, enjoy yourself! Your alcoholic's going to drink no matter what you do.
Your pussyfooting around does not reduce his
reasons for drinking; and it hurts you. It makes
you dependent upon him; it makes it easier for
him to drink and to wield his power over you.
• Renew old friendships and begin new ones.
The more you become a shadow of the sick alcoholic, the greater your destruction, and the
easier it is for him to continue drinking. You have
your own life to live and you must live it. If you
refuse to, you are allowing your alcoholic to destroy you and himself. With your resumption of
normal living patterns, your alcoholic will find
further excuses for drinking. Remember that he
is going to find them no matter what you do.
• *On some level* your rejoining the world will force
the alcoholic to compare his sick behavior with
the more normal behavior of others. *On some level*

rejoining the world will represent to the alcoholic a loss of control over you. You are changing; he is forced to accommodate; *he may decide to get well.*

You no longer have to threaten.
START saying what you mean and doing what you say.

• Explore all your options, examine the consequences of any actions you might take, then make decisions and *put them into action.*
• Say what you mean and mean what you say, and *if you say it, do it.* Only then will the alcoholic begin to believe you. Only then will he begin to take you seriously, which he must do if you wish to be influential in getting him to treatment. Be believable; be serious. Don't announce any intention unless you are sure to put it into action. Anything else renders you unbelievable.
• Threats diminish you! Threats feed into the alcoholic's grandiosity and help to keep him from feeling his need to change.

You no longer have to accept or extract promises.
START rejecting them.

• It isn't fair to ask for promises. The alcoholic can't keep them. Broken promises heighten his sense of inadequacy and cause him to feel unworthy of help.
• He cannot consistently modify his drinking, so he is neither believable nor trustworthy and won't be until he is treated. Why pretend other-

wise? By asking for or accepting promises, you are telling your alcoholic you think he can control his drinking. He can't! If you pretend otherwise, he will not see his powerlessness.

• Refuse to accept his promises. By not accepting and by not asking for promises from your alcoholic you are giving him a very important message. *You are telling him he is too sick for that.*

You no longer have to seek advice from the uninformed.
START your commitment to treatment and long-range goals of health.

• If family, friends, clergy, and professionals do not have knowledge specific to the disease—and they won't have without specialized education—they will not be able to help you and they may hurt. Families and friends will have only "home remedies" to offer; "home remedies" are no more effective for alcoholism than they are for cancer or any other serious disease. Consequently trying them will only increase your sense of failure. The exhortatiohs for greater demonstrations of will power so often delivered by uninformed clergymen and physicians do not speak to the disease; consequently they too increase everyone's sense of failure. Uninformed doctors also often prescribe sedatives and minor tranquilizers which serve only to prolong the progression of the disease while providing another chemical and the opportunity for a dual addiction.

• Adhere to your program of recovery even when it's painful! Stop looking for the easy ways out so often suggested by the uninformed. Continue your attendance at Al-Anon. If Al-Anon is not available, attend open AA meetings. Seek help from professionals in the field of alcoholism—professional alcoholism counselors, or social workers, clergymen, nurses, physicians, or psychologists who have received specialized education and training in the treatment of alcoholism. Go to any lengths to secure the help you need.

You no longer have to hide the fact that you are seeking help.
START telling the alcoholic that you are.

• Alcoholism is not a moral issue. It's a disease! Go for treatment and keep going when he tries to stop you. Your seeking treatment will represent to him a loss of his control over you and he will feel threatened. He will ridicule you, or threaten you, or plead with you or complain about you. He will do anything to make you stop seeking help. Don't stop!
• Your getting help shows your alcoholic that you care for him, that there is help available, that he is worthy of help and can be helped.
• Your going for help means you are serious and he knows it. His drinking won't be quite the same any more. It may seem to get worse for a while, but for sure, it won't be as much fun; you are ruining it!

You no longer have to nag, preach, coax, and lecture.
START *reporting his inappropriate actions to him.*

• He can't be coaxed or nagged out of a drink and he's beyond your lectures and sermons! There are no exhortations strong enough to counteract his craving for his fix, alcohol. Exhortations will serve only to make the alcoholic feel more defensive and inadequate. To be receptive to treatment, he must feel less defensive, not more so, and he must feel worthy of help.

• Look at his behavior: don't minimize it to yourself or to your alcoholic. Facts are facts! Report the facts of the alcoholic's behavior—his actions—to him the next day when he's sober, then drop the subject to avoid nagging. But keep the pressure on; the next day review the new actions, then drop the subject again, and so on. Remember that he was anesthetized the night before and may not remember much of his behavior. Your reports will refresh his memory. Report his actions matter-of-factly. Express your concern for him and point out that his actions indicate a need for treatment, a need for seeking outside assistance. As you report his behavior, he will put the blame elsewhere. Don't let him! Bring it back to him by maintaining the attitude and the words that no matter what anyone else did or did not do, it is his actions that are under discussion. *Nothing is as important as how he reacts to it.*

• Don't get into any discussions with the alcoholic

about whether he is an alcoholic or not. The point is, there are problems associated with his drinking that warrant outside help. Offer him the opportunity to see someone about the problems so that solutions can be investigated. If he refuses, end the discussion. It can be reopened next time.

You no longer have to allow the alcoholic to assault you or your children.
START protecting yourself.

● Do not let him assault you. He does not have that right. Don't give it to him.
● Call the police if necessary. Get an Order of Protection if necessary. Have him jailed if necessary. Leave him if necessary. Physical abuse destroys you both. Go to *any* lengths to avoid it.

You no longer have to be a puppet.
START detaching yourself.

● Stop jumping every time he pulls a string. No matter what strings he pulls. When you act like his puppet, you give him control and make him feel as if he's O.K. He's not O.K. He's dying. He can't see that he's sick if you act as if he's well!
● By responding to his demands, threats, pleadings, anger—any of his manipulations—with either acquiescence or emotional outbursts, you allow him to make you do things you don't want to do. Besides weakening your own sense of self-worth, you put him in the position of pup-

peteer. You make him your manager. He can't get well until he sees that he can't even manage himself, which he won't be able to see as long as he can manage you.

• Your alcoholic is an expert at pushing your buttons. He actually needs you to blow up and to be fearful of him or for him. He goes out of his way to get you to lose your cool. If you blow up, he has his justification for drinking. If you acquiesce, he is rescued once again from facing his behavior and its consequences. He wins another round in his fight to continue his destruction.

• If you concentrate on what is right for you, and therefore for him, by taking constructive action with the help and knowledge you are receiving, he no longer controls you. If you detach yourself from his sick or destructive behavior, you gain your freedom.

• You then change enormously. The alcoholic is forced to respond to your healthy changes with changes of his own. The odds are he'll choose sobriety—health for himself.

It is never too late to stop the old and start the new. The time to start is *now*. Perhaps the hardest part of stopping the old ways and beginning new ones is the underlying fear that the alcoholic won't be able to "make it" unless you do the very things you're supposed to be stopping.

To rid yourself of this fear, take a good look at the track record in terms of how well the alcoholic is actually "making it" today. Is it better now than two years ago, or five? Is he "making it" better now than then? You will probably discover that your helping has not interfered one iota with the destructive progression of his disease. With a closer look you will see that your helping only made it easier for him to continue drinking.

It is important also to review the record in terms of your own feelings, for you won't be able to make a change unless you believe it's right. Examine the responses you have been using, bearing in mind that it is your actions which will make or break you. How have they made you feel about yourself? Have they increased or decreased your sense of your own worth?

Do you feel shame, humiliation, fear, degradation, anger, resentment? Are you anxious? Do you feel sorry for yourself? Are your actions bringing you peace of mind, confidence, hope? Or is everything going from bad to worse?

Naturally, if your ways are working there is no need for change. It is only when you perceive that your ways are not working that you will see the need. And at that point any change will seem right, even if only because it's a change.

You may feel it isn't fair that you have to change; after all, he's the alcoholic! If he hadn't become an alcoholic, none of this would have happened and such incredible demands would not have been placed upon you. That may be true. Then again, something worse might have happened instead. Life is not fair. Your alcoholic doesn't think it's fair either. He would have chosen otherwise had he been able.

To respond effectively to your alcoholic, you will have to act in ways which seem unnatural and which will therefore be uncomfortable for you. The new acts will seem strange; some you've never been taught, and some you've been taught to avoid. But don't let that stop you. Alcoholism is an unnatural condition; the ways out of it are also unnatural. As you begin to act differently, you will start feeling differently. Pretty soon you will wonder how you ever lived the way you did.

Be prepared for flak from your alcoholic as you begin doing new things, acting in new ways. He will want you the way you were and will be very resistant to your changes. He will feel threatened because he knows that if you maintain your changes, he's going to have to change as well, and he does not want to change. He may very well muster up all his energies to subvert and thwart you any way he can. Hang tight! Have the faith that you can't lose by doing what you now know is right. You can only win.

Responding constructively to your partner's alcoholism will require the greatest effort you have ever put into anything in your life. And it's a daily effort, not a one-shot deal. It's the long haul you will be going for that will require you to break your life into manageable sections—days! Every day, for the day, with persistence and determination, concentrate on only those acts which you know have a chance. Let go of how your alcoholic responds. You will be able to measure the effects of your new actions only in retrospect, after you've been performing them for several months. It will not be the actions of one day your alcoholic will respond to, it will be your daily actions accumulated over a period of time, which you can best perform by concentrating only on what you have to do today—letting go of yesterday, putting aside tomorrow. A daily check list of actions that are effective in responding to alcoholism are provided at the end of this chapter. If you perform these actions, one day at a time, you guarantee your recovery, and very likely your alcoholic's.

It's all up to you. Your actions can either cause you to ·grow, bringing a resurgence of your energy, self-confidence, and peace of mind, or they can cause you to suffer further. Your actions as well can either perpetuate your alcoholic's disease or make possible his recovery.

Combating alcoholism and its destruction requires your greatest efforts. It can also bring you the greatest rewards you've ever known. Alcoholics can get "weller than well" and so can their spouses. You can come to act in ways you've never acted; you can come to feel in ways you've never felt. You can become beautiful and free!

GUARANTEED Rx
FOR RECOVERY

- You no longer have to run from the disease.
  Start learning the facts about alcoholism.

- You no longer have to blame the alcoholic.
  Start concentrating on your own actions—they are what will make or break you.

- You no longer have to control the alcoholic's drinking.
  Start concentrating on his need for treatment and *start* offering treatment.

- You no longer have to rescue the alcoholic.
  Start letting him suffer and assume responsibility for each and every consequence of his drinking.

- You no longer have to be concerned with the alcoholic's reasons for drinking.
  Start resuming a normal living pattern.

- You no longer have to threaten.
  Start saying what you mean and doing what you say.

- You no longer have to accept or extract promises.
  Start rejecting them.

- You no longer have to seek advice from the uninformed.
  Start your commitment to treatment and long-range goals of health.

- You no longer have to hide the fact that you are seeking help.
  Start telling the alcoholic that you are.

- You no longer have to nag, preach, coax, and lecture.
  Start reporting his inappropriate actions to him.

- You no longer have to allow the alcoholic to assault you or your children.
  Start protecting yourself.

- You no longer have to be a puppet.
  Start detaching yourself.